BY STRATIS HAVIARAS

FICTION
The Heroic Age (1984)
When the Tree Sings (1979)

POETRY
Crossing the River Twice (1976)
Apparent Death (1972)*
The Night of the Stiltwalker (1967)*
Berlin (1965)*
The Lady with a Compass (1963)*

EDITOR
35 Post-War Greek Poets (1972)
The Poet's Voice (1978)

* Published only in Greek

the.
heroic
age

Stratis Haviaras

SIMON AND SCHUSTER • NEW YORK

This novel is a work of historical fiction. Names, characters, places
and incidents relating to nonhistorical figures are either the
product of the author's imagination or are used fictitiously, and
any resemblance of such nonhistorical figures, places or incidents
to actual persons, living or dead, is entirely coincidental.

Copyright © 1984 by Stratis Haviaras
All rights reserved
including the right of reproduction
in whole or in part in any form
Published by Simon and Schuster
A Division of Simon & Schuster, Inc.
Simon & Schuster Building
Rockefeller Center
1230 Avenue of the Americas
New York, New York 10020
SIMON AND SCHUSTER and colophon are registered trademarks of
Simon & Schuster, Inc.
Designed by Eve Kirch
Manufactured in the United States of America
1 3 5 7 9 10 8 6 4 2

Library of Congress Cataloging in Publication Data
Haviras, Stratis, date.
The heroic age.
I. Title
PS3558.A783H4 1984 813'.54 84-1248
ISBN 0-671-49291-8

Excerpt from *Triumph and Tragedy* by Winston S. Churchill, copyright 1953 by
Houghton Mifflin Company. Copyright renewed © 1981 by the Honourable Lady
Sarah Audley and the Honourable Lady Soames. Reprinted by permission of
Houghton Mifflin Company.

For Elektra

2218375

◆ PART ONE ◆

the
children's
war

ἀπελευθέρωση. Εἶναι ὅμως καὶ ρεαλιστική:

Ὁ Πέτρος Ροῦσος, στὸ βιβλίο του «Ἡ Μεγάλη Πενταετία», ἀπευθυνόμενος πρὸς ἀριστερούς ἀναγνώστες καὶ προσπαθώντας νά δικαιολογήσει τό «ὄχι» τοῦ ΚΚΕ, ἰσχυρίζεται πῶς ἡ ἡγεσία του δέν ἀρνήθηκε τή συγκρότηση τοῦ Βαλκανικοῦ Στρατηγείου οὔτε τό τορπίλλισε. «Ζήτησε ἁπλῶς – γράφει – ἀναβολή τοῦ ζητήματος μέχρι νά δημιουργηθοῦν οἱ ὅροι». Γιατί αὐτές οἱ μασημένες δικαιολογίες; Ὁ ἴδιος ἀναφέρει ὡς ἑξῆς τούς λόγους πού ὦθησαν τό πολιτικό γραφεῖο τοῦ ΚΚΕ στήν ἀπόφασή του:

«Πρῶτο, νά στερεώσουμε τήν ἐθνικοαπελευθερωτική συμμαχία, νά μήν προκαλέσουμε δυσαναχέτηση τῶν συμμάχων μας στό ΕΑΜ καί σέ ἄλλους ἐνδεχόμενους συμμάχους μας. Δεύτερο, νά μήν ἐπισπεύσουμε ἔνταση τῶν ἀντιδράσεων καί ἐπεμβάσεων τῶν Ἄγγλων στήν Ἑλλάδα προτοῦ προλάβει νά στερεωθεῖ τό ἐπαναστατικό κίνημα

θανε τήν ἑλληνική, γιουγκοσλαβική καί

Γιουγκο...
σουμε ἀ...
ἀντιχιτλ...
ἂν θά μ...
σουμε σ...
καταχτη...

Μακεδ...

Ὁ Κώ...
μείχθηκ...
ἰδιαίτερη...
φοντα τ...
τήν ἐξήγ...

–"Ἀκου...
γοι πού...
λιτικό μ...
ὅτι τό Ε...
λουθούσ...
ματα. Δ...
λίγο πρὶ...
Διεθνής...
τῆς δέν...
ὅπως κ...
ἔδειχνε...
πολύ μ...
χρεωμέ...
σίες γι...
ἑνότητα...
θεῖ τό τ...
Τέμπο...
ὅμως δ...
χαιρία α...
Γιατί κ...
ὀρθωνό...
Γιουγκο...
αὐτά ὅμ...
ἕναν ὀ...
Καί κα...
του καί τά αὐτιά του γιά νά ἀκούσει, ὁ Κώστας Καραγιώργης συμπληρώνει:

– Ἐκεῖνο πού μᾶς τρόμαξε εἶναι ἄλλο: Εἴχαμε πληροφορίες ἀλλά καί ἀντιληφθή-

Ὁ Τίτο κατά

Καί τώρα ἕνα...
γνώση τοῦ Τίτο...
Τέμπο; Ἀσφαλ...
ὅσο τελικά ὅρι...
πρόσωπος τῆς...
σχεδιασμό στρα...

Ὥστε ὁ Τίτο υ...
Μεγαλοσέρβων...
γκοσλαβίας;

Ἡ ἀπάντηση,...
δοξο, εἶναι κατ...
στούς πολλούς...
μέ ἐντολή του...
τερα τά γιουγκ...
ψαν τό ἀντίθετο...
καὶ ἀδιάψευστα...

Ὁ Τίτο πράγ...
σύσταση Βαλκ. Σ...
κούς λόγους. Κ...
ὸν στρατι...
ακή. Ἀλλά...
οσέρβων σ...
κλοι – ὑπο...
οῦ θρασμ...
– γιά νά ἔ...
ν μηχανισ...
ησε νά τέ...
ραῆς ἐπικ...
λοκαίρι το...
ζωῆς ἤ θα...
Ὅταν πλη...
ἡ ἀντίδρ...
σε νά δια...
ραγγείλατ...
Τέμπο α...
ηγείο γιατ...
σωστό».

γράμμα π...
αμμίζει:

ἡ σημεριν...
ἡ ὁποιουδ...
αν λάθος,...
ἡ χαριστικ...
ολή του πρ...
δημιουργί...
ονησία».

μηνύματα...
ηγό του δ...
ά εἶχε λάθ...
τοῦ Σιάντ...
ει τό θέμ...
όριστικά.
ωστε ,τώρ...
ξάνοι ὅπως...
ονταν μπρ...
οπή: Ἡ ἰτ...
ὸν βαλκαν...
ς ἕνας ὀλό...
τῶν δυνα...
χώματα τῆς Γιου...
και τήν Ἑλλάδα...

Τό ΚΚΕ λέει:

> The moment was apt for business, so I said, "Let us settle about our affairs in the Balkans. Your armies are in Rumania and Bulgaria. We have interests, missions, and agents there. Don't let us get at cross-purposes in small ways. So far as Britain and Russia are concerned, how would it do for you to have ninety per cent predominance in Rumania, for us to have ninety per cent of the say in Greece, and go fifty-fifty about Yugoslavia?" While this was being translated I wrote out on a half-sheet of paper:
>
> | | |
> |---|---|
> | Rumania | |
> | Russia | 90% |
> | The others | 10% |
> | Greece | |
> | Great Britain | |
> | (in accord with U.S.A.) | 90% |
> | Russia | 10% |
> | Yugoslavia | 50-50% |
> | Hungary | 50-50% |
> | Bulgaria | |
> | Russia | 75% |
> | The others | 25% |
>
> I pushed this across to Stalin, who had by then heard the translation. There was a slight pause. Then he took his blue pencil and made a large tick upon it, and passed it back to us. It was all settled in no more time than it takes to set down.
>
> —WINSTON S. CHURCHILL, *The Second World War: Triumph and Tragedy* (Houghton Mifflin, 1953)

γκοσλαβίας". Ὑπάρχουν καὶ σήμερα ἀκόμη ὁρισμένοι τους πού λένε πώς καὶ ἂν ἀκόμα δέν ἐλευθερωνόταν ἡ Ἑλλάδα ἀπό τὸν ἰμπεριαλισμό, θά εἶναι ἐλευθερωθεῖ τουλάνι-

·1·

All day we'd been roaming the flooded fields for food. Five-, six-, seven-year-olds, ten-, twelve- and thirteen-. Just a dozen boys altogether, mostly ten to thirteen. It was hard to find a thing to eat; it was harder to steal. In the afternoon we tried to rob a farmhouse; we were beaten back. Those who couldn't run very fast were whipped as they ran away. The small ones sniffled. The older ones swore. We spent the night in the trees, pressing against one another to keep warm. It rained. At dawn we spat on a stone and flipped it: heads, we'd head northwest; tails, east of north.

Many others had done this before us. They'd leave the village, promising to return in a couple of days or so, but the promise of bread kept moving northward, east or west, sometimes even crossing the border into another country. "Back soon," they'd promise, but a few days later it no longer made sense for them to return.

Heads, west. Tails, east. We flipped the stone, but the stone fell into a puddle. After that we couldn't agree on anything. We dispersed, hoping at least to get rid of the five- and six-year-olds who cried most of the time, and who shouldn't have been allowed to leave the village in the first place.

When the sun came out I saw two rows of sharp yellow teeth across its blazing face. It reminded me of Uncle Jimmi's face. I stared at it until its light grew dim and my eyes ached, then I pressed north.

◄   ◄

It must have been a lucrative deal with CARE, the Red Cross, UNRRA, or was it the Marshall Plan, by which Uncle Jimmi had remembered the Old Country and sailed from New York with a shipload of flour for the hungry.

The occupation had been over for more than three years, but the civil war still raged. There were new massacres; more destruction in the name of freedom, in the name of justice, in the name of honor. . . . Terror, betrayal, and murder by the rightist Nationalists and the leftist partisans, the Andartes. We buried the dead regardless of the side they'd fought on, that the gods might at least pity the peaceable.

Uncle Jimmi's ship, the *Laconia*, docked at the mole on Holy Saturday, and we formed a long line, waiting. We had held out for days, for weeks, without bread or anything besides thistle stems and armyrikia, the succulents that grew in the abandoned salt flats. Our anticipation at the sight of the *Laconia* made our hunger more painful. Some of the old folk began to faint then, and others stepped over them and pushed to get to the front faster.

Hearing the commotion, Uncle Jimmi showed up on the deck, and, putting his hands to his mouth, he shouted at us to shut up and stop behaving like animals, "Or I'll dump the flour overboard and sail back to the States."

That was the first time I saw Uncle Jimmi: a tall man in his fifties, with a well-shaven face, wearing a white shirt, a straw hat and gold-rimmed sunglasses.

Aunt Evanthia waved to Uncle Jimmi, and for a moment he raised his glasses over his eyebrows and looked at her, but didn't wave back. Instead, he shook his head at the ongoing disorder and stepped down to where the flour was.

I stood in line with Aunt Evanthia, holding her hand, or

holding on to her sleeve, I don't remember for sure. I kept looking around for my little brother, Teo, who must also have been very hungry.

Those who were first in line were now hurrying back from the ship, carrying a sack of flour each, and I couldn't imagine where they found the strength. One of them, Barba Yannis, slowed down and asked Aunt Evanthia to wipe the sweat and the flour from his neck with his handkerchief, and while she did he confided to her that Uncle Jimmi was handing out different kinds of flour to different people.

"I couldn't tell which kind's the best," he whispered, "but how can one be fussy in a time like this?"

When our turn came, Uncle Jimmi recognized Aunt Evanthia, but he didn't kiss her and he didn't seem very pleased to see us. His face twitched and took on an awkward expression, a grimace that for an instant struggled to become a smile, but failed. He then turned to me, wondering who I was, and I knew he did so not out of real interest, but rather as an excuse to turn his eyes away from Aunt Evanthia.

My aunt explained that I was hers. "He's my sister's once, and mine twice," she said.

I pulled at her sleeve, looking into her eyes, and then looking around again.

"Yes, of course—there's little Teo too," she added. "He too is ours."

And where was her sister these days?

Aunt Evanthia didn't know, or chose not to tell. She was now staring at the flour silently. There were two stacks of it packed in burlap sacks, and Uncle Jimmi stood in between, one hand resting on top of each, but there was such nervousness in the way his fingers stroked the flour that I thought he was more determined to protect it than to give it away.

Was it true or wasn't it that Aunt Evanthia's sister, "your mother," had joined the other side? Uncle Jimmi, noticing a new stir of impatience in the crowd, raised his head above

Aunt Evanthia's and renewed his threat to dump the whole damned cargo into the bay. When he returned his attention to us he remembered that we hadn't answered his question.

"Who knows who joined what side, Cousin?" said Aunt Evanthia. "Look at us. Is this a time to talk about sides?"

"I'm afraid yes," he said. "I have information that your sister joined the left, which is the wrong side."

"We see no sides, Jimmi. We are hungry, and hunger's blind. Never mind the sister; the boy's innocent."

I pulled Aunt Evanthia's sleeve again.

"Yes," she said.

Uncle Jimmi didn't think that I was all that innocent. "Look into those eyes," he said, staring me down. "Aren't they the eyes of a little snake? A small snake now, a big snake tomorrow."

I worried that Aunt Evanthia might explode at that moment, but she kept silent.

Uncle Jimmi seemed to enjoy taking his time with us. "Cousin, let me tell you something. Why don't you go to the other side, stand in their line, see what the others can offer you?"

Aunt Evanthia put her arm around my shoulders, pressing me to her side. Once again she kept her silence.

"I'm afraid you don't see my point, Cousin. We have to draw the line. There are priorities, you know. The war's still going on, and we have to win friends—every ounce of wheat is crucial. Maybe next time, when the air's clearer. Besides, I don't want to be seen favoring relatives."

"Say what you have to say, Jimmi, but don't expect me to go home without flour."

"Ah, you should be thankful that you still have a home to go to, Cousin." Uncle Jimmi's face twitched, and he said, "Listen, you belong to the left, right? Now, hunger might not recognize sides, but we do, we have to, and you happen to be on the wrong side, that's all."

"I am not going home with empty hands, Jimmi. I hear that you are giving different kinds of flour to different people, as if they're livestock. Well, never mind that we are of the same blood, of the same family blood even. Never mind that, and never mind the best kind of flour. Just give us something, anything."

Uncle Jimmi's face twitched, but this time he managed to smile. Was he touched? I couldn't tell.

"Have it your way, Cousin," he said. "You win. But like the others who are still on the left, you too will have to make do with flour from the left side, the stack on my left. Right here," he said. "Turn around and I'll put a whole sack on your back. But remember my words, Cousin: the left side is the wrong side —always the wrong side."

At home Aunt Evanthia opened the sack and had a taste of the flour. It was the wrong flour, all right. Her face grew pale, and she turned the sack around, looking at the red stenciled lettering on the burlap. It read, RYE.

I was wondering what those letters meant.

Aunt Evanthia didn't know, either, but the flour tasted like secale to her.

"What's wrong with it, Aunt?" We'd eaten bread made from secale many times before.

"The fungus," she said. "There's a fungus that grows on the secale, which you'd better weed out before taking the grain to the mill." Aunt Evanthia sat in a chair, holding her head between her hands and staring at the flour. "He wouldn't dare!" she added in a weak tone.

"What happens if you don't weed out the fungus, Aunt?"

"Strange things happen. You eat the bread and you go crazy. The devil takes hold of you and shakes the wits out of you."

"But it's Good Saturday; tomorrow is Easter," I said. "The devil can't come, can't take hold of us. In a few hours' time we'll be going to church for the Resurrection service."

Aunt Evanthia was still holding her head, thinking.

Please bake it, I wished silently as I crawled into bed, lying on my stomach, pressing my mouth against the pillow. I fell asleep and dreamed that my little brother was on his way home to have supper with us. When I awoke the warm smell of fresh bread was everywhere. I sat up and leaned against the wall, waiting.

Aunt Evanthia walked in from the kitchen, carrying a large frying pan. "Unleavened and without salt," she said, putting the pan on the table. "God have mercy on us," she said.

I stretched out both hands for a slice, but she wouldn't hear of it.

"At the table!" she ordered, serving my helping.

As we ate, Aunt Evanthia began to weep.

I stopped eating, although the bread tasted fine to me. Why was she crying?

"To add salt," she said, licking her tears as they trickled down to her lips.

We started to laugh. Aunt Evanthia kept crying and licking her tears, and laughing, and I laughed so hard that tears came to my lips as well.

"There! Lick them now!" said my aunt, laughing.

And I licked my tears, which made the bread taste better, and the strength of the bread filled my blood, and the inside of my body felt like a field of rye waving in the afternoon breeze, and on each head of rye there were many blond grains but also two or three purple ones, and Aunt Evanthia said, "That's the fungus I was talking about, God have mercy on us," and I shivered and laughed, and the inside of my head felt like the sky, half of it night with a crescent moon and millions of flickering stars, and the other half sunny and blue, and when I looked around, the room itself and the table and the bread that was on the table were also divided, left and right, half night, half day. And from the dark side of the room guests began to arrive: Mother and Father, my little brother Teo who hadn't grown up in all the years since we'd seen him last, my cousin

Lambis sick with love for Lena who had married an older man and left town for a better life, and Great-Aunt Martha, shabby as ever, with a pipe hanging from her black tooth. And when they all joined us at the table, a cricket began to sing and I went looking behind the chest of drawers but could not find him, and in the daylight part of the room there were sparrows and a stream of small white butterflies, and a mouse went under the table sniffing for crumbs, a porcupine then, and a turtle cautiously, the Christmas turkey and the Easter lamb, and my father's last horse, cinnamon-colored and broad-chested like the month of August. And there were bread and bread crumbs for everyone at the table and under the table, and the horse grew larger, and the house so small that Aunt Evanthia opened the door and out we poured, out into the street to breathe. The air in the twilight was cool, and we saw more people there, Barba Yannis and others, and animals, more animals walking about like respectable citizens, equals among equals, and the birds that circled above us glowed as the last glimmer of the sun caught their wings and beaks, and Aunt Evanthia looked in a daze at the birds, saying, "What am I doing down here?" And she flapped her wings, and up she went, one with the birds, but I stayed below.

◄ ◄

Aunt Evanthia was my last relative. When she flew off, joining the birds and the shadows, I made the decision to join the next group of kids who were leaving town. I locked the house and gave the key to a neighbor, saying that I intended to be back in two or three days. The neighbor understood. We took off. We spent the first night in the trees. It rained, rained for hours. At dawn we split up, and the five- and six-year-olds were at a loss. Some tried to follow the older ones, but some of the nine- and ten-year-olds shouted at them to stay back, and even threw stones at them.

Around noontime four of us were on the same road again,

heading in the same direction. We pretended not to know one another, so I made up a new name for myself: Panagis. The others liked that, and changed their names to Minos, Andreas and Issaris. Minos, a five-year-old, had been born when the rest of us were already in the second grade. Issaris just couldn't leave him behind.

When they asked me where I thought I was going, I thought, Switzerland. My new name began to give me new ideas. Unbeknownst to me, Panagis wanted to give up his Greek nationality and take up residence in a truly civilized country, a country that didn't fight wars.

"Switzerland," I said.

Issaris and Andreas were impressed.

Minos seemed surprised. "I didn't know Switzerland was just across the border," he said.

We continued without further explanations, but something bothered me. Issaris didn't look like someone whose name is Issaris. Not that I knew anyone by that name before, not at all. I just thought that anyone whose name is Issaris ought to be taller and not be missing his left eye.

Andreas didn't agree. "Issaris is fine," he said. Andreas' own new name did little to improve his character, and there was no reason for me to hope that under that name he and I would agree on things more often.

I often compared people's names to the way they looked, and sometimes they just had the wrong names or the wrong looks.

Issaris was lean but not tall. His good eye blinked often, and, as though he doubted that his left one was missing, he often felt the sunken eyelid with the tips of his fingers.

And Andreas wouldn't miss an opportunity to defend Issaris. So when I finished explaining my theory about names and looks, Andreas wondered whether I was criticizing Issaris' name or his eye.

"Because if you don't like his eye and keep making jokes about it, I'll give you a black one," he said, showing me his fist.

Issaris glanced at Andreas, who immediately became nervous and, picking up a dry twig from the ground, put it between his front teeth to keep himself busy. There was something odd about the way Issaris glanced at people and made them aware of his scrutiny. Sometimes when he looked at me I had a feeling that it wasn't his good eye with which he saw me, but the ghost of his dead eye.

Minos had been lagging behind for some time, and then he stopped and sat down.

Andreas, who noticed it first, stopped and shouted at him irritably, "Well, what now?"

Minos put his hands between his feet and his sandals, staring at his toes. "I don't want to go to Switzerland," he pouted.

"He doesn't want to go to Switzerland. How do you like that?"

"Fine, let him go back," said Issaris.

"Tell me—I'm just curious—why don't you want to go to Switzerland?" said Andreas, restraining himself.

Minos was staring hard at his toes.

"Why?" asked Andreas again. "Too rich for you? Too civilized? Too clean?"

"I saw in a picture magazine how grownups in Switzerland scrub the kids every morning and evening," muttered Minos.

"I knew it!"

"And they don't have any sea there. All they have is lakes and mountains."

Andreas seemed alarmed. "That true?" he asked Issaris.

"My picture book says there's also a lot of snow—a lot of cold weather," confirmed the other.

"Might as well forget Switzerland," said Andreas.

Issaris and I lifted up Minos from under the arms, and we were on our way again.

The land ahead of us was bare. The summer sounds were all gone. Autumn had spread violently, startling the sparrows, sending the cranes and the wild geese hurriedly south. We breathed in the sharp air and, as if very little of it were left, we held it in, remaining silent. Here and there a small tree held its stiff branches upward without memory of summer, without remorse for its loss of memory. A sparrow, gray on gray, hid his beak, then his entire head, in the down of his breast, pretending to look for something, pretending to be someplace else.

·2·

Past the crossroads linking the two major towns of our province
we saw the Heraion, the ruins of the ancient temple and the
small theater, shining in the afternoon light. The theater was
still in pretty good shape, and many considered it to be the
oldest surviving testimony to our history. I tried to retell that
history by recounting the highlights in the theater's long life,
but I'd already forgotten the earliest episodes, and the first one
I could come up with took place around the time of the death
of our Savior Jesus Christ, when an earthquake caused extensive damages to the supporting walls and the propylaea. Our
country was then under the occupation of Rome, so it was the
Romans who had to do the repairs. Nestled on the hillside, the
theater looked like an open hand constantly receiving and dis-
persing sunlight. By the time Saint Paul visited here, spreading
the word of Christ, the marble seats of the theater had turned
rusty, and its circular stage was a puddle of mud.

Many years later the Franks took over most of the country,
and after the Franks the Venetians, and after the Venetians
the Saracen pirates from the north of Africa, burning everything but the theater—because the marble wouldn't catch fire
—and then the Turks came down, and the Turks removed
several marble seats to use them as lintels in a mosque they
built nearby to worship the Prophet. And when the revolution
broke out, and the Turks had to let the country go, the Allies

came: the English, the French and the Russians came, and our great-grandparents thought of tearing down the mosque and returning the seats to the theater, but they saw that the Moslem builders had carved some remarkable vines—or were they inscriptions in Arabic?—on the marble seats, so they decided to restore the theater without dismantling the mosque, and they cut new marble for the seats.

Now Andreas was in a feisty mood and did nothing to hide his dislike for the mosque and for the way I was telling the story. As it turned out, he didn't even care much for the theater. "Speak for *your* grandparents, not mine," he grumbled. His grandparents would have torn down the mosque gladly, or would have stuck a cross on top of its dome. Hadn't the Turks stuck all sorts of crescents on the domes of St. Sophia?

Minos said that his own grandfather, who had come from Smyrna as a refugee, used to say that the Turks weren't really all that bad—it was the war that turned people into animals. "My grandfather wouldn't tear down a nice mosque like that," said Minos.

"Not a mosque in Smyrna, anyway," chuckled Andreas.

More years went by, and the Italians who were the great-grandchildren of the Venetians who were the great-grandchildren of the Romans came to our country together with the Germans, and they recognized the Roman repairs in the supporting walls and the propylaea of the theater, and they set out to repair the repairs, which their allies the Germans thought a waste of time, although they too admired the architecture. But once the repairs were all finished, the German soldiers began to use the theater for meetings, or for sitting quietly to watch the sunset. It was then that our parents who had joined the Resistance thought about mining the foundations to blow up Germans, but in the end they didn't have the heart to destroy the theater.

"Your parents, not mine." Andreas' parents would have blown it up gladly.

The foreigners took turns. When the Germans and the Italians left, back came the English, and the English brought back the German Queen. By then our parents had been shot by the same Germans who watched the sunset, so it was our parents' younger brothers and sisters who went to join the Andartes, fighting on the mountains for bread and freedom. And one night they too came down and mined the theater to blow up what they called "the foreign locust" and the Queen's scum, but again no one had the nerve to sacrifice the theater, so no one fired the dynamite.

"That's because your uncles and aunts were too soft," said Andreas.

But the theater was still there.

And so were the Americans who had just replaced the English. "Aren't they supposed to be busy reopening the old airstrip on the other side of the river?"

"Farther up north."

The English and the Queen's scum had killed many Andartes and tricked thousands of others into laying down their arms, and a dozen or so concentration camps were full to capacity and beyond, but the English became exhausted before they could finish off the Andartes, so they handed the theater and the rest of the country over to the Americans and went home. But before that, one of the American soldiers who'd been to college made a snide remark to an English soldier, "What's the matter with you fellows, aren't these marbles good enough for the British Museum?"—which caused the greatest fistfight anyone ever saw around here. Now the Americans were all over the place, bringing in money and experts and equipment, the Truman Doctrine and the Marshall Plan, General Van Fleet and the Sixth Fleet, recruiting Nazi collaborators who had experience in tracking down the Reds, training the new Army and the Royal Air Force and the Royal Navy and other military and paramilitary units, helping the King and the Queen to save what was left of the kingdom, to save Greece from the Greeks.

The Corps of Engineers had been reopening the old airstrip farther up north so that American airplanes could bring in supplies or take off to bomb targets, "targets" being bands of Andartes on the mountains. Sometimes, when the weather was good, the shepherds saw American soldiers walking over to the theater to smoke and write letters to their families while watching the sunset.

"And who has the guts to blow it up now?" Andreas gazed at the white bowl of the theater gathering sunlight, and spat. "Dumb, good for nothing, silly stair going nowhere," he said.

Issaris, who'd been quiet for a while, rolled his only eye and cleared his throat. "Why don't you go ahead and blow up the dumb thing yourself and shut up?" said Issaris. We'd made up our minds to leave our town and province quietly, but Issaris would prefer to see the theater blown up than to see it pissed on.

Andreas turned, surprised at Issaris' challenge, and lifting his right pant leg, pretended to take a piss. There was a bitter grin on his face as he returned Issaris' challenge, and Minos thought there was going to be a fight any moment—I saw his lips tremble, his eyes about to fill up with tears.

Issaris made no move, assuring us that Andreas would probably end up pissing in his own shoes.

Andreas wasn't going to take that, and I wasn't going to be the peacemaker and end up getting punched by both of them, but Minos broke out crying loudly enough to divert everyone's attention.

"What's the matter with you?" Andreas barked at him. "You already forgot that you swore to behave like a grownup?" It was on that condition that Minos had been allowed to join Issaris and Andreas, and for a grownup crying was out and fighting was in.

"I'm hungry," cried Minos. "I want a slice of bread with some sugar on it."

"With sugar on it, too!"

Minos sat down and began to cry even more loudly. "Yes, sugar!" he said stubbornly. His face was so dirty that his tears were leaving two bright trails down his cheeks.

Issaris sat down next to Minos, sighing, as though weary of giving in. He then took out an imaginary pocketknife, cut a generous slice of imaginary bread, and spread a layer of imaginary sugar on it.

That was fine with me. I licked the extra sugar that spilled on my fingers, and I took a good bite.

Minos looked at Issaris suspiciously, looked at me, took a deep breath and started to cry again.

Issaris cut another slice.

"Easy with that sugar, now." Andreas took a bite, but his face was still sour.

Another slice, another handful of sugar on it—never mind that there won't be any left for dessert.

Reluctantly, Minos stretched out both hands, took the slice, then handed it right back. "First you've got to soak the bread."

"Whatever for?"

"It tastes better. And the sugar sticks to it and you don't lose any."

"You've already soaked it in your tears," sneered Andreas. "Now eat up or I'll rub it all over your face."

Issaris laughed. Once, when he was Minos' age, he happened to be playing in the neighborhood with a kid who was eating a slice of bread with sugar on it. Issaris was very hungry. That was the first year of the Occupation, when the Germans had taken everything away, so bread was rarely seen, and sugar was nowhere. Issaris was hungry. He stared at the bread and sugar so persistently that the kid cut a small piece and gave it to him. Issaris couldn't believe his eye. In fact, it was that eye, plus the ghost of his dead eye, that often made people be friendly to him; and that time Issaris was so sure of that and so

angry that he took that small piece of bread and sugar, and
instead of putting it in his mouth and eating it he rubbed it on
his eye.

We walked down the hillside, leaving Hera's temple and theater behind, and half an hour later we were climbing up the
dike on the left riverbank. The Mornos' source had dried up
many years before, and the only water running in the river
came from the spring thaw and the rainfall on the mountains.
Now, in spite of the heavy rains we had seen, there was only a
narrow stream of muddy water winding along the broad riverbed, and here and there a few pools and puddles infested
with frogs, leeches and a wide variety of crawling and flying
bugs. So the most recent rains must have fallen only locally.

From the top of the dike the plain looked endless, colorless,
with a few bare trees, a row of crooked telegraph poles and half
a dozen or so summer huts marking the view of the terrain but
failing to interrupt its flatness and lack of color. The sound of a
shepherd's reed in the distance made his small flock of sheep
and goats visible. The goats separated themselves from the
sheep seemingly by following the sound of their own bells. But
there wasn't even a small patch of green, and what the animals
fed on couldn't be anything other than last summer's weeds,
now dead and discolored by sun and water.

Past a bend in the river, behind the dike of the right bank,
we saw the big earth-moving machines of the Americans, clearing and broadening the old airstrip. There were yellow bulldozers, a crane and three dump trucks, plowing, pushing, loading
topsoil, unloading gravel, and cutting trenches on both sides of
the runway. We climbed down to the riverbed, hoping to get
past the construction crew undetected. Once we were down we
took off our sandals and stepped into a puddle, pulling out
water celery and other edible greens for our dinner. It wasn't a
filling meal, and soon enough Minos began to cry again, complaining that the water celery had given him cramps.

"It's probably all that sugar you ate," said Andreas.

Minos ran and pulled down his pants hastily behind a tree log, still crying, but Andreas kept an eye on him and when he saw him wipe his behind with a small white stone he warned him to watch out for scorpions. Minos pulled up his pants in a hurry and joined us, but he continued to hold his stomach and to cry, complaining about his hunger and his pain from the runs.

"You are a pain in the ass," said Andreas, adding, "I've already had enough of this baby shit. You hold on like a grownup, or back you go!"

"I'm hungry," protested Minos.

"I don't mind your being hungry. It's your crying that drives me nuts!"

"What do you want me to do—sing?"

Andreas was thinking about it. "It's an idea," he said.

"That's right, you've already tried crying and it didn't work," said Issaris. "Who knows? Singing might do the trick."

Minos was looking at me now, and I had to admit that singing could make the wheat grow faster, the horses paw harder on the threshing floor and the fists knead the dough more vigorously. Singing even made the oven hotter!

"Where? Where?"

"Let me see, now."

"Don't you worry," Issaris assured him. "If it's bread we'll find it."

Having to listen to Minos sing "Vulture" was a small price to pay. It was a little song of exile that we'd made up ourselves, but like so many other Greek songs, it was sung to a lively, uplifting tune:

> Mama Vulture builds her nest
> with feathers and twigs.
> Mama Vulture counts her chicks
> and she finds four missing.
> Mama Vulture preens her neck.
> Mama Vulture flays her breast.

> *Her husband drags out a carcass,*
> *crowing, "Lunchtime, lunch!"*
> *At five she has a fava,*
> *at six a bowl of lava.*
> *At seven she builds prisons,*
> *eight explains the reasons.*
> *Nine hops down to the wharf*
> *to see the little ones off.*
> *Midnight counts her children,*
> *but again she finds four missing.*
> *Tam-tam-tatam. Tatam-tam-tam.*
> *Tatam-tam. Tatam-tam.*
> *Tatam-tam-tatam!*

Once, I had asked my aunt Evanthia what exactly was the so-called "heroic age" in Greece, and she said that for men it's between six and fourteen years old. "At six," she said, "one is too old to be a child, and at fourteen he is too young to be a soldier."

As soon as he finished the song, Minos began to sniff the air to see if there was any fresh-baked bread nearby.

άπελευθέρωση. Εἶναι ὅμως καὶ ρεαλιστική:

Ὁ Πέτρος Ροῦσος, στὸ βιβλίο του «Ἡ Μεγάλη «Πενταετία», ἀπευθυνόμενος πρὸς ἀριστερούς ἀναγνῶστες καὶ προσπαθῶντας νὰ δικαιολογήσει τὸ «ὄχι» τοῦ ΚΚΕ, ἰσχυρίζεται πῶς ἡ ἡγεσία του δὲν ἀρνήθηκε τὴ συγκρότηση τοῦ Βαλκανικοῦ Στρατηγείου οὔτε τὸ τορπίλλισε. «Ζήτησε ἀπλῶς – γράφει – ἀναβολὴ τοῦ ζητήματος μέχρι νὰ δημιουργηθοῦν οἱ ὅροι». Γιατί αὐτὲς οἱ μασημένες δικαιολογίες; Ὁ ἴδιος ἀναφέρει ὡς ἑξῆς τοὺς λόγους ποὺ ὤθησαν τὸ πολιτικὸ γραφεῖο τοῦ ΚΚΕ στὴν ἀπόφασή του:

«Πρῶτο, νὰ στερεώσουμε τὴν ἐθνικο-απελευθερωτικὴ συμμαχία, νὰ μὴν προκαλέσουμε δυσανασχέτηση τῶν συμμάχων μας στὸ ΕΑΜ καὶ σὲ ἄλλους ἐνδεχόμενους συμμάχους μας. Δεύτερο, νὰ μὴν ἐπισπεύσουμε ἔνταση τῶν ἀντιδράσεων καὶ ἐπεμβάσεων τῶν Ἄγγλων στὴν Ἑλλάδα προτοῦ προλάβει νὰ στερεωθεῖ τὸ ἐπαναστατικὸ κίνημα στὴν Ἑλλάδα ἢ τουλάχιστον στὴ Γιουγκοσλαβία. Τρίτο, νὰ μὴ δημιουργήσουμε πρόωρα ἐμπόδια στὴν παγκόσμια ἀντιχιτλερικὴ συμμαχία, τὰ ὁποῖα ἄγνωστο ἂν θὰ μπορέσουμε τελικὰ νὰ ὑπερπηδήσουμε ὅσο βαστάει ὁ πόλεμος κατὰ τῶν καταχτητῶν».

Μακεδόνες καὶ Μεγαλόσερβοι

Ὁ Κώστας Καραγιώργης ὅμως, ποὺ ἀναμείχθηκε ἄμεσα στὸ θέμα,ὅπως εἴδαμε, σὲ ἰδιαίτερη συνομιλία ποὺ εἶχε· μὲ τὸν γράφοντα τὸ 1946, καθαρὰ καὶ σταράτα ἔδωσε τὴν ἐξήγηση:

–Ἄκου νὰ σοῦ πῶ: Ὑπῆρχαν πολλοὶ λόγοι ποὺ [...] λιτικὸ μ[...] ὅτι τὸ Ε[...] λουθοῦ [...] ματα. Δ[...] λίγο πρ[...] Διεθνὴς [...] τῆς δὲν [...] ὅπως κε[...] ἔδειχνε [...] πολὺ μεγάλες δυσκολίες. Πῶς ἦταν ὑποχρεωμένος νὰ κάνει κι' ἄλλες βαριὲς θυσίες γιὰ νὰ διατηρήσει τὴ συμμαχικὴ ἑνότητα χωρὶς τὴν ὁποία μποροῦσε νὰ χαθεῖ τὸ πᾶν. Καὶ δὲν ξέρω πῶς ὁ Τίτο καὶ ὁ Τέμπο ἔκαναν τοῦ κεφαλιοῦ τους, ἐμεῖς ὅμως διστάζαμε νὰ καταφέρουμε μιὰ μαχαιριὰ στὰ νεφρὰ τῆς μεγάλης συμμαχίας. Γιατί κάτι τέτοιο θὰ ἦταν ἂν ἀποκαλύπτα ὀρθωνόμαστε μαζὶ μὲ τοὺς Ἀλβανοὺς καὶ Γιουγκοσλάβους κατὰ τῶν Ἄγγλων. Ὅλα αὐτὰ ὅμως ἦσαν δευτερεύοντα μπροστὰ σὲ ἕναν ὀγκόλιθο ποὺ θὰ σοῦ ἀποκαλύψω».

Καὶ καθὼς ὁ γράφων τέντωνε τὸ λαιμό του καὶ τὰ αὐτιά του γιὰ νὰ ἀκούσει, ὁ Κώστας Καραγιώργης συμπληρώνει:

– Ἐκεῖνο ποὺ μᾶς τρόμαξε εἶναι ἄλλο: Εἴχαμε πληροφορίες ἀλλὰ καὶ ἀντιληφθή-

βανε τὴν ἑλληνική, γιουγκοσλαβικὴ καὶ

«... Ἡ σκέψη τῶν Γιουγκοσλάβων καὶ τῶν Ἀλβανῶν συντρόφων νὰ ἐπηρεάζουν πρὸς ὁρισμένη πολιτικὴ τὶς ἀντίστοιχες ἔνοπλες δυνάμεις τῶν ἐθνικῶν μειονοτήτων στὴν Ἑλλάδα (Σλαβομακεδόνων καὶ τσάμηδων Ἀλβανῶν) περιέκλειε σοβαροὺς κινδύνους γιὰ τὸ ἐθνικοαπελευθερωτικὸ κίνημα [...]

[At the present moment in world history nearly every nation must choose between alternative ways of life. The choice is often not a free one.]

[—HARRY S. TRUMAN, Speech before a joint session of Congress, March 12, 1947]

Ὅσοι τρέφουν αὐτὴ τὴν ἰδέα ξεχνοῦν ὅτι: Στὴ Γιουγκοσλαβία μὲ τὴν ἀπελευθέρωση ὑπῆρχαν 30 μεραρχίες σοβιετικοῦ στρατοῦ. Στὴν Ἑλλάδα μετὰ τὴν ἀπελευθέρωση ἦρθαν 3 μεραρχίες ἀγγλικοῦ στρατοῦ.

Ἀλλὰ πολὺ χαρακτηριστικὰ ὁ Πέτρος Ροῦσος παρατηρεῖ:

«Γιουγκοσλάβικα καὶ ἰδίως ὁρισμένα σλαβομακεδονικὰ στελέχη τῆς γειτονικῆς χώρας ἀψηφοῦσαν τὶς συνέπειες ποὺ θὰ 'χει σ' ὅλον τὸν ἑλληνικὸ ἀγώνα καὶ στὸν ἀγώνα τῶν βαλκανικῶν λεῶν ἡ ἄμεση υἱοθέτηση ἀπὸ μὰς τοῦ συνθήματος "ἑνιαία Μακεδονία στὰ πλαίσια τῆς νέας Γιουγκοσλαβίας". Ὑπάρχουν κι σήμερα ἀκόμη ὁρισμένοι ποὺ λένε τους κι ἂν ἀκόμα δὲν ἐλευθερωνόταν ἡ Ἑλλάδα ἀπὸ τὸν ἰμπεριαλισμό, θὰ εἶνε ἐλευθερωθεῖ τουλάχι-

Καὶ τώρα ἕνα [...] γνωση τοῦ Τίτ[...] Τέμπο; Ἀσφαλῶ[...] ὅσο τελικὰ ὅρισ[...] πρόσωπος τῆς [...] σχεδιασμὸ στρα[...]

Ὥστε ὁ Τίτο υ[...] Μεγαλοσέρβων [...] γκοσλαβίας;

Ἡ ἀπάντηση, [...] δοξο, εἶναι κατ[...] στοὺς πολλοὺς [...] μὲ ἐντολὴ του '[...] τερα τὰ γιουγκο[...] ψαν τὸ ἀντίθετο [...] καὶ ἀδιάψευστα [...]

Ὁ Τίτο πράγμ[...] σύσταση Βαλκ. Σ[...] κοὺς λόγους. Κ[...] ταν στὸν στρατι[...] ἦταν κακή. Ἀλλὰ [...] μεγαλοσέρβικοι [...] κοὶ κύκλοι – ὑπο[...] νιστικοῦ βρασμο[...] νήσου – γιὰ νὰ δ[...] τὸν τον μηχανισ[...]

Ἄργησε νὰ τὸ [...] τῆς ἀραιῆς ἐπίκ[...] τὸ καλοκαίρι τοῦ [...] μάχη ζωῆς ἢ θα[...] τῶν. Ὅταν πληρ[...] γίνει, ἡ ἀντίδρ[...] Ἔσπευσε νὰ δια[...]

«Παραγγείλατ[...] στὸν Τέμπο νὰ [...] ηγείο γιατ[...] ωστό».

[...]γράμμα το[...] [...]αμβίζει [...]

[...]ἡ σημερὶν[...] [...]α ὁποιουδ[...] [...]ς λάθος, ἡ χαριστικ[...] [...]λή του πρ[...] [...]δημιουργι[...] [...]λει ἀνοησία [...]

Τὰ μηνύματα [...] στρα[...]ηγὸ τοῦ δ[...] νος τὰ εἶχε λάβ[...] «ὄχι» τοῦ Σιάντ[...] πυρώσει τὸ θέμ[...] τήσει ὁριστικά.

Ἄλλωστε ,τώ[...] παρτιζάνοι ὅπω[...] βρίσκονταν μπρ[...] ἀνατροπή: Ἡ Ἰτ[...] Καὶ στὸν βαλκα[...] σποτος ἕνας ὁλό[...] γέρας τῶν δυνα[...] χώματα τῆς Γιου[...]

Τὸ ΚΚΕ λέει:

·3·

The sound of bulldozer and truck engines had grown louder. There was nothing to warn us that the site was off-limits, but we planned to get past it as fast as we could, anyway.

Just then I saw what I thought was a large heap of trash dumped into the river over the right-bank dike. From the looks of it, it was unlike all other heaps of refuse that we'd gone through before; this one was fresh, clean-looking, colorful.

"Fresh?"

"Clean?"

"Look at it carefully."

"It's colorful, all right," admitted Andreas. "It must be American."

We were heading toward the trash without even a token debate. Minos was now sniffing in that direction, and the rest of us kept our eyes fixed on the glittering mound as if trying to nail it down that way, to make sure it didn't move from where it was.

"Bread," said Minos. "I smell bread!"

"Easy, now." Andreas spread his arms to make us slow down. Several crows and a small dog were at work scavenging, and we couldn't afford a commotion.

"I've never seen any trash like that in my whole life!" A wild look in Issaris' eye.

A couple of crows turned, saw us, and took off.

"American," whispered Andreas. "Name it and it'll be there!"

"Bread!"

Two more crows took off, and the rest followed them soon. The dog wagged his tail at us. He wouldn't go away, but he wouldn't bark either.

We dug into the refuse with hands and feet, plowing through crushed cartons, boxes, empty cans of food and engine oil, sorting out beer bottles, tires, clothing, broken tools, and newsmagazines with such excitement that the dog was appalled and started to back off, turning his ears in this direction and that as if he feared the worst was yet to come.

A pair of headphones, odd pieces of cable and a spool of copper wire. Bent instruments, screws, empty rifle shells, nails. An assortment of small bottles still full of pills, powders, liquids and ointments, from which we could identify only aspirin, quinine and ammonia. Deeper in, where birds and dogs had not reached, we found a loaf of bread that had started to mildew, a few unopened cans and several boxes of neatly stacked crackers and biscuits. Other fantastic objects, shining and looking as good as new, and still others that had lived only part of their useful lives before they were discarded without thought of repair. The wristwatch didn't work—quarter of one. A pair of binoculars, but one of the lenses gone. Issaris gave them a try: perfect! Andreas found a brown army bag and the barrel of a broken rifle. Minos found a switchblade, but Andreas wouldn't trust him with it and he took it away. Then Minos found a small enameled pan. Issaris got a thermometer and a box of wet matches, another loaf of bread, already sliced and wrapped in paper, and a deck of playing cards. And I found a pair of leather gloves made for a person with two left hands. Minos got a pair of overalls that could fit all four of us together. Andreas a fountain pen that had run out of ink, and a pair of suspenders. Issaris a bottle of ink and a broken syringe. And I found a book that taught Greek from alpha to omega through pictures. We hastily threw everything we thought we could use into the army bag, and we were ready to run.

"Wait!" Using Minos' switchblade, Andreas cut a wide strap of rubber from the inner tube of a flat tire and showed it to us proudly before adding it to the bag. "Slingshots," he said.

We ran. We were thieves, and the bulldozers would come after us with their broad, shining blades and treacherous treads. Thieves, and if the bulldozers missed us, a squadron of fighter planes would catch up with us in no time. We ran. Without turning to look back, because if you run away from something and turn to look, chances are that you'll see it coming after you, or else you'll turn into stone. And if the planes didn't catch up with us, the machine-gun or rifle fire would almost certainly get us. We ran. Until Andreas and I, who carried the bag, ran out of breath and threw the bag to the ground. Then we threw ourselves down as well and rolled on our backs, laughing.

Minos and Issaris emptied the bag, and, first things first, they put aside the bread, the crackers, and the cans of food. Andreas flipped the switchblade open, crossing himself with it.

What did he mean by that? Thank God?

When Andreas opened the first can, I realized that the sign of the cross was meant to protect us from food poisoning.

"Carrots! Steamed in plain water—damn!"

"Whole onions! Also steamed in plain water!"

The third can was beans in a thick, sweet sauce. Andreas poured them into Minos' pan and started to work on the bread, carefully cutting out every green corner or spot.

The dog was lying on his belly a few steps from us. When our eyes met, he lowered his chin onto his paws and looked at each one of us shyly, and then yawned, stretching out his long ears all the way behind his head until they touched each other.

"*My* dog," said Minos.

"You've had enough bread?" said Andreas.

Minos picked up all the mildewed leftovers and threw them at the dog, who wolfed them down instantly. The dog was still hungry.

"Take him back to the trash," said Andreas.

As though having heard his name, the dog got up and went over to Andreas.

"Sit!" ordered Andreas.

The dog yawned.

"Trash!" said Minos.

The dog went over to Minos, wagging his tail.

His name had to be Trash.

"You feed him," said Andreas, handing Minos the carrots.

We went carefully through the spoils, sorting out every item by category for a final selection, saving besides the food some of the clothes and tools, and whatever medicine we thought we might need. We left out all the heavy or bulky objects regardless of their value. Then Andreas went to work, cutting thin strips of rubber for slingshots. Issaris was scanning the riverbed ahead of us through his "binocular," and Minos was busy washing the pan and talking to the dog.

And I looked at the afternoon sun and adjusted my new wristwatch to the right time.

We spent the night in a shallow cave that the water had dug out in the earthworks, and at dawn we continued our journey north. The sun rose in a cloudless sky that had already changed from pink to deep blue to light, and by ten, when I reset my watch once more, it was no longer autumn but a warm brilliant day of late summer. We started taking off our American clothes and putting them back into the brown bag that we carried in turns. Breathing in the mild air, feeling the strong sun on our faces and bare arms, we were as light as the sparrows that had already shaken off the first autumn chill from their wings, and as noisy. We were whistling and making jokes about anything that attracted our attention: the flies, the round shining stones, the broomweed and its hard bristle, infested with red spores and mosquitoes. But deeper in me lay quietly the knowledge that we had finally gone too far to return, and that it would probably be years before any one of us made it back to the hometown and country we were leaving behind. I began to speculate about the outcome of our journey, and about the fate of the other kids who had headed in different directions. Would we be able to cross the borders before the Nationalists sealed them? Would the Andartes help us?

The Nationalists, now with the American Mission on their side, were predicting an early victory. The Andartes, without even promises for help from the Russians, were talking about a long, long struggle.

Andreas finished making the last slingshot and gave it to me. Now it was his turn to carry the bag. I tried out my slingshot, aiming at a thicket of broomweed. Minos used a piece of insulated wire to make a collar and leash for Trash so that he wouldn't run away when our supplies came to an end. Trash did not object to being on a leash. On the contrary, he seemed pleased by it, and he led the way as though he'd sensed his master's wish, and adjusted to our pace, stalling once in a while to lift his leg and mark a big stone, a tree log or a weed. Issaris walked ahead, scouting. Whenever he saw someone crossing the river, he'd lower his binoculars and signal to us to hide.

After a midday snack of crackers and canned pudding, Minos washed the pan and decided to wear it as a helmet to protect his head from the sun. Minos was so pleased with Trash's intelligence and good nature that he kept talking to him, telling him stories about other pets he'd owned. Zavos was his most favorite dog. "When he was a small puppy, a big shepherd dog bit one of his legs, one of his hind legs—the right one, I think," said Minos. "And ever after he dragged that leg behind him, and the whole town made fun of him. So I wished that someone would cut off Zavos' broken leg," he said. "That way he wouldn't be stepped on all the time when he was around people." As it was, not only was he being stepped on accidentally and on purpose, but also when he got into a fight with another dog that dog always attacked Zavos' broken leg. Then, as if pain were not enough, Zavos had to suffer humiliation. When he went to pee at a tree or a pole, he wouldn't be able to lift that leg, and he'd pee all over himself instead, which mortified him and made him the smelliest dog in town. "People were throwing stones at him all the time," said Minos. And one day Zavos fell for a young bitch who also seemed to have nothing but contempt for him. In the beginning of the courtship, Minos even saw her turn around and give Zavos a bite on that same broken leg. But Zavos wouldn't give up. He followed her day and night, sniffing along, limping along, pausing to wet his leg and curse the day he was born, and when she barked at him, or bared her teeth, he'd slow down and raise his ears to assess the situation, then follow her again, at a distance. "This went on for many days."

We saw Issaris slow down while peering at something through his binoculars, and when we caught up with him he said he was trying to focus on what seemed to be a group of people, but they were too far away for him to tell who they might be and what they were up to.

Andreas asked for the binoculars to have a look for himself, but he said he couldn't see a thing.

"Close your left eye," said Issaris.

Andreas closed his left eye and adjusted the lens. "There," he said. "I think they're a bunch of kids."

"They look small because of the distance," said Issaris.

"No. They are kids," insisted Andreas. "Here," he said, handing me the binoculars.

They were kids. They were gathered near the right-bank dike as in a circle, some seven or eight of them, and I wondered if they weren't in the original group that we'd split from.

"Give me the binoculars. Let me have a look," said Minos.

We filled our pockets with small round stones for our slingshots and headed in that direction cautiously.

Minos started again to tell Zavos' story from where he'd left off, as if Trash had demanded it. "This kind of thing went on for days," said Minos. After a while the bitch became more tolerant of Zavos' advances. She didn't bite him, she didn't seem to mind him sniffing after her, and one afternoon Minos saw her standing in front of Zavos trustfully, if not encouragingly, to go ahead with what was on his mind. "That's what Zavos had been waiting for," said Minos. And Zavos jumped her, putting his forelegs on her back, but he still had trouble supporting himself on one hind leg only, and he kept falling back on his broken leg, and the bitch didn't know what was going on, what was the matter with him, and at the end she got angry and, turning around, she growled and bit him hard on that same crippled leg. "And that was the last time I saw Zavos," said Minos. Later on someone said that he'd seen a dog looking like Zavos lying dead in a ditch in the fields, but Minos didn't believe him. "I think somebody from another town liked him and took him along, and a doctor fixed his leg all right so Zavos can pee anywhere he wants without making a mess of himself, and jump any bitch that he likes," said Minos.

When we got closer to the kids who were gathered by the right bank, we saw that they were kicking and jabbing with sticks at another kid whose arms and legs had been tied around a treelog on the ground. They were between ten and twelve years of age. They did not look familiar. Now they had turned in our direction, raising their sticks as a warning to us not to get closer.

Andreas let the bag fall to the ground and put his hand into his pocket where he kept the switchblade. We took out our slingshots and stretched them out, aiming at the heads of the bigger kids. Andreas took another step forward.

"What's going on here?" he asked.

A tall, skinny kid from the other group took a step toward Andreas. Like Andreas, he kept his right hand in his pocket.

"Are you Bandit sympathizers, or Nationalists?" he said. The Nationalists always referred to Andartes as "Bandits."

"You answer my question first," said Andreas. "What's your name, anyway?"

"What's yours?"

"Andreas."

"Mine's Vasilis, and I am for the King."

"That's fine with me," said Andreas. "What's the story with him?"

"He's a Bandit sympathizer. He's our prisoner."

"Help! They want to cut my throat," cried the other, pushing to turn the log so he could see us. Unable to move, he went on crying and pleading for our help.

Andreas was staring at the kid who'd said his name was Vasilis. "That true?" he asked him calmly.

Vasilis was surprised. "None of your business," he said.

"Suppose he is a sympathizer. What are you going to do with him?"

Vasilis turned his face halfway around to exchange a meaningful look with one of his pals who stood behind him.

"Tell him," urged the other.

"First they'll have to tell us where they come from," said Vasilis.

Andreas wasn't sure whether or not he wanted to say where we were coming from. "Why?" he asked.

"Because you are not from around here. If you were you'd know what we do to Bandits and Bandit sympathizers that we catch."

We did know. It just hadn't occurred to Andreas and to the rest of us that what they were planning to do was to cut the kid's throat and take his head to the nearest Gendarmerie station to collect bounty. It didn't occur to us, because the kid was under fourteen and did not qualify. We'd heard many stories about the headhunters who went around the country hunting down Andartes and anyone friendly to them, and once we'd seen photographs of severed heads in the newspaper; but it was unheard of that children were taking the heads of other children for money. Everyone knew that the Gendarmerie had orders from the government not to pay a single drachma for the heads of children under fourteen. Either Vasilis and his pals didn't know the law or the law was different in that region.

Andreas shook his head. "You are going to cut his head off?" he said.

"That's what we do around here."

"You know who he is?"

"He says he's on his way to Yannina, where he has relatives."

"Was he armed?"

"No."

Andreas took out his switchblade and flipped it open. "You know what this is?" he asked.

The kids behind Vasilis came forward to have a better look at the switchblade. They were impressed.

"It's an American gutting machine," said Andreas, folding the blade in and flipping it open again. "A dangerous weapon," he added. He walked cautiously over to the other side of the log, from where he could see the prisoner's face. "I'll be damned!" said Andreas

"Who is he?" asked Minos.

"Well, you won't believe—it's Makis!" Andreas said.

"Makis?" Who was Makis? We didn't know anyone named Makis. And Makis was not a name. That's just it! It was a nickname for almost any male Greek name. That's just it.

"You are kidding me," said Issaris.

"Come see for yourself," said Andreas while trying to untie the prisoner's hands with his left hand.

"Don't," Vasilis warned him.

Andreas stood up, showing the switchblade to everybody, while Issaris untied the prisoner.

"His name is not Makis," said Vasilis. "His name is Avraam."

"Avramakis, Makis," said Andreas. "We're friends. We call him Makis for short."

Minos and I went closer to see Makis, who was rubbing his wrists and ankles.

"Andriko! Nikola!" said Avramakis, embracing us. Smart.

"I don't believe you," said Vasilis, his face red with frustration and anger. "He is our prisoner." He then turned to his pals. "Are you just going to stand there looking and do nothing about it? What's going on?" he said.

The kids did not move.

"You know who my father is?" he shouted at us desperately.

"No, but I have a pretty good idea," said Andreas.

Andreas had risen to the occasion; he was our leader, all right.

"My father's a professional headhunter," announced Vasilis.

"Mine too," said the kid who stood next to him. "We've been waiting to meet them here."

"Good!" said Andreas. "So pretty soon you'll all find out it's against the law to cut the throat of anyone who's only eleven years old."

"What'd you want us to do, wait for him to become fourteen?" muttered Vasilis.

We kept staring at Vasilis' pocket, trying to imagine why he kept his hand in it. No one thought he might be carrying a knife or a pistol, for if he was he would have tried to use it before we released his prisoner. And yet he still kept his right hand in his pocket.

Andreas sat down on the log. "Tell me," he said to Vasilis calmly, "how do you go about cutting somebody's throat, anyway?"

Vasilis was silent.

The kid next to him said, "Where did you find that knife?"

"I'll tell you if you tell me first how you were going to cut my friend's throat," said Andreas.

"You tell first where you got that knife," said Vasilis.

Andreas turned to me. "Tell them," he said.

I would not trust them with anything, not even with the location of that American dump. "My Uncle Jimmi brought it all the way from New York," I said proudly. "He's a gangster there."

"Tell us where's your town, and we'll ask his uncle to send you one, too," said Issaris.

"You're teasing me," said Vasilis.

"Honest," said Issaris. "What do you have to lose?"

Vasilis was confused. "It's over there," he said shyly, pointing beyond the left bank of the river. "The name of the village is Katouna," he said.

"What's your name?" said Andreas. "Uncle Jimmi can't send you the knife if he doesn't know your family name."

"You won't go tell the Gendarmerie?" said Vasilis.

"Why bother? You are not a Bandit sympathizer, are you?"

"Oh, no. I was just thinking . . ."

"His name's Tranos," said the other kid. "Vasilis Tranos."

"Fine," said Andreas. "Now tell me how you go about cutting somebody's throat in Katouna."

"Show him," said the same kid to Vasilis.

Vasilis hesitated for a moment, then pulled his hand from his pocket, revealing—what? the lid of a tin can, which had been folded in two for extra thickness. Its edge was as jagged and sharp as the can opener had left it.

"With that?"

Vasilis flashed his terrible weapon in the air. It made a swishing sound and stopped just short of Andreas' face. "Cuts better than most knives," he said.

"Don't," said Andreas. "Don't ever use this thing. What you need is a real knife. Like this. And if you're a nice kid, Saint Basil will bring you one."

I put the slingshot into my pocket and lifted the bag to my shoulder. After having gained some distance, we looked back.

Vasilis and the others were still there, still at the same spot, facing our way like little white statues in a cemetery.

Once he regained the circulation in his hands and feet, Avramakis offered to carry the bag, and I handed it to him gladly.

"You shouldn't have given those kids your real name," I said.

Avramakis smiled. "Who said I gave them my real name?" And then he said, "Where to, old friend?"

·4·

A black spot in the strong afternoon light. It grew. It rose with the heat of the stones. A tendril, then a stump, a tree already struck by lightning.

"A cross," said Issaris once he'd focused the binoculars.

And it was a slender black cross in the middle of the riverbed. But it soon moved. A woman in black, hopping on the hot stones. Barefoot on the hot stones.

"And she's headless," said Issaris, handing me the binoculars.

"She must've run into the headhunters," whispered Andreas.

She was headless. We stopped. The dog began to bark, and Avramakis had to help Minos restrain him. I took out my slingshot and loaded it.

"She's coming this way," said Avramakis, shuddering.

We shuddered. Trash raised his fur. When the woman's head popped up again through the collar of her dress, her face was mustached and bearded. It was the face of a young monk.

He was a young monk. With big dancing leaps he stopped a few meters short of us, a wild look in his brown eyes. He brought his index finger to his lips: "Shh. Blessed be those who ask no questions after the answers have been exhausted." A soft voice, considering the strained expression of his face and his stringy limbs.

We asked no questions.

"Silence. Disturb not the temperate, for they carry the gold to a temper that has no return. . . ."

We'd even stopped breathing.

". . . But let not silence accumulate for long or it may become as offensive as gold."

"Father," said Andreas in a tone that was as soft as the monk's, "where is it, the gold?"

The monk jumped as though he'd stepped on a thorn. He took a step to the right and dragged his left foot and his body slowly in the same direction. Painfully, as though his insides had suddenly collapsed, he sat down and let his head drop to his chest. "Where is the gold indeed?" echoed his voice. "And where are my seven stars—the tetramorphs?" His head jerked up once more, his eyes piercing. "Four, but not just four. Four and twenty elders on one side, and on the other side the mountains: men lying on the ground dead or living filled with terror. Listen. . . . Do you hear the galloping horses? Gloomy the mountains, and the moon eaten away by consumption, and the stars break up into pieces. Notus, Boreas, all the winds mix their breaths and grind the blood-red coal to powder—the very cloud you breathe. Listen to the trumpet. . . . Woe, woe, woe to the inhabitors of the earth. Ships and wrecks blown down, engulfed. Beyond the sea a multitude of trees and plants consumed by fire! A river beyond, men drinking on the bank, but what river and what do they drink? In the midst of this smoke, locusts with faces of men and hair of women and teeth as the teeth of sharks; they have tails of scorpions and stingers in their tails. And out of their mouths issue fire and smoke and brimstone. Under their feet a crowd of men slain, and others like you and myself take flight, running backward in terror—do you hear? I hear . . . I hear you. . . . I am not afraid of you." The vision having faded away, the monk's eyes focused on our faces now. "You are terrified!" he said triumphantly.

We were scared. The dog, who was cowering behind Minos all this time, now began to bark at the monk.

Slowly, the monk lay down on his side. He seemed to be
falling asleep. We approached and looked at him closely. The
dog sniffed him all over and began to lick his wrists and neck,
which had not been washed for a long time. He had gone to
sleep, breathing weakly. A few minutes later he was shrinking
away as if the stones had eaten their way into the dark of his
body, as if the stones shone beneath his body, until he was no
more than a black spot in the dazzling afternoon light.

The frogs: V*rekekex koax-koax* . . . An hour or so before sun-
down, when the light had become softer and the air cooler,
hundreds of frogs started to leap out of the puddles and arrange
themselves around the edges on the damp sand or on stranded
lumps of algae, clearing their puffed-up throats, rehearsing
their individual or choral parts for the evening concert, which,
as we were about to find out, would include swarms upon
swarms of other musicians and singers that hovered above the
water in dense but ever-changing formations, humming, buzzing, chirping, scraping or screeching without a conductor or
moderator or any sense of moderation whatever.

"It's like Lake Yannina," said Avramakis, wiping his sweating
brow.

I wondered if someone shouldn't relieve him of the bag.
Avramakis was frail. The weight of the bag seemed heavier on
his shoulder, and as he held it from the top with his left hand
his arm looked bony, without any muscle, and his neck thin
like the neck of a cockerel. His straight black hair kept falling
over his eyes, hiding them. But now and then his big brown
eyes shone through from behind his hair, animating his entire
face. Avramakis admitted to having lied about many things in
order to save his life during the past couple of years, in fact he
claimed to have become an expert liar, but he insisted that the
story of his having been born in Yannina was true. And he did
not believe that any members of his family were still there.
After that, he wanted to tell us the story of Ali Pasha, the
Arslan, the "Lion of Yannina."

"Never mind," interrupted Andreas. "Everybody knows Ali Pasha. Everybody knows how he tricked the Turks, and how in the end he was outtricked by the Sultan, who knifed him in his own castle in the lake island."

"Wrong, wrong," said Avramakis, laying down the bag. "Here, you carry this for a minute so I can think better, and I'll tell you exactly how it happened. You see, most of the people know about Ali Pasha from the stories they've read in magazines, but in Yannina people still remember the real story—the history."

"That's impossible," said Andreas, lifting the bag. "How can they remember something that happened a hundred and fifty years ago?"

"Good point," mocked Issaris. And then he said to Avramakis, "Promise you won't give up on us soon, too, and go back to join the cutthroats."

"I promise," laughed Avramakis.

And Andreas wondered, "Did I say something wrong?"

Avramakis insisted that it wasn't Ali Pasha, but Kyra Frosyni, the most beautiful and trusted among his wives, who was murdered in the lake castle by the Sultan's agents. Ali himself had been stabbed to death in Grand Vizier Khurshid's tent, where he and Khurshid were supposed to work out their differences. His head was then cut off and sent to Constantinople. But that was only the end of Ali Pasha's long life, and Avramakis had no intention of making a long story short. So he started from the beginning, with Ali Pasha's own father, who was a landowner at the foot of the Klissura Mountains in Albania, and how the other local chiefs envied him and in the end killed him and took over his lands, how Ali's mother formed a brigand band but was not able to take revenge and recover the family's property, until Ali himself was old enough to make his own army. But after he killed the killers and took back his fields, he also took theirs and other people's, and as his wealth grew so did his army. And so he moved to take over one province after an-

other, but he was clever enough not to offend the Sultan, and
to prove his loyalty he kept sending rich gifts to Constantinople. Once he was through with Albania he moved south to
Greece, grabbing the Sultan's provinces from the Sultan's
men, in the Sultan's name, conspiring now with Napoleon and
now with the English. And the Sultan was outraged and got
some support from the Russians, but it was already too late:
one of Ali Pasha's sons had just taken over the Morea in his
father's name, spreading his authority all over Greece.

"And he still sent presents to the Sultan," said Avramakis.
"What a fox he was."

Now the Sultan sent armies against him, but Ali Pasha kept
crushing them, and once he even sent the Sultan some of the
spoils he'd taken from his defeated men. "He really didn't want
to offend the Sultan," said Avramakis, "but he couldn't help it.
The only lands around that he could conquer belonged to the
Sultan."

Funny. Ali explained this in a letter to Khurshid, the Sultan's
Grand Vizier, who seemed to understand. "Maybe now is a
good time for us to straighten out our affairs," said Khurshid.
Despite Ali's age (he was eighty by then), he accepted the invi-
tation, and his meeting with Khurshid turned out to be very
friendly. But on his way out of the Grand Vizier's tent, Ali was
stabbed in the back, and whoever stabbed him—some say it
was Khurshid himself—used the same knife to cut off his head
and send it to the Sultan.

"But wait until you hear the story of Ali Pasha's two sons,
Veli and Mukhtar, and how they were murdered by the Turks,"
said Avramakis.

"Never mind about Veli and Mukhtar," said Andreas. "Tell
us about your family. Why aren't they in Yannina anymore?"

"My family," said Avramakis, sighing.

"The truth," said Andreas.

"My parents were Hebrews," said Avramakis. There were

many Hebrews in Yannina before the war. When the Germans came, his parents wanted to join the Andartes on the mountain, but the elder of the community told them not to because that would make the Germans angry, and they'd use it as an excuse to punish all the others. Well, the elder was wrong. The Germans didn't need an excuse. The Greeks saved some Hebrews, but most of the others were rounded up and sent to Germany, to the ovens. Avramakis had heard that the Germans made soap out of Hebrews, but he didn't believe they washed their hands and faces with it.

"Were your parents sent to Germany?" asked Minos.

"They escaped from Yannina, and they paid a mule trader to take me to Thebes," said Avramakis.

"How old were you?" asked Minos.

"About your age: six. So I remember everything." Avramakis' parents went to Thrace, where they knew people from the fur trade. They thought Thrace, which was occupied by the Bulgarians, was safer, but Bulgaria itself was occupied by the Germans. Each month, the Bulgarians had to deliver to the Germans a certain number of Hebrews. Avramakis was afraid that his parents had been taken to Bulgaria, and from there to Germany. "The truth is that they didn't come back after the war," said Avramakis.

As family stories went, it sounded just like our own, for each one of us had lost his parents during either the German occupation or the civil war that followed the occupation, my mother being perhaps an exception. It had been just the year before that people had spoken to me about her as though she were still alive and fighting with the Andartes, or in hiding.

We went on silently for a while. The western sky was changing. A small white cloud had taken the shape of a spiral, the upper end of which seemed to have hooked into the sun as if in an attempt to pull it down into its funnel and hustle it out of sight, doing away with the ritual of a prolonged setting. Trash barked at the cloud once, and afterward busied himself with snapping at those insects that strayed from their swarm to attack us.

As we approached the large shallow pool that occupied most of the width of the riverbed, both the number of insects and their attacks on us increased dramatically. For a while we laughed it off, trying to make a joke of it, pretending to engage the little mean squadrons of gnats, mosquitoes and other flying water bugs in a boxing match, but they seemed to have the upper hand right from the beginning, and they won the first round in almost no time. Andreas threw the army bag down and handed out to us whatever pieces of clothing he could find in it. We swatted at the insects, downing dozens of them at a time. In spite of this, their numbers continued to grow as, wave after wave, they split from the gray cloud that hovered over the green water to mount successive assaults on us from all sides.

"We've got to run!" shouted Andreas. "Take the other end," he said to me, his left hand already having taken hold of the top end of the bag. "The rest of you run ahead, clearing the way," he added.

We ran. It was awful. We looked to see if we could find a goat path to climb up the dike, but there was none. We tried anyway, only to turn back after having gone halfway up. We ran. Alongside the dike. Panting. Avramakis and Issaris swatting their way through the thick air, Minos being forced to run as fast as the dog, who went ahead snapping, barking and trying to break away from his possessive master. Finally Minos let go of the leash and joined the fight with Avramakis and Issaris. The narrow path they opened closed rapidly after them, each new stream of insects recoiling like a hydra head to strike the three from the rear, then to turn for a head-on attack on Andreas and myself, who were handicapped by that bag dangling between us. We defended ourselves, striking back at the monster with our free hands and our cries. They were no use. I shook my head right and left, trying to keep my eyes and mouth shut, leaving my nostrils and ears undefended. We ran, screaming with fear and pain. But the worst was not yet over. Within the next few moments the main body of the swarm moved to block our way, and the air became so thick that the last rays of the sun could not penetrate it. It was as though the air had taken a visible body and was eager to show its pulse and its muscle, its twisting limbs at each point of severance, and its furious power of regeneration. It could strangle us, suffocate us, bite and sting us to death, devour us whole. And as its body blocked our view and the light about us, so did its collective voice obliterate all other sounds and noises, even our forceful steps on the stones, even our own voices, for the sound of the swarm had become so piercing, it felt as if it had taken residence in our brains, as if the swarm itself had entered our brains, and our brains were the swarm. I tried thinking of the swarm not as a monster but as many individual insects. It didn't work. Besides mosquitoes and other small bugs, there were dragonflies, black water flies, and beetles with hard armored wings that crashed into our faces and every bare spot of our bodies with such a blind ferocity that we often fell down, or stepped on each other as we lay writhing on the ground. A thought flashed through my mind: It's hopeless. It was not my thought but the suggestion of the swarm itself that had entered my brain. "Stop fighting, it's no use," whispered the little voice inside my brain. "Close your eyes now, and you'll see: it's so easy, so easy, so easy . . ." But then another little voice shouted, "Ammonia! Get that ammonia, stupid!"

"Ammonia!" I was on all fours, searching for the bag.

Andreas was crawling on the stones, pulling at the bag, dragging it along. "What's the matter with you?" he shouted.

"The ammonia!" I shouted back. "There's a bottle of ammonia in the bag!" I found the bottle, unscrewed its cap, spilled some of its contents onto my arms, cheeks, chest, legs. The acid smell attacked my nostrils and eyes violently. But that was nothing compared to the incredible sting that I felt all over my skin. I let out such a scream that all the others crawled to my side to see what had happened to me. Still screaming with pain, I spilled some of the ammonia at them.

"Close your eyes, and rub it all over," I yelled. I went on pouring more in their hands.

"It stings!"

"God, it stings!"

We were crawling around, rubbing our arms and legs, while streams of tears ran down our cheeks from the ammonia gas and the stinging it caused in the insect bites that covered every part of exposed skin. Noticing a change in the light, I looked up and saw a hole in the swarm, and through the hole I saw the sky. The insects had retreated, and the deafening sound subsided, but the gray cloud still loomed overhead, and the hole in it offered no more than the disquieting comfort of our being in the eye of the storm. We were stunned, but it occurred to me that if we didn't seize the opportunity to gain some distance from the pool before the ammonia had completely evaporated, the swarm would come back to finish us off.

"Let's get going!" I spilled some ammonia on our clothes this time, and we were on our way again. Soon the pool was behind us, and so was the great body of insects, which remained suspended above the water, waiting for other victims. Once we felt safe enough, we all decided to take a break to scratch. Avramakis said we shouldn't scratch for more than a minute at a time, because we'd run the risk of skinning ourselves alive. We started to scratch. First softly over the many swollen spots, bumps, red and white blotches. Then a bit harder in between. Later very hard all over. But as the scratching spread, so did the wild itch through our contaminated blood. After that we stood in single file and scratched each other's backs.

"More!" cried Minos. "A little to the right. No, not so high —lower!"

"Harder!" shouted Issaris. "Don't you have any nails?"

Avramakis was last, without anyone behind him. We turned

around and carried on in his direction for another half minute. We could not stop. We scratched wildly, letting out all sorts of grunting and purring sounds. What a strange, tyrannical sensation, that itch, and what a relief and pleasure to scratch, and scratch, until the teased blood came to the surface and the skin could take no more. We spent a few more minutes getting to the forgotten spots such as elbows and armpits, lips, and behind the ears, and inside the palms of our hands. We lay on our backs, panting. It was then that the sun finally reached the mountain line, surrounded by yellow, orange, red, violet and blue bands of haze.

"Listen," said Minos.

We followed the barking sound until we spotted Trash near the left-bank dike. He was running around a mule or a horse that was probably tied onto a stone and could not leave. There were two baskets fastened one on either side of his saddle.

Issaris took out his binoculars and scanned the vicinity, to see where the owner of the mule might be. "Nobody," he said.

We loaded our slingshots, approaching with caution. When we got there, Minos took hold of the dog and pulled him aside. Docilely Trash quieted down. Andreas went straight to the mule to check the contents of the two baskets.

"Whatever it is, it's covered with bugs," he said. "It's got to be food," he said.

Issaris, Avramakis and I went around a small pool nearby to see if there was anybody behind the broomweed. And it was there that we found the owner of the mule. He lay on his back, his face and hands completely hidden by insects. Crossing his chest were two cartridge belts. Under his left leg, his German rifle. His feet were soaking in the green water. We were still standing by, staring at him, when Andreas and Minos joined us again.

"Get me that bottle of ammonia—quick!" said Andreas.

I opened the bottle over the man's face, and most of the insects flew away, while others tumbled down or caught in the stubble of his cheeks. His face was so swollen by the bites that we could not open his eyes. Andreas tried again until he suc-ceeded in pulling the lids of one eye apart and holding them open for a moment with his thumbs. We saw the brown pupil glide to the center of the eye under a layer of mucus. Was it trying to focus? Andreas jumped back, frightened.

"He's still alive," he said. He then went back, and with Avra-makis' help he pulled the two cartridge belts off the dying man's chest. As they lifted the upper part of his body, we saw the bloodstain and the bullet wound in his back.

"Let's check the baskets," said Issaris.

We went back to the mule. Issaris and I pushed one of the baskets up while Andreas and Avramakis unfastened the other. They put it down. It was still full of insects. When we took the second one down, once again I opened the ammonia bottle over the baskets until the insects had flown away, and we looked in. We stepped back, stumbling onto one another, hold-ing on to one another, terrified.

"What's in them?" asked Minos, stepping on tiptoe to see for himself.

"Hold it right there!" Issaris blocked his way.

In the meantime, Avramakis had turned his face the other way, throwing up violently.

Andreas and I waited for a minute, then decided to have another look: Inside each basket were the severed heads of four or five young men and women.

◄ ◄

In the copper twilight, we helped Minos and Avramakis onto the saddle and handed them our army bag. Issaris and I pulled the mule forward by the harness, following Andreas, who walked ahead armed with the rifle and cartridge belts of the dying headhunter. The dog kept up with our pace alongside the mule, his leash crawling between his legs like a small ser-pent.

As the light of day diminished and the first stars shone in the darker blue of the sky, the faces we'd just seen, the same young faces, came back to us, a faint glow in the night air, lighting our way out of the river. Faces of the martyrs, each leaning against the other as in old ikons, sorrow slanting their eyes as centuries before. And yet one could tell that a few hours earlier, before the dark set in in their eyes, there was compassion in their eyes; before the dark filled their mouths there was hope in every word they uttered. They were young, and they would remain young as the gods had intended. The hours passed slowly, but that glow stayed with us all night. Now we were their witnesses, and we would live to tell, as their faces aged within ours, with hairs stuck to the cheeks and between the lips, with the horizon around the neck blackening, to show how the day must come to an end before it can begin again.

άπελευθέρωση. Είναι όμως καὶ ρεαλιστική:

Ὁ Πέτρος Ροῦσος, στὸ βιβλίο του «Ἡ Μεγάλη Πενταετία», ἀπευθυνόμενος πρὸς ἀριστερούς ἀναγνῶστες καὶ προσπαθώντας νὰ δικαιολογήσει τὸ «ὄχι» τοῦ ΚΚΕ, ἰσχυρίζεται πὼς ἡ ἡγεσία του δὲν ἀρνήθηκε τὴ συγκρότηση τοῦ Βαλκανικοῦ Στρατηγείου οὔτε τὸ τορπίλλισε. «Ζήτησε ἁπλῶς – γράφει – ἀναβολὴ τοῦ ζητήματος μέχρι νὰ δημιουργηθοῦν οἱ ὅροι». Γιατί αὐτές οἱ μασημένες δικαιολογίες; Ὁ ἴδιος ἀναφέρει ὡς ἑξῆς τοὺς λόγους ποὺ ὦθησαν τὸ πολιτικὸ γραφεῖο τοῦ ΚΚΕ στὴν ἀπόφασή του:

«Πρῶτο, νὰ στερεώσουμε τὴν ἐθνικοαπελευθερωτικὴ συμμαχία, νὰ μὴν προκαλέσουμε δυσανασχέτηση τῶν συμμάχων μας στὸ ΕΑΜ καὶ σὲ ἄλλους ἐνδεχόμενους συμμάχους μας. Δεύτερο, νὰ μὴν ἐπισπεύσουμε ἔνταση τῶν ἀντιδράσεων καὶ ἐπεμβάσεων τῶν Ἄγγλων στὴν Ἑλλάδα προτοῦ προλάβει νὰ στερεωθεῖ τὸ ἐπαναστατικὸ κίνημα στὴν Ἑλλάδα ἢ τουλάχιστον στὴ Γιουγκοσλαβία. Τρίτο, νὰ μὴ δημιουργήσουμε πρόωρα ἐμπόδια στὴν παγκόσμια ἀντιχιτλερικὴ συμμαχία, τὰ ὁποῖα ἄγνωστο ἂν θὰ μπορέσουμε τελικὰ νὰ ὑπερπηδήσουμε ὅσο βαστάει ὁ πόλεμος κατὰ τῶν καταχτητῶν».

Μακεδόνες καὶ Μεγαλόσερβοι

Ὁ Κώστας Καραγιώργης ὅμως, ποὺ ἀναμείχθηκε ἄμεσα στὸ θέμα, ὅπως εἴδαμε, σὲ ἰδιαίτερη συνομιλία ποὺ εἶχε μὲ τὸν γράφοντα τὸ .... τὴν ἐξήγηση ....

–"Ἄκου ...... γοι ποὺ μ ...... λιτικὸ μα ...... ὅτι τὸ ΕΑ ...... λουθούσε ...... ματα. Δε ...... λίγο πρὶν ...... Διεθνής κ ...... τῆς δὲν θ ...... ὅπως καὶ ...... ἔδειχνε π ...... πολὺ μεγ ...... χρεωμένο ...... σίες γιὰ ...... ἑνότητα χωρὶς τὴν ὁποία μποροῦσε νὰ χαθεῖ τὸ πᾶν. Καὶ δὲν εἶχε πὼς ὁ Τίτο καὶ ὁ Τέμπο κάναν τοῦ κεφαλίου τους, ἐμεῖς ὅμως διστάζαμε νὰ καταφέρουμε μιὰ μαχαιριὰ στὰ νεφρὰ τῆς μεγάλης συμμαχίας. Γιατί κάτι τέτοιο θὰ ἦταν ἂν ἀποκαλυπτα ὀρθωνόμαστε μαζὶ μὲ τοὺς Ἀλβανοὺς καὶ Γιουγκοσλάβους κατὰ τῶν Ἄγγλων. Ὅλα αὐτὰ ὅμως ἦσαν δευτερεύοντα μπροστὰ σὲ ἕναν ὀγκόλιθο ποὺ θὰ σοῦ ἀποκαλύψω».

Καὶ καθὼς ὁ γράφων τέντωνε τὸν λαιμό του καὶ τὰ αὐτιά του γιὰ νὰ ἀκούσει, ὁ Κώστας Καραγιώργης συμπλήρωσε:

– Ἐκεῖνο ποὺ μᾶς τρόμαξε εἶναι ἄλλο. Εἴχαμε πληροφορίες ἀλλὰ καὶ ἀντιληφθή-

«... Ἡ σκέψη τῶν Γιουγκοσλάβων καὶ τῶν Ἀλβανῶν συντρόφων νὰ ἐπηρεάζουν πρὸς ὁρισμένη πολιτικὴ τὶς ἀντίστοιχες ἔνοπλες Δυνάμεις τῶν ἐθνικῶν μειονοτήτων στὴν ...... θανε τὴν ἑλληνική, γιουγκοσλαβικὴ καὶ

...... του. Στὴν Ἑλλάδα μετὰ τὴν ἀπελευθέρωση ἦρθαν 3 μεραρχίες ἀγγλικοῦ στρατοῦ.

Ἀλλὰ πολὺ χαρακτηριστικὰ ὁ Πέτρος Ροῦσος παρατηρεῖ:

«Γιουγκοσλάβικα καὶ ἰδίως ὁρισμένα σλαβομακεδονικὰ στελέχη τῆς γειτονικῆς χώρας ἀψηφοῦσαν τὶς συνέπειες ποὺ θὰ 'χει σ' ὅλον τὸν ἑλληνικὸ ἀγώνα καὶ στὸν ἀγώνα τῶν βαλκανικῶν λαῶν ἡ ἄμεση υἱοθέτηση ἀπὸ μᾶς τοῦ συνθήματος "ἑνιαία Μακεδονία στὰ πλαίσια τῆς νέας Γιουγκοσλαβίας". Ὑπάρχουν καὶ σήμερα ἀκόμη ὁρισμένοι τους ποὺ λένε πὼς καὶ ἂν ἀκόμη δὲν ἐλευθερωνόταν ἡ Ἑλλάδα ἀπὸ τὸν ἰμπεριαλισμό, θὰ εἶναι ἐλευθεωθεῖ τουλάχι-

---

Ὁ Τίτο κατὰ

Καὶ τώρα ἕνα γνώση τοῦ Τίτο Τέμπο; Ἀσφαλ ὅσο τελικὰ ὁρίσ πρόσωπος τῆς σχεδιασμὸ στρα

Ὥστε ὁ Τίτο υ Μεγαλοσέρβων γκοσλαβίας;

Ἡ ἀπάντηση, δοξο, εἶναι και στοὺς πολλούς μὲ ἐντολή του τερα τὰ γιουγκι ψαν τὸ ἀντίθετο καὶ ἀδιάψευστα

Ὁ Τίτο πράγμ σύσταση Βαλκ. Σ κοὺς λόγους. Κι ταν στὸν στρατ ἦταν κακή. Ἀλλ μεγαλοσέρβικοι καὶ κύκλοι – ὑπο νιστικοῦ θρασμ ἡσου – γιὰ νὰ δ τὸν τὸν μηχανισ

Ἄργησε νὰ τ τῆς ἀραιῆς ἐπικ τὸ καλοκαίρι το μάχη ζωῆς ἢ θ τῶν. Ὅταν πλη ...... ἀντίδ ...... σε νὰ δια ...... παγγείλα ...... Τέμπο για ...... γείο γιατ ...... κωστό».

...... ράμμα τοῦ ...... αμμίζει:

...... σημεριν ...... ὁποίοβ ...... λάθος, ... χαριστικ ...... λὴ του πρ ...... δημιουργί ...... ησία».

...... ανύμισα ...... γό του Δ νος τὰ εἶχε λάβ «ὄχι» τοῦ Σιάντ πυρώσει τὸ θέμ ...... τήσει ὁριστικά.

Ἄλλωστε ...... παρτιζάνοι ὅπως βρίσκονταν μπρ ἀνατροπῆ: ...... Καὶ στὸν Βαλκα ...... σποτος ἕνας ὁλ ...... γέρας τῶν δυνι ...... χώματα τῆς Γιου ...... καὶ τῆς Ἑλλάδ

Τὸ ΚΚΕ λέει:

BELGRADE—The Yugoslav National Assembly has passed by acclamation a seven-point resolution directed against the "campaign of slander" by the Russians and Cominform countries and their "attempt to incite the Yugoslavs to revolt against their government."

The whole assembly—comprising the Federal and People's councils in joint session—and all spectators in the public galleries rose to their feet, clapping, cheering wildly and shouting the name of Marshal Tito as the four-day session ended. . . .

—Reuters dispatch, October 1948

·5·

The air grew colder, the sky more distant in November. We took care not to be seen by peasants, though we always envied them for having a house, and a bowl of hot soup on the table. Sometimes during the night we'd see a light in the distance and imagine a house with smoke coming out of its chimney, but then as we walked on the little light would climb higher and higher until it reached the top of a hill and vanished down the opposite slope, or it continued to climb until it lost itself among the stars. We traveled mostly by night; and if a star let us down we fixed our course by another star, and pressed on, until that star too disappeared or changed direction. We often stopped, listened, and holding our breaths we watched shadows of armed boys and girls slip over the contours of the rock northward. And in the morning we'd look at the highway down below and see columns of Nationalist troops led and followed by armor and artillery units, heading in the same direction. We traveled by night to keep warm. And when the sun came out we huddled on the windless side of the rock, feeding on berries and trying to get some sleep with our eyes half open. The sun would soothe our eyes, and we'd hear familiar voices calling our names, names that were not really ours any longer, and sometimes we would see apparitions, countenances that were neither recognizable nor entirely unfamiliar, spreading a certain iridescence over us as if they were relatives, brothers and sisters we'd never seen or even known we had, and others who were as close to us as neighbors: fishermen, craftsmen, farmers, and birds, birds pecking at seeds of the wind, and fish that swam a bit higher, higher above us, that is, as if the whole mountain-side were submerged.

The sound of the wind whistling through evergreens, and a sound of goat bells. A vertigo, an awful sickening in the blood as I awoke. I first saw his eyes: calm, steady, piercing. The rest of his face, his hair, arms and clothing had the color and tex-ture of the rock: gray, dusty, old-looking. Thin wrinkles of a darker gray pulled his cheeks downward and back as on an ancient mask. One after the other, Minos, Avramakis and Is-saris opened their eyes, tightening their hold of one another's hands. Andreas, who'd been all curled up on his left side, stirred, sniffing the air.

"The mule!" he said, jumping up.

"The dog!" echoed Minos.

The rifle and the cartridge belts were gone, too.

"God-given, devil-taken," Issaris murmured to himself.

When we all stared at the goatherd, he looked as innocent and gray as the rock. "Andartes," he said. "They take only what they need."

"Did you see them?"

"I see everything."

"You must be seeing a lot of things that you really don't care for," said Issaris.

"A lot of people," said the goatherd.

"Thieves," said Andreas.

"The Nationalists call the Andartes 'Bandits,' " said the goat-herd. "Are you Nationalists?"

"We are nothing," said Andreas. "Nothing"—the standard smart answer.

The goatherd shrugged, saying nothing.

Minos went around, looking for the dog, shouting, "Trash . . . Trash . . ."

"We're just passing through," said Issaris.

"That's what everybody says—'passing through,' " said the goatherd, rubbing his unshaven chin. "The Andartes and the Nationalists going north, and the refugees going south: all passing through."

"You get to meet a lot of interesting thieves," said Andreas.

"We've heard that the Nationalists are evacuating many villages because of the war," said Avramakis.

"Because the villages are helping the Andartes," said the goatherd. He then opened his bag and took out a small head of cheese and half a loaf of bread, saying, "Be my guests."

Having something to eat made everybody feel better, and when our host asked us whether we were headed south or north, we didn't mind telling him. We were headed north but did not want to get caught in the fighting.

The goatherd didn't understand. He said, "Yes," but he only meant "I hear you; now tell me how do you propose to go north and not get caught in the fighting."

"The reason we're headed north is that we're sick and tired of the war," said Avramakis.

The goatherd did not take too long to come up with the right question, and when he asked it he was so pleased with himself there was a grin on the lower half of his face. "How far north?" was the question.

"All the way," said Avramakis.

"All the way out?"

"And way past," said Andreas.

"One ought to be cautious these days," said the goatherd. "But if you don't trust the Andartes any more than the Nationalists, you might be in trouble. You'll have to cross their lines, you know."

"We know that," agreed Andreas.

"Then you must also know they're out recruiting boys like you all the time."

We knew that also.

"But they're not supposed to force you to fight on their side if you don't want to, or if you don't have any training," added the goatherd.

Still, they didn't have their training camps on the mountains for nothing.

"We'll take the risk," said Andreas.

And Issaris added, "If we stayed behind we'd be in the Queen's camps by now."

The goatherd was thinking. "There's someone else here you must talk with before you go," he said, and, pressing his weight against his staff, he stood up and straightened his matted wool cape on his shoulders. "Come," he said. "He's not far from here—and he's educated. He's been up north, fighting."

Andreas hesitated for a moment, then decided to go along, and the rest of us followed them, carrying the bag. Just on the other side of the rock, some fifty meters off the goat path, we stopped by the opening of a shallow cave, and the goatherd went in.

"Mr. Philon," he called.

We went closer. A man covered in lambskins raised his head, and the goatherd helped him sit up and lean against the wall. A stench of rotting flesh assaulted our nostrils as we approached. He was young, but drained of blood and aging rapidly. His right shoulder hung like a broken wing under the covers, betraying the location of the festering wound.

"Don't call me 'Mister,' " he pleaded with the goatherd. He looked at us, but he couldn't see our faces well, for the light came in from behind us. "Don't call me 'Comrade' either," he added.

"These boys are heading north," said the goatherd. "They'll have to cross the lines and the borders, and I thought maybe you could give them some advice."

"Please," said Issaris.

"I'll talk to one of them only. The others can take a walk," said the man whose name was Philon.

Andreas moved forward, and the rest of us went down to the path, where Minos started to look for the dog. When the goatherd rejoined us, Issaris took the opportunity to ask him how badly Mr. Philon was hurt.

"Only God can save him, but I doubt that He will," said the goatherd.

"That bad, eh?"

"He doesn't believe in anything anymore," said the goatherd, trying to explain why God wouldn't save Mr. Philon.

"How did he get that wound, anyway?" I asked.

"A shot from assassins. He was in the Party, you know." The goatherd went on to say that Mr. Philon had discovered a box full of documents, mostly letters between Stalin and Zachariades—the Secretary General of the Party—that had something to do with ending the war by destroying the Andartes army from within. Mr. Philon took off to warn General Markos, but the others caught up with him. Just as they caught up with Ares in the previous round. The goatherd went on, repeating everything he'd been told but had not always understood, and we listened attentively, understanding even less.

And what did he mean to say about the end of Ares? That he'd been killed by headhunters, but only after the Party had betrayed his hideout to them?

"That's what Mr. Philon said. He found that out from the documents," said the goatherd.

"But why?"

The goatherd didn't know. Mr. Philon had explained it to him, but he'd forgotten. "It doesn't matter," he said.

This was the first time that someone other than the sworn enemies of the Andartes was suggesting to us that the Party, and even Stalin himself, wanted the revolutionary army destroyed, more or less as the Germans did from 1942 to 1945, the English from 1945 to 1947, and the Americans from 1947 to who knows when.

"I don't get it," said Avramakis.

"Barba, have pity on us," said Issaris.

And I was so confused I could do nothing but look around to make sure that Minos didn't get too far from us while looking for Trash.

"Ares, and the Andartes, and the Party have been together in this all along," said Avramakis.

"And so has Stalin," said Issaris.

Awkwardly, the goatherd scratched his chin. "That's what I thought, too, but Mr. Philon found proof that this is not so."

"Do you trust Mr. Philon?" asked Avramakis.

"Can you mistrust someone who's dying?" Content that he'd come up with the right answer, the goatherd walked down the slope to turn his flock back.

The mountain wind brought a smell of carob and smoke trees. Ahead of us the mountains looked incredibly tall, their peaks blue from the cold.

The goatherd came back and sat down quietly.

Avramakis and Issaris looked depressed, even tired.

And I, wondering about Andreas and worrying about Minos, who had just disappeared around the other side of the rock, took a few steps downhill, and, hiding behind the shrubbery, I lifted my pant leg and pissed right between a storax flower and a round red stone.

Andreas came back and asked if we were ready to go. He looked grim and eager to get going.

We were ready. We glanced at the goatherd once more as he took a reed out of his bag and, pursing his lips around its mouthpiece, began to play. And then it was hard to tell the difference between his music and the hissing wind that grew stronger as the sun waned. After a while we turned to look at him once more, and we saw that he'd begun to blend in with the rock, to become part of the rock, and suddenly we could not tell him apart from the mountain.

We told Andreas about our brief political discussion with the goatherd, but he refused to let us know anything about his conversation with the man in the cave, whose name was Philon, until Issaris asked him if the subject of the Party had come up at all.

Andreas said, "Yes," it had, but Philon only made bad jokes about it and pretty soon he seemed to be drifting into a delirium, so it was difficult for him to make much sense.

"What do you suppose is the matter with him?" said Avramakis.

"Fever," said Andreas. "I even remembered the medicine we salvaged from the trash pile and offered to give him some for his wound, but he said it was too late for medicine. He said all he needs now is a brain enema so he can die in peace. Bad news," said Andreas.

"What else? What other bad news did he give you?" said Issaris.

"Strange things. He said things about Stalin and his pipe, Churchill and his cigar, Truman and his dentures—I mean, real dirty jokes that weren't funny at all."

"Anything about crossing the lines? Crossing the border into Serbia?"

"How did you know?"

"Come on, tell us," said Issaris.

"He said, 'Ask Zeus to change you into birds—that's about the only way you can cross the lines and the border.' "

"Very funny," said Avramakis.

"I'm telling you," said Andreas.

"What else?"

"Nothing."

"You're lying."

"How did you know?" It was hard to tell whether Andreas was admitting to having lied or if he was mocking Issaris.

"Are you trying to hide something?" said Avramakis.

Andreas turned and looked at me, as though I was the one who'd dared challenge him. "You spoke to me?" he said, looking as mean as could be.

I felt the blood rising to my head, my throat drying, and I was about to answer him, to tell him once and for all what a cauldron-head I thought he was, but the sound of someone's fart beat me to it, and everyone except Andreas burst out laughing.

It was Minos, and no one would let Andreas punish him. As for me, I was completely out of danger, for Minos' single musical note had made any outburst of mine unnecessary.

Issaris let something like a minute pass, and then he said as calmly as he could, "So what else did he say?"

"Nothing," said Andreas. But he then gave in: "Oh, something about Marshal Tito joining the pack—whatever he meant by that: some argument with Stalin. Some deals with the Americans . . . sealing the border and helping the Nationalists finish off the Andartes—it really didn't make any sense. If it did, I wouldn't have minded talking about it."

"Tito making a deal with the Americans? That's ridiculous!" said Avramakis.

"Sealing the border and helping the Nationalists finish off the Andartes? He must be pulling your leg," agreed Issaris.

Andreas had thought so himself. Soon, though, he became restless again, as if he couldn't wait for the first opportunity to be nasty. So I slowed down, joining Minos, whose trailing behind usually kept him out of trouble.

▲ ▲

Later that night Issaris told us a dream he'd had just before waking to find the goatherd staring at us. A hawk had come down from the sky like an arrow, and when it touched down Issaris saw that it was after a cockerel that scratched at the surface of the rock, pecking at seeds. Issaris jumped, but it was already too late. There goes the stupid chick, he thought, and the next thing he knew the cockerel hung in midair from the hawk's talons.

"That's how they do it, all right," said Andreas.

"And then?" asked Minos.

"The hawk flew toward the shore. There were cliffs. Somehow, I'd been there before. And then I thought I heard someone call my name. It wasn't my real name, but in the dream I thought it was my name. Also, the voice calling me did not come from the cliffs but somewhere inside my ear."

"What else did the voice say?" asked Avramakis.

"Nothing, just my name. But I knew it had something to do with the cockerel, so I ran after the hawk. It'd flown behind the cliffs. I ran, climbed down the rock, and I scared the hawk off. I found the cockerel right on a thin strip of sand between the sea and the rock, hopping awkwardly to avoid the water. The hawk had already pecked out its eyes. It hopped to avoid the water and beat its wings, running against the rock, and falling back into the water, and then against the rock, time after time, and there was nothing else it could do, and I felt awful for not letting the hawk finish the job."

"Why didn't you wring its neck and put it out of its misery yourself?" said Andreas.

"I guess I didn't have the nerve. I felt so awful about it that I woke up."

Avramakis began to clear his throat. "That's a strange dream," he said. "What would you do if you were in Issaris' place?"

Minos would have saved the cockerel and taken it home to care for it.

"Home?" Issaris laughed.

I would have wrung its neck and given it a proper burial.

Avramakis would have left it there without wringing its neck, just like Issaris.

Andreas would have killed it and eaten it.

"A blind cockerel?" Issaris was appalled.

"Why not?" said Andreas. "Would its meat be bad just because it had lost its eyes?"

"Something like that," said Issaris angrily.

Avramakis was getting impatient. "All right, all right," he said. "You can go on arguing forever, but when you are in the middle of a dream you don't have choices. Besides, Issaris' dream was not about eating or not eating the blind chick."

"Oh? So you know what it was about," said Andreas, nudging Issaris.

"I think so," said Avramakis. "My grandmother could explain any dream."

"So what's this one all about?"

"I think that the cockerel is Issaris, and in a way the rest of us," said Avramakis.

"But the rest of us are not missing any eyes," said Minos.

"Shut up and let him finish," laughed Issaris.

"Being blind in a dream means being helpless," continued Avramakis. "We're all helpless because of the war."

"The hawk," said Andreas.

"It could be a vulture."

"What about the sea and the rock? What are they supposed to mean?"

"Well, the sea must be Greece because we are leaving it, and the rock must be the borders."

"Does that mean that the borders are sealed off?" said Issaris.

"It means that you were worrying about it. It also means that you predicted what that man Philon told Andreas about Tito and Serbia."

"You and Mr. Philon better be wrong," said Andreas.

"What if we're not?"

"I hate to think. On the other hand, there's still Bulgaria and Albania."

"But that means many more days of traveling," said Avramakis.

"What about Turkey?" threw in Minos.

"Never mind Turkey and Bulgaria," said Avramakis.

"I thought you were going to Yannina," said Issaris.

"So did I," admitted Avramakis.

"You were not putting us on with all those stories about Yannina, were you?" I asked him.

"No. There's really no one left from my family there. I didn't lie. I swear."

"Look, he swears. What else do you want?" said Issaris.

"All right, all right."

"What about your house? Don't you have a house there?" said Andreas.

"The Germans looted it and burned it to the ground."

"I'm glad you're coming with us all the way," said Issaris, putting his arm around Avramakis' shoulders.

"Unless you decide to go through Bulgaria," said Avramakis.

There was no reason to go through Bulgaria or Turkey, which were too far to the east. If we couldn't cross the border into Serbia, we all agreed to try to sneak into Albania, then maybe reach Italy by boat. Avramakis said that that would be the shortest way to France and Spain, but we could get stuck in Albania for a long time. We knew nothing about the situation on either side of the border except that the Greek-speaking villages of southern Albania were friendly to the Andartes, and that near the town of Skopje was a new refugee camp of about five hundred kids from the northern Greek provinces.

If the border to Serbia had been sealed off, we all agreed that Avramakis should become our official dream interpreter.

A little before dawn we heard a dog barking out in the fields. Minos was sure it was Trash, and he started calling his name. Trash caught up with us in no time, carrying something like a bird in his mouth. He went straight to Minos and dropped it at his feet. It was a wild pigeon.

"Where have you been? Where did you get this?" said Minos.

The dog began to jump up and down, licking Minos' hands and making all kinds of noises.

"Simple," said Issaris. "He went hunting. He let the thieves take our mule away, but he brought back a bird for dinner."

·6·

We had left the mountains of Sterea Hellas behind, and for the past two nights we'd been in the great plain of Thessaly, trying to avoid the roads and the Nationalist convoys that headed north around the clock. Instead we traveled through the fields, digging now and then for cabbage roots and potatoes that we peeled and ate raw. One morning we came upon a huge solitary rock, some one hundred meters tall, with a red building nestled on its peak. It was a monastery, the Monastery of St. Anna, as we were soon to learn. A mist, a pearly glow, covered the landscape, and just before sunrise broad shafts of light fanned out from the promontory's red crown as in old icons. The hospitality of these monastic communities had been famous for centuries. The monks and the nuns never ate meat, eggs or butter, but they always had vegetables and grain, olives and raisins from the lands they cultivated down below on the hillside. We decided to approach, hoping the good saints might see us and send someone down in the windlass with some bread and olives.

As we got closer we heard someone, a child or a young girl, shouting obscenities somewhere in the mist near the foot of the promontory. Soon we were crossing a cemented canal that must have been the boundary of the monastery's property as well as the main drainage and irrigation conduit for the fields below the hillside. We dried our feet, and, putting on our shoes, we began to approach again with caution. The mist shifted now, creeping over secondary troughs and boulders, but we still couldn't see anyone. The shouting went on, though, and we could hear clearly enough to tell that these obscenities were not among the ones we knew, and that they were probably made up on the spot to fit the occasion. We took a few more steps in the direction of the shouting. It was then that the mist thinned out just ahead of us, and we saw her, not more than twenty meters away. She was about thirteen and looked like a Gypsy: dark skin and hair, old jacket, long skirt with large yellow flowers, no shoes on her feet. Her voice was rough, and as she shouted she looked upward, shaking her fists at the monastery.

"*Mavroukes!* Whores of Missir! Bloodsucking, devil-worshiping *lamies!* May you sit your fat asses on porcupines! May Saint George put his spear up your slits!" were her last curses before she heard us approaching. And when she turned around and saw us she reached down to a leather bag that lay by her feet and took out a pistol. It seemed ridiculously big and heavy in her hands as she took aim at us.

"Don't shoot, we're friends," said Andreas, heroically protecting the rest of us with his body.

"Friends!" mocked the Gypsy girl, spitting in front of her feet.

"Honest," said Andreas.

"You won't try to do it to me?" By this time the gun weighed so heavy in her hands it didn't point any higher than the spot where her spittle had landed.

"Do it to you?" Andreas turned to us, raising his eyebrows with significance. "What do you know?" Then back to the Gypsy: "I'd say you have too high an opinion of your charms."

Noticing that her gun was pointing to the ground, the Gypsy girl lifted up its barrel with her left hand, keeping the forefinger of her right hand fast on the trigger.

"Say that again!" Either she'd missed Andreas' point or she'd understood it too well.

"No," said Andreas, showing her the palms of his hands. "We won't do it to you. I swear."

"Are you Christian? Make the sign of the cross," she demanded.

Andreas made the sign of the cross.

"What about them?" she said, pointing the gun at the rest of us.

Minos, Avramakis, Issaris and I made the sign of the cross so fast that the Gypsy girl burst into laughter. "You are not going to the monastery, are you?" she said.

"Why? Are soldiers up there?" asked Andreas.

"Worse than soldiers."

"Andartes?"

"Worse than Andartes: vampires!" said the Gypsy.

"Vampires!"

I closed my eyes not to see Andreas raising his eyebrows again.

"Sucking blood and worshiping the devil," I heard him say.

"How did you know?" Her skin was smooth and evenly dark, and not dirty-looking, as most Gypsies looked to non-Gypsies, and her eyes were big and green—an unusually bright green that I was sure no other Gypsy, or non-Gypsy, could match.

"Isn't that what vampires are famous for? Besides, I just heard you saying that," said Andreas.

"Who are you shouting at, anyway?" asked Issaris.

"The nuns," said the Gypsy girl. "But they're not real nuns. They're bitches, witches, vampires and whores."

"Bitches, witches, vampires and whores," repeated Andreas.

"Once upon a time there were real nuns up there, but one of them left the monastery to join the Andartes, and for this Saint Anna cursed the rest of them to become bitches, witches, vampires and whores."

"Just because one of them joined the Andartes, or because the rest of them didn't?" wondered Issaris.

"The monk told me all about them," went on the Gypsy girl. "They pricked his thumb with a needle and they sucked off all his blood. They almost drove him mad, too, but a week ago he climbed down the rock and ran away. I tell you, it wasn't easy. There are vultures' nests on the cliff, and I saw birds as big as turkeys attacking him, but he made it all right. The phony nuns warned him that no one had ever gone down the cliff alive, but he made it all right—I saw it with my own eyes."

"Sure, sure," said Andreas. "But what are you doing here, calling them names and shaking your fists at them? Don't you have anything else to do?"

"I'm trying to get Kitso back," said the Gypsy girl, lowering her eyes. "He's still up there and they won't let him go."

"Who's Kitso?"

She said she and Kitso were engaged to be married, but the bitches, witches, vampires and whores had been sucking off his blood and bone marrow for nine days and nights. Kitso had gone up in the windlass to show them his merchandise of black cotton fabrics, but now that the monk had run away he was the only man left to them and they wouldn't let go of him. Her long black hair and big green eyes made her look pretty the way only some grown-up girls look pretty, but she wasn't any taller than the rest of us, and she didn't have any breasts yet.

"Are you telling us the truth?" said Andreas.

What a dumb question, I thought to myself.

"I think she's cuckoo," said Avramakis.

"The monk was cuckoo, but that's because those bitches, witches, vampires and whores sucked off his blood and his marrow," said the Gypsy girl. And, raising her pistol once more, she aimed at Avramakis, saying, "If you call me cuckoo again I'll shoot you!"

"It's all right, he didn't mean to say that," said Issaris.

And Andreas said, "We saw that monk a few days ago. He was cuckoo, all right."

"He told me if I could see Kitso now I wouldn't recognize him, because all day long they work him like a slave, drawing water from the cistern for them, and in the night they take turns sucking off his blood and his marrow, and he's like a ghost."

"The monk was cuckoo, but you believed everything he told you?" said Andreas.

"Why not? He looked like a ghost himself."

She was right, the monk did look like a ghost. We all looked at one another, not knowing what to say, and Issaris was pointing to Minos, who'd just fallen asleep by his side.

"Who knows?" said Andreas. "Maybe those nuns are onto something up there."

"Thanks for nothing." The Gypsy girl was disappointed.

And Avramakis said, "It's like those silly stories about the Hebrews putting little Christian babies into barrels fitted with nails, to drain away their blood."

"What? You don't even believe *those* stories?" The Gypsy girl was outraged.

We just looked at her, trying hard not to laugh.

"Well, they nailed Jesus Christ, didn't they?" she shouted at us.

"With special nails made by Gypsy blacksmiths," said Avramakis.

"So you think I'm cuckoo, eh?"

Seeing that the gun was pointing at him, Avramakis said nothing.

"Say it," she said.

"I think you're cuckoo," said Issaris bravely, and he ducked.

In the quietness of dawn the shot sounded like thunder, echoing twice around the promontory. But the bullet missed both Avramakis and Issaris. In the meantime Minos had jumped up from his nap, screaming, and Andreas had thrown the Gypsy girl to the ground, struggling to take her gun away before she had a chance to fire it again.

At that moment we heard the church bells of the monastery chiming in earnest, and we looked up. And when we looked down again, the pistol had changed hands.

"Fucker," she spat at Andreas, standing up again, dusting off her skirt.

"What?"

"Fucker. Just like your mother," she said and, swinging her fist, hit Andreas in the face so hard that he fell back, bleeding from the nose.

That was funny, and I heard someone giggle, but Andreas' armed hand was by my feet and I could not resist the temptation to snatch the pistol from him and to hide it behind my back. I thought that might put an end to the confusion, but it didn't: Andreas and the Gypsy girl went on fighting; Issaris was yelling at Minos that everything was all right and that he ought to stop behaving like a spoiled brat; the dog was barking at everybody and everything; the church bells were still chiming; and Avramakis was looking at the monastery and at the same time shouting something to me, but I couldn't hear, and to tell the truth I didn't want to hear and to look up. Because. Because I thought he might just be trying to divert my attention and grab my gun. But when the stones began to fall nearby, we all stopped fussing and ran to take cover. Looking up at the promontory, we saw the nuns throwing stones at us. Alerted by the chiming of the bells, which began when the shot was fired, they had gathered behind the parapet, throwing stones, and the vultures left their nests in the cliffs and hovered over the battlefield, eager to keep it clean. If one of those stones found its target, a second stone would have been one too many.

We ran some fifty meters away from the rock, and turned

around to look. Now the stones fell short of reaching us, and we began to make fun of the nuns, who looked so little and so far away.

"Bitches," said Andreas.

"Witches," said Issaris.

"Vampires," said Avramakis.

"Whores!"

"Whores of Missir!" shouted the Gypsy, shaking her fist at the nuns, who soon ceased fire and went back to take turns on poor helpless Kitso.

And then the sun hit the monastery, only the monastery, lighting it as though lifting it from the rock, so that for a moment it looked all cut off from the earth, and still not part of the sky. We sat down, leaning against our elbows and peering at the floating Monastery of St. Anna and the deep, cloudless sky, forgetting our differences and our troubles. And the mist dissolved and drifted off to the fields down past the canal, leaving the ground fresh-smelling and moist.

Then the Gypsy girl began to sniffle again. She lay on her stomach, and, resting her head on her right arm, she looked away from us, as though she wanted to hide her tears.

I thought maybe we ought to empty the gun and return it to her.

Andreas agreed, on condition that she promise not to fire at us again.

And Avramakis said, "If she can fire an empty gun—Oh, forget it."

I walked around the Gypsy and saw that there were no tears in her eyes. "Don't," I said to her, handing her the empty gun.

"I didn't mean it," she said.

"I'm not talking about your firing at us."

"Oh?"

"I'm talking about crying. Too many tears will ruin your precious eyes," I said.

Not only did she miss my point, but, as though I'd just reminded her that sniffling works wonders, she started to rub her
eyes and to make sniffling noises all over again.

"Why are you crying now?"

She wouldn't say. She went on rubbing her eyes and crying,
but she couldn't come up with any tears.

"What's wrong?" I said.

"He's dead," she muttered. "Kitso."

"Kitso is dead? Come on."

"What's going on there?" said Andreas.

"I think our troubles are just starting," predicted Issaris.

"Who are you to worry about me, anyway?" said the Gypsy.

"I've been saying that to myself for the past hour," said Issaris.

"How do you know that Kitso is dead?" I said.

"Look, he's not made of iron," said Issaris.

"Sometimes I can tell," said the Gypsy. "I could tell when
my mother died; and when my father and my baby brother
went the next day, I knew that also."

"When did that happen?" asked Issaris.

"You don't really think that the nuns did Kitso in, do you?" I
said.

She turned around, looked at Issaris, and decided that his
question was more important than mine. "Some three months
after Kitso and I went on our own, one evening, while I was
outside the tent, cooking, I heard myself saying, 'Zaphira, your
poor mother's just bit the dirt.' "

"And she actually died?"

"Is that your name? Zaphira?"

"What about Kitso? Did you just hear your own voice, saying
that Kitso too bit the dirt?"

Everybody was asking questions. And Zaphira, if that was
her real name, could pick and choose which question to answer.

"Kitso said, 'What?' He thought I was crazy, but I wouldn't

waste another minute arguing with him. I got into my wagon and took hold of the traces, hoping that he'd stay put, minding the pot on the fire, but he could tell I wasn't joking, and in the last moment he jumped in, leaving everything behind. He was really a clever one. We traveled all night and most of the next day. Middle of November, and it was pouring all the while, and when we found my father's tent we were soaking wet and shivering. That was near Kephalari, down south by the spring of Inachos. My mother, she was dead, all right. She'd been pregnant and she made a little boy. But there were no Gypsy women around to help, and my father didn't know what to do and he kept on drinking, so pretty soon my little baby brother, he died, too. When Kitso and I got there, my father wouldn't let us bury the dead ones. He said he knew a secret way to bring them back. He must have been drunk, or else he'd gone mad —but not completely, mind you, because he also found the opportunity to whisper in my ear the secret place he'd been keeping my dowry. He lugged the bodies out into the rain, swearing to bring them back to life by sunrise. Kitso and I kept hearing all kinds of strange sounds, but we weren't supposed to leave the tent and we couldn't see what my father was doing. It sounded like singing and crying, dancing and jumping around, but the rain was making a lot of noise also. The wind and the rain went on all night. Kitso and I lit a small fire to dry our clothes and keep warm. I was tired and I was getting sleepy, but all of a sudden I started to tremble, and I said to myself, 'Zaphira, your father has just croaked, too.' It was a little just before sunrise, and Kitso and I decided to go out, and we found him dead, my father. All three bodies nicely washed in the rain, and none came back."

Her name *was* Zaphira.

"But how did he die?" asked Andreas.

"With his knife. It looked so strange where he'd left it, in his chest, without a drop of blood anywhere."

"Look," said Andreas, without pointing at anything.

"And now Kitso is dead," said Zaphira.

"Hard to believe," said Issaris.

After Minos, Avramakis was the next to fall asleep during this conversation, and I myself had difficulty keeping my eyes open.

"Wake me up," I said or meant to say, but I doubted that anyone was looking at me. Issaris, Andreas and Zaphira kept talking, and I pretended to listen and understand everything, but I was really at a loss, sinking deeper and deeper into sleep, the kind of sleep that overwhelms even the coldest part of one's body, and the last thought one has before sleeping becomes the beginning of the first dream. "Wake me up when you're ready to go," and "Be quiet," is what I meant to say, or said, remembering that Zaphira had the gun and Andreas the bullets, and Issaris enough brains to keep the two of them apart.

ἀπελευθέρωση. Εἶναι ὅμως καὶ ρεαλιστική;

Ὁ Πέτρος Ροῦσος, στὸ βιβλίο του «Ἡ Μεγάλη Πενταετία», ἀπευθυνόμενος πρὸς ἀριστεροὺς ἀναγνῶστες καὶ προσπαθῶντας νὰ δικαιολογήσει τὸ «ὄχι» τοῦ ΚΚΕ, σχυρίζεται πὼς ἡ ἡγεσία του δὲν ἀρνήθηκε τὴ συγκρότηση τοῦ Βαλκανικοῦ Στρατηγείου οὔτε τὸ τορπίλλισε. «Ζήτησε ἁπλῶς – γράφει – ἀναβολὴ τοῦ ζητήματος μέχρι νὰ δημιουργηθοῦν οἱ ὅροι». Γιατί αὐτὲς οἱ μασημένες δικαιολογίες; Ὁ ἴδιος ἀναφέρει ὡς ἑξῆς τοὺς λόγους ποὺ ὤθησαν τὸ πολιτικὸ γραφεῖο τοῦ ΚΚΕ στὴν ἀπόφασή του:

«Πρῶτο, νὰ στερεώσουμε τὴν ἐθνικοαπελευθερωτικὴ συμμαχία, νὰ μὴν προκαλέσουμε δυσανασχέτηση τῶν συμμάχων μας στὸ ΕΑΜ καὶ σὲ ἄλλους ἐνδεχόμενους συμμάχους μας. Δεύτερο, νὰ μὴν ἐπισπεύσουμε ἔνταση τῶν ἀντιδράσεων καὶ ἐπεμβάσεων τῶν Ἄγγλων στὴν Ἑλλάδα προτοῦ προλάβει νὰ στερεωθεῖ τὸ ἐπαναστατικὸ κίνημα στὴν Ἑλλάδα ἢ τουλάχιστον στὴ Γιουγκοσλαβία. Τρίτο, νὰ μὴ δημιουργήσουμε πρόωρα ἐμπόδια στὴν παγκόσμια ἀντιχιτλερικὴ συμμαχία, τὰ ὁποῖα ἄγνωστο ἂν θὰ μπορέσουμε τελικὰ νὰ ὑπερπηδήσουμε ὅσο βαστάει ὁ πόλεμος κατὰ τῶν καταχτητῶν».

Μακεδόνες καὶ Μεγαλόσερβοι

Ὁ Κώστας Καραγιώργης ὅμως, ποὺ ἀναμείχθηκε ἄμεσα στὸ θέμα, ὅπως εἴδαμε, σὲ ἰδιαίτερη συνομιλία ποὺ εἶχε μὲ τὸν γράφοντα τό...

...θανε τὴν ἑλληνική, γιουγκοσλαβικὴ καὶ

... Ἡ σκέψη τῶν Γιουγκοσλάβων καὶ τῶν Ἀλβανῶν συντρόφων νὰ ἐπηρεάζουν πρὸς ὁρισμένη πολιτικὴ τὶς ἀντίστοιχες ἔνοπλες δυνάμεις τῶν ἐθνικῶν μειονοτήτων στὴν

> PARIS—One of the inalienable rights of man, the chairman of the United Nations Social Committee has ruled, is the right to go to lunch on time.
>
> The committee, debating a draft of a declaration of human rights, was held in session a half hour past the regular 1 P.M. lunch time by an impassionate speech. . . .
>
> —Associated Press dispatch, November 1948

τὴν ἐξήγηση...

– Ἄκου...

για ποὺ φι... λιτικὸ μα... ὅτι τὸ ΕΑ... λουθούσα... ματα. Δε... λίγο πρίν... Διεθνής... τῆς δὲν θ... ὅπως καὶ... ἔδειχνε...

πολὺ μεγάλες δυσκολίες. Πῶς ἦταν ὑποχρεωμένος νὰ κάνει κι᾿ ἄλλες βαριὲς θυσίες γιὰ νὰ διατηρήσει τὴ συμμαχικὴ ἑνότητα χωρὶς τὴν ὁποία μποροῦσε νὰ χαθεῖ τὸ πᾶν. Καὶ δὲν ξέρω πῶς ὁ Τίτο καὶ ὁ Τέμπο κάναν τοῦ κεφαλιοῦ τους, ἐμεῖς ὅμως διστάζαμε νὰ καταφέρουμε μιὰ μαχαιριὰ στὰ νεφρὰ τῆς μεγάλης συμμαχίας. Γιατὶ κάτι τέτοιο θὰ ἦταν ἂν ἀποκαλυπτόμασταν μαζὶ μὲ τοὺς Ἀλβανοὺς καὶ Γιουγκοσλάβους κατὰ τῶν Ἄγγλων. Ὅλα αὐτὰ ὅμως ἦσαν δευτερεύοντα μπροστὰ σὲ ἕναν᾿ ὀγκόλιθο ποὺ θὰ σοῦ ἀποκαλύψω».

Καὶ καθὼς ὁ γράφων τέντωνε τὸν λαιμό του καὶ τὰ αὐτιά του γιὰ νὰ ἀκούσει, ὁ Κώστας Καραγιώργης συμπλήρωσε:

– Ἐκεῖνο ποὺ μᾶς τρόμαξε εἶναι ἄλλο: Εἴχαμε πληροφορίες ἄλλα καὶ ἀντιληφθή-

Ὅσοι τρέφουν αὐτὴ τὴν ἰδέα ξεχνοῦν ὅτι: Στὴ Γιουγκοσλαβία μὲ τὴν ἀπελευθέρωση ὑπῆρχαν 30 μεραρχίες σοβιετικοῦ στρατοῦ. Στὴν Ἑλλάδα μετὰ τὴν ἀπελευθέρωση ἦρθαν 3 μεραρχίες ἀγγλικοῦ στρατοῦ.

Ἀλλὰ πολὺ χαρακτηριστικὰ ὁ Πέτρος Ροῦσος παρατηρεῖ:

«Γιουγκοσλάβικα καὶ ἰδίως ὁρισμένα σλαβομακεδονικὰ στελέχη τῆς γειτονικῆς χώρας ἀψηφοῦσαν τὶς συνέπειες ποὺ θὰ 'χει σ᾿ ὅλον τὸν ἑλληνικὸ ἀγώνα καὶ στὸν ἀγώνα τῶν βαλκανικῶν λαῶν ἡ ἄμεση υἱοθέτηση ἀπὸ μᾶς τοῦ συνθήματος "ἑνιαία Μακεδονία στὰ πλαίσια τῆς νέας Γιουγκοσλαβίας". Ὑπάρχουν καὶ σήμερα κάμποσοι ὁρισμένοι τους ποὺ λένε πὼς κι ἂν ἀκόμα δὲν ἐλευθερωνόταν ἡ Ἑλλάδα ἀπὸ τὸν ἱμπεριαλισμό, θὰ εἶνε ἐλευθεωθεῖ τουλάχι-

Καὶ τώρα ἕνα γνώση τοῦ Τίτο Τέμπο: Ἀσφαλ... ὅσο τελικὰ ὅρι... πρόσωπος τῆς σχεδιασμὸ στρα...

Ὥστε ὁ Τίτο υ... Μεγαλοσέρβων γκοσλαβίας;

Ἡ ἀπάντηση, δοξο, εἶναι κα... στοὺς πολλούς... μὲ ἐντολὴ του... τερα τὰ γιουγκ... ψαν τὸ ἀντίθετο... καὶ ἀδιάψευστα...

Ὁ Τίτο πράγμ... σύσταση Βαλκ. Σ... κους λόγους. Κ... ταν στὸν στρατ... ἦταν κακή. Ἀλλ... μεγαλοσέρβικοι... κοὶ κύκλοι – ὑπο... νιστικοῦ θρασ... νήσου – γιὰ νὰ δ... τον τὸν μηχανισ...

Ἄργησε νὰ τό... τῆς ἀραιῆς ἐπικ... τὴν καλοκαίρι το... μάχη ζωῆς ἢ θα... τῶν. Ὅταν πλη... γίνει, ἡ ἀντίδρ... σε νὰ δια... αγγειλατ... έμπο ιο η... γείο γιατ... ωστό».

ράμμα τοῦ... μιίζει:

... σημεριν... ὁποιουδ... ο λάθος, ... ἡ ἀντίδ... χαριστικ... του πρ... δημιουργ... λεῖ ἀνοησία».

Τὰ μνήματα... στρατηγό του δ... νος τὰ εἶχε λάβ... «ὄχι» τοῦ Σιάντ... πυρώσει τὸ θέμ... τήσει ὁριστικά.

«Ἄλλωστε, τώ... παρτιζάνοι ὅπως... βρίσκονταν μπρ... ἀνατροπή: Ἡ Ἰτ... Καὶ στὸν βαλκαν... σποτος ἕνας ὁλό... γέρας τῶν δυν... χώματα τῆς Γιου...

·7·

In the dream, Zaphira had a Gypsy wagon, Andreas a fine mule, and Issaris enough brains to put two and two together.

Zaphira, who didn't need any rest, sat in the driver's seat, and, taking the trace into her hands, she said, "Go ahead and stretch out, and mock the dead, for all I care! But I'll have to wake you up around noon to feed Tsiftis."

Tsiftis was the mule.

When after a while the rocking stopped and I opened my eyes, I saw that we were still lying on the straw mattress inside the wagon. Closing my eyes, I went back to sleep, but a few moments later Zaphira lifted up one of the canvas flaps in the back, letting in enough light to make everybody jump up.

"Out!" shouted Zaphira.

This couldn't be part of the dream. The ceiling of the wagon was tall enough for someone to stand up, but Andreas chose to crawl to the exit, and Issaris followed him in the same fashion. And then the dog tried to get out, but Minos grabbed him by the tail.

"Somebody better come up with an explanation," I said.

"I remember getting into the wagon this morning, but nothing else," said Avramakis. "I was asleep." He yawned.

Minos and I didn't even remember that much. And where had the mule and the wagon come from?

"They must belong to that crazy Gypsy," said Avramakis. "But I've no idea where they were hidden."

"They were under the bridge," said Zaphira, opening one of the flaps again. "Get out now, we have work to do."

Minos let the dog go.

It was a sparkling autumn day, neither cold nor quite warm, but the morning damp was gone and the plain, empty now except for a few cabbage and cauliflower fields, seemed to be made mostly of light. Half lost in that light, in the distance, we saw Andreas and Issaris cocking their slingshots. Quickly Avramakis got hold of Trash, and Minos put him on the leash. On the other side of the wagon Zaphira was picking up sticks for a fire while keeping an eye on the mule, which was already unharnessed and feeding on the short grass. Without turning to look, Zaphira went on giving orders: under the driver's seat there was a box and in it, among other implements, a cooking pot and a big wooden scoop; she wanted them out. Also the salt container and a bag of dried hot peppers.

"Your wish is my command," said Avramakis, saluting like a soldier.

Zaphira spat and turned to me. "You take Tsiftis down there into the ditch where the grass is taller and thicker," she said.

"*Ja wohl!*" I replied, clicking my heels.

"Now, you, Sporos . . ."

Minos frowned. He a spore? "My name is Minos," he said.

"Sporos! Inside the wagon there's an old black coat. It's hanging from a nail on the left side. Look in its pockets and you'll find a refugee."

Refugee was a lighter with a long cotton wick and no fuel. It had been brought to this coast of the Aegean by refugees from Asia Minor, and it was the surest way to light a cigarette or start a fire, unless you ran out of flint.

"My name is Minos."

"Sporos!"

"*Scrofa!*" said Minos, tying the dog onto a wheel and climbing into the wagon.

In the distance, half lost in the intense light, Andreas and Issaris began to shout with excitement, and the dog broke loose and ran, barking, in their direction.

Avramakis followed me to the ditch, where there was running water, and, filling a flask for the road, he whispered to me that he'd just discovered some more bullets under the driver's seat. "That means her pistol is loaded again," he said.

I wondered if Zaphira was crazy enough to shoot at us again.

Avramakis thought she was. "She looks all right now, but she can go off anytime; and if she doesn't try the gun she'll try something else."

Avramakis and I decided to steal Zaphira's gun and keep it away from her for as long as we were her guests, but first of all we had to sit down with Andreas and Issaris and find out what kind of deal they'd made with her, how they'd convinced her to quit cursing the nuns and give us a ride north.

Once again we heard Andreas and Issaris shouting and the dog barking. All three of them were returning to the wagon, and Minos was running toward them, skipping, and flapping his little arms like wings. "A rabbit!" someone said, and Zaphira stood up to see.

A rabbit! Issaris had hit him with his slingshot, and Trash ran him down in the cauliflower field and Andreas made him stop dancing on his tail with a quick chop on the back of his neck, and Zaphira took out a special skinning knife from her leather bag, saying she always wanted a rabbit skin for her seat. And Minos, Avramakis and I had to start the fire, clean the cauliflower and fetch more water for the cooking. Ah, meat!

Every one of us knew that in better times, when there was bread, we used to make the heavenly taste of cheese last twice as long by taking three bites of bread to one of cheese; that when there was olive oil we used enough of it in cooking vege-

tables, and it didn't matter that we didn't have meat; and that
when we had fish only Christ could increase it so that everyone
at the table could have more than a bite. But when there was
meat and the meat was rabbit, the meal had no need of oil,
potatoes, bread or the blessing of Christ, for the rabbit somehow increased itself in the pot three or four times—without
help from the teaser of the poor, the devil, either. And so when
the time came to add that snow-capped, ever-budding and blos-
soming, fart-smelling cauliflower to the pot, Zaphira changed
her mind and left it out for anyone interested in it to eat it raw.
Ditch water, salt from faraway seas, and juicy rabbit, that's all.
A meal. So delicious it made us wonder where Christ might be
in that hour, what Christ might be having for supper.

Afterward, Andreas joined Zaphira up front in the driver's
seat, and Minos, Avramakis and I took the opportunity to corner Issaris in the back.

"All right," said Avramakis. "Question number one: What
happened back there while the three of us were dozing off?"

"That's right, you missed that part," said Issaris.

"Well?"

"We didn't make any funny deals, if that's what you think."

"Let's have the whole story."

"There really isn't much. Once Zaphira decided that the
nuns had finished off Kitso, she thought, and rightly so, that it
was time to move on. Nothing wrong with that."

"Nothing wrong with that. But how did she decide that the
nuns finished off Kitso?"

"That I can't answer," said Issaris. "That's her own business.
Gypsy magic," he said.

"Question number three," I said.

"Fine," said Issaris without waiting to hear what question
number three was. "When she asked where we were heading,
and we told her, Zaphira said, 'That's out of my way,' and we
said, 'Too bad.' She said, 'I can take you as far north as my
wagon can go, you know,' and I said, 'I know.' She said, 'What

are you going to do for me?' and Andreas said, 'If you take us as far north as your wagon can go? We'll kiss you where only your mama's kissed you. We'll kiss your ass.' "

"Ha!" said Minos.

"Ha!" said Issaris. "She took out her pistol, aimed at Andreas and pulled the trigger: *click*—it was empty."

Avramakis looked at me, shaking his head. "Empty," he said.

"And what did Andreas say?" To Minos it was just another extraordinary story.

"You should be able to guess," said Issaris. "Andreas took out of his pocket one of the bullets, and, pointing it toward Zaphira, he said, 'Bang!' "

Turning to me, Avramakis raised the thumb of his right hand and, pointing his index finger at me like a gun, said, "Bang!" And then, turning to Issaris: "If Andreas leaves Zaphira alone, she's going to reach for something in the box under her seat that will make your hair stand on end," said Avramakis. And he said, "You should be able to guess what it is."

"Come on, tell me," said Issaris.

"You should be able to guess."

We were having fun. Lying on the filthy straw mattress, feeling every pothole and stone that each of the four wooden wheels hit, belching and tasting the rabbit's aftertaste time and again, each question and answer and all the chuckles in between, wondering what was the price that Andreas and Issaris had agreed to for the ride.

"There's got to be a price. Everything has a price," said Avramakis.

"Probably a small price."

"But you really don't know what it is."

"Right again," admitted Issaris.

"And you went ahead and agreed to it without knowing what it is and without asking the rest of us?" shouted Avramakis.

Issaris rubbed his only eye as if guilt made it itch. "What can I tell you?" he said. "She made it sound like it was a small thing.

A little favor or something. She promised to tell us soon, maybe in the evening," said Issaris. "But whatever it is, you can leave it to Andreas and to myself. How's that?"

"I can't promise anything without knowing what it is," said Avramakis.

We dozed off some more, and just before it became dark we all took our slingshots and went out to see if we could kill any birds as they settled in the shrubs for the night, but we returned to the wagon with nothing at all. All we could afford for dinner was cabbage and artichokes, which Zaphira would not waste the time to cook. Also, the sky had become increasingly cloudy in the afternoon, and there was a smell of rain in the air. Zaphira was in a hurry to get us to a safe place for the night.

At that time Andreas joined the rest of us, leaving Zaphira alone up front, and Avramakis took the opportunity to mention his discovery of more bullets under the driver's seat.

"That means she's loading her pistol again right now," said Issaris.

"I told you it'll make your hair stand on end—didn't I?" said Avramakis.

"Very funny," said Issaris.

"Funnier than you think." Andreas smiled, pulling the pistol from inside his shirt and showing it to us proudly.

"What happened?"

"Simple," he said. "She trusts me."

"Ah," sighed Avramakis. "There's a proverb that says, 'Madness does not go to the mountains, it goes to people.' "

Issaris laughed. "First she breaks his nose, and then she trusts him with the gun."

"Don't be jealous," said Andreas. "I had a long talk with her, and she might not be as crazy as you think."

"Did she ever explain to you why Kitso went up to the convent without taking the pistol with him?" asked Avramakis. "Because if he did, he wouldn't have any problem getting down again."

"No," admitted Andreas. "The truth is that she doesn't bother to explain a lot of things."

And there was something else: once Zaphira made up her mind that Kitso was dead, how come she never wept, never shed real tears, never went into mourning?

"That I think I know," said Andreas. "You see, she and Kitso used to stare into each other's eyes a lot, and their fathers were good drinking pals and agreed that the kids ought to marry each other. But when the kids went on their own, a lot of things didn't work, as they say. According to her, their breaths just didn't match. You know what that means."

"Each one thought the other had foul breath," I offered.

"I think Kitso took to drink and tried to do funny things to her, or he beat her too often, and—that's it!—she kept the gun for her own protection."

"If things went that bad, how come they didn't separate? After all, they weren't even married," said Issaris.

"Hard to disobey the old folks," said Avramakis. "The Hebrews are that way, too."

"And I guess she must have had a pretty good dowry," Andreas went on. "She kept saying that Kitso had a hungry eye, a greedy eye, and that she had a hard time keeping him from searching for the dowry money. Zaphira pretended that she didn't know where her father had stashed it, but Kitso never really believed her because she didn't even show an interest in looking for it."

"Somehow, Kitso sounds more and more real all the time," said Avramakis. "I wouldn't be surprised to find out she really knew someone like him."

"And if he was such a son of a dog, why should our friend bother to mourn him?" said Andreas.

"*Our* friend?" repeated Avramakis.

"He was talking to me," joked Issaris.

Somehow, Zaphira sounded less and less crazy all the time,

but we decided that at least one of us should be keeping an eye on her.

"Let me take care of that for a couple of hours," said Issaris, and he moved to the front.

"Here, take this." Andreas offered him the pistol.

"Thanks, I have my slingshot."

A couple of hours later it was a couple of hours darker and the rain was a couple of hours nearer. The wind blasted the sailcloth against the arched wooden ribs of the ceiling, forcing it to swell, and the air felt cold and clean, bringing in news of the earth under the weather—a distant warmth that mixed with the dark soil which, even though sealed for the coming winter, kept producing: radishes, cabbage, broccoli, turnips, and that snow-capped, ever-budding and -blossoming edible coral, the cauliflower.

Tired out, the mule had begun to balk, and Zaphira had to crack the whip a few times, but then she gave in and decided to let Tsiftis rest a little while, although the rain was still coming our way and we had at least three kilometers to go before we could count on a decent shelter, or a higher elevation that would be useful if floods came.

Zaphira said that nearby was a cemetery that was shared by two villages, both of which had been evacuated by the Nationalists late last summer. The villages were north and south of the cemetery and at equal distances from it, so we even had a choice.

We decided to flip a button. But first we wanted to get out of the wagon and pee, and feel that strong, moist wind, and smell the news of the rain.

"No peeing," said Zaphira.

"What?"

"No peeing." And before we could jump out she cracked the whip, and the mule pulled again forward, but some two hundred meters later we stopped again, and Zaphira said,

"Here's the cemetery." And she said, "The grass grows taller around here—guess why."

It was too dark to see the cemetery—only its white gate, and the darker-than-night cypress trees rising throughout the lot. We decided to pee in the opposite direction.

But Zaphira came after us. "Wait, wait, I've got a plan," she said.

"A what?"

"Two years ago we joined up with a family of Gypsies that had camped near here, and in the middle of the night some of the kids came to take a stroll among the graves and the cypress trees—it was great fun!"

"And what does that have to do with not peeing?" Issaris had trouble holding it any longer.

"Some of the kids were so scared they peed in their pants. If they'd peed before they went in nobody'd know they'd gotten scared," said Zaphira. "And the kids who got scared and peed in their pants didn't get to pick a good-looking girl for themselves."

"Girls didn't have to go in?"

"Of course not. Girls had to go around picking up dry twigs for the fire, because when the boys came out of the cemetery they were shivering."

"What about the kids who wouldn't go into the cemetery at all?" asked Minos.

"Ah, those! We put skirts on them. We dressed them like girls and made fun of them. So if any one of you is going to take a stroll in the cemetery, he shouldn't pee beforehand."

"Say that again?" said Andreas.

"Just wait a minute!" said Avramakis.

And Issaris mumbled, "I can't believe this."

"Scared, eh?" said Zaphira.

"Who? Me?" Issaris, Andreas and Avramakis protested in a chorus.

·8·

Issaris asked to go in first, because he had difficulty holding his pee, but also he was interested to hear from her in detail about his choosing a good-looking girl for himself after his stroll in the cemetery.

"No details," said Zaphira.

"But what if more than one of us make it back dry?" worried Andreas.

"They'll qualify as well," said Zaphira. "No first-come-first-served deals."

"Yes, but—"

"You're asking too many questions," Zaphira cut him off. "The rain is coming any minute now and we can't waste more time."

"*Scrofa*," hissed Minos.

"It's all right if you don't go in," I whispered in his ear.

"Well, I'll be back in a minute," said Issaris, taking a small step forward toward the gate.

"One more thing . . . " she warned him.

"What?"

"I've heard there's a well in there," said Zaphira. "It's supposed to be covered with a set of planks, but I wouldn't count on it."

It was too dark for anyone to see the expression on Issaris' face, but I could imagine it: left eyelid fluttering; temple above

85

right ear shuddering; Adam's apple lowering in his throat with difficulty as though his throat were too dry to swallow.

"Be careful," said Andreas.

"Shut up!" Issaris thanked him.

It was too dark for anyone to see Issaris beyond the cemetery's gate, and dark enough for anyone to turn back, but a noise from farther in proved that Issaris was doing all right. He'd just run into a tree or a gravestone, which he had then kicked, muttering a little prayer or something less pious. A new noise, this through the dense foliage of cypresses: a night bird dashing from tree to tree, as if to spread the word that there were intruders, perhaps even gravediggers, in the cemetery. Up nearer the sky the pointed treetops, darker than the night, exhaled an ancient breath of retsin.

Issaris came back, rubbing his arms. "It's another world in there," he said, his teeth chattering.

"What is it like? I'm ready to go in," said Andreas.

"Cold," said Issaris. "And all kinds of strange things keep crawling over your feet."

"Try washing your feet more often," advised Andreas. He was about to take off, but Zaphira stopped him.

"I'll take that gun now," she said. "You can have it again when you're back."

Andreas handed her the gun, and in a couple of minutes he was shouting at us from deep inside the cemetery, "Stop throwing stones! Somebody might get hurt!"

"What's he talking about?"

"Strange," said Issaris. "I too heard a couple of them falling nearby, and I thought you were trying to make things more difficult." And, turning the other way, he lifted his pant leg and took a long pee.

Minos shuddered. "It must be ghosts."

"What else?"

"That well," said Zaphira to Issaris. "Did you stumble on it, by any chance?"

"No. I was lucky, I guess," said Issaris. And he said, "Who goes next?"

"Avramakis," said Minos.

But Zaphira doubted it. "I'll be surprised if he makes it," she said.

"I hate to surprise you," said Avramakis, "but if I don't go you're going to say that I've no guts, right?"

"Right."

When Andreas returned, no one could convince him that we hadn't thrown any stones at him. "Give me back that pistol," he said, shaking.

"Never mind the pistol," said Zaphira. "Tell me about the well."

Inside the cemetery, Avramakis was comforting himself by whistling an old lively tune.

"Are you trying to wake everybody up?" shouted Andreas.

"The well," repeated Zaphira. "Is it there, or have they filled it in?"

"It's there, all right. But the lid was pushed aside, and I'd have fallen in if I couldn't see in the dark."

"How come you didn't tell Avramakis about it?" said Minos.

"Because the well is covered now," said Andreas, kicking him gently.

Avramakis returned, explaining that he whistled only because he was bored, and not that he was scared or anything.

"You heard any stones being thrown at you?"

"Several, but none of them hit me."

"Then how come there's blood all over your neck?" said Andreas.

"It's from bad jokes," replied Avramakis.

So Andreas turned to me and put his hand on my shoulder. "You are stalling," he said.

It was dark, all right, and the darkness was damp, and the dampness sharp, penetrating. The wind had quieted down, though, a sign, I thought, that the rain was about to start. I stretched out my hands in front of me in case I ran into a tree, but the ground was uneven and covered with dry vines and weed, and a couple of times I lost my balance and almost fell. I breathed in the pungent scent of pine and moist earth, listening to and then wondering about the slight noises around me and how they diminished as soon as I turned my attention to them. I could feel the touch of things even before I touched them, while my eyes refused to grow more accustomed to the dark. When the first stone fell, I stopped and stood still, terrified. I closed my eyes as if my eyelids could shelter my entire body. When I started to move again, I ran into a tree. Two more stones fell. Cypress cones. Feeling my way around trees, mounds, small tombstones, and wooden crosses, I returned to the main walkway and from there hurriedly to the gate. The others had already entered the wagon, ready to take off.

The rain came down suddenly between the cemetery and Skirakon, the abandoned village that we chose to spend the night in. Zaphira was driving from inside the wagon, which increased the chances of our getting lost in the night, but both she and the mule had been there before and did not hesitate at crossroads or where a road split in two. It was exciting to hear the driving rain crash onto the canvas and all around on the bare land, while we were safe inside. Not that we didn't feel for the mule, who was drenched and had to struggle to pull the wagon through the mud.

Just before reaching Skirakon, Andreas brought up the subject of our stroll inside the cemetery. "All for nothing," he said, annoyed.

"Try to prove you're a man and you really get yourself into trouble," said Avramakis. "Remember my words."

Zaphira drove without showing interest in the discussion.

"If that's the case, maybe we should do something to prove that we aren't men," said Issaris.

"That's easy," I said. "All we have to do is pee in our pants."

"I wonder what ever happened to all those good-looking girls," said Issaris.

"Zaphira! What happened to all those good-looking Gypsy girls?" said Andreas.

"I never promised you more than one girl," Zaphira said calmly.

"One for all?" wondered Issaris.

"One for all and all for one," said Avramakis.

Zaphira laughed. "What's wrong with that?"

"Give me back the gun and I'll tell you what's wrong with a deal like that," said Andreas.

"Not yet," said Zaphira.

"You promised to give it back to me once I came out of the cemetery."

"You're going in again tomorrow morning," said Zaphira.

"What?"

"You having trouble with your hearing?"

"What am I going back into the cemetery for? is what I'm asking."

"To return the favor for the ride," said Zaphira. "You promised to return the favor."

On entering Skirakon we saw neither lights nor houses. Since we knew that the town had been evacuated, we couldn't imagine any people waiting for us, either. So our anticipation must have had something to do with finding shelter for the night.

We found a stable and a bale of dry clover for Tsiftis, and a fireplace kitchen in which Minos and I got a fire going while the others lit Zaphira's storm lamp and went in exploring the house. We needed dry clothes; we needed carob pods and raisins to make the last head of cabbage we'd saved more palatable; and we needed lambskins or blankets for the night. We found nothing. Issaris and Avramakis took off again to see if they couldn't break into a few neighboring houses. Then Andreas went out to fill a pot with rainwater, and Zaphira got busy quartering the cabbage and preparing her kitchen implements and assortments of spices. Once the pot was on the fire, she took off her clothes and spread them around to dry. All her clothes!

We stared. At the reflection of the orange flames. Over her face. Neck. Shoulders. Chest. Stomach. Belly. Thighs. Knees. Shins. Feet.

"I bet you've never seen before a good-looking Gypsy girl without her clothes on," said Zaphira, smiling.

"No-o-o-o!" Minos, Avramakis and I replied in one voice.

"Are you going to keep yours on? Would you three billy goats rather catch pneumonia and die?"

"No-o-o-!"

Zaphira turned around, letting the fire warm up her back and buttocks. "I still can't believe it," she said, looking around at the bare walls.

We took off our clothes, wondering what she meant by that. In the meantime Trash took the best spot before the fireplace, yawning.

"Oh, look at you!" Zaphira laughed.

We looked at ourselves.

"What is it you can't believe?" I asked.

"That I'm inside a house. This is the first time I've been inside a real house," she said.

We had no reason to dispute that. City people and peasants alike never let Gypsies into their homes.

"Well, what do you say now that you have been inside one?" said Avramakis.

Instead of answering his question, Zaphira stared at his crotch. "Say, why are you hiding your peepeni?" she asked, laughing.

"My what?" Avramakis blushed.

"Come here, let me have a good look at you here in the light. You have a funny-looking one, don't you!"

"What's so funny about it?"

"Ha! It's all peeled off." She laughed.

"Don't touch!" warned Avramakis.

"I can peel mine, too," Minos said proudly, and he started to pull back the skin of his little penis.

"So what do you think about being inside a real house?" I asked Zaphira, to see if I could change the subject.

"I think one gets to see many more pricks than one sees outside," she said.

Andreas and Issaris returned, lugging in several goatskins and a couple of army blankets, and a tin box half full of surprises, which they insisted on keeping sealed until we were through our meal. But first they had to stare at Zaphira as if it had never crossed their minds that she could be beautiful.

Feeling their eyes on her body, Zaphira pressed her stomach in with her arm, and, turning the upper part of her torso slightly toward us, she showed us her tiny breasts.

Issaris and Andreas began to applaud. "I'd have sworn to God you didn't have any of those yet," said Andreas.

"Your turn," said Zaphira. "Let's see now what *you* have to show us. And you too," she said to Issaris.

The two of them spread the goatskins and the blankets on the wooden floor, and, taking each piece of clothing off, they placed them next to ours by the fire.

Then Issaris showed himself to Zaphira: front view and rear view. "Mostly bones," he admitted. "Somehow, everything I eat turns to bone."

Andreas went and stood in front of the fire next to Zaphira. He had a close look at her, smiling.

Zaphira elbowed him between the ribs, laughing. Her cheeks were red and her eyes clear and shining. She threw back her hair, glancing at each one of us as though measuring our admiration or self-confidence. "When are you all going to make a choice?" she asked.

"A choice of what?"

"A good-looking girl," she reminded us.

"Not much of a choice," said Avramakis.

"I choose you," said Issaris.

"So do I," said Andreas.

"First come, first served," said Issaris.

"No favors," Zaphira declared. And then to Andreas: "Why me?"

Andreas was surprised to have been challenged, but he recovered in no time, saying, "Because you're wild."

Zaphira liked that, and her eyes moved to Avramakis.

"Pass," said Avramakis.

"What?"

"How come nobody's asking the dog?" said Avramakis.

Zaphira didn't like that.

"Pass," repeated Avramakis. She had teased him earlier, and now he was getting even with her.

"So do I," I said.

"So do you what? Pass?"

"No. I choose you."

"Oh," said Zaphira. And she said, "How come?"

"Because you are unique," I said.

"What's that supposed to mean?"

"That you are one of a kind."

Zaphira went on smiling.

"And because you have a nice round ass," I said.

Minos burst out laughing, and the dog jumped up and began to bark.

"You want to squeeze my ass?" said Zaphira.

"And your little breasts too."

"But I'll squeeze your peepeni," she threatened.

"It's a deal."

"Eh, what about us?" protested Andreas. "You said, 'No favors.'"

"I have only two hands," explained the Gypsy.

◂ ◂

After dinner Andreas opened the mystery box and handed out the goodies; dried figs and slices of quince. We chewed slowly, smacking our lips in ecstasy. We chewed, cracking every tiny fig seed between our teeth, to make sure no fig tree took root in a tooth cavity. We stretched out on the soft goatskins in a circle, touching toes and tickling one another's feet, to make sure our excitement didn't go away too soon and sleep didn't put an early end to that day. Soon, though, the fire settled to a few glowing embers, and the layer of ash began to increase, covering their glow too soon, too early.

"Out there in the stable," said Zaphira, slapping Andreas' hand that must have been creeping too close to her thigh.

"Want to go play there?" Andreas wished aloud.

"No special favors! I was talking about a bunch of grapevines I saw there. They looked dry. They must be from last April's pruning."

"I saw them, too," said Avramakis.

"You go get them, and I'll feed the fire," offered Minos.

Avramakis went and brought in the sticks, saying that Tsiftis was doing fine, and what a good-natured mule he was.

"You're telling me?" said Zaphira. "That's why he got that name." And turning to Minos: "Sporos, keep that fire going slow so it can last long."

"I'll save one of these for your ass," murmured Minos, holding out one of the sticks. He then went on to build a little pyramid over the embers.

Avramakis blew at it gently, and the sticks caught fire.

They twisted and hissed, issuing rings and jets of smoke from their core before surrendering to the flames with a crackling sound. On one of those sticks was an ant. Slowly, the flame had begun to pursue it toward the upper end of the stick, which trembled and bent right and left. Following that motion, the ant went round and round, all the while climbing up as in a groove, until it reached the end and had nowhere else to go.

We watched. If the ant took a leap, it would land in the middle
of the fire. If it stood still, the flame would soon leap at it,
swallowing it together with the last bit of the stick. The ant
moved its tiny antennae in all directions, undecided. We
watched, saying nothing. In another moment it would be over,
all over. Just then, Minos stretched out his hand and snatched
the unburned tip with the ant still on it. His intervention was
so spontaneous that even Minos himself was surprised by it.
Zaphira's own hand had jerked toward Minos' as though to stop
him, but now it was too late for that and she just stared at him
with amazement, if not admiration. In the meantime, the ant
had advanced on Minos' hand, which it was determined to
explore, now climbing up the steep hill of a knuckle, now van-
ishing in a crag between two fingers. Minos couldn't be more
pleased with himself. He looked at each one of us, and then I
noticed the same leaf of flame that would have taken away the
ant still dancing in the pupils of his eyes. The ant returned to
the back of Minos' hand, ran all the way up to the promontory
of his thumb, slipped on the terrace of his thumbnail, and
started down again toward the inside of his fist, which looked
as dark and inviting as a cave. But Minos kept on turning his
hand gently so that he might not lose sight of his new friend,
since he could not put a friend of that size on a leash.

·9·

Early in the morning Zaphira drove us back to the cemetery. The sky had cleared, and when the sun came out, embracing the last stretch of the plain, it more than made up for the colder weather that had set in after the rain. Unlike the night before, nobody shuddered at the suggestion of taking a stroll among the graves. We tied the dog to the gate and went in, wondering what Zaphira might mean to do this time. We walked on the soaked earth around mounds and crosses and cypress trees, following Zaphira, who wanted to find the well, and Andreas, who had stumbled on it last night.

"Who needs a well in a cemetery anyway?" wondered Minos.

"Zaphira does," said Issaris.

"The ghosts," said Andreas.

"The flowers," argued Avramakis.

"The gravediggers."

"Look!" Minos picked up a couple of cypress cones from the ground and examined them. "Are these the stones that the ghosts were throwing at you last night?" he said,

Issaris went and kicked at the trunk of a cypress. Several cones fell, one hitting Andreas on the shoulder. "The answer to your question is yes," said Issaris. "Congratulations! You have just won the right to choose a nice-looking Gypsy girl for yourself, even though you'd have peed in your pants seven times if you'd strolled in here last night."

95

"Yak!" said Minos.

"Last night's stones, this morning's apples," remarked Avramakis, examining one of the cones. "What do you know!"

"Except, even the ghosts can't find their target in the dark." Andreas rubbed his shoulder.

When we got to the well Zaphira wondered what might have happened to the rope and the bucket that ought to be there for drawing water.

"You are not going to drink that water, are you?" said Andreas.

"No," said Zaphira.

"Who is?" said Andreas. "Who needs that water after so much rain?"

"Your brain," said Zaphira. And she said, "I bet the rope's fallen in." She pushed the lid to the side, looking down into the well: "Can't see a thing. But I have the right piece of rope in the wagon, right under the seat."

"What do you need the rope for?" said Andreas.

We got on our knees to look into the well, but the water smelled as if there were dead animals in it, and we had to turn our faces away.

When Zaphira came back she tied one end of the rope around the nearest tree, and, offering the rest of it to Andreas, she said, "Now return the favor for the ride."

"So that's what it was," said Issaris.

And Andreas just couldn't believe his ears. "What do you want me to do?" he said.

"Climb down. Find a small tin box. Bring it to me."

"Me? In there?" Andreas shuddered.

"Terrific!" Issaris shuddered.

"What's in the box?" asked Minos.

"And where is it? In the bottom?" Andreas was getting sick to his stomach.

"It must be," guessed Zaphira.

"And how am I supposed to get to it? After last night's rain the water in there must be two meters deep."

"Dive," said Zaphira.

"And the water stinks—there must be dead rats in it," Andreas complained, and his eye stopped at Issaris. "You promised to return the favor, too," he said. "How come you don't volunteer?"

Issaris put his hand into his pocket and took out a button. "It has to be you or I," he said. "You want to call it?"

Andreas examined the button. Its front side was polished and had an anchor embossed on it. The reverse was plain.

"Flip it," Andreas agreed. And while the button was in the air he called, "Tails."

On the ground, the button showed its polished side with the anchor.

"You lost," said Issaris.

"And here's the tail." Zaphira handed him the end of the rope.

Silently, Andreas took off his clothes. He then made a loop and, passing it over his head and arms, fastened its knot by yanking the rope in front of his face.

Issaris, Avramakis and I agreed to lower him down and wait for his signal to pull him up.

"Make sure you don't get too close to the edge," Andreas warned us. "It's all soaked, and the last thing I want is all three of you landing on top of me."

We had let go some seven meters of rope and Andreas must have just reached the surface of the water, when we heard his voice telling us to hold. Minos and Zaphira were on the opposite side of the well, on their knees, looking into it. There went a few moments of silence, then we heard Andreas' voice again:

"Pull!"

"No!" Zaphira shouted back at him. "Dive for the box!"

"Pull me out of here, I'm choking!" yelled Andreas.

"Don't," said Zaphira. "Don't pull him out yet!"

We pulled hard at the rope, and Minos was stretching out his hand for him. Soon he was out, and we saw that he'd brought along the end of another rope.

"And this is *your* tail," he told Zaphira, handing it to her. He was pale and shaking. We helped him untie himself and put on his clothes.

"What happened down there?" asked Issaris.

"This must be the rope that fell in," said Zaphira.

"There's also a body in there," said Andreas, his teeth chattering. "A dead man, do you hear?" He then took the rope from Zaphira and turned to us. "That's what stinks in there!"

"A man's body?" Zaphira had turned yellow.

We stared at the rope.

"Not this," he said. "I mean the body that's tied to the other end."

"You tied the body to the rope?" said Zaphira.

"No. He's tied the same way I tied myself—under the arms," said Andreas. "He drowned days ago."

We all turned to Zaphira, who looked as shocked and puzzled as the rest of us.

"Well, let's pull him out," she said.

"Let's," said Andreas, gathering all the loose rope, which was just enough for three more pairs of hands to take hold of.

We pulled, and felt the lifeless body rising from the water and bumping along the way on the muddy wall. When the dead man's face peeked at us from the well's edge, it was all puffed up and covered with dirt. Issaris and Andreas moved forward without letting go of the rope, and, getting onto their knees, they lifted the corpse out and laid it on the ground, face up. Somehow, its stench wasn't unbearable, so we went on breathing freely. But then we saw Zaphira stepping back and crossing herself, and only then did we notice the small tin box hanging from the drowned man's belt.

"My dowry!" said Zaphira triumphantly, pointing the pistol at us.

"All right, all right," said Andreas. "Just put that gun away."

"Give me the box!" she said, aiming at Andreas' face.

"You come and get it yourself." And, turning to the rest of us, Andreas added, "Let's just get out of her way."

We stepped back and watched Zaphira approach and try to unbuckle the dead man's belt. It wasn't easy. The corpse was so bloated that she had to put the gun down, and, pushing at the swollen stomach with her foot, she pulled hard at the free end of the belt. At last, the hook came off. At last, the little tin box was hers. It must have felt very heavy to her hands as she lifted it up, and the thought of it made her smile. Her dowry. It was all hers. She raised her eyes to us in reconciliation, but, as if she remembered something else, something that had been in the back of her head all along, she glanced at the dead man's face, and, pulling out a handful of grass, she wiped off some of the mud that covered his eyes and mouth. We saw her own mouth twitch, her own eyes blink in disbelief.

"Kitso," she muttered. "Little Christ, it's Kitso!" And leaving box and pistol behind, she ran toward the gate.

Andreas dashed after her, and we saw him catching up with her and rolling with her on the ground.

Issaris picked up the pistol and made for the box, but Avramakis beat him to it.

"In theory," whispered Issaris, "the gun can demand and take the money."

"What are you, some kind of theoretical gangster?" whispered Avramakis.

"Let me see," pleaded Minos. "I've never seen a dowry before. Come on, let me see."

"Silence," said Issaris. " 'Disturb not the temperate, for they carry the gold to a temper that has no return.' "

"The monk!" remembered Avramakis.

The monk had also said, "But let not silence accumulate for long or it may become as offensive as gold."

"Maybe the monk wasn't that crazy, after all," said Issaris.

"Do you think he knew that Kitso was after the money?" said Avramakis.

"Somehow."

"But how did Kitso climb down from the promontory?"

"The same way the monk climbed down."

"Probably during the night, too," said Avramakis. "Clever."

"I wouldn't call him that," said Issaris.

Andreas had now managed to pin down Zaphira, and, having twisted both of her arms in back, he forced her to return with him, shouting at her, "You did him in, didn't you?"

"No!" Zaphira was yelling back and struggling to free herself.

"Oh, you killed him, all right," insisted Andreas, pushing her forward.

"No, that's a lie!"

"All right, everybody calm down now and see if we can't sort this thing out." Avramakis moved in, making sure everybody saw the gun in his hand.

Zaphira looked now at the tin box and now at Kitso. She turned and spat to the side and sat down on the wet ground, facing away from the dead man.

"What happened, Zaphira?" said Avramakis, pushing the little tin box closer to her.

"I wish to God I knew," she said sadly.

"She pushed him in and then got us to help her retrieve the gold—that's what," said Andreas.

"If I knew that he'd drowned trying to steal my dowry, I wouldn't have asked anyone to help me take it out of the well," said Zaphira, wiping her nose along her sleeve.

"Why not?"

"It belongs to Kitso now, because he died for it."

"I don't believe you are saying this," said Andreas.

Zaphira searched into her bag and pulled out a shoestring, at the end of which was tied a small key. "Open the box," she said, handing Andreas the key.

Andreas tried the key, but it wouldn't work. "Rusted," he said.

"Break it open, then. Who cares?"

Andreas inserted the tip of his switchblade under the box's lid and pressed upward until it popped open. "Gold!" Andreas' hands became so nervous that they suddenly lost their grip on the box, which tipped over, spilling the glittering coins to the ground.

Gold! We drew close, trying to see, to feel the heaviness, smoothness and softness of it between our fingers and teeth. There were fifty pieces altogether, each one showing Saint George on his horse spearing the dragon, and Zaphira glanced at them but refused to touch them, since they were the property of the dead.

Immediately, Minos threw the coins he held back into the box and wiped his hands on his pants.

Andreas looked at Zaphira, clearing his throat. "You sure you didn't do him in?" he said.

"I swear," said Zaphira, crossing herself.

"But how did he get in there with the loop under his arms if someone else didn't hold the other end of the rope up here?"

"Maybe he meant to tie the other end around the cypress tree, but in the last moment he forgot to do so," said Issaris.

"He wasn't that stupid," sneered Zaphira. "But maybe he tied it to the tree and it came loose while he was trying to climb up—who knows?"

"Maybe that crazy monk," said Avramakis.

"Maybe he knows something, but he couldn't have walked here with Kitso and have turned around and gotten as far south as the Mornos in just three days," said Andreas. And he looked at Zaphira again. "You sure you didn't do Kitso in?"

"You say that one more time and I'll kick you in the eggs," she yelled, throwing a cone at him.

Now it was Avramakis' turn to clear his throat to get some attention, and when everyone was ready he announced that he had had enough of that conversation and wondered when we might be getting on our way.

"Soon, soon," said Andreas. "But first we've got to decide what we're going to do with these coins."

"Same as what we're going to do with Kitso," said Zaphira. "Bury them. In the same grave."

Avramakis wondered if one had to be so worthless to be so rich.

And Issaris said, "What do you know. Last night's gold, this morning's lead."

But Andreas wasn't ready to give up the gold, not yet. "All right, I've got it!" he said. "Kitso is in bad need of a decent grave, and we can be of help. We can provide the best spot in the cemetery, and even pray to the good Lord to forgive him for all that greed and stupidity. He's rich, he can afford anything. And we're going to take another hour or so and get him the best burial anyone can have for fifty gold coins. What do you say?"

Less than an hour later we were on our way, having just given Kitso a poor man's burial near the well. Zaphira had given up her dowry of gold for nothing, but the dead groom would leave nothing to us. So we didn't bother looking for the best spot in the cemetery, or making a fancy cross to mark the grave with, and as for prayers, they were brief and silent, and when the moment had come to shovel in the dirt, covering corpse and gold alike, only Andreas wept, mumbling something about how precious all those Saint Georges would have been to us at the border—if we were ever to cross any border to anywhere.

◂ 10 ◂

Zaphira had given up her dowry of gold for nothing, but she kept her word to take us all the way up north, as far up north as secondary roads allowed, beyond which point loomed the mountain range of Grammos. Zaphira thought we'd be coming to that point by the next morning, unless we all agreed to stop for the night. We would not stop. We planned to take a few short breaks for the sake of the mule and to do our best to start our climb in the morning, hoping to reach the border or at least to make contact with the Andartes before dark.

Throughout that last leg of our trip we made several efforts to persuade Zaphira that her future was with us, but every time she laughed.

Issaris said, "Look, your mother and father are gone, Kitso and the gold are gone, and we're your only friends."

"Some friends!" said Zaphira.

Andreas said, "Listen, we're as good as a family—we've even had family fights. How about it?"

And Zaphira just spat.

"Why not? We're as good as Gypsies," said Avramakis.

"And better!" said Minos.

But Zaphira said, "Ha!"

Then Minos said, "Maybe she wants to get married."

"Nobody will marry her without a dowry," said Issaris.

"But we will—won't we?" said Andreas.

"We'll certainly think about it," said Avramakis.

"And we'll never do it to her—will we?"

"The thought will never cross our minds."

"How about it?"

"Come on, say yes, Zaphira."

"Forget it."

In the early evening we made a stop near a chapel, and while the mule grazed in a shallow trough Zaphira made an effort to convert us to the Gypsy way of life and to see if we couldn't stick together and carry on, roaming the country and making the best of it more or less as we had been doing in the past few days.

"The best, you said?" said Andreas. "Here we are again without even a head of cabbage for dinner, and you're talking about making the best of it? Don't make me laugh!"

And Zaphira said, "Look, sometimes the best of it can be pretty bad."

"I can see it now," said Issaris. "Another month without washing with hot water and soap, and we'll even *look* like Gypsies."

"Dirt helps, but it isn't everything," said Zaphira.

And Avramakis said, "I should hope so."

"Right," agreed Zaphira. "Everything can be dirt, but dirt is not everything."

"But it is something," said Andreas. "Your point is well taken."

"Sometimes a little dirt and a funny shirt or scarf can save your life," said Zaphira. "When you look funny they don't bother to shoot at you."

"I'm not sure about that, but I'll sure do something about it next time someone points a pistol at me."

"You want to wash, go ahead and wash yourself," Zaphira said resignedly.

"Listen, all I care for is to save my skin," said Issaris.

"Then stay with me," said Zaphira.

"What about food?" remembered Minos.

"Food's not everything, either," said Zaphira. "You can really teach yourself not to mind being hungry."

"I know," said Andreas. "Nastredin Hodja, the famous Anatolian sage, almost taught his donkey to live without eating."

"Almost," said Avramakis.

Later in the day the Trikala–Kastoria highway came into view and we saw another convoy of Nationalist trucks in the distance, heading north while small armies of refugees went the opposite way on mules, donkeys, wagons and on foot, disrupting the flow of traffic. Then for some time the country road ran alongside the Aliákmon, the river whose waters came down the slopes of the two great mountains, Grammos on the west and Vitsi on the east, forming Lake Kastoria and traveling a long distance east, all the way to the Gulf of Thermaïkós, near Thessalonike.

The landscape continued to change. This was north country, stony but fertile, with an abundance of blue in the air blended with everything in sight: trees, water, mountains and hills. The kind of blue that always made me glance at the backs of my hands to see if they too had begun to turn bluish. But the north wind had not yet become icy. So when I glanced at my hands I saw only how much they'd changed in shape and size, how delicately long and bony they'd grown, and how their being inactive for so many weeks made them seem awkward, sad and, most of all, embarrassed. Then I put my hands into my pockets and looked into myself, the way one looks around from room to room, not because he's trying to find something or other that's gotten misplaced, but to reassure himself that everything's in order. Everything was. Except that the light on everything had diminished. As though the shutters had been drawn shut or the flame of the oil lamp lowered for economy or in mourning, and the familiar countenances of people and the furniture had receded into a permanent dusk. So much for inside the house, and the outside must have been worse, even more bleak, for when I saw him who responded to the name I no longer had, staring into my eyes, I was surprised that he still existed, that he continued to grow up secretly, and, no matter how hard I tried, I found nothing to say to him.

That night Zaphira made one more effort to win us over to her side, saying, "Once you get used to Gypsy life it doesn't matter which country you live in."

"That bad, eh?" said Avramakis.

"Come on, you haven't seen anything yet."

"I've seen Gypsy life, and I've seen Gypsy death," brooded Issaris.

"And I've seen enough Gypsy cabbage and cauliflower," added Minos.

But Zaphira said, "Even if you have to go to bed on an empty stomach every once in a while, you know it won't be the end of the world."

"When was the last time that you slept in a bed?" asked Andreas.

"On the the other hand, even if you die from hunger it won't be the end of the world," said Issaris.

"Very clever," Zaphira spat. "But smart talk can take you only so far, and then you'll start to remember *my* words."

We were determined to cross the border and seek a better life in another country, but if we got stuck in the war zone we'd surely wish we had listened to Zaphira.

We stopped by another chapel and lit the tin oil lamp that hung from the ceiling in front of the icons. The oil was gone, and the herb wick that sat in the bottom of the lamp glowed instantly and instantly was consumed by the flame. The face of Christ and every saint's face on the icons had been slashed time and again by bayonets, and the Mother of God was riddled by submachine-gun fire.

Zaphira crossed herself and, as if it had just dawned on her that we were getting close to the front, asked for her pistol.

We left the country road, which would have taken us straight

to the Nationalist encampments around Kastoria, and picked
an even smaller dirt road heading west, between the villages of
Nestorion and Mesopotamia. We bypassed the road sign and
the road to Mesopotamia on the left, and the sign on the right
side of the road, where the traveler going to Nestorion had to
turn. The rest of the way was unknown even to Zaphira, but it
couldn't be very far. Andreas lit Zaphira's oil lamp, and, emptying the American bag on the floor of the wagon, we went
through the whole pile of things, examining and reappraising
each item carefully. We rejected everything that was heavy or
bulky, saving some of the clothes, the medicine, and the ear-
phones, around which Avramakis hoped to build a crystal radio
someday. By the time Andreas put out the light, two-thirds of
our American treasure still lay on the floor, soon to become
Zaphira's.

By then the dirt road had come to an abrupt end. Ahead of
us soared the massive wall of the mountain. We got out of the
wagon and gazed at it, at its dark outline where the stars kept
watch, kept their flickering vigil on either side of the border,
the other side still far from us, still invisible. Here we were, at
the end of the road, at the end of the ride, trying to read one
another's face in the dark, one another's mind, finding nothing
to say. We'd wait around for the dawn, hoping that the new
day would somehow make it easier for Zaphira to decide what
to do, and for us to say "Thanks" and "Goodbye" without hurt-
ing her feelings and risking being shot at again.

We spent the last hour before dawn waiting. We found a flat
spot on the rock and, sitting down, drew closer together, hugging one another, squeezing faces, shoulders and legs together
to keep warm. Even the dog found a place for himself, and,
curling up on the ground, he rested his chin on Minos' right
foot, letting his ears flap down as though he'd sensed that there
wouldn't be anything worth listening to for a while, and he
yawned until his jaws clicked. Minos felt the pressure on his
foot and pulled his foot out of the way. Slowly, gently, Trash

turned a bit to his left and, lowering his head, rested his chin on Minos' foot once again. All six of us, and the dog seven, held together as though having become one, and I was convinced that during that hour we all had the same feeling and the same thought, that we could very well close our eyes and keep them closed, trusting that if one of us felt different the others would know it immediately. There was no peeking. We kept our eyes closed even when we sensed the first weak reflection of light in the eastern sky, even when that light had increased enough to make our eyelids tremble. And the dazzling sun peeked at us from the faraway hills, and it was morning.

ἀπελευθέρωση. Εἶναι ὅμως καὶ ρεαλιστική;

Ὁ Πέτρος Ροῦσος, στὸ βιβλίο του «Ἡ Μεγάλη Πενταετία», ἀπευθυνόμενος πρὸς ἀριστερούς ἀναγνῶστες καὶ προσπαθώντας νὰ δικαιολογήσει τὸ «ὄχι» τοῦ ΚΚΕ, ἰσχυρίζεται πὼς ἡ ἡγεσία του δὲν ἀρνήθηκε τὴ συγκρότηση τοῦ Βαλκανικοῦ Σ-ρατηγείου οὔτε τὸ τορπίλλιασε. «Ζήτησε ἁπλῶς - γράφει - ἀναβολὴ τοῦ ζητήματος μέχρι νὰ δημιουργηθοῦν οἱ ὅροι». Γιατί αὐτὲς οἱ μασημένες δικαιολογίες; Ὁ ἴδιος ἀναφέρει ὡς ἑξῆς τοὺς λόγους πού ὤθησαν τὸ πολιτικό γραφεῖο τοῦ ΚΚΕ στὴν ἀπόφασή του:

«Πρῶτο, νὰ στερεώσουμε τὴν ἐθνικοαπελευθερωτικὴ συμμαχία, νὰ μὴν προκαλέσουμε δυσανασχέτηση τῶν συμμάχων μας στὸ ΕΑΜ καὶ σὲ ἄλλους ἐνδεχόμενους συμμάχους μας. Δεύτερο, νὰ μὴν ἐπιστεύσουμε ἔνταση τῶν ἀντιδράσεων καὶ ἐπεμβάσεων τῶν Ἄγγλων στὴν Ἑλλάδα προτοῦ προλάβει νὰ στερεωθεῖ τὸ ἐπαναστατικὸ κίνημα στὴν Ἑλλάδα ἢ τουλάχιστον στὴ Γιουγκοσλαβία. Τρίτο, νὰ μὴ δημιουργήσουμε πρόωρα ἐμπόδια στὴν παγκόσμια ἀντιχιτλερικὴ συμμαχία, τὰ ὁποῖα ἄγνωστο ἂν θὰ μ...

θανε τὴν ἑλληνική, γιουγκοσλαβική καὶ

Ὁ Τίτο κατὰ

Καὶ τώρα ἕνα γνωση τοῦ Τίτο Τέμπο; Ἀσφαλ... ὅσο τελικὰ ὅρι... πρόσωπος τῆς σχεδιασμὸ στρα...

Ὥστε ὁ Τίτο υ... Μεγαλοσέρβων γκοσλαβίας;

Ἡ ἀπάντηση, δοξο, εἶναι κατ... στοὺς πολλοὺς μὲ ἐντολή του τερα τὰ γιουγκ... ψαν τὸ ἀντίθετο καὶ ἀδιάψευστα

Ὁ Τίτο πράγμ... σύσταση Βαλκ. κοὺς λόγους. Κ... ταν στὸν στρατ... ἦταν κακή. Ἀλλ... μεγαλοσέρβικοι

Μακεδ...

C Κώ... μείχθηκ... ἰδιαίτερη... φοντα τ... τὴν ἐξήγ...

—Ἀκου... γοι πού λιτικό μ... ὅτι τὸ Ε... λουθοῦ... ματα Δ... λίγο πρί... Διεθνής... τῆς δὲν ... ὅπως κα... ἔδειχνε ... πολὺ μ... χρεωμέν... σίες γι... ἑνότητα ... θεῖ τὸ τ... Τέμπο ... ὅμως δι... χαιριά σ... Γιατί κά... ὀρθωνό... Γιουγκο... αὐτὰ ἐμ... ἕναν ἀγ...

Καὶ κ... τοῦ καὶ τὰ αὐτιὰ του γιὰ νὰ ἀκούσει, ὁ Κώστας Καραγιώργης συμπλήρωσε:

—Ἐκεῖνο πού μᾶς τρόμαξε εἶναι ἄλλο: Εἴχαμε πληροφορίες ἀλλὰ καὶ ἀντιληφθή-

---

> Throughout the 1948 campaigns and in the winter operations, the United States and British military advisers studied the effectiveness of the Greek combat aircraft. They, as well as the RHAF (Royal Hellenic Air Force), recognized the need for an aircraft capable of carrying heavier bomb loads. In March 1949, their studies and further, more intensive investigations led to the June decision to obtain 40 SB2C-5 Helldiver aircraft from the U.S. Navy for use in the bandit war. Another tactic for improving the combat aircraft effectiveness was the use of napalm. After successful study, the Operations Division, JUSMAPG, believed it was highly desirable for the RHAF to use napalm against enemy targets. The United States provided a six-man team to train the RHAF in the proper handling and effective use of the weapon with the standard Spitfire, and work began in May 1948. The first successful test of a napalm tank on a Spitfire occurred in mid-September 1948. Some RHAF pilots objected to carrying this type of ordnance, and many Greeks opposed the use of it at first. Although limited use of napalm began in the summer of 1948, it was not until late 1948 that it began to supplement other types of ordnance.
>
> —Project No. AU-411-62-ASI, *The Employment of Airpower in the Greek Guerrilla War, 1947–1949*, by Concepts Division, Aerospace Studies Institute

---

μακεδονια ... γκοσλαβίας". Ὑπάρχουν καὶ σήμερα ἀκόμη ὁρισμένοι τους πού λένε πὼς καὶ ἂν ἀκόμα δὲν ἐλευθερωνόταν ἡ Ἑλλάδα ἀπὸ τὸν ἰμπεριαλισμό, θὰ εἶνε ἐλευθερωθεῖ τουλάχι-

Τὸ ΚΚΕ λέει:

·11·

When God created the world,
The city of Lyxouri and so many other places,
He said, Now, son, I must create the people.

That's how the funny poet from Lyxouri had imagined the beginning of it all, but almost everyone else agreed on a different version: In the beginning God created the world, and in the end He shook off the muck from his hands, and the muck that fell into the sea came to be Greece and its islands. It made sense: leftovers. Muck. All those islands, all those mountains, were just grains of sand in the scale of Zeus. As for us people, they say we were too small to be seen, and only the size of our deeds brought attention to us. Deeds of war and such. Apparently, at some point or other we had attracted so much attention that the gods themselves came to live here, meaning to keep an eye on us. What I never understood was, how could the gods live on a mountain which to their scale was no bigger than a grain of sand?

All morning long we'd been climbing up a grain of sand that must have been second in size only to Mount Olympos. At the beginning it looked like an average-sized mountain, but once we'd reached the top we saw that there was another peak to climb to, and then another, and still one more. Deceptive little grain of sand.

The sky was overcast, and as we continued to climb the light wind became increasingly colder, and we kept adding on clothes. American clothes from our bag, regardless of size, which felt nice but made the climbing difficult. The sky was overcast, but down below, just past Kastoria, the lake that had the same name reflected the sun in a perfectly cloudless sky. Farther up north there would be two more lakes: Lake Prespa, divided among Greece, Serbia and Albania, and the Lesser Prespa, just south of the Serbian border—two more drops of brackish water in the great scale of Zeus.

I was still thinking about grains of sand and drops of water and Zeus himself when we reached the fourth peak, so I wasn't surprised to see that the next one higher up was shrouded by a small white cloud. Somewhere beyond that cloud, sitting on top of that peak and that cloud, the gods were debating the war, the course of the war, who deserved to win and why, who to suffer defeat or what. By then probably only Athena was still on the side of the Andartes, but even she wouldn't mention the word "victory," I thought, only "peace," only "an end to the strife," while the others demanded that the lesson be total, that those who had sought to destroy the order of things be dealt with once and for all.

"Trash!" said Minos.

Once again we joined hands to make sure we didn't lose one another, for the mist was getting denser as we continued to climb, and we couldn't see a thing beyond two or three meters.

"Trash!" Minos would slow down to wait for the dog, who had run out of breath and was trailing. Minos was accusing Trash of plotting to run away and go back to team up with Zaphira.

"Don't you wish!" gasped Andreas.

A few hours ago we'd left Zaphira behind without goodbyes,

tears or even a farewell fight. She thought we were crazy trying
to cross the war zone and the borders. And we thought she was
crazy no matter what she did. And the last thing she did, when
Issaris warned her not to try to bring back to life Kitso and the
gold ("See what I mean: don't you go back to that cemetery
and dig them up!"), was to lift her skirt way up and slap her
buttocks, saying, "This way for Kitso and the gold, and this way
for you!" Under that skirt Zaphira wore nothing. Not one of
the others believed then that we'd never see her again, and
only I said that we might not live long enough to see her, or
anyone else we'd ever known.

Thudding of distant cannon fire, and echo thudding twice.
Past the mist and the cloud, and the hidden fifth peak, down
the other side: the war. It would creep up the going-down side,
or we'd climb down its going up. Hard to imagine injury and
death by steel so far away.

Driven by a gust of wind, the mass of the cloud shifted
enough to leave a clearing in the sky, through which the sunlight came down in broad shafts, crowning the hard ridge and
a dozen or so boys and girls who stood motionless against the
deep blue of the heights. They were all there, all wearing thick
wool sweaters and khaki odd jackets, coats, fatigues and trousers that once belonged to German, Italian or English uniforms, all armed with rifles, hand grenades and cartridge belts
of the same origin. Soon a new cloud moved in, and one of the
boys appeared to have long hair and a beard that were as white
as snow. A girl who was talking to him all that time now
reached out and stroked his beard, smiling. Quietly, we crawled
some more on our stomachs, then paused, listening.

It was then that we were ordered at gunpoint to stand up and
climb the rest of the way to the top with our hands raised. Our
captors were a boy and two girls not older than fifteen. We
were led to the gathering, and there were no more mountains
to be climbed, only wind and cloud, dense streams that came
down on us, brushing our cheeks and hair with powerful fin-

gers of air. Their faces, with healthy cheeks and stubborn lips, had turned toward us. People were so free on the mountains, they could be gods.

"Not now; turn back!" a boy wearing a worker's cap ordered us.

Two other boys, gagged, wrists tied behind their backs, lay still on their sides, waiting.

One of the two girls pushed us back, then, pointing downward with her weapon, ordered us to sit.

"Who are those prisoners?" asked Andreas.

"Be quiet," said the girl.

"Is that a trial going on?" asked Avramakis.

"You don't want to know."

"What will happen to them?" asked Issaris.

Minutes later there were four, five shots, and the dog began to bark. We jumped to our feet, shaking.

"Spies," announced another girl who had been sent by the young chief to question us.

Our faces had turned pale, and Avramakis covered his mouth with his hand as though to stop himself from speaking or from getting sick.

"Are you spies, too, or what?" she demanded. Her war name was Scorpaena. Once she'd heard our story she told us to follow her down the back side of the mountain, and soon enough we were in a cave where the Andartes kept their provisions: cases of ammunition, carob pods, olives layered on beds of thyme, yellow onions and garlic, a sack of hazelnuts, a steel drum of water.

"The food belongs to those who fight," announced Scorpaena.

"Sting number one," whispered Issaris. They hadn't given her that name for nothing.

". . . Not for spies or social parasites," she added.

Sting number two!

"Most of you are old enough to join the revolution, but I can tell that you won't. All that you care about is saving your skins and filling your food bags. Shit bags!" she said.

Sting after sting. What could we say? We said we weren't very hungry. We still hadn't recovered from the thought of the two prisoners having been shot, and already had begun to worry about our own lives.

Only Minos wondered if there weren't any leftovers for the dog.

"Leftovers? Leftovers of what? Roast lamb? Is that what you think we are feasting on up here?" Scorpaena shouted at him. "What's your name, anyway?"

Minos did not answer. He lowered his eyes and tightened his lips to hide their trembling.

"Are you going to cry now?" she shouted at Minos again. "Are you a man, or what? Oh, never mind, go ahead and give your dog some hazelnuts. He's probably more useful to society than the rest of you."

Before leaving us there, Scorpaena ordered us to get some rest, as she thought we'd be moving north by nightfall, and she cautioned us to watch our language, because the Party representative in their group stood for discipline. The Party representative was the boy wearing a worker's cap. From Scorpaena we also learned that their commanding officer, the young man with the white hair and beard, whose war name was Capetan Aetos, had sent two teams to recruit boys and girls from the villages, and as soon as they returned we'd head north again to rescue a large group of kids who were being kicked out of Serbia. Scorpaena said that Serbia was now called Yugoslavia, and that was that. Serbia, which recognized and helped the Andartes, was no longer there. What was there was Yugoslavia, and Yugoslavia did not recognize the Andartes. So Mr. Philon was right after all: Yugoslavia, which had trouble dealing with Stalin, needed American help. To qualify for that help it had better cooperate with the Greek Nationalists, not with the Andartes. Mr. Philon was right all along: Yugoslavia would cooperate. It would return to Greece any Greek children that could be located north of the border, and make sure to seal off that border until the war south of it had ended.

Minos wondered if we weren't better off down south.

We tried to rest but couldn't. There were those two prisoners. Those shots. That Party representative, and his idea of discipline. The sealing off of the border. And how did Capetan Aetos expect the Yugoslavian authorities to release any kids to him rather than to the Nationalists? Was Marshal Tito already cheating on his new allies? And what would become of us?

We tried to rest but couldn't. Four of us sat down, leaning against one another's backs, worrying, while Minos busied himself with trying to teach Trash how to stand on his hind legs and salute like a soldier.

It was almost dark inside the cave when Scorpaena returned with the news that one of the recruiting teams had been ambushed outside Argos Orestikon and that three out of the four Andartes had been killed. The second team had just made it back, but with no more than a dozen new recruits, most of them boys between eight and eleven years of age. Soon we were marching north once more: down and up and down the mountain, single file, often holding hands with the new recruits, who were crying and pleading with Scorpaena to let them go back to their villages. What was the matter with them? Hadn't they followed the Andartes voluntarily?

"Be quiet or you'll get us all into trouble!" warned Scorpaena.

One of them whispered to me that they'd been rounded up at gunpoint and taken away against their and their parents' will. Another said that the Andartes had threatened to burn down the village if the village didn't help the Andartes. But then two girls confided in Avramakis that their parents were convinced that the right was with the Andartes, and that they would be better off on the mountain.

A cold cloudy night, the dark air filled with the scent of

hardwood. It was around midnight when we stopped before a footbridge over a tributary of the Aliákmon to be joined by a young Ikarian man who'd been assigned the job of escorting any volunteers and some of the refugees from Yugoslavia to a secret training camp on Mount Grammos. All others, "parasites and juveniles," as Scorpaena put it, would head west and cross the border into Albania, just south of Corcë. Then Scorpaena described the Ikarian, whose war name was Pelekys, as "the tallest boy you'll ever see in this war," and we looked up, scanning the night sky among the oak trees. The sky was still cloudy and the birds were quiet. Pelekys' arrival was announced by the rustling and breaking of lower branches of those trees, but even that made him very tall, and when we saw the upper part of his body and his head looming above us we shuddered, and Trash began to back off, growling. I wondered what he might look like in daylight: Herakles? Ajax? Cyclops? Or that giant of not so distant an era, who was intimidated by regular-sized people like us, and spent most of his time alone, making pancakes in his cave? I personally favored the idea of Herakles, although I could tell that Pelekys was too young to have a beard. Also, unlike Herakles, who wore a lion skin ever since he'd slain the lion of Neme, Pelekys seemed to wear a sheepskin. On a second look it turned out to be the traditional *fylaki* of Ikaria, a backpack made from a sheepskin sewn back together so as to preserve the original shape of the animal, except that the forelegs were tied to the hind legs to make the necessary shoulder loops, and the head had been left out so that the neck would serve as the open top of the bag. In Pelekys' case, the animal must have been a great big ram.

We followed Scorpaena's cautious steps on the narrow bridge over the gorge and the river while Pelekys waited behind until every one of us had reached the other side. He then got to his knees and crawled the entire length of the footbridge like a baby.

"Why'd he do that?" Minos wondered aloud.

"Vertigo," replied Pelekys.

"What?"

Without saying another word, Pelekys picked up Minos with his left hand, flung him into the air over his head, and caught him again with his right hand.

Giggling, Minos crept his way onto the giant's shoulders, where he made himself at home in hopes of getting a free ride. "Me, no vertigo," he said.

"You, watch out for low-flying enemy planes," warned Issaris, who had taken charge of the dog, since its leash was now too short for Minos to hold.

We walked on quietly as the night air became colder and colder. Fatigue began to set in. Just before we'd left the cave Scorpaena had handed out wool sweaters and socks, and let each one of us plow through a pile of used shoes and army boots until we all came up with matching pairs, in exchange for which we gladly left our sandals. Now we were in good enough shape to brave the winter, and if we were lucky, by the time we'd broken in those new used shoes we'd be into Albania and maybe even out of it.

A faint, gray light filtered through the cloud, separating the cloud from the mountain, and soon afterward we heard the buzzing of airplanes in the distance. We left the path to take cover under the tall oak and fir trees, and there Issaris and I noticed that Minos was no longer perched on Pelekys' shoulders. What could have happened to him?

The young giant shrugged, grinning. "He must've got caught in a branch, or maybe knocked down by one," he said. And then he turned around, showing us his bulging *fylaki*. Cold and tired, Minos had slipped into the large sheepskin, where he'd been rocked to sleep by his benevolent host.

Soon the sound of the planes faded away, but Scorpaena motioned us to stay put.

"I think they're coming," whispered Pelekys, putting a hand behind his ear.

Through a low-perching cloud, among the trees: two young women armed with submachine guns, then several kids. One, two more women followed by many more kids, hiding and showing up again around the trees, panting, looking at us and panting, coming around to join us, three or four at a time. The armed women, who weren't older than sixteen, said the children ought to number seventy-three: twenty-eight girls and forty-five boys. Scorpaena counted the newcomers, counted again. They were all there: seventy-three of them—all under fourteen.

Out of the cloud they came, and the littlest ones spoke no language. Parting from the cloud as the first light of day filtered through the cloud: born in Argos, children of Danae, and they spoke no Greek. Born in Athens, children of Athena, and they spoke no Greek, or any other language. From Thessaly and from Thessalonike, and they spoke no Greek. Achaeans, Messenians, Spartans. Moslems from Thrace, Armenians from Volos, Hebrews from Thebes and Yannina—spoke neither Greek nor Turkish nor Armenian nor Hebrew nor even Serbian.

"Eh?" they asked.

"Ha," or "Ai," they answered.

"Pa," they said. "Pa" and "Ba," they said.

They said, "Ts" and "Ah," and "Vai" or "Vava."

"Oooo," and "Ooh," they said.

And if one kept asking questions, they said, "Shh."

And others were just crying. That they all knew: Dorians, Moslems, Armenians, Jews, Wallachians.

Out of dawn's low-perching cloud, wearing burlap or khaki, courtesy of the dead. Goatskin, or unmatched boots twice their size, and no socks on their feet. Their fingernails were as blue as their lips, and the soles of their boots laughed. Their lips they preferred to keep sealed. Anthoula from Ferrae. Varant from the vineyards of Corinth. Litsa from Pelion. Aristos from Pella. Şükrü from Xanthe. Simos and Stephanos from Vasilikon. Maritsa from Veroia: don't say "Ai," say "*Nai*." Don't say

"Ts," say "*Ohi.*" Don't say "Mam," say "*Psomi*" and "*Artos*" for "bread," say "*Nero, neraki*" for "water." Don't say "*Oooo,*" don't say "Ooh," say "*Cryo*" for "cold." *C-r-y-o, c-r-y-o, c-r-y-o* . . just the sound of it turned their lips bluer.

For years they'd camped outside Ljubojno north of the border, by Lake Prespa, and people there spoke no language, not even the Slavomacedonian, so the littlest ones didn't even learn to speak that. People showed their tongues, but spoke no language. They showed their hands, beat their breasts, scratched their heads, picked their noses, crossed themselves, but spoke no language. And their eyes stared at each other, but they could not see. At Ljubojno they had no bread, baked no bread to have a name for it; and they had no milk, and no name for milk; no meat, and no name for meat; no name for eggs. And the fish from the lake tasted brackish.

A young woman teacher had been assigned to the camp to teach Greek after she'd been wounded in the battle, but she didn't live long, and when she died the language went, too. From time to time the children thought of crossing the border into Greece, but were afraid that the Queen's soldiers would pull off their fingernails with pliers, or slash their skin and throw salt in their wounds, or roast them on the spit like Easter lambs, the way the Turks had roasted the monk Athanasios who refused to lay down his arms and serve the Sultan. And yet just four days ago, orders had come from Belgrade to send the children south, to hand them over to the Queen.

One of the kids who did speak some Greek was Varant, an Armenian. He'd come from Velo, a refugee village near Corinth. His parents were survivors of the slaughter in Turkey, his grandparents having fled to Asia Minor from Persia. Varant's mother had died during the German occupation, and his father had joined the Andartes. Two years ago, Varant ran away from the orphanage to search for his father, but he soon got caught in the fighting, and the Andartes sent him off to Ljubojno.

Pavlos' family was from Alexandroúpolis. His father was a

tobacco grower and had not joined the Andartes, but the Nationalists found that he was a distant relative of Markos, the Field Commander of the guerrilla army, and they killed him for it. They also sent his mother off to a detention camp on the island of Trikeri, so Pavlos was left alone and he set out to find his uncle the Field Commander. He too ended up in Ljubojno when the general sent a message to him, saying that now we were all brothers and sisters, and for that reason he should not ask any favors from him. Pavlos understood but he'd never forgiven his uncle, and his dream now was to travel to Italy someday and become an Italian because he hated war and loved pasta, and, besides, he preferred to be called Paolo.

At first it wasn't easy to tell the girls apart from the boys, because they all wore the same kind of clothing and their hair was clipped as short ("lice-control short"), but soon enough I began to notice certain glances and gestures that boys would have nothing to do with. The girls, even at a second look, were not shyer than the boys, but whether they talked or not they seemed to be more thoughtful and expressive than the boys. They spoke in lower tones, but their voices had a clearer sound, and once you'd heard their names you wondered how come you weren't sure from the beginning that they were girls. One of them was Marina. And the next thing I knew after I'd heard her name and wondered how I hadn't realized from the start that she was a girl was that there couldn't be another boy or girl like her.

Several times throughout the day we heard the buzzing of airplanes beyond the mountain to the east, often accompanied by bomb explosions, the echo of which made the branches of the trees shudder. Scorpaena thought we should spend the day under those trees and resume our journey at nightfall.

Andreas, Avramakis and I decided to go around and meet some more of the newcomers, although many were exhausted from the night-long march and, curling up in small groups, were trying to keep warm and get some sleep.

·12·

Three or four kilometers before we reached the Albanian border south of Corcë, Pelekys and the new recruits, having failed to enlist any of the kids from Ljubojno, left for the secret training camp on Grammos. Then one of the seven young women under Scorpaena's command, who had left an hour earlier to make sure we didn't run into a Nationalist detachment, came back to say that everything was clear. We climbed down the last hillside, and in less than an hour's time we were approaching the Albanian outpost. It was still dark when Scorpaena went in to talk to the officer in charge, and when she returned she said we had to wait. The officer was trying to reach his superiors by phone for permission to let us enter. Scorpaena did not like it. This was the first time that the border guard required permission. Scorpaena went back to see what was taking the officer in charge so long. He said he was having difficulty getting through to headquarters.

We had to wait. We began to hop on our feet to keep warm. Soon we'd be crossing the border to safety, and before noon we'd be reaching Corcë, where, as in most southern Albanian towns, most of the population was Greek or Greek-speaking, and the children's camp there was run with special care. Shivering from the cold, trying not to fall asleep in the cold, at one point we heard Scorpaena and the officer in charge shouting to each other:

"Shame on you, Prapas!"

"It's not my decision, Comrade."

Before long, we knew that the headquarters at Corcë had to call Tirana to authorize the entry, and the answer from the capital was negative.

Scorpaena talked briefly with her women, and then she announced that we were going in. We gathered behind the women, who had formed a two-row shield, and followed them. Most of the children didn't know what was going on.

"Prapas!" shouted Scorpaena as we approached the invisible borderline.

The officer came out of the shack accompanied by two armed border guards.

"The children are coming in, Prapas. Don't try to stop them." She readied her Bren, and the rest of the women did the same.

There was a clicking of weapons on the other side of the border as well, but Prapas' voice sounded conciliatory: "Wait, wait, Comrade."

"Don't stop them, Prapas!"

"One minute," said the officer, approaching our side. "The children won't be any safer in Albania, Comrade. There's going to be war here as well."

"Rumors," retorted Scorpaena.

Prapas glanced back at his guards and then spoke in a lower, confidential tone: "Listen, I am Greek, too, Comrade. I'd do anything to help, but the Corcë camp was secretly evacuated the other night."

"Go on," said Scorpaena.

"You don't know about it, do you?"

"What happened? Where did they take the children? Come to the point, Prapas."

"To Russia, I think."

"To Russia?"

"Word has it they're building a big camp—Tashkent or Siberia. Word has it that your war's been decided outside Greece, Comrade, and if any Andartes cross into Albania, they'll be sent straight to Russia. Our government is afraid the war might spill over into our side. You ought to have known better, Comrade."

There was a long silence, and at some point Prapas returned to his side of the border. One after another the birds began to get restless in the tall trees above us, shaking off the dampness from their wings, clearing their throats and trying out their voices. And one of the women was heard muttering something like "Russia is nowhere" or "Russia is better than nowhere," but Scorpaena just stared at her, saying nothing.

Right behind me, Minos and Trash were looking up at the trees, lost in the increasing commotion of the birds, which now flew from branch to branch and from tree to tree, ready to cross borders and purposes in any direction they pleased.

◀   ◀

North is always up, and south down. Turning around, we headed south again, but down south turned out to be higher up than any point north we'd ever reached. It was up and higher up, and higher-higher up a mountain that's called Grammos. We traveled day and night, following the wooded strips for protection, holding still and pretending to be trees and rocks each time an enemy plane flew low overhead. And when we started again, we were a long centipede that crept its way up so slowly that it seemed not to be gaining distance. When you looked at each pair of feet and how one foot stepped in front of the other with such determination and precision in spite of the uneven terrain, this simple function appeared to be at once silly and fascinating.

"I'm getting tired," said Avramakis.

"Walking within yourself is much easier, but then you don't get to see the country," I said.

"Unless, of course, you're a Hebrew," said Avramakis.

"Why?" The question came from Perdika, one of the armed women who walked behind Avramakis.

"Why? Because the Hebrews don't have a country of their own, except when they imagine one, that's why," replied Avramakis.

"You're wrong," said Perdika. "Now they do have a country of their own. It's called Israel."

"How do you know that?"

"I heard it on the radio."

"That true?"

"Why should I lie?"

"When did all that happen?"

"I am not sure exactly when, but recently . . . two, three months ago," said Perdika.

"I can't believe it," said Avramakis. "But if it's true, and if we lose Greece to the fascists, we can all go to Israel," he added, turning to me.

"Sure. Via Siberia and Tashkent."

I began to observe the dog, how differently the dog walked, putting two paws in front of the other two paws, following Minos, whose own two feet were the smallest ones among those of the centipede that crawled its way up patiently, steadily, without ever gaining any distance.

The following day I had a chance to get close to Marina again. She'd been talking with Fotis, a fourteen-year-old who had lost his right arm in an explosion, but when I joined them Fotis sort of slowed down and eventually joined two others: Trakas and Pavlos, who were his pals.

"Fotis is always talking to those who know some Greek," offered Marina as an explanation.

I looked at her as she spoke, amazed at how beautiful she was in spite of two years of hardships. The general impression coming from her eyes, the sound of her voice, her pale skin and the way she moved about was one of calmness and kindness, and of a refinement that she'd probably inherited from her mother's family line. But her black hair and eyebrows gave her an air of boldness, so that no one would mistake her grace for passivity.

"What are you up to?" I asked, and, realizing my slip, I hurried to correct it: "I mean, he, Fotis."

"Actually, he's the only one of us who wants to fight, but he can't because he has only one arm," said Marina.

"And what about the talking?"

"It has to do with us. There are more than thirty thousand Greek children in Serbia, Albania, Bulgaria, Romania, Poland and Czechoslovakia, you know, and Fotis wants to make sure that they are not forgotten by the rest of the world."

"That's interesting. The Queen and her friends are saying the same thing."

Marina turned and looked at me straight in the eyes, questioningly. "The Queen?"

"You haven't been listening to the radio. The Queen says all those kids were rounded up by the Andartes and taken outside Greece to be trained in guerrilla warfare and then cross the border to conquer the country on behalf of international Communism."

Marina was surprised. "That's not true," she said. "Some left on their own, and others were entrusted to the Andartes by their parents or other relatives to save them from the bombs."

"And from the Queen's own army that sent thousands and thousands of kids into what they call 'special camps,' 'children's cities' and 'reform centers.' "

"But it's not a lie that many of those kids actually crossed the border south to fight on the side of the Andartes, is it?"

"I guess not. But they weren't forced to. They were volunteers. At least that's what we were told."

"There have been children who said they were taken away by the Andartes against their will, right?"

"There are a few of those right here, among us," I said.

Marina's ability to be fair to the best of her knowledge was remarkable. She had been born in Nafplion, down south, but after her parents were deported to the island of Kea she moved to Meliti just east of Florina where she had relatives, not knowing that the worst part of the civil war would take place in the northern provinces. The rest of the story was familiar: the villagers would be forced to help the Andartes, then suffer reprisals from the Nationalists, then join the Andartes, or trust them with the safety of the children.

"Safety? What safety?"

"Get down, get down!" Scorpaena and her women ran back and forth frantically, pushing everyone to the ground.

Airplanes. Flying low over the mountainside, they came and went, heading eastward. In the distance we heard the rattle of antiaircraft guns and saw the small puffs of smoke in the air. The planes changed formation and, circling the slope at an even lower altitude, began to strafe their invisible challengers.

Moving on, we soon had a glimpse of the last stretch of our journey: the steep, windy summit of Grammos, already covered with snow. Elsewhere, the hard ridges were glazed with ice, and the icy wind blew the fresh snow away to lower peaks and crags. Down below, the last trees, like the remnants of a devastated army, bowed their hardy branches southward as though peering into the purple haze of the horizon for reinforcements.

Once we left those trees behind, we had to crawl along the shaded side of a ridge, clutching onto a line of thick rope that led us all the way up to the boys who had thrown it down to us. These boys, all six of them, were diggers from Naxos, who'd been assigned to extend a large cave in four different directions.

We spent the rest of the day in that cave, eating carob pods and taking naps, or watching the Naxians at work. Four of them were using long steel rods with sharp flat ends, which they rotated in their hands as they probed at the face of the rock, slowly boring holes in it. At night they filled these holes with dynamite sticks, and blasted. The other two boys were responsible for the maintenance of the tools and for cutting the loose boulders to pieces small enough to be moved out of the way. The following morning they'd clear the site for another set of holes and another blasting. The Naxians had always been known as expert well and tunnel diggers, and these six, who were brothers and cousins, seemed to know the rock and their tools better than they knew one another. They had rods and levers, pickaxes, mallets and chisels, sledgehammers, wedges and several steel mesh pads that muffled the sound of blasting and kept the rock from flying in every direction. We noticed, though, that while we were there the Naxians hardly did any work, as they turned to stare at the girls every few minutes and then to whisper and chuckle about them. And Scorpaena, who noticed that also, remarked that the Naxians were notorious for more things than wells and tunnels.

In the evening we moved again, but only after Scorpaena assured us that our final destination was just on the other side of the peak. Once the tunnels were completed, all these outposts would become directly accessible. Climbing down the southern slope was much easier, but the dog slipped on a strip of ice and became so frightened that Minos had to drag him all the way to the next cave.

Once we were all in, Scorpaena and two of her women rolled up a big stone to block the entrance, and another woman lit an oil lamp. We looked around, up and down. The cave was dry and spacious enough to hold as many as two hundred people. On one side there were stacks of firewood and a dozen portable tanks of kerosene. On the other, piles of blankets and clothing, crates and cases of ammunition, medical and other supplies.

Soon there was a fire going. We wrapped ourselves in army blankets and gathered around it to warm up and to dry our feet. Scorpaena said that this was the only cave she knew where the smoke from the fire presented no problem. We looked at the smoke going straight up and disappearing through the

cracks of the ceiling. If the smoke going straight up meant that
Zeus was on our side, we were in good shape. But where did
the smoke go? Not out. Did this mean that Zeus was hiding
somewhere in those cracks? If so, his eyes would be filling with
tears anytime now. Scorpaena said that no one had ever seen
any smoke rising from the peak outside. All we had to do to be
safe was to keep the entrance of the cave blocked, and to make
sure that no sparks flew in the direction of the oil and the
ammunition. If we were lucky we wouldn't have to move again
before the worst part of the winter was over, but Scorpaena
said it was up to Capetan Aetos and to headquarters to decide.

The smoke went straight up without the slightest wavering,
and then there was no smoke at all, only the glowing embers
and their irresistible power to mesmerize eyes and hands, to
draw our eyes and hands in its direction as the sun draws the
leaves and blossoms of the plants across the sky.

I stared at the glowing embers, wondering how much the fire
knew that I did not, until my eyes and hands turned to ashes,
and I drifted into sleep, feeling stark naked but warm, and
beneath the ashes safe.

Capetan Aetos saw no reason to have us moved. With the
Andartes concentrating now around Mount Vitsi and Mount
Grammos, there weren't many places left to move to. We spent
a few days resting in the cave, and then some of us volunteered
to help in the tunnels of Tsarno. The Naxians drilled and
blasted, and we carried the stones outside for the drywalls and
other fortifications. Several of the girls, including Marina, had
been assigned to Dr. Mathios, who was busy setting up a first-
aid clinic in the west wing of the tunnel, which had already
been completed. Dr. Mathios looked too young to be a real
doctor, and we soon found that he'd been a medical student at
the University of Athens, but he'd never finished his studies
and his internship. Marina was learning to be a nurse, taking
care of sick children and dressing wounds without fainting. At
the end of the day we returned to the smaller cave, where we
ate our dinner and talked by the fire before turning in.

In January, Pelekys and some two hundred recent recruits
who'd just finished their basic training joined the work force at
Tsarno, building drywalls and battlements. None of them was
an experienced mason, though, and the very first wall they
raised suddenly began to wobble while several kids were still on
the scaffold. Pelekys rushed to the scene and held the wall until
everyone had climbed down safely. Then the wall tumbled
down all at once, burying him underneath, and we thought

he'd been crushed to death. Not so. In a moment he was on his feet again, dusting off his sleeves and pants legs, giving instructions on how to build a better wall with the same old stones. Papanikas, a young deacon who'd left the Monastery of Athos on the Holy Mountain to fight on the side of the Andartes, called Pelekys "the new Samson" and advised him to resist getting a haircut before the war was over. But Selene, one of the young girls who stood guard at the main entrance of the tunnel, laughed, saying that the secret of Pelekys' might was definitely not in his hair.

The worst part of the winter came toward the end of January and lasted for about six weeks, during which constant snowfall and icy winds from the north put an end to travel, and the only means of communication with the rest of the world was the radio. Because of the weather, the second section of the tunnel to be completed was the east wing, the exit of which was much closer to our private cave, so that after each day's work we were still able to leave the work site and join the others. The cave was a welcome change after a day's work in the tunnel, and soon enough we began to call it Tatoi, after the summer palace of the royal family.

During those bleak weeks when no one came from the outside world, and nothing much happened that wasn't part of the work and the general wartime discipline, just around the time that some of us began to worry that springtime might never come, one of the Naxians, whose name was Sfekas, and Nike, one of the young girls under Scorpaena's command, fell in love with each other, and once again the people at Tsarno heard time ticking, and the promise of spring began to sneak up on us in our dreams. Now, falling in love wasn't all that strange a thing among the Andartes, and therefore it wasn't considered to be much of a handicap, interfering with one's sense of duty and dedication to the struggle for freedom. But with Sfekas and Nike it wasn't just a matter of falling in love. It was a matter of slipping, and stumbling, and falling, even of flapping of wings and flying, a matter of never again touching ground, a matter of daydreaming, and sighing, of hugging and necking, and falling asleep in midair—which created problems for many who lived and worked there. And since Sfekas was in charge of equipment maintenance, the drilling of holes slowed down, and so did the blasting, and only the building of walls went on unhampered, first because there were plenty of stones, and second because our masons were inexperienced and worked cautiously, trying at least to make walls that did not collapse before the bombs hit them. Little by little Sfekas and Nike were consumed by their passion, or so it seemed to the rest of us, and as there was no privacy in the tunnel they became bolder and bolder, showing no regard for others and no sense of shame whatever, heeding no advice in the name of decency and good taste, even in the name of the revolution. For it wasn't just hugging and kissing, and whispering and giggling; it was real rubbing and squeezing, and all kinds of funny things going on between them, and now and then there was moaning and fast breathing, and some of those who couldn't help catching a glimpse or two swore that the two lovers had found a way to make love without undressing, but that was not true. What was true was that the two of them did everything short of making love, which is why Sfekas had an uninterrupted erection for two straight weeks. Everyone noticed that amazing erection, and Nike herself was so proud of him that she often put both her hands along the inner side of his left thigh, feeling his stretched-out penis, then showing its length to whoever happened to be passing by and especially the girls of her age, shouting, "Look! Have you ever seen anything like this?" And Sfekas would giggle, pressing his thighs together and saying, "Easy, now," and "Ouch!"

One evening, on our way to the Tatoi cave, Marina and I saw Nike and Sfekas kissing. We approached to have a closer look at them. Nike rested her back against the rock, and Sfekas leaned against her, his left hand around her waist, his right squeezing her left breast. Their lips were glued together. There was rhythm in their kiss, a breathing rhythm that allowed their lips to move about in spite of their being glued together. As they kissed, I became aware of their body odor, a deep warmth like May, the smell of fields after spring thaw or after drought. Marina's hand sought mine, and as I turned everything else seemed far, far away. Someone moved the nearest oil lamp to the opposite wall of the tunnel, and huge slanting shadows rearranged themselves on the scaled rock. Then Marina and I kissed and silently walked toward the next light, where we kissed again. We did this three more times and again outside the tunnel on our way to Tatoi. Out there the air was so cold that I thought our lips might freeze together. They didn't.

In the next few days many more kids began to fall in love. It happened as though love were contagious, and the Party representative had to radio HQ that the crisis was getting out of hand, reaching epidemic proportions, undermining the morale of the revolutionary army. If love was a disease, no doubt the Party representatives were completely immune. HQ ordered "quick and decisive action to combat the outbreak by searing off all vestiges of this bourgeois affliction."

Capetan Aetos moved fast to interpret and enforce the orders, the "searing off," before the Party representatives had a chance to do so themselves. Accordingly, Sfekas and Nike would not be allowed to see each other for three months, or until the tunnels were all completed. The young Naxian would concentrate on equipment maintenance, and Nike would be restricted to Tatoi, teaching the little ones and supervising the younger girls who slept there. At the same time, Tatoi would be off-limits for any boy over twelve. From our group only Minos could continue to enjoy the luxury of the small cave and the company of girls. There were protests, but Capetan Aetos' decision was final. Still, the Party representatives went on to complain that these measures did not set an example, that Sfekas and Nike had gotten away with murder, that the bourgeois gangrene had not been seared off once and for all. "Gangrene? Now, now, Comrades." Capetan Aetos would see to it, with a red eye if necessary, that the orders were carried out to the letter. In the meantime, everybody back to work. "You too, Comrades."

We went to work: some carrying stones and building fortifications, others being trained how to use them. Work kept us warm. The fighters were divided into many small groups, led by young officers who'd studied at the mountain war academy or distinguished themselves in battle. There were artillery and antiaircraft units, drilling in target-finding without firing a shot, infantry battalions specializing in engaging large detachments of enemy, and commando platoons constantly devising and testing homemade weapons and surprise attacks. Besides the medical facilities, supervised by Dr. Mathios, there were classes for reading and writing, and a small network of spies, coordinated by the Party representatives who reported regularly to Headquarters. Weekdays, we pretty much ignored them; Sundays we had to listen to their prepared speeches and commentary, making even those who didn't disagree with them feel bored or embarrassed. For those who agreed with them resented being taught what they already knew and believed, and those who did not agree resented having to listen. To avoid conflict, Papanikas held Sunday services at seven in the morning, a good hour and a half before the Party sermon began. In the afternoon everybody hopped and stretched out to Swedish gymnastic exercises, and then gathered to play or watch chess matches, which we were told were highly esteemed in Russia.

From time to time I'd run into Marina, who worked in Dr. Mathios' clinic and slept in the Tatoi cave, but our meetings were brief and we were careful not to attract the attention of spies. And time slowed down again, and the promise of spring receded again in the future. Issaris, Andreas, Avramakis and I were so discouraged we didn't even feel like talking to one another, and when we did talk we always ended up blaming one another for the mess we'd gotten ourselves into. The truth was that getting stuck with the Andartes was much worse than we thought it would be. Once in a while we even wondered if we wouldn't have been better off in a Nationalist orphanage, or in the Queen's "children's cities." Work kept us warm, but the nights were still long and the night dreams unpleasant.

One Sunday morning, following a Party sermon about discipline and responsibility, Sfekas took me aside and asked me if I could keep a secret.

"For me keeping a secret is a matter of discipline and responsibility," I assured him.

Sfekas looked back over his shoulder, to see if someone was within hearing range, and then he whispered in my ear, "Look, I've got to get in touch with Nike. I've worked out something really exciting, but I need someone to pass the message to her."

That wasn't any easier for me than it was for him. "How can I give her the message?"

"By way of Marina. Look . . . while I was working in the south wing I found a new cave—a narrow pass running eastward for some distance. I calculated lengths, angles and elevations, and I thought maybe I could blast an exit near Tatoi without causing too much commotion."

"Blast an exit? Without commotion? You must be out of your mind."

"Look—"

"Sfekas, please, forget the whole idea. It smells of disaster."

"Listen to me—"

"No, you listen to me: this is dangerous, and Party watchdogs want blood. Why don't you talk to Marina yourself?"

"Sh. I've already blasted," whispered Sfekas, a wild smile in his eye.

"Blasted through?"

"Through and through—at the same moment the others were setting off the dynamite in the south wing."

"Nobody heard it?"

"Nobody heard it, nobody saw it, nobody will ever know."

"Except me."

"Except you and Marina." Sfekas' eyes shone; his voice trembled with excitement. "You and Marina can get together in it, too. But no one else—no one!" Sfekas took out of his pocket a folded sheet of paper and put it into my hand. "Map and directions," he whispered. "When the four of us are ready, we'll work out a schedule. You'll see," he said, and he hurriedly took off for equipment maintenance.

From the following evening on, Sfekas and Nike began to get together regularly in their love nest. But Marina was not willing to meet me there. Too dangerous for her. And, besides, she now thought she was too young to be in love. When one reason is not enough, the matter is not ruled by reason.

I couldn't see Marina long enough to change her mind. If I had been able to see her, I knew well how to go about it. First, I'd avoid sounding like Party representatives trying to push someone a little further down the line. Second, I'd just tell her that if I was old enough to be in love with her, she couldn't be far from being old enough herself. The next time we saw each other briefly was in the west wing, near the center, where she worked, and as though she'd read my mind she said to me shyly, "You will wait for me, won't you?" What could I say to that? I blushed, lost my voice, waved to her and hurried off to my work area, stumbling several times along the way.

After work I wrote Marina a love letter, which I then tore into tiny pieces. I tried again, writing, "I'll wait for you, but how long?" and I tore that one up also. The message I sent her the next day with Minos was, "Late spring—early summer: red anemones and red poppies." Even the Party representatives wouldn't have minded it, but Marina did not answer.

Sfekas and Nike went on meeting secretly almost every night till spring, till May, when the last wing of the tunnel system had been opened and the fortifications at each portal completed. Then, keeping his word, Capetan Aetos allowed the two lovers to reunite; but by that time Nike was triumphantly pregnant.

Spring came late to the mountains and never inside the tunnels. But as soon as the weather improved, more and more bands of Andartes began to travel, bringing in more supplies, while enemy reconnaissance planes flew overhead, checking out our defenses.

Meanwhile, Minos had such a hard time keeping the dog happy inside the cave that he almost quit trying to teach him to stand at attention and to salute.

And Issaris had finally located a fragment of gallium, and the headphones we'd salvaged from the American dump were put to proper use as a component of a crystal radio, which could receive songs and propaganda from both warring sides, but could play to only one person at a time, so whoever happened to wear the phones had to repeat everything for the rest.

The government Armed Forces Radio Station, broadcasting from Thessalonike, always made a big point about the American support in the war effort, listing fat figures of military and economic aid, new types of fighter planes and bombers, new weapons, experts, advisers and training programs—all part of the new bilateral agreements between the United States and Greece. America agreed to deliver. Greece agreed to receive.

On the other side, Radio Free Greece blasted the Truman Doctrine and the Marshall Plan, exposing the imperialist crusades of Uncle Sam and his murderous puppets, the former Nazi collaborators who ran the government in Athens, the dumb King Paul and the vicious Queen Frederika—or Freaka, as the Andartes preferred to call her—even that turncoat frog, Tito.

The Armed Forces Radio broadcast in formal Greek, Radio Free Greece in everyday Greek. The Nationalist speakers declared that the United States of America was determined to support the Athens government all the way. The rebel speakers quoted Stalin's warning to Americans: Hands off Greece! The

Nationalists said they had a quarter of a million men under arms, ready to sweep the northern mountains clean. The rebel radio boasted that over the winter Grammos had been turned into an impregnable fortress before which the fascist apologists would no doubt bite the dust. But then at the end of each day's broadcasts, the two sides played the same national anthem.

And the news that newcomers brought to Tsarno was even more confusing: Uncle Sam's support to the Nationalists was real and generous, but Uncle Joseph sent the Andartes only promises. Still, when the first clashes took place down below near Lake Prespa, the Andartes won. According to Pelekys we were going to win every battle, because the right was with us. It helped hearing someone like Pelekys say that with so much conviction. Others thought it was General Markos' decision to make up for the loss of escape routes into Serbia and Albania with fortifications such as Tsarno that was paying off. The small bands could still pick the time and place to engage the Nationalists, attack isolated garrisons for their weapons, ammunition and food, and, if pursued by superior forces, call for reinforcements and retreat toward the nearest stronghold. But then came more Party representatives, three serious-looking kids, bringing new instructions and orders from Headquarters, and some of us stopped whatever we were doing in order to think and rethink, while others stopped thinking altogether. Which only meant that some were more confused than some others. Word went rapidly around that General Markos had suddenly become ill and that Zachariades, the Secretary General of the Party, had replaced him as field commander of the rebel army. No doubt, the Secretary General had some ideas of his own on how to run the war. The new orders and instructions called for the abandonment of guerrilla tactics. From now on all military operations were to be conducted by the book, which meant the book the Nationalists had been using all along. So those who stopped thinking seemed to say, Well, the right is still with us. While those who stopped whatever they were doing in order to rethink declared, Now only the right is with us.

The new Party representatives took up residence at Tsarno to see to it that the Secretary General's instructions were followed to the letter, and one of the three kids returned to Headquarters once a week to report on all positive and negative developments. Capetan Aetos himself had no direct access to the Secretary General/Field Commander.

At some point Papanikas held a liturgical service in the tunnel, at the end of which he invited anyone who wished to receive Communion to step forward. Nobody seemed to be sure about Papanikas' offer, but a few boys and girls did step forward, although they had not abstained from food and the use of weapons that morning. But then some of those who'd made it a daily routine to think everything through twice wondered if the fugitive deacon from the Holy Mountain weren't delivering the last rites to us. One of those was Pelekys. But Pelekys was also one of those who'd stepped forward: one step, but what a step! Leaving the others way behind. Breathing down on Papanikas' neck. Refusing the spoonful from the trembling hand, but wresting the chalice from the other hand of the deacon, and emptying the blessed mix of bread and old wine down his throat, whispering, "If I go, He goes."

If Papanikas had meant to offer the last rites to those who still believed in Christ, he too must have been among those who had not stopped thinking, because the following week several rebel brigades launched an attack on the city of Florina, an attack that had been planned and ordered by the Secretary General himself, and it turned out to be a disaster. The Nationalist forces not only defended the city successfully, inflicting heavy casualties on the attackers, but they also went on the offensive, pursuing the rebels all the way to Mount Vitsi.

It was after that battle that Andreas, Issaris, Avramakis and I, and most of the kids between twelve and fourteen who had not volunteered for training in November, went to report for

duty, leaving it to Capetan Aetos and to Scorpaena to decide
whether we could still learn to use weapons or be assigned to
other tasks. The air inside and outside the tunnel and the cave
smelled sulphur-sharp, but the right was still with us. Having
the right on our side mattered, and yet we'd begun to fear it
might no longer make any difference.

One morning, the Armed Forces Radio announced the exe-
cution by firing squad of a dangerous anarcho-Communist
woman named Lambrini Randa-Kaplani, who was born on the
island of Ikaria, and whom Pelekys knew. She was the seven-
teenth woman to be shot in the courtyard of the Averof Prison
in Athens in the past seventeen months, but many hundreds of
women had been sentenced to death by the special military
tribunals throughout Greece, and the sentences were carried
out regularly in prison courts, abandoned quarries and army
detention camps. Only a few at a time, though, so that the
salvos would not be heard outside the country.

It was new retsin and ancient sulphur, that sharpness in the
morning air. Year-old odors buried in deep snow and now freed
again in the midst of spring. Crushed stone and thyme. Spent
shells and mountain tea. Bandages soaked in ouzo. Small fires
put out in haste. Then Radio Free Greece announced the formation of an international brigade that could link up with us in
as little as two weeks. In case we lost anyway, Papanikas offered
another chance at Communion to those whose step was shorter
than Pelekys'. Sure enough, the three Party representatives
didn't miss out this time.

And it was on that very same day that we reported for duty,
a brilliant summer day that we glanced at briefly as we ran from
the Tatoi cave to the tunnel, that after so many weeks of training by Minos, Trash finally stood up on his hind legs and,
raising his right paw to his ear, barked once, and saluted.

άπελευθέρωση. Είναι όμως και ρεαλιστική; θανε την έλληνική, γιουγκοσλαβική και
Ό Πέτρος Ρούσος, στό βιβλίο του «Ή
Μεγάλη «Πενταετία», άπευθυνόμενος πρός
άριστερούς άναγνώστες καί προσπαθώντας νά δικαιολογήσει τό «όχι» τοΰ ΚΚΕ,
ίσχυρίζεται πώς ή ήγεσία του δέν άρνή-
θηκε τή συγκρότηση τοΰ Βαλκανικοΰ
Στρατηγείου οΰτε τό τορπίλλιασε. «Ζήτησε
άπλώς - γράφει - άναβολή τοΰ ζητήματος
μέχρι νά δημιουργηθοΰν οί όροι». Γιατί αύ-
τές οί μασημένες δικαιολογίες; Ό ίδιος
άναφέρει ώς έξής τούς λόγους πού ώθη-
σαν τό πολιτικό γραφείο τοΰ ΚΚΕ στήν
άπόφασή του:
«Πρώτο, νά στερεώσουμε τήν έθνικο-
απελευθερωτική συμμαχία, νά μήν προκαλέσουμε δυσανασχέτηση τών συμμάχων
μας στό ΕΑΜ καί σέ άλλους ένδεχόμενους
συμμάχους μας. Δεύτερο, νά μήν έπισπεύ-
σουμε ένταση τών άντιδράσεων καί έπεμ-
βάσεων τών Άγγλων στήν Έλλάδα προτοΰ
προλάβει νά στερεωθεί τό έπαναστατικό
κίνημα στήν Έλλάδα ή τουλάχιστον στή
Γιουγκοσλαβία. Τρίτο, νά μή δημιουργήσουμε πρόωρα έμπόδια στήν παγκόσμια
άντιχιτλερική συμμαχία, τά όποία άγνωστο
άν θά μπορέσουμε τελικά νά ύπερπηδή-
σουμε όσο βαστάει ό πόλεμος κατά τών
καταχτη-

Καί τώρα ένα
γνώση τοΰ Τίτο
Τέμπο; Ασφαλ
όσο τελικά όρίσ
πρόσωπος τής
σχεδιασμό στρα
Ώστε ό Τίτο υ
Μεγαλοσέρβων
γκοσλαβίας;
Ή άπάντηση,
δοξο, είναι κα
στούς πολλούς
μέ έντολή του -
τερα τά γιουγκ
ψαν τό άντίθετο
καί άδιάψευστα
Ό Τίτο πράγμ
σύσταση Βαλκ. Σ
κούς λόγους. Κ
ταν στόν στρατ
ήταν κακή. Άλλ
μεγαλοσέρβικοι
καί κύκλοι - ύπ
νιστικοΰ βρασμ
νήσαν - γιά νά δ
μηχανισ
σε νά τ
ής έπικι
καίρι τοι
ώής ή θ
ταν πλη
άντίδρ
σε νά δια
αγγείλατ
μπο να
γείο γιατ
υστό».

Μακεδον

Ό Κώσ
μείχθηκε
ίδιαίτερη
φοντα τη
τήν έξήγ
-Άκου
γοι πού μ
λιτικό μα
ότι τό ΕΑ
λουθούσα
ματα. Δε
λίγο πρίν
Διεθνής τ
τής δέν ε
όπως καί
έδειχνε
πολύ μεν
χρεωμένο
σίες γιά
ένότητα
θεί τό πα
Τέμπο κ
όμως διο
χαιριά σι
Γιατί κάτ
όρθωνόμ
Γιουγκοσ
αύτά όμω
έναν όγκ
Καί κα

WASHINGTON, June 19.—Athens reports to the State Department indicated today that the Greek Army, profiting from
Yugoslav Premier Tito's split with the Communist Information
Bureau (Cominform), was gaining a definite upper hand for the
first time over the Communist-led guerrillas.

The guerrilla combat forces have been reduced from a peak
of 25,000 to around 18,000, with women making up an estimated 40 percent of the fighters, the reports said. A substantial
number of the rest were said to be young Greek boys, recently
returned from communist camps in the Soviet Satellite Balkan
States. . . .

Women in the rebel ranks, reports indicate, are often fierce
fighters but are mostly poorly trained, as evidenced by failure
to take cover when under fire. The young boys, found in rebel
ranks in increasing numbers, were said to be mostly lads "kid-
napped" by the rebels in the last two years and sent back
to fight the Athens government after Communist indoctrina-
tion. . . .

Greece currently has some 225,000 men under arms. A reor-
ganization recommended by Lieut. Gen. James A. Van Fleet,
chief of the United States military mission, has begun to show
results, American officials say.

—Associated Press dispatch, June 1949

του καί τά αύτιά του γιά νά άκούσει, ό Κώ-   γκοσλαβίας". Ύπάρχουν καί σήμερα άκόμη
στας Καραγιώργης συμπλήρωσε: όρισμένοι τους πού λένε πώς καί άν άκόμα
- Έκεΐνο πού μάς τρόμαξε είναι άλλο;   δέν έλευθερωνόταν ή Έλλάδα άπό τόν ίμ-
Είχαμε πληροφορίες άλλά καί άντιλαμφθή-   περιαλισμό, θά είνε έλευθερωθεί τουλάχι-

·14·

In the early summer of 1949 the Andartes fought dozens
of battles throughout the northern mountain regions, and
although Radio Free Greece kept announcing victory after
victory the truth was, as we soon learned, that the concentration of large Nationalist armies equipped with new weapons was forcing the guerrillas to retreat to fortified positions
on Beles, Vitsi and Grammos, waiting for the main summer
offensive.

I saw hundreds of young fighters arriving every day at
Tsarno, which was Grammos' largest fortress, crowding the
areas designated for encampment, or taking positions in nearby
crags and behind boulders. Nuts from every nut tree, as the
saying went: swarthy little boys, and girls whose breasts hadn't
swelled yet and who couldn't be told apart from the boys; black-
haired children from the southern parts, their arms and faces
already tanned; yellow-haired Dorians, Ilyrians, Macedonians,
Thracians, agile islanders and a wild assortment from the lesser
tribes along the borders of Albania, Serbia, Bulgaria, Turkey . . .

"Where to, Cousin?"

"Anywhere under the sun, Cousin."

"Where to, little patriot?"

"Where there's land there's country."

"And you, little friend, little comrade?"

"Give me a place to stand and I'll give this earth a good jolt."
Tsarno was the last place to stand. Not a very good place,
just better than no place at all. Capetan Aetos, Scorpaena and
other unit captains worked day and night to accommodate the
newcomers with sleeping quarters, food and ammunition, and
either assigned them to a post as a unit or, if that unit had lost
more than half of its fighters, to other incomplete units.

Issaris, Andreas, Avramakis and I had been assigned to Perdika, who was in charge of the supply of weapons and ammunition. When the attack came, we would be responsible for the
west exit and immediate surroundings, making sure the Andartes never ran out of artillery shells and bullets. For that
purpose, we were given some training in estimating the time
between sorties and artillery attacks, so that we could decide
when it was best to go out and when to run back, take quick
cover or wait inside the tunnel. By the end of June there were
more than five thousand Andartes on Grammos. The newcomers were everywhere. They had strengthened our forces, improving our chances to survive, but they'd also brought the
taste of defeat from Vitsi, and for that we resented them and
often avoided talking to them. But before long we began to
recognize some of the new faces, and if the summer offensive
held off for a few more weeks we were sure to make new friend-
ships.

One Sunday noon, following the Party sermon, I ran into
Marina again. This time she took my hand, and with shining
eyes she told me that she was very proud of me for having
volunteered to carry ammunition in the upcoming battle.

"If anything happens to us, remember that you are my best
friend," she said.

I felt my knees weakening, and a breath of cold air crawled
behind my right ear. The place was littered with broken bodies
and I was searching, wondering which one I would identify
first, hers or mine. I closed my eyes and shook my head, finding
nothing to say.

"But if nothing happens to us, you and I will become more than friends by the end of this summer."

Nothing would happen to us. And the end of the summer was only two months away.

Marina smiled, squeezing my hand, and when I saw her again two or three days later she still had the same smile on her face, and her eyes shone with the same pride and confidence.

Another day, Minos, Andreas, Issaris, Avramakis and I were eating bread and olives together, and at one point Issaris said, "I suppose there's a good chance some of us will never make it all the way."

"What do you mean by that?" questioned Avramakis.

"People get killed in the war."

"But we won't be fighting," Minos reminded him.

"Worse, we'll be running out there like rabbits, and the others will do the shooting."

"We can always use our slingshots," mocked Andreas.

Nobody laughed. Nobody even said another word after that. Gradually, though, I was beginning to agree with Issaris: people always died in the war, and not just those who fought it. Why should we be an exception? When Marina mentioned that possibility to me the first time I was startled, even scared; but in the next moment I was thinking only about the end of the war, the end of summer, and about a long lovely autumn of holding hands and kissing.

◀ ◀

The first major attack came on the fifth of August. The Nationalists had taken their positions just south of the border, so as to block any attempt on our part to cross into Albania, and they began to pound the ridges with heavy guns. Later in the morning, when the low clouds dissolved, they called in the Air Force. From inside the tunnel we heard the great explosions somewhat muffled through the rock, but their message vibrated all the way to our brains. On that first day of the attack, half a dozen kids were injured from stones that came loose from the arch of the tunnel, but that was all. Out in the open there were no casualties. The Nationalists gave away their positions without pinpointing ours. Our own artillery didn't respond until nightfall. Then our reconnaissance and sabotage teams loaded several mules with explosives and took off, hoping to penetrate enemy lines. Issaris, Andreas, Avramakis and I carried war supplies and food without incident to the fighters, and at night we became messengers, crawling up and down the rocks with directives and instructions about changes in tactics, and new initiatives. We got to know the rocks around the west exit quite well, but the still-hot shrapnel from artillery shells was all over the place, and it made our crawling and climbing up and down more difficult.

For five days and nights the Nationalists blindly bombarded Grammos and the Tsarno ridge, causing very little damage, while our cannon fire kept finding its target even in the dark. If our intelligence reports were correct in assessing the enemy strength at ninety thousand men and five thousand tanks, trucks and artillery pieces, how could our guns miss the target? On the eleventh day of August both artillery and air attacks stopped. We seemed to have won that round, but we wasted no time celebrating. There were wounded to be brought in, and repairs to be made to the drywalls outside the portals, and the Naxians took the opportunity to move their equipment to the slopes, drilling and mining one mountain pass after another. If and when a commando and infantry assault on our positions did materialize, hundreds of enemy troops would be destroyed by exploding rock. Up above, installed side by side with our antiaircraft guns, were the strange-looking wooden catapults, capable of hurling barbed-wire coils and boulders at the approaching enemy. The boulders were intended to trigger avalanches of stones just as the Nationalist commandos appeared to climb up the last five hundred meters to the tunnels. I couldn't wait to see them at work.

When our reconnaissance teams returned to Tsarno, we learned that the enemy forces were now thrown against Mount Vitsi. There were some seven thousand Andartes concentrated on Vitsi, and Scorpaena thought that the five-day attack on us must have been diversionary. Once they'd taken Vitsi they'd turn back to deal again with Grammos. But others doubted that the seven thousand would get caught by surprise, and the Party representatives ordered Scorpaena to quit speculating aloud.

Then while the battles raged at Vitsi the Party representatives handed out a leaflet urging us to fight to the end. It further said that despite enemy propaganda to the contrary, Russia was still on our side, and the battle of Vitsi would be won. In the meantime, international brigades were on the way to come and fight on our side. "We'll pursue the fascist apologists all the way to Athens," shouted the representatives as they handed out the leaflets.

Issaris rolled up his eye. "What are we to do first? Fight to the end, or take Athens?"

Some of us laughed, but most of the kids wanted to believe that the gods had tipped the scales of war in our favor, therefore the final victory had to be ours. "We'll fight to the end," they said, and they meant it.

On August 17 a messenger arrived with news from Vitsi, but he wasn't allowed to talk to anyone other than the Party representatives. Afterward there was a brief announcement, saying that the Third Nationalist Army Corps had turned to launch an attack on Mount Beles, which was held by a smaller guerrilla force, and that several thousand Andartes were giving up their positions at Vitsi in order to reinforce Grammos.

"We won at Vitsi, we'll win at Beles and Grammos too!"

Once again, Issaris couldn't keep his mouth shut. "If the fascist apologists bit the dust at Vitsi, how come they're attacking Beles and Grammos?"

This time nobody laughed, and a couple of kids were heard saying, "Shhh."

But hours later, late at night, the survivors of Vitsi began to arrive, and the truth could not be kept secret any longer: the Nationalists had taken Vitsi, had even taken Beles. It was the new planes and the new bombs—rockets and incendiaries— and their incredible accuracy, that decided the battles. The fortifications did not hold. The napalm blasted and burned through everything, and it went on burning. It was this fire that prevented hand-to-hand combat, this fire that separated the two sides for hours on end, allowing about four thousand Andartes to escape.

They were starved, blackened by the napalm smoke, burned. They'd left their dead and their heavily wounded behind. They'd fought with hope, and fought well. They would fight again, and without hope. "The Greeks know how to live; but if life doesn't meet their standards they also know how to die."

"Are you a Greek? Do you know how to live, little comrade?" a young woman asked Minos.

I took Minos by the hand, and we went to the dispensary to see Marina at work. The area was crowded by wounded and sick newcomers, but there was order and a remarkable efficiency in the first-aid section and the whole medical section, where hundreds of straw mats had been lined up in rows of five for those who might need extensive treatment. Under a big oil lamp, on a sturdy wooden table, Dr. Mathios operated on a wounded fighter, relieving him of a shell fragment or bullet lodged in the back of his right thigh. Others had to wait in a long line. Several boys supervised that line, giving priority to those with multiple or serious injuries, trying to comfort as best they could others who'd suffered phosphorus burns, for which there was no remedy.

Marina was busy at work in the first-aid section, and we moved on without trying to get her attention.

Minos was quiet.

"What are you thinking about?" I asked.

No answer.

"Are you getting sleepy?"

"All those boys and girls . . ." he said.

This time I was the one to be silent.

"These Greeks haven't learned yet how to live, so they don't know how to die either."

It made perfect sense.

"Just like me," added Minos.

·15·

It was past midnight, and as I lay down between Issaris and Avramakis, trying to sleep, I heard a little voice whisper to me, "The fire that will start on this mountain will never go out." And it was this same voice that finally put me to sleep, and this same voice that woke me up in the morning: "The fire that will start on this mountain will never go out."

"Sounds like a dream to me," said Avramakis, the official interpreter of our sleep-world. "You don't have to be completely asleep to be dreaming, you know."

"All right, suppose it was a dream. What does it mean?" said Issaris.

"Simple," said the expert. "The fire is the upcoming battle, and we'll never see it go out, because we won't live to see the end of it all."

Andreas did not like it. "Just a minute," he said. "He can dream anything he wants, but he can dream only for himself."

"Now one is all," said Avramakis.

"Dream for yourself, speak for yourself," argued Andreas.

"I for one don't know how to die," Minos remembered.

"Fine. You're excused," said Issaris.

"He'll have plenty of opportunity to watch and learn," said Andreas.

"One-all," repeated Avramakis. "But this doesn't mean that the dream will necessarily come true," he added.

When the final battle for Grammos began and the fires leaped to the sky, I remembered my dream and this conversation, and I doubted that any one of us, whether he knew how to die or not, would live to see the great napalm flames subside. More likely they'd burn and burn, eating away at the body of Greece. When the battle began in the small hours of August 25, it wasn't that the gods were setting out to decide our lives and the fate of Greece. The gods had already decided; and the battle for Grammos, and the fire, and the burning-forever was their decision. And the gods themselves caught fire and burned in the battle for Grammos.

▲   ▲

The artillery attack came from north and south at the same time. The first objective of the enemy was to push our forces together so that our concentrations would become visible and an easier target from the air. The enemy did not achieve this objective. Our fighters refused to abandon their posts on the mountainside, and the only large concentration of our forces was inside the tunnels. But the Nationalist field guns and new planes had enough firepower to destroy most of our positions outside the tunnels within three days. In the meantime the Albanian border had been sealed off on both sides, so that neither escape nor assistance was possible. And the same was true for Yugoslavia. We were asking ourselves: how would the international brigades reach us?

The long-range guns hit the ridge in a pattern that seemed to spare nothing. Everything qualified as a target, and everything was hit. And the space between targets was a hailstorm of shrapnel and broken rock. By the end of the third day it was suicide to be out of the tunnel, and as the planes began to drop their steel drums of napalm higher and higher on the mountain, and to aim their rocket and machine-gun fire at the last ring of our defense outside the portals, Perdika ordered us to stay in, limiting our assistance to the crews that fired the guns

at the west exit. When the Nationalist commando units would
begin to climb up the last stretch to Tsarno, followed by regular
troops, hundreds of our reserves would move to meet them at
each exit with more machine-gun and small-arms fire. They
would fight to the end, and we'd go with them. If the enemy
troops broke through and invaded the tunnels, Perdika would
fire at what was left of our munitions and blow the whole thing
up.

"Stop to think now," I told myself, but there was no longer
time to think, and Death had already entered the tunnels—not
as an enemy but as an observer, counting heads, taking inven-
tory of everything, like a buyer of property, or an inheritor,
arriving at the scene of transaction a little before the appointed
hour, making sure that no one was going to cheat him of what
was rightly his.

"Stop to think now," but there was no time. Death sat next
to Marina to see that the relief she and the doctor offered to
the wounded was tentative, that Marina and Dr. Mathios did
not cheat him out of what would be rightly his at the appointed
hour.

"Stop to think now." How had I gotten so far and yet nowhere? How had I, even I, allowed myself to be counted in,
without will, without fate or face? But it was too late for thinking, and all I could hope for was a totally thoughtless act that
could make a difference, that could make sense.

I stopped trying to think, and watched through the frame of
the portal the destruction as far as the eye could see, the blasting of the mountain and the deluge of fire, the scene ever
changing as masses of dense black smoke blocked one part to
reveal another.

Twice on the fourth day of the attack the west-exit crews
were hit by machine-gun fire from the air, and twice we saw
planes go down. Issaris, Andreas, Avramakis and I removed the
dead and carried the wounded to the dispensary. We were
stunned by the ways the bodies of the young fighters were

broken, and we carried them and cared for them in total confusion. Their blood flowed from their wounds, their mouths and nostrils, and then stopped flowing, their limbs collapsing oddly as though disjointed. And the sound of the guns, and the great explosions that reached our ears through the trembling rock like age-old trees being uprooted, made it hard for us to listen to their pain, to their last words. Blood and more blood anointed our brows, seeped through our shirts and thickened slippery between our fingers. Death came and went that day and the next. It touched the young fighters' eyes and blinded them; touched their legs, hands, and entire arms, and severed them; whispered in their ears and deafened them; unbuttoned their shirts, and their bowels tumbled forth, trembling; stroked their short hair, setting it on fire. And others burned down below in the crags, burned and burned like candles, like young pines in a firestorm—for there were no real trees at such heights.

I saw birds flying upward through the smoke, their wings in flames. I saw the Naxians, climbing down the portal before anyone could stop them, to repair the wiring of their mines, in a hail of rock fragments. I saw Pelekys, unrestrained by the six or seven hands that stretched out to seize him, climbing down to repair the protective drywall and bring back the disabled gunners. And others burning in midair, at the far end of the line, we lifted them up, flame issuing from their mouths; and the rope itself caught fire and broke in midair. I saw the rope breaking in midair and the kids, spattered with burning tar, falling. What else did I see? Papanikas, trying to give Communion to the dying. Some received it gratefully, some refused it: boys and girls who did not believe in Christ, or had already died. And the blood became sticky between my fingers; it would not dry.

On the fifth day hundreds of young fighters armed with small weapons and bayonets took positions at the exits, waiting for the enemy commando units, the mountain climbers, but the

planes were still dropping steel drums of napalm, feeding the
fire outside and making it impossible for any ground troops to
approach. Then there were several strafing sorties, and the
defenders of the west exit stood up, abandoning their cover and
sending barrage after barrage of machine-gun and rifle fire at
each approaching plane, and we saw smoke trailing three of
them as they flew overhead. Two other fighter planes, having
been hit by the east-exit defenders, crashed within view. There
were heavy casualties on our side: once the drywalls in front of
the portal collapsed, the enemy pilots could direct their machine-gun fire inside the tunnel, mowing down the young Andartes by the dozen.

As we removed the bodies between air attacks, a wounded
girl with whom I had talked once, but whose name I could not
remember, pushed her Bren gun my way. "Take it." She closed
her eyes, opened them again, and added, "Don't dishonor it."

Avramakis helped me pass the strap of the small, heavy
weapon over my head and left arm.

Later on, as more and more bodies lay scattered about the
west exit, and as I couldn't think of a better way to fulfill the
wounded fighter's wish, I took that Bren and buried it under a
pile of stones.

Late-hour news and rumors began to circulate among the
fighters as they fought, among the wounded and the dying:

The Naxians had not returned from the mission they under-
took against their commander's orders: they'd probably de-
fected to the enemy.

Nike, five or so months pregnant with Sfekas' child, had been
with Perdika at the munitions storage, but Perdika reported
that she'd disappeared the night before.

Pelekys, who'd climbed down to repair the drywalls, had not
come back to the portal; but another fighter was heard saying
that he'd seen our giant catching a steel drum of napalm in the
air and hurling it down the cliff to the enemy.

Scorpaena, who at the end of the other war had traveled on foot, at the age of ten, from Bergen-Belsen to Thessalonike and had gone on fighting for Bread-Freedom-Justice for five more years, had hurled herself from the cliff of the north exit.

The so-called "international brigades" couldn't get through the lines because they never existed. Only a few hundred Greek-Albanians managed to sneak past their border guard, but they were beaten back by the Nationalists in no time.

And for some strange reason, some dispute not made clear, the Party spies had taken Capetan Aetos aside and had shot him.

Issaris, Andreas, Avramakis and I tried to stay close to one another, and once in a while we glanced at one another as if searching for familiar signs, a smile, a word, an idea—anything, but there was nothing there, and it occurred to me that maybe our quiet preparations to die had been completed, and if the end didn't come soon we might even fail to recognize one another.

Toward evening, Issaris, Andreas, Avramakis and I took two more wounded fighters to the dispensary, and we were on our way back to the west exit when a great gust of compressed air coming from that direction threw us down. There was a vast explosion right at the portal, within the portal, a direct napalm hit, judging from the blackness of the smoke that rushed toward us, and Avramakis or I said, "This is it!"

"Let's run to the south exit," shouted Andreas, plugging his ears.

The south exit reminded me of Tatoi, the smaller cave where Minos and a lot of other small children had been put up for safety. "Let's try the Sfekas Pass," I shouted, ready to run. And then I remembered Marina.

"Let's," agreed Issaris.

"But if it's damaged we'll turn back and continue south, right?" shouted Andreas.

The smoke was rushing in faster than we could run, and by the time I found Marina the others had been swallowed up by it.

"See you there," one of them—I think Avramakis—shouted to me.

Smoke filled my eyes and mouth, choking me, and wherever I stepped there were bodies, wounded fighters coughing, moaning, crying.

"Quick!" I said to Marina, pulling her by the arm.

"What! I can't," she resisted.

"Come with me now. You promised," I shouted at her, coughing.

"Not yet," she said and turned her attention to the wounded.

"But you promised . . ." I was at a loss.

"When the war's over."

"The war *is* over. Can't you see?"

"My place is here," insisted Marina, leaving no doubt that she meant it.

"Please, there's no time," I tried again, struggling for breath.

"Go away!"

A new denser mass of smoke pushed its way between us, separating us. Coughing and crying, I stumbled, and fell, and crawled over the lean bodies writhing and twitching on the floor of the tunnel, and then I stood up and, holding my breath, followed the left wall south, determined to locate the secret pass which Sfekas and Nike had used as their love nest.

Darkness, the vast chemical night, poured forth, a black swelling intestine now taking the shape of the tunnel, rushing right and left, up and down, filling every pocket of space, every crevice, swallowing every bubble of air. The mountain convulsed, shuddering from the explosions. Loose chunks of rock rained constantly from the ceiling.

The Sfekas Pass had not caved in, and although Issaris, Andreas and Avramakis had not put back the stone that blocked its entrance, little smoke got in. I breathed, breathed again, and started down. The pass sloped down, and the smoke wanted to go up. I breathed and walked on all fours, and went on breathing. Somewhere before the exit, before I ran the last stretch to Tatoi on the scorched ground, the bombardment stopped and only the heat and the chemical smell and the sound of the raging fires were there.

It was over, all over, I thought. At day's end every child will have to return home. Tell me that this was no war, no real war. What was it that had started it all, anyway? A piece of candy? An unkind word? For a brief moment I had turned elsewhere, and I thought, listen now to the sparrows' last noise of the day as they settle in the bush for the night. Tomorrow everything will be forgotten, I thought. Tomorrow it's going to be a better day: Saturday, maybe Sunday.

I was sure it was over, but I was wrong. For as soon as I reached Tatoi, the whole mountain shook more violently than ever, and the top of the Tsarno skull came off, bursting and spewing fire, stone and flesh, aborting its belly full of dreams and dreamers.

Look now at that crater, I thought, and tell me: what did Perdika think about when she fired her Bren at the munitions dump as she promised? Look now at that crimson sky, at that scorched mountain, and tell me: where's Marina? Where are the others—so many others? What is left?

And a sparrow looked down from the sky, and there was nothing, not even a single twig, on which to perch for the night.

peace and reconstruction

άπελευθέρωση. Είναι όμως καί ρεαλιστική;

Ὁ Πέτρος Ροῦσος, στὸ βιβλίο του «Ἡ Μεγάλη Πενταετία», ἀπευθυνόμενος πρὸς ἀριστεροὺς ἀναγνῶστες καὶ προσπαθώντας νὰ δικαιολογήσει τὸ «ὄχι» τοῦ ΚΚΕ, ἰσχυρίζεται πως ἡ ἡγεσία του δὲν ἀρνήθηκε τὴ συγκρότηση τοῦ Βαλκανικοῦ Στρατηγείου οὔτε τὸ τορπίλλιασε. «Ζήτησε ἁπλῶς – γράφει – ἀναβολὴ τοῦ ζητήματος μέχρι νὰ δημιουργηθοῦν οἱ ὅροι». Γιατί αὐτὲς οἱ μασημένες δικαιολογίες; Ὁ ἴδιος ἀναφέρει ὡς ἑξῆς τοὺς λόγους ποὺ ὤθησαν τὸ πολιτικὸ γραφεῖο τοῦ ΚΚΕ στὴν ἀπόφασή του:

«Πρῶτο, νὰ στερεώσουμε τὴν ἐθνικοαπελευθερωτικὴ συμμαχία, νὰ μὴν προκαλέσουμε δυσανασχέτηση τῶν συμμάχων μας στὸ ΕΑΜ καὶ σὲ ἄλλους ἐνδεχόμενους συμμάχους μας. Δεύτερο, νὰ μὴν ἐπισπεύσουμε ἔνταση τῶν ἀντιδράσεων καὶ ἐπεμβάσεων τῶν Ἄγγλων στὴν Ἑλλάδα προτοῦ προλάβει νὰ στερεωθεῖ τὸ ἐπαναστατικὸ κίνημα στὴν Ἑλλάδα ἢ τουλάχιστον στὴ Γιουγκοσλαβία. Τρίτο, νὰ μὴ δημιουργήσουμε πρόωρα ἐμπόδια στὴν παγκόσμια ἀντιχιτλερικὴ συμμαχία, τὰ ὁποῖα ἄγνωστο ἂν θὰ μπορέσουμε τελικὰ νὰ ὑπερπηδήσουμε ὅσο βαστάει ὁ πόλεμος κατὰ τῶν καταχτητῶν».

Μακεδόνες καὶ Μεγαλόσερβοι

Ὁ Κώστας Καραγιώργης ὅμως, ποὺ ἀναμείχθηκε ἄμεσα στὸ θέμα, ὅπως εἴδαμε, σὲ ἰδιαίτερη συνομιλία ποὺ εἶχε·μὲ τὸν γράφοντα τὸ 1946, καθαρὰ καὶ σταράτα ἔδωσε τὴν ἐξήγηση:

– Ἄκου...

«... Ἡ σκέψη τῶν Γιουγκοσλάβων καὶ τῶν Ἀλβανῶν συντρόφων νὰ ἐπηρεάζουν πρὸς ὁρισμένη πολιτικὴ τὶς ἀντίστοιχες ἔνοπλες δυνάμεις τῶν ἐθνικῶν μειονοτήτων στὴν Ἑλλάδα (Σλαβομακεδόνων καὶ τσάμηδων Ἀλβανῶν) περιέκλειε σοβαροὺς κινδύ-

γοι ποὺ ...
λιτικὸ μ...
ὅτι τὸ Ε...
λουθούσα...
ματα. Δ...
λίγο πρὶν...
Διεθνής ...
της δὲν ...
ὅπως κα...
ἔδειχνε ...
πολὺ με...
χρεωμέ...

> On one occasion a general informed me by telephone that his troops had discovered a cave, high in the mountains, full of very small children, all half-dead from cold and hunger. . . . Of these children only a few survived; all the others died on the way down.
>
> —FREDERIKA, QUEEN OF THE HELLENES,
> *A Measure of Understanding*

σίες γιὰ νὰ διατηρήσει τὴ συμμαχικὴ ἑνότητα χωρὶς τὴν ὁποία μποροῦσε νὰ χαθεῖ τὸ πᾶν. Καὶ δὲν ξέρω πως ὁ Τίτο καὶ ὁ Τέμπο κάναν τοῦ κεφαλιοῦ τους, ἐμεῖς ὅμως διστάζαμε νὰ καταφέρουμε μιὰ μαχαιριὰ στὰ νεφρὰ τῆς μεγάλης συμμαχίας. Γιατί κάτι τέτοιο θὰ ἦταν ἂν ἀποκάλυπτα ὀρθωνόμαστε μαζὶ μὲ τοὺς Ἀλβανοὺς καὶ Γιουγκοσλάβους κατὰ τῶν Ἄγγλων. Ὅλα αὐτὰ ὅμως ἦσαν δευτερεύοντα μπροστὰ σὲ ἕναν ὀγκόλιθο ποὺ θὰ σοῦ ἀποκαλύψω».

Καὶ καθὼς ὁ γράφων τέντωνε τὸν λαιμό του καὶ τὰ αὐτιά του γιὰ ν' ἀκούσει, ὁ Κώστας Καραγιώργης συμπλήρωσε:

– Ἐκεῖνο ποὺ μᾶς τρόμαξε εἶναι ἄλλο; Εἴχαμε πληροφορίες ἀλλὰ καὶ ἀντιλήφθη-

θανε τὴν ἑλληνική, γιουγκοσλαβικὴ καὶ ὑπῆρχαν 30 μεραρχίες σοβιετικοῦ στρατοῦ. Στὴν Ἑλλάδα μετὰ τὴν ἀπελευθέρωση ἦρθαν 3 μεραρχίες ἀγγλικοῦ στρατοῦ.

Ἀλλὰ πολὺ χαρακτηριστικὰ ὁ Πέτρος Ροῦσος παρατηρεῖ:

«Γιουγκοσλάβικα καὶ ἰδίως ὁρισμένα σλαβομακεδονικὰ στελέχη τῆς γειτονικῆς χώρας ἀψηφοῦσαν τὶς συνέπειες ποὺ θὰ 'χει σ' ὅλον τὸν ἑλληνικὸ ἀγώνα καὶ στὸν ἀγώνα τῶν βαλκανικῶν λαῶν ἡ ἄμεση υἱοθέτηση ἀπὸ μᾶς τοῦ συνθήματος "ἑνιαία Μακεδονία στὰ πλαίσια τῆς νέας Γιουγκοσλαβίας". Ὑπάρχουν καὶ σήμερα ἀκόμη ὁρισμένοι τους ποὺ λένε πως καὶ ἂν ἀκόμα δὲν ἐλευθερωνόταν ἡ Ἑλλάδα ἀπὸ τὸν ἰμπεριαλισμό, θὰ εἶνε ἐλευθεωθεῖ τουλάνι-

Ὁ Τίτο κατὰ

Καὶ τώρα ἕνα
γνωση τοῦ Τίτο
Τέμπο; Ἀσφαλὰ
ὅσο τελικὰ ὁρίσ
πρόσωπος τῆς
σχεδιασμὸ στρα

Ὥστε ὁ Τίτο υ
Μεγαλοσέρβων
γκοσλαβίας;

Ἡ ἀπάντηση,
δοξο, εἶναι κα
στοὺς πολλοὺς
μὲ ἐντολή του ·
τερα τὰ γιουγκ
ψαν τὸ ἀντίθετο
καὶ ἀδιάψευστα

Ὁ Τίτο πράγμ
σύσταση Βαλκ. Σ
κοὺς λόγους. Κ
ταν στὸν στρατι
ἦταν κακή. Ἀλλ
μεγαλοσέρβικοι
κοὶ κύκλοι – ὑπὸ
νιστικοῦ βρασμ
νήσου – γιὰ νὰ ἐ
τὸν τὸν μηχανισ

Ἄργησε νὰ τ
τῆς ἀραιῆς ἐπικ
τὸ καλοκαίρι το
μάχη ζωῆς ἢ θ
τῶν. Ὅταν πληρ
γίνει, ἡ ἀντίδρ
Ἔσπευσε νὰ δια

«Παραγγείλατ
ζμπο α τ
ρεῖο γιατ
στό?».

Διλημμα το
μίζει:
σημερίν
ὁποιοαδηδ
λάθος,
χαριστικ
ἡ τιμὴ του μ
ημιουργί
σία».

νήματα
στρατηγό του δ
νος τὰ εἶχε λάβ
«ὄχι» τοῦ Σιάντ
πυρώσει τὸ θέμ
τήσει ὁριστικά.

Ἄλλωστε ,τώ
παρτιζάνοι ὅπως
βρίσκονταν μπρ
ἀνατροπή; Ἡ Ἰτ
Καὶ στὸν βαλκα
σποτος ἕνας ὁλ
γέρας τῶν δυνα
χώματα τῆς Γιου

Τὸ ΚΚΕ λέει·

·1·

A barrage of machine-gun fire sounded, and I felt my entire body convulse, my head, arms and legs jolting upward as if I were a puppet awakened on stage by a jerk of my strings. Other naked limbs jumped on both sides of me and over my face and bare chest. Had they discovered our hideout? Were they finishing us off on the spot? "Mama," whispered a weak voice nearby. A word I hadn't heard in a long time. I was searching its silent echo as my lips met and parted twice, blowing two weak syllables into the air, like kisses. But whom were those kisses meant for? For a loaf of bread and a bowl of sugar, perhaps; but the bread had already turned green from mildew, and the sugar was actually salt. A bird came next, a warm bird, but I couldn't stretch my hands toward it, and before I knew it the bird had gone up in flames. A sweater, then, a wool sweater to hide the chills and to quiet down the cramps in my stomach. Was there time? Was there still time? The outline of a figure against the window, against the dusk. Her hands are knitting a small sweater, and her index fingers are needles with which she knits. The day comes to an end. Is there still time? She lights the kerosene lamp to continue the knitting while there is still time. That light too comes to an end as it consumes the last drop of oil. She moves back to the window to knit by the moonlight. She won't hurry. Slowly, while the mind wanders, she'll bring that sweater to flawless completion. She doesn't look at the clock. What keeps the time is the wool in her hands and her mind's wandering: a second or so per stitch, but several stitches per thought. And how often does she look at her knitting? Her eyes are deep-set, slanted a little at their outer corners, almost beyond hope, by now perhaps even beyond sorrow. Her eyes are the tips of her fingers, and when she parts her lips she is not about to sigh and give away her thoughts, but to slow down the mindless momentum of her fingers, the needles. By morning she might discover that the back of the sweater is a bit longer than it needs to be, a bit longer than the front, anyway, so she'll prudently undo a few rows, as though attempting to undo time.

A second, deafening barrage rang out, scaring my eyes open. The cave—was it a cave?—looked small and symmetrical, its vaulted ceiling lined with corrugated tin. A number of us lay crowded on straw mattresses on the floor, all naked, a pile of bones wrapped in stained yellow skin. We had no cheeks, nor stomachs and buttocks—just skulls, cheekbones, rib cages, kneecaps and shins, the eyes unusually large in their sockets. The lips, having shrunk like fabric, kept the mouths half opened and the teeth bared. The hair had been clipped short or had fallen out. When the second barrage sounded, the bones began to stir, mingling or tangling: feet over faces, legs under arms, backs over thighs. Somewhere under the bones a few weak cries: "Mama, mama." Issaris, Minos, Andreas and Avramakis were not there, or else had shrunk beyond recognition. And all the girls were missing. I made an effort to crawl, but couldn't. The ceiling was vaulted and lined with corrugated tin sheets: the common, quick, inexpensive construction used in military installations.

Soon, the gate at the far end of the building opened up, flooding the interior with daylight. It rushed in, piercing our eyes, and our half-open mouths gave out a sigh, a sound so deep and distant that I, even I, thought it was coming from a well, a basement. All hands moved slowly over the faces, covering the eyes. When the gate clanged shut, I saw two boys wearing navy uniforms and gas masks walk toward us. Each one carried a small tank strapped to his back, and, pumping with the right hand at a lever, he extended a thin rubber hose toward us with the left, spraying a solution that smelled like camphor and gasoline over our heads. The cloud of mist began to settle on us in no time, stinging our eyes and skin and causing violent coughing. We coughed, scratched and cried, hoping it wouldn't be long before the poison did its work. By the time the sailors left, the coughing ceased and I felt a pleasurable numbness crawling over my skin. I reeled, gazing at the vaulted ceiling through the saltwater that had gathered between my eyelids.

It must have been hours later that once again we were awakened by the same machine-gun-like rattle, except this time I also heard the end of another sound, a sound of hard objects rolling down the roof, and it occurred to me that someone outside must have been throwing a handful of stones onto the tin roof each time we were supposed to be awakened for a visitor. If so, any moment now the gate would open again and the sailors would walk in with more insecticide or some torture of another kind, or death by real machine-gun fire. Still shaking, I clasped my hands together, breathing deeply. The air still smelled of DDT.

The gate opened and everybody covered his eyes, but no sailors showed up this time. The gate was kept open. Bones stirred, creaking, limbs moved slowly over slow limbs like cold worms, and as the eyes became accustomed to the light a few eyelids blinked. In the opening of the gate stood a dark figure: a man with both hands raised in front of his face as though covering his eyes; a newcomer, perhaps, someone who could not bear the sight of us and had to cover his eyes before they got used to the sight, or at least to the darkness inside. *Click*, it wasn't his hands that covered his face, but a camera. He held it before his face. The photographer didn't see us but the camera focused at us. *Click*—its metal eyelid blinked time and again, its glass eye scanning the bones, scanning the stained skin and the bared teeth, but the photographer didn't see a thing. He took a few short steps backward, and the gate began to close. A last *click*, then the gate was closed shut like the eyelid of a huge camera, but neither the photographer nor anyone else saw the sight.

·2·

He was introduced to us as Ensign Koliopoulos of the Children's Royal Navy. A straight-faced, well-fed kid who must have spent a good part of his life learning and obeying the Rules. His at-ease posture was so stiff one couldn't imagine him standing at attention; for his backbone was so well trained to be straight that it arched backward. And he held his hand behind his ass as though he were hiding something important from us. Ensign Koliopoulos' speech to us went like this:

"Children of Greece: Long live the King! Long live the National government! Long live the victorious armed forces! Today, depending on your cooperation with the Royal Navy, could be the first day of your repatriation. I am well aware that some of you were forced by the Bandits to abandon your families and schools and take up arms against your country; that some others only followed their parents who already were Bandits; and still others got caught in the crossfire and accidentally found themselves in the camp of the enemy. Finally, there are those among you who joined the enemy bands by choice, motivated by the same criminal passion: to enslave our nation to the Red Menace."

Ensign Koliopoulos of the Children's Navy took a deep breath, wiped his brows and lips with his handkerchief and, staring at some of us with considerable contempt, went on to say, "Now, of course, you are the sad remnants of a rebellion

163

that has been defeated, crushed. Obviously some of you are
more guilty than others, and should expect your punishment
to be harsher. But none is totally innocent. We believe that
every one of you has been contaminated, infected. What are
we to do with you? The truth of the matter is that either accidentally or knowingly you have lost the right of choice. So it is
up to us to determine your fate. Let me give you a hint or two:
you may never run away again; you may never again aim your
murderous weapons at Mother Greece. War, famine and disease have already taken a heavy toll. Thousands of youths like
you perished in this war in total ignorance. May the soil that
covers them be light, for they might have known better. But
you who still live may never run away and aim your weapons
at Greece. We will teach you better and you will learn. Greece
is forgiving. Greece will always be ready to receive you back
into her bosom. But not before your blood is decontaminated,
not before your minds are cleansed, not before your hearts
throb again with national pride. The Children's Navy has accepted the difficult task of your reeducation on one condition:
that we'll have a free hand with you. But remember: at the end
it will be up to you how long and harsh or how short and
painless this period of transition will be. At the end Greece will
offer you a contract, and it will be under her terms that you
will be allowed to return to her bosom. Until then I wish you
quick recovery—and, of course, good luck. You will need it."
Ensign Koliopoulos wiped his mouth as though he'd just finished eating a soft-boiled egg, and turned to his subordinate,
Petty Officer Kotevas of the Children's Navy, nodding.

"Dismissed!" yelled Kotevas.

Most of us leaned back on our straw mattresses; a few looked
around in confusion. Since we were unable to stand on our
feet for more than a few minutes at a time, Koliopoulos and
Kotevas had allowed us to remain seated during the speech.
We remained dismissed, waiting for our lunch of black-eyed-
bean soup and galleta.

From the navy doctor who had examined us twice in the past month, we'd learned that all the girls who survived had been transferred to another camp while we were still in the hospital. The infants and most of the four- and five-year-olds had been found dead in the cave. Others died in Kastoria as the doctors fought to revive them. Minos and Avramakis had still been in the hospital when Andreas and Issaris were taken away, soon after their frostbitten legs had been amputated. Avramakis knew that Andreas and Issaris were dead. Minos guessed otherwise. The rest of us were recovering slowly. And it was just as slowly that the death of so many who'd been close to us, especially the death of Andreas and Issaris, was catching up with us.

Minos, Avramakis and I developed complications beyond the obvious pains and aches of frostbite, but we were careful not to complain about anything, for fear of amputation. Minos had dizzy spells and psoriasis on the backs of his hands. Avramakis was confusing his words so badly that even he was aware of it when it happened, so he ended up trying not to talk very often or for long. And I could not remember anything about the last two months of our hiding in the Tatoi cave, during which we ran out of provisions and the mountain was covered again with ice. Day and night we had nightmares, and the smaller kids seemed to cry all the time. But we were recovering. Our bodies were growing healthier and stronger every day. And then I noticed that the stronger we got, the worse we began to feel about the ones we'd lost. It was as though every bit of life that returned to us was a gift from those who died, and I began to wonder: Why Issaris and not I? Why Andreas and not Avramakis? Why Marina, Scorpaena, Capetan Aetos, Papanikas and Pelekys, and not Zaphira, Fotis, Pavlos, Polyvios and Trakas? From time to time I would sense the eyes of the dead watching me, and I'd struggle to build a face around two eyes that seemed familiar, and I'd ask, "Tell me what I can do to ease your pain," but the eyes looked at me and did not answer, and in the end I recognized those eyes as mine. Slowly, painfully, I began to understand that I might have to spend the rest of my life sharing their silence and trying to read in my own eyes what it was that the dead left unfinished.

Avramakis thought that my problem was severe but not serious. "Listen," he said, but no other words came from his mouth.

"Go on," I encouraged him.

"Forget it," he said after a while. "I lost it. I thought it was under my tongue, but I can't find it anywhere."

And Minos wouldn't pay any attention to what I had to say, since he wouldn't listen to anyone talking about the dead. As it turned out, he was busy developing a theory of his own, according to which Andreas and Issaris had not died in the hospital, but simply transferred to Methana, a hot-springs resort where people from all over the country went to obtain treatment for certain ailments or to convalesce. At Methana, Andreas and Issaris were reunited with Marina and other girls, so they weren't lonely. Minos could see them taking hot or cold baths at the springs, or lying down and heaping mounds of mineral mud over their bodies. Thanks to that treatment, Andreas and Issaris would not have to have their legs amputated.

·3·

For three more days we lay on our straw mattresses, resting and worrying about our upcoming punishment.

I spent several hours each day with Minos and Avramakis, trying to remember what had happened during the last two months of our hiding in the Tatoi cave, but none of their descriptions and stories sounded right, or even possible. Not so much because Avramakis kept mixing up the wrong words in everything he said, and Minos simply refused to believe that the thousands of kids who'd made the final stand and lost the battle were all killed, but because my own mind felt exhausted and more than ever before confused. I was determined to memorize some of those stories.

Minos and Avramakis insisted that after the war had come to an end and while we were hiding in the cave, the five of us (including Andreas and Issaris) had sworn to lie about everything if we were taken prisoner by the Nationalists. Sworn to lie! Big general lies as well as little ones, and lots of uninteresting details plus a few irrelevant anecdotes here and there, which take one's attention away from the big lies. No, I didn't remember having sworn to lie. Minos and Avramakis swore that I swore.

"I am telling you, I don't remember a thing."

"You're lying."

"Look," said Avramakis. "The five of us—"

"We're only three now."

"And we're going to be even fewer if you tell them the truth. Anyway, the three of us met somewhere between Trikala and Meteora while searching for our parents who'd been forced by the Andartes—"

"Bandits," Minos corrected him.

"That's right, we've got to be careful about things like that too." Avramakis went on. According to his version, my father and mother had been dragged out of our house by the Slavo-Communist bandits, because they were known to favor the return of the Bast—"Oops! I mean the King," Avramakis corrected himself.

"Wait a minute . . ."

"You've got to lie."

"Not about my parents I won't."

"Look. Just before the war, during a tour in the countryside, the King had shaken your father's hand, and from then on he became a royalist. Simple," said Avramakis.

"My father wasn't that stupid."

"Fine, but others were. It'll stick, I promise."

Minos could not wait to get to the anecdotes part. Could he relate again the one about his dog Zavos who kept peeing from under his crippled leg? Minos was unsure, because that was a true story.

"Go ahead, throw it in," approved Avramakis. "Now, what about your family?"

"No family," answered Minos.

"Good. What about your town?"

"I don't remember it."

"What was the nearest town that you recall swimming in?" Avramakis asked again.

"Eh?" Minos thought the nearest town was Lamia, but he didn't recall anything about swimming. Lamia was not by the sea.

Avramakis himself would mention nothing about his family

being Hebrew, or about his house in Yannina. His parents had nothing to do with the fur trade. They just owned mules and made their living by transferring goods for merchants from one town to another. Once, they stopped to spend the night at an inn near Xylokastro, and when Avramakis woke up in the morning he was told that his parents and the mules with the merchandise had been taken away by the Andart—("I mean, the Bandits"). The innkeeper still lay on the floor with a knife wound in the back of his head.

"A knife wound? In the head?"

"Details," explained Minos.

"I guess they'd aimed at his neck but missed," offered Avramakis.

"Is that a true story?"

"Now it is," said Avramakis.

Back to my family: my own parents were supposed to be farmers. We lived in the country, near Tripolis. On Saturdays we used to go to the haymarket to sell eggs, cauliflower, onions and braids of garlic. In the spring months it was lettuce, scallions and dill.

"Details," said Minos.

"You can change them, but not during the interrogation," warned Avramakis.

We were still lying on our backs, conspiring, when Fotis, Polyvios and Pavlos came crawling across the concrete floor to talk to us.

Fotis, panting from the effort of having to use his only arm to move forward, started off. "The three of us have been thinking." He looked at Pavlos and Polyvios and then at the rest of us, allowing a brief pause. "The idea is to do something to help the kids," he said then. "And I think the best way to go about it is to run a trial trial."

"A what?"

"A rehearsal for our defense in the upcoming trial," said Fotis.

"What trial?" Had I missed something?

"Who said there's going to be a trial?" Avramakis' eyes were twice as big, as though he spoke with his eyes.

"I think there's going to be a military tribunal as soon as we can stand on our feet, and they won't even appoint a lawyer to our defense," interrupted Fotis.

Avramakis seemed to be searching for the right words to keep on arguing, but he couldn't come up with any. "Are you sure about that?" he said at the end, meekly.

Fotis didn't even bother to answer.

"What are they going to do to us?" asked Minos.

"Nothing," said Avramakis, before anyone else could answer that question. "They'll probably deport us all to Methana for mineral mud baths."

"What I am afraid is they'll probably try to turn some of us against the others," said Fotis.

"And we've got to make sure nobody becomes witness for the prosecution," added Polyvios.

"How can you stop anybody who intends to do that?"

"We'll talk to everybody," said Fotis with conviction. "We'll tell them that if no one cooperates, the court won't be able to prove our guilt, and we'll all be acquitted or get away with light sentences."

"That's why before the real trial we're going to have a trial trial," said Pavlos.

"A rehearsal," explained Polyvios. "Just to make sure there will be no surprises—if you see my point."

Surprise! It was only minutes after Fotis, Pavlos and Polyvios had gone on to convert more kids to their plan for a trial rehearsal that the gate burst open, and in came Ensign Koliopoulos and Petty Officer Kotevas to inform us that we had more than forfeited our right to a so-called "fair trial," and therefore any activities such as preparing to defend our case in a court of law was unnecessary.

How did they know? Had they been eavesdropping on us?

"Quiet!" shrieked Kotevas.

"I am referring specifically to Emergency Laws 375 and 509, which in addition provide for administrative deportation or incarceration at remote islands and military camps of all persons charged with sedition, insurrection and other crimes against the territorial integrity of our nation, or the established order and the social system, namely the Constitutional Monarchy," Ensign Koliopoulos went on. He then placed his crop under his left arm and, unbuttoning his breast pocket, produced a document. He glanced at it, and again at us with a slow turning of his eyes from left to right. "This," he said, showing us the typewritten, stamped and signed sheet of paper, "is the order for your deportation according to Emergency Laws 375 and 509. It has been issued by the Ministry of the Interior and bears the signature of the Deputy Minister for Public Order. Other orders will designate the particular location of your exile and specify methods of discipline and reeducation, diet, physical fitness and so on." Ensign Koliopoulos now moved his right hand over his left breast pocket and reached under his arm—a rapid succession of gestures, aiming at an exchange of the two symbols of power, the Ministerial Order and the officer's crop. "Any questions?" And before anyone could think of one, Ensign Koliopoulos added, "Dismissed!"

"Dismissed!" echoed Petty Officer Kotevas.

• 4 •

Late at night on New Year's Eve, we were awakened by several seamen recruits of the Children's Navy and led without explanation to the railroad stop outside the navy stockade. We spent the very last minutes of 1949 wondering in the cold whether or not this was our transfer to a detention camp in accordance with Emergency Laws 375 and 509 and in compliance with the executive order of the Minister of the Interior, cosigned by the Deputy Minister of Public Order.

We boarded the train right at midnight—the beginning of a new year and a new decade. It was a cargo train, probably returning from Xanthe. We packed an open car, accompanied by Petty Officer Kotevas and six seamen recruits armed with rifles. Kotevas said they had orders to shoot to kill, but said nothing about the circumstances under which that might take place. We were very crowded, but the car was open. And the stockade lay behind us, getting smaller and smaller, almost beautiful in the moonlight.

Past the barracks . . . past the camp . . . past the barbed-wire fence of the base . . . past the shadows of the moon . . . past any army truck and a house . . . past an arch and a sign, blue on white: LONG LIVE THE QUEEN! . . . past another: LONG LIVE THE ARMED FORCES! . . . past a third: LONG LIVE THE NATION! . . . past a small concrete bridge, and a dark stream underneath . . . past that thought . . . past another about the past, and the future a mystery. . . . Past a row of telegraph poles . . . a disabled tank and a tree . . . a wartime checkpoint abandoned as pointless . . . past the point . . . past the past . . . past a sign: WELCOME, and another sign: TO KAVALLA . . . past the last of the open country—and the city looks small: small houses; peeled, pocked marked walls; tiled roofs, not very steep, considering the snow; small windows behind the shutters; and beyond the windows the weak oil lamps and the meek "Happy New Year!" from one remaining member of the family to another. . . . Past the night patrol with the slow, rhythmical step . . . past one empty street and another . . . past the school . . . past the church . . . past the city hall and the city . . . and suddenly the air turning salty and sharp. . . . Three expansion joints each breath, two, two, and one, and a final one on the brakes, metal on metal the brakes, and stop, before the train can enter the sea—and the stopping steam underneath our feet goes *fssst!*

Sit quiet. Sit still. Take advantage of the stop to breathe in the wet salt of the night.

I felt the sea rushing into my body from every pore, filling me, and inside my veins I recognized the tickle of seaweed and minnows. And then mermaids and Tritons, sea horses and ancient ships began to surface in my eyes, and I may very well have cried from pleasure, for I knew that this was the first and last time that the sea would take a swim within me.

And Kotevas was no longer there. "Where's Officer Kotevas? Did he get off?"

"Talking to a Coast Guard officer."

An even colder breeze blew from the direction of the harbor, checking one car of the train after another, then it took a halfhearted whirl in the empty square and, bypassing the Military Police, went from house to house, perhaps to spy on the remaining members of each family, or to wish Happy New Year to them.

"Now," whispered Minos, opening his eyes.

"Now what? Are you dreaming?"

"Silence!" Kotevas and a Coast Guard officer were standing behind us at the door, counting heads.

Out in the harbor a chain rattle and the sound of an anchor plunging into the water made everyone turn.

"How did you know?" I asked Minos.

"I counted to a hundred."

The ship, a dark mass with a single light on the bridge, was almost too big to maneuver about. It took half a turn in place and released its second anchor. Slowly, it began to approach the docking area.

"How many times did you count to a hundred?"

"A hundred."

Kotevas was now giving orders to two of his men to stand by the door of the car, letting out three of us at a time. A second pair of seamen recruits were to be stationed halfway between the ship and the train. Petty Officer Kotevas himself would be at the ramp, seeing to it that our boarding was orderly. As soon as the first group of three reached midpoint, a new group would be released. That way no more than two groups of three would be heading toward the ship at a time.

"No running, stalling or turning to look back," warned Petty Officer Kotevas.

"Yes, sir."

"You will do nothing at all to attract attention."

"Yes, sir, Petty Officer Kotevas."

"Ready? I will be waiting for you by the *Lemnos*."

"The what?"

"The name of the ship."

"Happy New Year, Petty Officer Kotevas."

"Shut up!"

We boarded the *Lemnos* quietly, as ordered, without ever turning to look back. The *Lemnos* was a troop carrier that looked old enough to have been decommissioned three wars ago, but like any ship in the Royal Greek Navy it had to sink before it could be decommissioned.

Another petty officer of the Children's Navy, already aboard the ship, came down the ramp to receive the prisoners.

Kotevas handed him the documents.

"Fifty-two male detainees at time of embarkation—Petty Officer Palioras in charge."

Kotevas and Palioras saluted each other and shook hands.

"All in order, then?"

A salute, a countersalute, and Kotevas was running down the ramp, at the end of which the Coast Guard officer was saying something that no one heard.

"This way to first class," chuckled a seaman apprentice, handing each of us a small card with a stenciled number and pointing down the stairwell.

I was number A-227.

We went down three flights of stairs, on each level of which another seaman apprentice showed the way with a motion of his left hand, waving it before his face as though fanning himself.

It was hot, engine-room hot, past the bottom of the stairwell, and the last door brought us to the source of that heat: the engine room itself and the crowded space around it, a large horseshoe tracing the ship's stern, packed with hundreds of kids between eight and fourteen. We stopped, waiting for the rest in our group, and when they came they pushed us deeper in, and the last two seamen apprentices we saw looked and smelled like the prisoners they guarded.

·5·

A few bodies moved drowsily, but farther on our way was blocked and we had to step on arms and legs to get through to the sink that was mounted on the opposite wall. The kids who slept or who had been trying to sleep for some time were soaked in their sweat, and their faces looked yellow in the dim lighting. Some of them didn't even move when they were stepped on. And when the foot did find empty space to step, the floor was slippery with vomit.

I counted twenty-three kids standing in line for a drink of water, although the water seemed to be too hot even for washing. In the water line we learned that the ship had been sailing for four days, picking up groups of detainees from several ports on the mainland. Most of the kids were with the Andartes when the army captured them, and they were being deported as Bandits and dangerous Communists. Many had lost their parents in the war, and others had been told that their fathers and mothers had already been deported to other camps on uninhabited islands. Markos, who'd joined the line, told Fotis that all prisons and uninhabited islands were overcrowded with political prisoners, and he'd heard that there were even ships like the *Lemnos* that had been loaded with prisoners and sailed day and night without destination, or anchored in the middle of the sea waiting for instructions because there was no room left on land for any more prisoners.

Another kid, Leonis, told us that some two dozen detainees on the ship were about to be released as innocent of wrongdoing against Mother Greece. Two kids, Razis (number A-94), and Zaphiris (number A-95), were let go because they were Gypsies.

Mincs, Avramakis and I glanced at one another, surprised, and Avramakis said, "Did I hear Zaphiris, or Zaphira?"

"Zaphiris," repeated Leonis. "If you're looking for girls in here, you're out of luck."

"We knew a Gypsy girl by that name, that's all," explained Avramakis.

Leonis had heard that the government was going to put the smallest ones into an orphanage, give some of the others up for adoption, and assign the rest to public services such as the City of Athens Gas Distribution Department, the Sanitation Department, the National Bureau of Fisheries and who knows what.

And who knows what was in stock for the rest of us. The ship was out of the harbor now, heading south, probably to the port city of Volos, where the two dozen innocent ones were to disembark, and a new group of prisoners would come on board to replace them.

"That Gypsy kid, Zaphiris—what does he look like?" Avramakis asked.

"Just like any other Gypsy," said Leonis. "Dark skin, black hair, brown eyes."

"How old?"

"About nine. You'll see him before he gets off."

We looked around. The kids must have talked for hours on end with each new group coming on board, and now they were seasick, sleepy, uninterested, depressed.

"If only they'd let us go up on the deck," Leonis wished.

For us, joining a larger group was some sort of reassurance. The more we were, the safer we seemed to feel, as though

sharing the same fate with three hundred others was not as bad
as with fifty or fewer. But for the others the opposite seemed to
be true: when the first group boarded the *Lemnos*, Petty Officer
Palioras and the sailors addressed each one of them by name,
and now they couldn't tell who was who, and Leonis said
whether the seamen addressed them individually or collectively
they just shouted at them, "You!"

The water was too hot to wash with, so we just drank some.
Afterward I leaned back against the vibrating steel wall of the
engine room, feeling the sweat trickle down my chest and sides.
Gradually the conversation ceased. Only here and there a
sleepy voice, slow and tired and distant, persisted: three words
for a question, one for an answer. One or two words for a
second question, no answer at all. Even when the last question
had been asked and the last word spoken, one or two voices still
hung in the air, wordless, aimless.

Suppose there is no island left for us in the Aegean, I
thought. Suppose the *Lemnos* was only meant to anchor and
rust in the middle of nowhere, with us rotting in its stomach
slowly . . . or suppose they sink the *Lemnos* and its trouble-
some cargo—the prisoners. The Germans had done this just
before their surrender, sinking their prison ships in the Baltic,
and the English just after the war, sending down half the population of Megiste, a tiny island between Rhodos and Cyprus.
Why shouldn't the Greeks do the same? Ah, to be a Gypsy! To
have nothing, neither island nor country, not even a handful
of dirt—for beyond bloated words and emotions, that's what
countries are: handfuls of dirt with fancy names. How stupid I
was not to follow Zaphira.

I went on and on, supposing, considering one lost chance
after another, weighing handfuls of dirt, slowly getting drowsy,
thinking of going to the sink for another drink of water and
postponing it for the sake of a thought about cold mountain
springs. But even that changed into a thought about hot

springs and flatlands, and before I knew it I found myself at Methana, where Andreas, Issaris and Marina were now rising from the mud on their own legs, healed, now taking a dip, rinsing their bodies in the sparkling seawater.

·6·

It must have been five or six in the morning that I jumped up screaming and wiping my eyes, thinking they were filled with blood, for I'd just dreamed about the last battle and the taking of Tsarno, and everything in the dream was red: the mountain and the enemy planes, the bombs and the explosions; and red, blood-red, the bodies blasted into the air together with stone or strewn on the scorched slopes. My eyes were clear of blood, but the red had already spilled into the bowels of the *Lemnos*, bloodying everyone and everything even outside that dream. And the knowledge spilling out of the dream was that what I'd just witnessed had nothing to do with Minos' and Avramakis' versions of what had happened in the Tatoi cave during the last two months of our hiding there, for my memory of those two months had just returned. Before I knew it, I was filled with visions, sounds and meanings, in the same way that the sea breeze had filled my body a few hours earlier, or the way one enters a certain room in a house, a room that hasn't been opened for a long time and is full of objects—furniture, toys, books and old photographs—each object a story to remember. But in this case I was the house and the room, and I entering, I seeing the forgotten objects, and I remembering: Here was the scratchy sound of the crystal radio—our only contact with the outside world, although only one of us could listen to it at a time: frequent patriotic speeches that made us sick. And here

180

was Fotis, wanting to destroy the little radio. It took Trakas no time to solve the problem of our frustration over the propaganda, by talking back to the radio and convincing anyone who listened to it to do the same. " 'The bosom of Greece,' my ass!" Trakas would comment. "The old bag doesn't have any bosom left." Or: "Tell his Majesty the King and his Majesty's Prime Minister to go piss." But Marina was not there. Within a few weeks many boys and girls became close friends with one another, but Marina was not there and I didn't care to have another girl as a close friend. At the end of October our provisions ran out. In November there was the first snowstorm, which turned out to be endless, and the icy wind came, freezing over the rock—our breaths turning to icicles up on the ceiling, our arms and legs beginning to shake from cold and hunger. Here were pneumonia and bronchitis, fever and the coughing of blood. Then even the smell from our makeshift toilet in the far end of the cave froze and stopped being a sanitary problem; and when the first deaths occurred the same thing happened: the bodies froze before decomposition could begin, and we didn't have to risk getting out of the cave to bury them. We just put them up, facedown, on the left side, where the girls used to sleep before they moved with us so we could all be a little warmer. Here the whispers and the holding of hands under the blankets, and there I, curled up between Minos and Avramakis, constantly aware of Marina's absence. Here was the diminishing warmth and the numbing of limbs from body to body, and here the crying of the little ones day and night. And many died disbelieving death, and many more fearing and fighting death every moment. Here finally the diminishing of tears and the uneasy quietness, then a few more hours of relative peace before the rest of us went to sleep and some never woke. Those who did wake found themselves in a different place, face to face with a world that would take them time to accept and to be accepted by. Here lying on our backs and resisting sleep, or dreaming of resisting sleep, watching through a web of frost between our eyelashes the icicles hanging from the ceiling, and how much bigger and more succulent they'd grown in the past few days. Succulent: like the roots of certain trees. . . . Maybe this cave was not up on a mountain but in a plain, where the trees grew tall and their roots were sweet and tender enough to eat. But they were too high up, and we were too weak to make a pyramid with our bodies to get to them. . . . Later I saw a frosty glow through the ceiling—and here was the translucent ceiling and the sky beyond overcast, and when I closed my eyes and opened them again I knew that the opaque sky was actually a river: light and water thick like mercury, like pearls, flowed lazily southward while one school of minnows after another swam upstream in bright silvery formations. And here was the bottom of a small boat crossing the river, the gentle dip of the oars leaving a set of ripples on either side—the left side obscured by the shadows of the boatman and his passenger. I decided to follow the river downstream, but my neck had stiffened from looking up, and as it turned out I was already in that boat—and here was the boatman again, steering his vessel across the quiet water westward, the west bank of the river muffled in dusky fog.

·7·

Those people, objects, events and dreams kept pouring back in, and I spent most of the new day remembering, or checking on certain details with Minos and Avramakis to make sure I wasn't making up or changing anything along the way. But Minos and Avramakis weren't too excited about the return of my memory; on the contrary, they seemed to get increasingly annoyed at my discoveries and subsequent inquiries, until sometime in the afternoon Avramakis shouted at me that everything I remembered was more or less the way everything happened, and would I please find something more interesting to do for the rest of the day. And the next time I opened my mouth to ask a question, Avramakis pretended to be sleeping and Minos was already snoring. But I went on remembering, talking to myself, trying to answer my own questions, now getting upset and now pleased, until toward the end of the day I found myself exhausted and miserably depressed. Avramakis may well have known something about remembering that I did not.

Afterward, Leonis dropped by to show us the little Gypsy, Zaphiris, who stood in the water line. "That's your man," he said to Avramakis. He was not our man, nor did he have anything in common with our woman. Zaphiris was small, about nine, and had none of the lovely features of Zaphira, so he couldn't even be a cousin of hers. We saw him for the second

183

and last time later that night when we awoke to the grinding noise of the anchor chain and the excited voices of the kids who were about to disembark. The *Lemnos* was soon docking at Volos. Waiting by the stairwell, ready to race upstairs and out into the cold quiet night, were the "innocent ones," stenciled numbers A-75 through A-99.

"Who's that one?"

"I can't see from here."

They'd stayed by the door, near the two seamen apprentices who guarded the door, ever since our group had come on board at Kavalla; and although the entire horseshoe around the engine room was jammed, they'd managed to stick together and even look like a separate group from the rest. They succeeded in this by avoiding associating too much with any one of us, and by talking a lot among themselves, even though they must have exhausted whatever they had in common in a few hours' time. All this and their being in a less unfortunate category than us seemed to be an embarrassment to both sides, even to the two seamen apprentices guarding the door.

"On the double!" we heard Petty Officer Palioras' voice coming down the stairwell.

And the two seamen apprentices began to let the kids run upstairs one at a time, after checking their numbers.

"That one toward the end of the line."

"I'm not too sure. . . . I think, number A-95."

"No, no. His name!"

"Oh, I think that's the other Gypsy I told you about: Razis," said Leonis.

"You're crazy, Razis is the other one, the nine-year-old. This one is Zaphiris—" And, staring at me with a wild look in his eyes, Avramakis said, "I mean—God, I can't believe it!"

Leonis shrugged. "So I made a mistake."

In the meantime, as though he heard his name, the real Zaphiris turned our way, glancing at us with his bright-green eyes and smiling.

"Zaphira!"

"Zaphira!"

Minos, Avramakis and I rushed toward the stairwell, only to be intercepted by the guards who'd just let Zaphira through the door. We saw her little bare feet run up the stairs, and we turned back.

"So you made two mistakes." Avramakis pointed two fingers against Leonis' chest like a pistol.

"He sure looked like any other Gypsy to me," said Leonis.

"She!" said Avramakis.

"You're putting me on," said Leonis. "She sure looked like any other Gypsy to me," he repeated.

How could he say that? Her hair had been clipped short like the rest of us in the ship, and the clothes she had on were a boy's clothes all right, but how could he miss those eyes and the way she looked at you, especially when she smiled? The way she moved her body, those small tanned feet running up the stairs and out of the ship to freedom?

"So I made a mistake," repeated Leonis.

"Two!" Minos shouted at him.

Goodbye, A-84, we wish you good health and good luck with your job at the Gas Distribution Department at Keramikos. Farewell, A-90 and A-91, may yours be a bright career in the Bureau of Fisheries. A-76, we wish you a full stomach, not an upset one in the Public Stockyards. And may our stomachs become accustomed to rough seas. A-78, A-93 and A-99, you are too small to be on your own, and adopted parents are better than no parents at all. A-87, A-88 and A-96, A-97, A-98, you look too weak to be on your own (and it's hell out there), so the roof of the orphanage will be better than no roof at all over your heads. A-80, A-81, we wish you fair weather in the seven seas as merchant marines; and Razis and Zaphira, we wish you open roads and borders. And you may wish fair weather to us who are sailing tonight to an island that may not yet be charted.

Less than an hour after we'd left Volos we were still talking and arguing about Zaphira and her new appearance and her apparent refusal to wish us fair weather, for the north wind had picked up and become more noticeable as it blew over quarter port, and that meant that our sailing east was already causing much discomfort to our empty stomachs. If there's anything worse than throwing up, it must be trying to throw up while there's nothing in your stomach.

But how did Zaphira happen to be in that ship, disguised as a boy? Why was she arrested and then let go, and what was the story with Razis? What was she up to now that she was again on the loose? No one knew anything, except A-129, Matsoukas, whom Leonis once saw talking to her, soon after she and Razis came on board the *Lemnos* at the island of Oinousai. Matsoukas first swore that Zaphiris was one hundred percent boy, and then said that the two Gypsies had been arrested by the Coast Guard for trying to sneak into Turkey in a small boat. The Coast Guard officer thought they might be fugitives, but he didn't find anything against them and decided to ship them to the mainland.

"That's all?"

That's what Zaphiris told him before he settled down with the other kids who got out at Volos. Neither of the Gypsies talked very much, not even to their own group, and Zaphiris spent a long time snoozing because he was seasick.

"Especially since we came on board," said Avramakis.

The more I thought about that second encounter with Zaphira, the more incredible it seemed to me, and I began to wonder if there was a secret meaning in it. A little more than a year ago we went to the mountain against her advice, and we paid a heavy price for it—in fact, we were still paying. Now she and we were heading in opposite directions again: she to freedom and we to a prison camp. Was she still trying to tell us something?

"In a way," said Avramakis.

"Well, when are we going to start learning from her?"

"All right, last year we had a choice, but we were stupid. This time around we don't even have a choice," protested Avramakis.

That was true enough, but I went on thinking about Zaphira and I speculated about seeing her again, since I felt convinced that there would be at least one more meeting in the future.

Volos had contributed only three kids to the lot. We asked them how come there weren't more, whether the rest of them had been loyalist-royalist, and one of them said, "Leave us alone, we're not in the mood for silly talk like that."

The north wind and the waves now beat the *Lemnos* with such violence that we, even though we were on the lowest level, could feel each blow and responded unwillingly by rolling over one another like pigskins filled with wine. We listened to the creaking of the salt-eaten ribs of the *Lemnos*, a terrifying noise that sounded to us like the ship's breaking up and sinking. At some point even the two seamen apprentices began to vomit, their eyes wide open and bloodshot, their faces yellow and sour like lemon.

"Have you counted to a hundred yet?" Avramakis asked Minos.

"What for?" asked Minos. But then he remembered, and, wiping his mouth on his bare arm, he said, "Now."

"What? Going down!"

"No, the wind stopping."

But the wind wouldn't stop. It went on and on for the rest of the night and most of the following day, and the ship wouldn't go down, either.

·8·

Many of the Greek islands have little children islands by their side: Skyros, the mother island, has a little daughter island, Skyropoula. And Spetsai has Spetsopoula; and Serifos, Serfopoula. Anaphi, one of the prison islands, has a very-little-boy island, Anaphopoulo, which is too little even for a little boys' prison. Then there are a few parent islands that have disowned their children because their children opposed them: Paros—Antiparos. Psara—Antipsara. Melos—Antimelos. Paxoi—Antipaxoi. Kithera—Antikithera. Kalamos, a parent island, was named after the reed that had thrived on its soil for centuries. Antikalamos, its unprincipled child, stood about four nautical miles to the east, and it detested the reed and anything growing on soil and water. Antikalamos could afford no soil or fresh water on its back. It had a head, a back and a tail of stone, but the head and the tail were submerged, and all we could see from the ship was its bent back of stone, a hard reddish stone swept clean by the strong briny wind and disinfected daily by the cloudless sun. If there had been a prophecy that after so many centuries of isolation and punishment by the elements Antikalamos would someday be inhabited, that day had come, because Greece had run out of islands for isolation and punishment, had run out of stone.

"Welcome to Antikalamos, the place of your exile," said the

stone. "According to archaeologists, in ancient times it used to
be one of the Kalamae, a chain of islands that broke up during
a major geological upheaval in the second millennium. Therefore it is natural to suppose that some of the islands that sank
at that time were interspersed between Kalamos and Antikalamos. As for the entire region, it is still considered to be geolog-
ically young and unstable, prone to violent quakes and volcanic
eruptions. The climate conforms to the general conditions of
the entire Aegean and eastern Mediterranean: temperate, with
seasonal winds, and rainfalls in the late autumn and throughout the winter. Throughout its glorious history our country has
used several uninhabited islands such as Antikalamos to rid
itself of subversive and seditious elements, in short any individual or group of individuals who threaten peace or the prevailing
social order," said the stone. "It is a humane practice, and as
such it has failed more than once to guarantee the safety of our
national institutions and of the law-abiding subjects, but
Greece refuses to abdicate from this civilized tradition." And
the stone coughed, and the dark sea slapped its hard reddish
cheek, but the stone wasn't through yet. "The Royal Navy has
already assembled and installed the facilities in which you must
live when not at work in the quarry. There are two barracks for
your guardians, and six large tents for yourselves. We will supply your rations of foodstuffs and water, but you will be responsible for the preparation of your meals. Only those who work
will eat. I repeat, only those who work will eat, and the work
amounts to hard labor. The only ship that you will see anchor-
ing at Antikalamos will be the *Nikaia*, bringing your monthly
provisions in exchange for the product of your work at the
quarry. Also once a month you will be visited by a medical
doctor, and when necessary by a priest. For those among you
who will succumb to the hardships of exile there will be funeral
services, but the burial will take place at sea. Petty Officer
Palioras and I will see to it that your reeducation is replete with

mental and physical discipline. . . ." The stone went on and on. Its rank and name was Ensign Tsakalos of the Children's Navy, commanding officer of the Antikalamos Camp.

Later we marched to the campsite, where we were greeted by two flags, one Greek and one American, that flapped in the chilly wind on twin poles. Down below, mounted on a concrete base that resembled a headstone, a marble slab read:

THIS INSTITUTION
ESTABLISHED BY THE QUEEN'S FUND
AND THE AMERICAN MISSION
IS DEDICATED
TO THE IDEALS OF FREEDOM AND DEMOCRACY
1950

The six tents had been installed at about a hundred meters from the flags, forming a broad circle around them. Past the tents, to the east, were the barracks: a quonset divided into dorms for Ensign Tsakalos, Petty Officer Palioras and a dozen seamen recruits and apprentices of the Children's Navy, and a much larger one partitioned into offices, kitchen and canteen, an assembly room, and several smaller rooms that were as yet undesignated.

Ensign Tsakalos was a balding sixteen-year-old with reddish skin and reddish small round eyes through which he squinted as though he needed prescription glasses but refused to admit it. On the left side of his chin stood at attention two moles: a mother mole and a child mole.

Soon after our arrival we were divided into six groups of forty-seven, each group assigned to a separate tent, and while Ensign Tsakalos and Petty Officer Palioras held their first private conference we took time to locate the outhouse. It was a partitioned tin shack, three units in all, at the far end of three waiting lines of kids, north of the tents. Past the outhouse, to the left, a barbed-wire fence and a red-lettered sign warned that the northernmost tip of Antikalamos was off-limits.

DANGER—DEATH
ENTRY
STRICTLY
FORBIDDEN!

As we stood in line meditating on the positive influence of outhouses throughout the history of Greek civilization, we heard Trakas and Dionysis, who were just ahead of us, count and recount dates on their fingers, adding up months into years, and years into more years. Minos looked at Avramakis, and he seemed about to ask what all that counting of years was about, but Avramakis stopped him.

"Never interrupt someone counting on his fingers, because he might lose count and have to start all over again."

Minos said, "Oh."

Avramakis said, "They're also counting nautical miles."

Minos said, "People always say things like Don't interrupt someone who's counting, or Don't interrupt someone who's drinking, because he might choke to death."

Avramakis said, "It depends on what one's drinking."

Then Trakas announced that according to his calculations Antikalamos was too small to take the shit of three hundred inhabitants and not go down like most of the Kalamae.

"All right, so let it roll down to the sea," said Dionysis.

"That's just it!" shouted Trakas. "According to my calculations, in eleven short years it'll make a floating bridge all the way to Kalamos."

"A shit-bridge to freedom!" pondered Dionysis. "I can see the inscription on marble: 'This bridge, made possible by the Queen's Fund and the American Mission in Athens, is dedicated to the ideals of freedom and prosperity, 1950–1961.'"

·9·

Trakas' calculations were all wrong, as he overestimated the size of our rations, which turned out to consist of no more than a cup of black-eyed-bean soup and a piece of dried bread for lunch, and a cup of black-eyed-bean soup and a piece of dried bread for dinner. The Sunday Special was to be a cup of navy beans and three olives each. Now, according to Trakas' revised calculations, it would take that "bridge" eleven years just to roll down to the sea. And the years on Dionysis' revised sign read: "1950–2061."

The following day was Navy-Beans-and-Olives Day. Early in the morning we saw Ensign Tsakalos start his motorboat, and we thought this meant he went to church on Sundays, but when he got back from Kalamos around noon he brought along five more prisoners—all transferred from the camp of Leros, all experts in quarrying and stonecutting. These were Kyrillos and Lambros, originally from Paros, and Dikaios, Paskalis and Sfekas, originally from Naxos. Minos, Avramakis and I, originally from nowhere, had to sit down when we recognized two of the three Naxians, feeling as though someone were playing a dirty joke on us. On their part, the Naxians were neither surprised nor glad to see us, and in any case they wouldn't talk about the past. Were the other four killed? How did the two of them survive? And Nike? What about Nike? Paskalis and Sfekas

192

wouldn't say. They wouldn't talk about the past, and as we were part of that past they'd rather not talk with us about anything.

But Monday was Hard-Labor Day, and after a few hours of going about the island the Naxians picked out a spot on the western shore for the quarry and began to prepare their equipment and to wipe their hands on their trousers.

"Solid as the devil," mumbled Paskalis, stroking the smooth surface of the rock.

"Can't do anything without furnello," said Sfekas. "Cakes or sticks—I don't care," he said. "We've got to blast our way in."

The Parians went farther down near the water, arranging and inspecting their tools, an assortment of straight and serrated chisels, small to medium mallets, steel rulers and triangles, plumb lines, levels, pencils and chalk. We followed them around, listening to their comments, and pretty soon we knew what exactly the finished product of labor was supposed to be: thousands of perfectly cut stones measuring twenty by twenty by forty centimeters, for the restoration of a church on Kalamos.

The division of labor wasn't easy to settle. Some had to be assigned to the Naxians and some to the Parians; most would be busy clearing the quarry after each blasting, by moving the best-looking rocks to the stonecutters and dumping the useless debris into the sea. For that we needed shovels and wheelbarrows that had been ordered from Kalamos but had not yet been delivered. Finally, several kids had to be assigned to the kitchen to prepare our meals. As for the little ones, they were to carry water and to do all sorts of errands.

Fotis didn't like the division of labor. "Not fair," he remarked.

"On the other hand, what is?" said Trakas.

"Not even the weather," agreed Polyvios.

"We've got to get organized," said Fotis.

"There he goes again."

"If we don't make decisions, others will be making them for us," said Fotis.

I was among the ten kids assigned to the stonecutters. We spent the first morning clearing and leveling the worksite and learning all about tools, their use and their maintenance. In the afternoon, the Parian stonecutters rolled two small boulders from the shore and began to trim them, while the ten of us stood around watching. In less than twenty minutes the two boulders had been turned into fifty-centimeter cubes. That more or less was the preliminary work that we would be doing in a few days. Satisfied with the results, the two masters went ahead with the fine work, using finer chisels with a serrated edge and smaller mallets. Mastro-Kyrillos, a graying fifteen-year-old, was more gifted or experienced than his colleague, and he always seemed a little bit ahead of the other. Mastro-Lambros was somewhat younger, but he was wise enough to go on learning from his senior rather than to compete with him. Still, he was catching up fast. Laughingly, Mastro-Kyrillos sat on top of his stone and ran his pencil all around his ass, drawing its outline on it, which looked like the letter omega, and then he started to chisel again. Mastro-Lambros did exactly the same, drawing a smaller omega. First things first: each of the Parians had to make a comfortable work seat for himself.

We were given special soap for seawater to wash ourselves and our clothes, but swimming was strictly forbidden. Half of the seamen recruits or apprentices would be patrolling the camp and the worksite, reporting any violations that came to their attention, apprehending transgressors or shooting to kill.

I wondered about that "kill" and looked around, but no one else seemed to be wondering about it, and Prassinos, one of the recruits, just stared at me, grinning. No doubt Prassinos would shoot to kill.

That day we saw Petty Officer Palioras on several occasions. Palioras was tall enough to be an officer, but not talkative enough to be a Greek, and we wondered: was he a European, a barbarian, or a mere fascist? Avramakis thought that the petty officer was not talkative enough simply because he did not know how to talk. But that would make him a barbarian.

"I guess so," admitted Avramakis.

Ke-kes thought that the petty officer didn't talk very much because he was too embarrassed to show his gold-capped teeth.

And Minos said, "We'd all be more pissed at him if he talked."

But I doubted it. Palioras was a type that I had seen before: pretentious because ignorant, vicious because pretentious, he trusted neither his words nor the sound of his own voice, and he ended up using silence to solicit respect, if not fear. I knew him; I'd seen him before. I feared him. Who was the greatest flatterer the world had ever known? He'd become the friend of Palioras.

Avramakis was to join the many who were assigned to move stones and debris from the quarry, and Minos was to be a water boy. After washing, we climbed up the hill together, straying briefly to explore a part of the island that we hadn't yet seen. There was little to be seen, and even less to be explored. Antikalamos was incredibly little. So little that from the circular yard where the flags were one could see the coastline around the island, except the northernmost tip, which was fenced and terraced downward. Here, then, was the only spot on Antikalamos worth exploring. But exploration wasn't everything, and by that time I knew that every little island wasn't meant to be an earthly paradise—not that I wasn't disappointed at the size, bareness and poverty of Antikalamos. Still, the word "island" meant a piece of land surrounded by the sea, so the sea here is as important as the land, if not more important. And the sea looked lovely and various, blue here, a different blue there, bluish and greenish and dark, foam-crested and wine-crazed, olive-calm, many-mirrored and withdrawn, expansive, many-storied and perilous, and, after the peril, quiet, hollow and content. And so the best and most interesting part of the island was the sea. The sea that was contained and boundless, easy to be with and inaccessible, much like our own bodies and the very body of Greece.

·10·

"All right, take this here stone; it's yours—it has your name written all over it. You know anything about stones? You know why this one has your name on it? No-o-o-o. But you better find out soon so you won't lose your tools and end up hauling rubble from the quarry. If you're born to be a stonecutter you'll live to see hundreds, thousands of stones with your name written on them—you'll live a long life. But you never hit a stone over the head with your mallet. If you hate the stone, the stone breaks up, because it can't take the hate. Understand? No-o-o-o, you don't understand. You are stupid, but that's all right with the stone. For the time being. But if you're a hater, the stone will never forgive you. It'll break up in the middle or it'll make you miss and break your own foot. All right, so you can read your name on it, and you know that if you hate the stone it's like you hate yourself. Wrong? So far so good. The next thing you do—No! not that! Wait! As I was saying, the next thing you do is listen to the stone. That's right, you put your ear on it and listen. If the stone trusts you it'll whisper something to you, but I can't tell you what because each stone speaks a different language. On second thought, I'll give you a hint, because I don't think you're a stone-hater, you're just stupid: some stones say, 'Here, put the edge of your chisel right here, and give it this angle, and strike gently.' If you listen and understand, and do what it tells you, the right piece will come off, no more, no less. Understand? I don't believe you, but go ahead, give it a try anyway."

Mastro-Kyrillos had guessed right; I wasn't a stone-hater. If I were one, I'd be in deep trouble, for the whole island was one big rock. And I was stupid enough not to understand everything that the stone whispered to me, and most of the times I ended up cutting the wrong part of the stone, or missing the stone altogether—the mallet having first missed the chisel. In a world where the stones whispered instructions, mallets and chisels seemed remarkably undisciplined.

The other nine apprentices in stonecutting were learning as slowly and painfully as I was, and after some more advice and supervision the Parians set out to do their part, which was cutting and finishing blocks to twenty by twenty by forty centimeters for a running wall, and to twenty by twenty by twenty for corners. Mastro-Kyrillos worked fast, as though trying to keep pace with a fast-speaking stone. He'd place his steel angle on top of the rough stone and draw a horizontal and a vertical line, marking forty and twenty centimeters respectively. He'd then turn the angle upside down and repeat the pencil lines and the measurements. Chisel in the left hand and mallet in the right, he'd listen for advice from the stone and cut clear of the pencil side after side, then shave off each surface with a broad comblike chisel that left white stripes behind it. Mastro-Kyrillos' first block looked perfect. It even had a smooth molding on either side of each corner which, besides making a striking contrast with the pockmarked surface of the sides, brought more attention to the symmetry of the block. A few minutes later Mastro-Lambros was finishing his first piece. But Kyrillos did not start on a second stone right away. He stood up and stretched, and walked around, supervising our work, giving advice on how to handle tools, how to secure the stone between one's feet, and how to look at it while you worked without getting any flying chips in your eyes. Still, many continued to be injured by the sharp fragments, and Leonis even managed to deliver a direct hit on his left ankle, which nearly crippled him. Mastro-Kyrillos examined it and shook his head.

"Helots of Beelzebub!" he said.

Leonis grinned. "Looks bad, eh?"

Mastro-Kyrillos grinned back. "Bad enough for you to come to work tomorrow. Only if you work every day will you learn how to handle the tools, and your muscles and bones will get used to the strain. Goofing off makes everything tougher," he said.

I couldn't tell whether or not Leonis would be able to walk to work the next day, but if I had a choice I'd rather take the day off and wander around the island looking at the stones and thinking, looking at the sun through the clouds and thinking, looking at the sea and thinking . . . until the sun went down and there was nothing to look at any longer, only to think, one or two things worth thinking about.

· 11 ·

Sometime during that night I awoke, wondering why the northern tip of the island was fenced and off limits, and why the sign warned, DANGER—DEATH. I was still lying down, slowly going back to sleep, and at the same time trying to find my way out of the tent. "The outhouse," I heard my voice saying, and I reeled, but then, acknowledging the soft wind and the solitary murmur of the sea, I thought I'd staggered out into the night. Then, just before getting to the outhouse, I changed direction and headed toward the forbidden area. When I got there I pulled the barbed-wire coils apart to protect my face and advanced a left foot and a right shoulder forward. But while I was dragging my right foot inside the coils as well, the upper arch of the wire came abruptly down and hooked onto the back of my shirt. I lowered myself, pulling sideways, tearing my shirt. Catching another wire that I felt scraping the nape of my neck, I pushed upward with my right hand and down with my left, to make an opening. There were coils within coils, and each time I pushed or pulled one section away from me another snapped back to take its place. Now there was one pressing down on my neck and another up against my crotch, and still another hooked to my stomach, the rusty spikes probing into my skin, cutting me. I stopped, took a breath, tried to move toward the far arch of the coil, but once again I ended up worsening my situation. I lifted up my right foot and stepped down, pushing

two or three wires to the ground, then carefully got hold of as
many other sections in my hands, pushing them as high above
my head as I could. I couldn't move forward. The wire across
my stomach blocked my way. I tried to go back, but then another section came snapping onto the back of my legs. Exhausted. I lowered my arms, leaving the upper sections to rest
on my shoulders. And it was then that the coils, having been
forced to wind and catch onto one another, suddenly un-
twisted, returning to their original places and trapping me
tightly, and at the same time lifting me up and flipping me over
in a half-circle. I was bound hand and foot in the air, facing up
and westward.

Each new effort to disentangle myself made the spikes press
deeper into my skin. I quit trying. I watched the stars. Many
years ago I'd seen a beetle caught in a web. A lizard came by
and thought him dead. An owl came along and thought him
stupid. He was neither; he watched the stars. When at dawn
the stars began to fade in the stronger light, the beetle tried to
click his wings and flip and land on his feet, but his wings were
stuck. He wondered about the spider. He lay on his back trying
all day, knowing it was a matter of time, and in the evening he
resigned himself to it and gazed again at the stars. I never found
out what happened to the beetle, whether or not the spider
climbed all the way down from the stars and delivered him.

And what would happen to me? What would a spider whose
web is made of barbed wire be like? I closed my eyes and let my
muscles relax, although that seemed to make the spikes pierce
deeper into my neck and stomach.

"Who's that over there?"

"I don't know."

The sunlight had crept softly over the rock, finding me. I
opened my eyes to the sky, and my muscles grew rigid. There
were more sounds, kids running toward me from the outhouse
and from the tents.

"There! There!"

Then a familiar voice: "What happened?" Avramakis'.

"I don't know."

"Don't try that with me, pal."

"You-ah. . ."

"You must've been sleepwalking again."

Again? I'd never sleepwalked in my life.

"That's it," said Avramakis. It was final.

More steps, more voices approaching, panting.

"I've seen him walk around in his sleep before," Avramakis was swearing to someone I could not see.

"Sure!" The voice of Petty Officer Palioras.

"Please, be careful, he hasn't snapped out of it yet."

"Sure, sure." Palioras ordered everybody to disperse and whispered his instructions to a seaman apprentice: "Psgldnatsir-chrfst."

Once his superior was gone, the seaman apprentice, who was no other than Prassinos, stretched out over the wire so he could see my face and said, "We're going to let you hang in there until you get to be as dry as codfish, and as smelly."

Prassinos was so young, I doubted that he ever had a chance to play hide-and-seek, kick-the-can, wood sticks or clay marbles. More likely his first toy was a real rifle.

"Unless you try to escape," he added.

I was too tired to follow him.

"Bam!" said Prassinos, imitating the sound of a gunshot. He then forced the barrel of his rifle under my right arm and pretended to fire again: "Bam!"

I glanced at his sweating face with the corner of my eye, trying to understand.

"Bam! Bam!" he said again, smiling, but he didn't fire.

·12·

For some time I'd been noticing something past the outer corner of my left eye. I couldn't turn my head or eye farther to the left, but I could tell that it was out of my eye, far away and above the sea: a white or light-gray spot that wasn't a seagull. I moved my head right and left, expecting the spot to vanish. It did not. I closed my eyes and opened them. It was there. Fixed in the lucent morning sky just above the sea. It could only be the town of Kalamos. Gray because it hadn't been whitewashed for years. The war. The earthquake. The rumor that Saint Thalassios, the martyr and protector of the island, no longer performed miracles. The formerly white town of Kalamos. The graying old parent of Antikalamos. It only takes the clearest atmosphere, and the sun falling on it from the right angle.

"I could blast your brains out, if I wanted to," threatened Prassinos.

He could, but he wouldn't. My body was numb and I wondered whether or not I could go to sleep for a while.

"My superior officer said I can blast your brains out anytime I want to."

" . . ."

"Well?"

" . . ."

It wasn't sleep that I'd gone to, and yet when I heard Prassinos cutting the wires with a pair of pliers, and I opened my eyes, I felt as if I were waking up from a deep midday slumber. Two other seamen apprentices were helping untangle me, and two more boys stood by silently at some distance. When I was cut loose I recognized Tsakalos and Palioras. Kalamos had vanished from the horizon, but then the sun had moved to the other side of the sky and was about to set. I had managed to take the whole day off from work and waste it.

"Shame on you," I said without opening my mouth.

The two seamen carried me all the way to the barracks, where the kids, having finished another day's work, waited in line for their dinner. They left me lying on my back on a table. I was sore, stiff, unable to walk or even stand on my feet.

"Look at him!" shouted Tsakalos. "I want all of you to have a good look at him. The next time one of you tries to get through the wire to the restricted area, he will not be brought back alive. What lies past the wire is a military secret, but if somehow you found out what it was, you'd be grateful for that barrier and warning. As for him, there seems to be evidence that he only dreamed about going through the barrier, that in fact he was caught in it during his sleep. Therefore, I have ordered no further disciplinary action. You may proceed with your meal."

Minos and Avramakis helped me sit up and have some bean soup. I could tell they admired me for what I'd attempted, and that made me feel embarrassed. Then Avramakis wanted to know the truth.

"You are not really a sleepwalker, are you?"

"I don't think so."

"Then why did you do it?"

"I really don't know."

Trakas' admiration was even greater. "When are you going to try again?" he whispered.

"I really don't know."

"But you are going to try again, aren't you?"

". . ."

While we ate, a rumor went around that the restricted area past the fence was actually a German minefield that hadn't been cleared after the war by the Allies or the Coast Guard or the Navy. Now, who could start a rumor like that? I wondered if Tsakalos and Palioras weren't passing state secrets to us, after all. And I wondered if Tsakalos and Palioras shouldn't be court-martialled, if as a result of it none of us was blown to pieces.

Afterward, as I lay on my straw mattress in the tent, slowly falling asleep, I heard that several more kids had seen the town of Kalamos that morning, and Varant insisted that he even got all kinds of whiffs in the wind that blew from the same direction: smells of winter flowers, home-cooked meals, real bread and sweets. I took a deep breath, but I found nothing unusual in it. Neither chrysanthemums nor cabbage-and-rice, nor black bread and corn cake, nor even black-eyed-bean soup, of which I could easily have gulped another small bowl.

· 13 ·

The Naxians had been allowed to use a small number of dynamite sticks under supervision, and they produced enough red stone to keep the two master stonecutters and their ten apprentices busy for a while. Once the rhythm of work had set in, the Parians ordered more tools and picked another ten kids to be trained in stonecutting. Trakas and Pavlos were among them.

On the fourth Sunday after we arrived on Antikalamos, a small navy ship, the *Nikaia*, anchored near the stacks of stones that we had finished, bringing, as Ensign Tsakalos promised, our monthly supplies of fresh water, beans and galleta, as well as religious and medical services. Paparigas and Dr. Delaportas had been assigned by the Greek government to provide these services to every prison and detention camp in the Aegean, so the two of them went around from island to island, seeing to it that the rehabilitation of political prisoners and detainees was replete with medical supervision and spiritual guidance. That year, the detention-camp population in the Aegean was estimated between 23,000 and 223,000. We unloaded the supplies and attended church service in the assembly room of the main barracks, then lined up to be examined by the doctor.

"You are fine," he said. "You're just fine. No problem here. Hm . . . hm," he said. And "Nothing wrong with your chest. Breathe in and hold your breath. What are you brushing your teeth with?"

206

". . ."

"Never mind, you can exhale now. You're just fine."

Some complained about their old frostbites, others about coughing, sore throats, headaches.

"Take aspirin. And don't stare at me; I don't have any with me."

Still others complained about upset stomachs, dizzy spells, weakness.

"This is from hunger, and hunger is not a disease. There is nothing I can do about it."

In the afternoon, while loading the Nikaia with stones, we learned from a sailor that the restoration of the Church of St. Thalassios, the patron of Kalamos, had already begun, and that the islanders hoped to complete the project by the end of the summer, in time for the saint's festival. The sailor said that Saint Thalassios was a renowned healer of demonics and all sorts of lunatics. Which Polyvios was eager to confirm. He'd heard about it from the barber of his village, who used to take his retarded son to that festival every year, but he'd never made the connection, he'd no idea that the island of the festival was Kalamos.

Minos, Avramakis and I slipped out of the gathering, and when the last stone had been transferred into the ship we decided to take a walk along the shore.

We had come to a place on the shore where the rock and several algae-dressed boulders formed a small, shallow pool. The seawater was constantly sneaking in and out of it among the stones, but it was protected enough from the waves to have attracted a good number of sea creatures such as little crabs, hermit crabs, shrimp, a school of minnows and a couple of long orange-colored worms that crawled on the bottom with hundreds of tiny white legs. Near the worms, partly buried in the sand, was a strange-looking scavenger fish with tentacles hanging down on either side of its mouth like a mustache, waiting in ambush. The shrimp too were hard to keep track of, for they were very small and transparent and swam erect and with amazing speed when in danger, flinging themselves from one end of the pool to the other. Under the stones, between the stones, lurked the little crabs; their round, stony eyes gleaming in the dark water, their flat bodies moving rapidly sideways, the largest claw extended in the front, always ready. Higher up, stuck on the exposed top of a stone, were sea snails and limpets. We spent a little time observing the creatures and their habits, their way of going about the business of getting their food and protecting themselves, and how they all seemed to fit nicely into their tiny community.

But this is not how Avramakis saw it. "What do you know?" he said, scratching his head. "They even have little concentration camps for marine life!"

· 14 ·

Those of us who had been assigned to the stonecutters were learning to handle our tools so well that we hardly injured ourselves anymore, and the number of blocks we trimmed for the Parians kept increasing each week. One day I felt so confident about my new skills that I asked Mastro-Kyrillos' permission to go on and finish each stone I started, rather than do only the preliminary work.

"So you think you can become a master stonecutter?" he said.

"I'm pretty sure I can."

"You've been watching me work, but that's not enough. No one can learn much without asking questions, and you are not a question-asker. If you are too proud to ask questions you'll never become a master stonecutter."

"I didn't want to take your time."

"The time belongs to those who take it. You are not too proud to ask questions and listen to advice?"

"I swear."

"Have you been listening to the stone?"

"It was the stone that told me I ought to try."

Mastro-Kyrillos stood up, dusted off his pants, took two brand-new chisels out of his canvas bag and handed them to me. "Try," he said. "If you break the stone I'll take the tools back. If you break the tools, I'll break your neck."

I tried, asked questions, and listened to the stone, and asked and tried again, and I didn't break the stone, but I didn't get its corners and sides straight either. And Mastro-Kyrillos didn't take my tools away, and since I hadn't broken the tools he didn't break my neck either, but he thought that my stone looked like a piece of Turkish delight after someone had squeezed it.

And he said, "I'll tell you what."

"What?" I could hardly hear my own voice.

"You'll sit on that stone while you cut the next one. That's how I learned."

It worked like a horsewhip. It made my back and my ass hurt, but my next stone was better and, as I guessed he'd do, Mastro-Kyrillos told me to use that one as a seat while I struggled with the third one. It took me many more stones and days to get rid of that backache while improving my skills, and to present my first perfect stone to the masters.

"It's pretty good," conceded Mastro-Kyrillos. "But."

I stopped breathing.

"Now you'll have to destroy it," he said.

"Not I."

"If you don't break that stone to pieces your next one won't be as good."

I thought I was being tested, so I said, "It will be even better."

"Mastro-Kyrillos is right, you know," said Mastro-Lambros.

"But what will the stone say?"

"Do as he tells you."

"But I am not a stone-hater."

"The stone already knows that," said Mastro-Kyrillos. "But there's more for the stone to learn."

Now it was the stone's turn to sit in a lumpy seat. "Learn what?"

"That from now on you won't destroy a stone by accident, by mistake."

"I won't destroy one for the fun of it either."

"Ah, he's not to be a real stonecutter," said Mastro-Kyrillos, throwing up his arms.

"I know what you mean," said Mastro-Lambros.

"Well, you can keep that stone and give up your tools, or give up the stone and earn the right to cut a few more," offered Mastro-Kyrillos.

It had to come to that. Either/or. "What if I threw it into the sea instead of breaking it?"

"Noooo."

It was a lost cause: "Would you at least destroy it yourself?"

"Noooo!"

"On my behalf."

"Noooo!"

I raised the mallet up high, but Mastro-Kyrillos stopped me. "Aren't you going to listen to the stone first?"

Was I supposed to help the stone commit suicide? I put my ear on it, thinking, This is going too far; but at the same moment the stone spoke to me. A whisper that sounded like *Sfffft*, and I could tell right away that it meant "Soft" or "Softly." I looked at my stone again, and for the first time I saw a fine crack running diagonally along one of its sides. Amazed, I turned to Mastro-Kyrillos.

"Do what the stone tells you," he said.

And I raised the mallet again and touched the stone softly at the center, and the stone coughed and broke in two. I stared at the pieces, wondering if I didn't deserve to sit on them while struggling to finish my first truly perfect stone; but Mastro-Kyrillos and Mastro-Lambros had already gone back to work, content that my stone had gotten what would have been coming to it sooner or later.

And Ke-Ees, who until that moment had witnessed the entire drama without saying a word, exclaimed, "C-c-c-crack! A perfect stroke, Mastro-What's-Your-Name."

· 15 ·

The production of stones continued to increase, but the rations of black-eyed-bean soup and galleta remained the same, and most of us began to lose weight again. Hunger, like an invisible stonecutter, kept chipping away at us. Then by the middle of March production started to go down.

It was around the middle of March, on a mild spring morning, when instead of going to work we were herded into the assembly room of the main barracks and ordered to keep quiet until further notice. The assembly room had no windows and Palioras put the padlock on the door, so we couldn't see what went on outside. It must have been sometime between nine and ten when suddenly we heard children marching in the direction of the square. At first we thought they might be a new batch of detainees, but their marching and the song they marched to didn't make sense.

"Maybe they're already reeducated," said Leonis.

"Boy Scouts!" shouted Ke-kes from the front end of the assembly room.

"What?"

"I'll c-c-c-cut my throat if this isn't a Boy Scout song!"

Boy Scouts? Here? Where from? Whatever for?

"Beats me. They must've c-c-c-come on an excursion or something."

"Excursion? Here?"

There were more sounds: steps; laughter; voices, some speaking Greek and some foreign. We picked out words such as "phoenix . . . ashes . . . exemplary . . . Madam . . . a multipurpose building . . . progress . . . side by side . . ." and then something that we couldn't be more unprepared for: "Your Majesty . . ."

"Your what?"

"*Her* what!"

"Majesty?"

"Is that what they call it now?"

"It?"

"Her what."

"Shut up!"

Ke-kes and I moved to the far end of the room, joining Minos and Avramakis, who were chatting with the Parians. Mastro-Lambros had been peeking through a nail hole in the tin and kept rubbing his eye.

"He says he saw the Queen and an American general go by, and some of those silly old bags who wear green sunglasses and collect for the Queen's Fund, but he won't let anybody else have a peek," said Avramakis.

"It's the Q-q-q-queen, all right," said Ke-kes. "What about the k-k-k-kids?"

"Well-fed, well-dressed, well-behaved—like rich kids going on an excursion," said Mastro-Lambros.

"Boy Scouts!" said Ke-kes, slapping his knee.

"What I want to know is what're the Queen and the American general up to, showing their faces in this godforsaken place?" said Mastro-Kyrillos.

"They're just visiting to inspect the camp and the quarry," said Avramakis. "They have reporters with them, photographers. . . . Tomorrow we'll all be in the papers."

"Oh, sure. What I can't figure out is those Boy Scouts."

"We're locked up in here, and who's out there greeting our eminent guests? A bunch of Boy Scouts from K-k-k-kalamos. Beats me too," confessed Ke-kes.

"And I thought you knew everything," said Mastro-Kyrillos.

"Nobody knows everything. Not even Fotis," said Minos.

"C-c-c-come here, you, where did you learn to talk like that?"

"Fotis taught him," said Leonis.

Avramakis was thinking. "The Boy Scouts instead of us. . . . Are the Boy Scouts supposed to be us? I'd say yes, they're supposed to be us. But the Boy Scouts don't know they're supposed to be us, and the Queen and the general don't know that the Boy Scouts aren't us. Only Tsakalos and Palioras know that the Boy Scouts don't know they're us—"

"Wait, you've got me confused," protested Mastro-Kyrillos. "Why the Boy Scouts instead of us?"

"Because we look too awful for the Queen," said Avramakis.

"That's it!" agreed Ke-kes.

"I don't get it," said Mastro-Kyrillos.

"Have you seen your face in the sea lately?" said Ke-kes.

"I tried to, but the sea was choppy," laughed Mastro-Kyrillos.

"That was your face," said Ke-kes.

"You are a comedian, aren't you?" laughed Mastro-Kyrillos.

"Me? Only half of the time."

"And the other half? What do you do the other half, you're serious?"

"No. The other half I'm busy trying to avoid words that start with k-k-k-kappa."

άπελευθέρωση. Εἶναι ὅμως καὶ ρεαλιστική;
Ὁ Πέτρος Ρούσος, στὸ βιβλίο του «Ἡ
Μεγάλη Πενταετία», ἐπευθυνόμενος πρὸς
ἀριστερούς ἀνενόστες καὶ προσπαθῶντας νὰ δικαιολογήσει τὸ «ὄχι» τοῦ ΚΚΕ,
ἰσχυρίζεται πὼς ἡ ἡγεσία του δὲν ἀρνήθηκε τή συγκρότηση τοῦ Βαλκανικοῦ
Στρατηγείου οὔτε τὸ τορπίλλισε. «Ζήτησε
ἁπλῶς – γράφει – ἀναβολή τοῦ ζητήματος
μέχρι νὰ δημιουργηθοῦν οἱ ὅροι». Γιατί αὐτὲς οἱ μασημένες δικαιολογίες; Ὁ ἴδιος
ἀναφέρει ὡς ἑξῆς τοὺς λόγους ποὺ ὤθησαν τὸ πολιτικὸ γραφεῖο τοῦ ΚΚΕ στὴν
ἀπόφασή του:

«Πρῶτο, νὰ στερεώσουμε τὴν ἐθνικοαπελευθερωτική συμμαχία, νὰ μὴν προκαλέσουμε δυσαρεσκήτηση τῶν συμμάχων
μας στὸ ΕΑΜ καὶ σὲ ἄλλους ἐνδεχόμενους
συμμάχους μας. Δεύτερο, νὰ μὴν ἐπισπεύσουμε ἔνταση τῶν ἐντ δράσεων καὶ ἐπεμβάσεων τῶν Ἄγγλων στὴν Ἑλλάδα προτοῦ
προλάβει νὰ στερεωθεῖ τὸ ἐπαναστατικὸ
κίνημα στὴν Ἑλλάδα ἤ τουλάχιστον στὴ
Γιουγκοσλαβία. Τρίτο, νὰ μὴ δημιουργήσουμε πρόωρα πρόβλημα στὴν τεραστία
ἀντιχιτλερική συμμαχία τὰ ὁποία ἄγνωστο
ἂν θὰ μπορέσουμε τελικὰ νὰ ὑπερπηδήσουμε ὅσο βαστᾶ ὁ πόλεμος κατὰ τῶν
καταχτητῶν».

Μακεδόνες καὶ Μεγαλόσερβοι

Ὁ Κώστας Καραγιώργης ὅμως, ποὺ ἀναμείχθηκε ἄμεσα καὶ θέλα ὅπως εἴδαμε, σὲ
ἰδιαίτερη συνομιλία ποὺ εἶχε μὲ τὸν γράφοντα τὸ 1946, καθαρὰ καὶ σταράτα ἔδωσε
τὴν ἐξήγηση.

–Ἄκου
γοι ποὺ μ...
λιτικὸ μα...
ὅτι τὸ ΕΑ...
λουθοῦσα...
ματα. Δε...
λίγο πρὶν...
Διεθνής ...
τῆς δὲν θ...
ὅπως καὶ ἀποδείχτηκε. Αὐτὸ τὸ γεγονὸς
ἔδειχνε πὼς ὁ Στάλιν ἀντιμετώπιζε ἀκόμη
πολὺ μεγάλες δυσκολίες. Πὼς ἦταν ὑποχρεωμένος νὰ κάνει κι' ἄλλες βαριὲς θυσίες γιὰ νὰ διατηρήσει τῆ συμμαχικῆ
ἑνότητα χωρὶς τὴν ὁποία μπορούσε νὰ χαθεῖ τὸ πᾶν. Καὶ δὲν ξέρω πὼς ὁ Τίτο καὶ ὁ
Τέμπο κάναν τοῦ κεφαλιοῦ τους, ἐμεῖς
ὅμως διστάζαμε νὰ καταφέρουμε μιά μαχαιριά στὰ νεφρὰ τῆς μεγάλης συμμαχίας.
Γιατί κάτι τέτοιο θὲ ἦταν ἂν ἀποκαλύπτα
ὀρθωνόμαστε μαζὶ μὲ τοὺς Ἀλβανούς καὶ
Γιουγκοσλάβους κατὰ τῶν Ἄγγλων. Ὅλα
αὐτὰ ὅμως ἦσαν δευτερεύοντα μπροστὰ σὲ
ἕναν ὀγκόλιθο ποὺ θὰ σοῦ ἀποκαλύψω».

Καὶ καθὼς ὁ γράφων τέντωσε τὸν λαιμό
του καὶ τὰ αὐτιά το για νὰ ἀκούσει, ὁ Κώστας Καραγιώργης εἶπε:

– Ἐκεῖνο ποὺ μᾶς τρόμαξε εἶναι ἄλλο·
Εἴχαμε πληροφορίες ἀλλὰ καὶ ἀντιληφθή-

θανε τὴν ἑλληνική, γιουγκοσλαβική καὶ

... Ἡ σκέψη τῶν Γιουγκοσλάβων καὶ τῶν
Ἀλβανῶν συντρόφων νὰ ἐπηρεάζουν πρὸς
ὁρισμένη πολιτική τὶς ἀντίστοιχες ἔνοπλες
δυνάμεις τῶν ἐθνικῶν μειονοτήτων στὴν
Ἑλλάδα (Σλαβομακεδόνων καὶ τσάμηδων

ATHENS—Martial law in Greece, imposed during the civil
war with Communist guerrillas, has been completely lifted,
Premier John Theotokis announced. He declared the country
"100 percent ready" for the coming elections. . . .

—Reuters dispatch, February 1950

Κοινὸ Βαλκανικὸ Στρατηγεῖο καὶ νὰ κατα-
λάβει τὴν ἐξουσία, ἀ λὰ Γιουγκοσλαβία;
Ὅσοι τρέφουν αὐτὴ τὴν ἰδέα ξεχνοῦν ὅτι:
Στῆ Γιουγκοσλαβία μὲ τὴν ἀπελευθέρωση
ὑπῆρχαν 30 μεραρχίες σοβιετικοῦ στρατοῦ. Στὴν Ἑλλάδα μετὰ τὴν ἀπελευθέρωση
ἦρθαν 3 μεραρχίες ἀγγλικοῦ στρατοῦ.

Ἀλλὰ πολὺ χαρακτηριστικὰ ὁ Πέτρος
Ροῦσος παρατηρεῖ:

«Γιουγκοσλάβικα καὶ ἰδίως ὁρισμένα
σλαβομακεδονικὰ στελέχη τῆς γειτονικῆς
χώρας ἀψηφοῦσαν τὶς συνέπειες ποὺ θὰ
ἔχει σ' ὅλον τὸν ἑλληνικὸ ἀγῶνα καὶ στὸν
ἀγῶνα τῶν βαλκανικῶν λαῶν ἡ ἄμεση υἱοθέτηση ἀπὸ μᾶς τοῦ συνθήματος "ἑνιαία
Μακεδονία στὰ πλαίσια τῆς νέας Γιουγκοσλαβίας". Ὑπάρχουν καὶ σήμερα ἀκόμη
ὁρισμένοι τους ποὺ λένε πὼς καὶ ἂν ἀκόμα
δὲν ἐλευθερωνόταν ἡ Ἑλλάδα ἀπὸ τὸν ἰμπεριαλισμό, θὰ εἶνε ἐλευθερωθεῖ τουλάχι-

---

Ὁ Τίτο κατά

Καὶ τώρα ἔνα
γνώση τοῦ Τίτο
Τέμπο; Ἀσφαλ...
ὅσο τελικά ὁρίσ...
πρόσωπος τῆς
σχεδιασμὸ στρα...
Ὥστε ὁ Τίτο υ
Μεγαλοσέρβων
γκοσλαβίας;
Ἡ ἀπάντηση,
δοξο, εἶναι κα...
στοὺς πολλοὺς
μὲ ἐντολή του ·
τερα τα γιουγκ...
ψαν τὸ ἀντίθετο
καὶ ἀδιάψευστα
Ὁ Τίτο πράγμ...
σύσταση Βαλκ. ...
κοὺς λόγους. Κ...
ταν στὸν στρατι...
ἦταν κακή. Ἀλλ...
μεγαλοσέρβικοι
κοὶ κύκλοι – ὑπο...
νιστικοῦ βρασμ...
νήσου – γιὰ νὰ ...
τὸν τὸν μηχανισ...
Ἄργησε νὰ τ...
τῆς ἀραιῆς ἐπικ...
τὸ καλοκαίρι το...
μάχη ζωῆς ἡ θα...
τῶν. Ὅταν πλη...
γίνει, ἡ ἀντίδρ...
Ἔσπευσε νὰ δια...
...αγγείλατ...
...εμπο νὰ
...ειο γιατ...
...οτό».
...άμμα το
...μίζει:
...σημερin...
...ὁποιουδ...
...λάθος,
...χαριστικ...
ἐπιστολή του π...
«Ἡ δημιουργί...
λεῖ ἀνοησία.
Τὰ μηνύματα ...
στρατηγό του δ...
νος τὰ εἶχε λάβ...
«ὄχι» τοῦ Σιάντ...
πυρώσει τὸ θέμ...
τήσει ὁριστικά.
Ἀλλωστε, τώρ...
παρτιζάνοι ὅπως
βρίσκονταν μπρ...
ἀνατροπή; Ἡ Ἰτ...
Καὶ στὸν βαλκαν...
σποτος ἕνας ὁλ...
γέρας τῶν δυνα...
χώματα τῆς Γιου...
...των 'Ελλάδ...

Τὸ ΚΚΕ λέει:

· 16 ·

We didn't fit anywhere, not even on Antikalamos. What was to become of us? We now expended more energy than we took in from our meals, and if things went on like this much longer our existence would sink so low that dreaming would again become the only evidence of life.

During their visit the Queen and the general had praised Tsakalos and Palioras for the great work they'd done in a short two and a half months, and the kids who were supposed to be us and did not know it looked in top shape as they stood at attention, saluting the dignitaries and cheering:

"Long live the Queen!"

"Long live General Van Fleet!"

"Long live the Royal Navy!"

"Long live the American Mission!"

After the speeches, the kids offered the Queen a lovely bouquet of wild anemones. Where did they find them? In two and a half months we hadn't seen even a blade of grass on the island. Anyway, the official photographer took a good shot for the papers: the wild anemones and the happily tame children, completely rehabilitated and restored to health. The children, the future of Greece. Unbeknownst to Greece, we were crowded into that so-called "multipurpose building," telling jokes. Soon, though, the distinguished visitors were off to the royal speedboat *Arrow*, and the Boy Scouts to the *Nikaia*, and

we were released to go to work. But before that, just before
Paliora: unlocked the gate and let us out, Minos wanted to
know what exactly that American Mission was, and Şükrü the
Turk offered to tell him, on condition we wouldn't give him a
hard time—whatever he meant by that.

We promised not to hit him, but Trakas warned him to watch
his language.

"*Yavas-yavas*," said Şükrü in Turkish. "I always take my time
when I speak foreign languages."

"*Yavas-yavas*," said Trakas.

"Whole thing started with this Gheneral Van Flit, when Truman Pasha dispatched him here to save Yunania—"

"The name is *Hellas—Grecia*," interrupted Pavlos.

"*Merc*," said Şükrü. "To save Hellas not from the Turks but
from the Helenes themselves."

"Well said, Şükrü!" Fotis approved.

"*Merci*. But, you know, first thing this gheneral found was
the Greeks didn't have civilized shithouses. In America they
have little white thrones that you sit on so your legs don't get
tired, and when you've finished you pull on a little chain, and
everything goes down the pipe and disappears, and you never
see it again."

"That's true," said Fotis.

"Thanks. But here, like in Turkey, you have to go behind a
bush or behind a rock to empty yourself, and there's no way to
make your hot-cross bun disappear."

"Eh, Mehmed!" shouted Ke-kes.

"My name is Şükrü."

"I know but you're also supposed to tell us about the American Mission, not about shit."

"Same thing," said Şükrü.

There were laughs here, and the gathering of listeners doubled in no time.

"So what happened?"

"The gheneral had to go behind a rock. He was supervising

the troops outside Konitsa, and the bushes were all burned down from the bombs, so he had to go behind a rock—are you following me?"

"We're trying, we're trying," said Trakas.

"There he emptied himself, but when he pulled up his pants and buckled his belt, and he started to go, he heard a little thin voice calling him from behind: 'Psssst, pssst, Gheneraaaal . . .' The gheneral turns around, and what he sees?"

"A boa constrictor," said Trakas.

"That's close."

"A hot-cross bun," said Minos.

"*Aferin!*" exclaimed Şükrü. "He saw his own hot-cross bun, rearing its head and talking to him: 'Gheeeneraaaal . . . where do you think you are goooiiing?' Gheneral Van Flit couldn't believe his eyes and his ears, so he stood there stone-faced, just staring at the thing. 'Gheneral, ah, my Gheneral, please, don't leave me here in the wilderness,' it said again."

"What did the general say?" asked Minos.

" 'My, my, I think I forgot to wipe myself,' " said Trakas.

"*Yavas-yavas.* The gheneral said, 'Shhh . . . be quiet . . . what do you want from me?' 'Take me along. It's so cold out here and there's a war going on.' 'But I can't.' 'Of course you can. You made me. You can't just walk out on me like that.' 'What do you want me to do?' 'I know plenty about military matters, and, besides, I am American. I even know English.' 'No denying that.' The gheneral went back and forth, shaking his head: 'Whoever heard . . .' and so on. 'Take me along, I tell you, or I'll talk. I'll scream!' 'No screaming, please,' said the gheneral. 'Give me a minute to think.' 'I can fight Commoonism, too,' said the thing. 'All I want is to serve a cause, have a mission in life—any mission.' "

"Aha!" shouted Trakas.

" 'A mission, a mission . . . How about the *American* Mission?' said the gheneral. '*Tamam!* But what do I have to do?' 'Just be yourself. We'll get you an office in the palace, or in the

Parliament, or in our own embassy. You'll do absolutely nothing. But nothing would be done without your seal and signature either. What do you think? You like it?' 'Sounds exciting. When do I start?' said the thing. And the gheneral said, 'When you're ready.' And that's how the American Mission in Athens came to be," said Şükrü. And he said, "*Tamam!* That's the end of it."

In a couple of weeks' time, when the *Nikaia* arrived again with our monthly supplies, we had a chance to learn how close to truth Şükrü's words had been. Because of the strong winds, the *Nikaia* was unable to anchor near the quarry and instead had to wait on the northeastern shore of Antikalamos until the weather improved. On the second day the sailors were allowed to come ashore, and one of them told us that there had been new elections in the country, and a change in government. Plastiras, the new Prime Minister, had promised general amnesty, but he'd already run into opposition from the palace and the American Mission.

"*Skata!*" said Varant, Pavlos, Leonis and Trakas, as in a chorus.

"*Skata,*" echoed Avramakis.

"I told you, didn't I?" said Şükrü.

"What else can you tell us? What's going to happen now, Mehmed?" said Trakas.

"The name is Şükrü," said the Turk. "Bring me a little spring goat. Light a fire and put the goat on the spit. Then bring me a flask of Samos wine, the red kind, and when we're through eating and drinking I'll read the signs on the goat's shoulder blade, and I'll tell you what's going to happen."

"But, Şükrü, we don't have any kindling for the fire, and, besides, the wind's too strong to light a fire," said Minos.

"Heh!" said Şükrü. "Where did you learn to talk like that? You're only a little kid. Anyway, I guess we must wait until the weather gets better."

But the weather didn't get better, and the *Nikaia* returned to

Kalamos the next morning when the Coast Guard radioed that
a major storm was building up in the area. Hour after hour the
wind gathered force and blew over the open sea, stirring and
swelling the body of the water into high waves as if it had found
a way to enter the water itself, while masses of black cloud
swept low over the island. The wind hissed and whistled relent-
lessly. We listened to it, shuddering, wishing we were on the
mainland.

That night the sides of our tent flapped in and out, pulling
furiously at the metal stakes that were wedged in the bedrock,
and as the wind rushed inside the tent itself, blowing and
stretching the sailcloth like a parachute, we heard the driving
rain, or was it the seawater that the wind had lifted off the high
waves, and we huddled in the dark, waiting for the storm to
pass, worrying that the worst was not yet over.

·17·

The answer came later that night when a great sound rose from the sea, and the rock of Antikalamos began to shift and rearrange itself in the water. Then the sea gulls came inland, thousands of birds roaming the dark air, now screeching, now clawing and pecking at our tent, and we let go of one another's hands and clutched the central pole, the ropes and the hem of the canvas, struggling to keep our tent down. Our weight and strength couldn't match the ferocious wind. Suddenly there was a lull as though a bubble of calm weather or a vacuum hovered above the rock, but we didn't relax our grip, and a moment later the twisting wind came down, pulling everything up, the pegs having first come out of the ground and the entire tent blown way up in the air with most of us dangling from the roped hem of the canvas. I always wanted to fly, but this wasn't exactly flying. The tent was like a parachute, falling upward or zigzagging down. At any moment we could be dashed against the rock or could take the plunge into the stormy sea. Then, as I considered the advantages of the sea over the rock, I felt the ground scraping the soles of my feet and I took that opportunity to let go of the rope. I rolled, counting the stones on the ground with arms and legs, four-five-six and one that slapped my face, and another that grated my chest, until I ran into one kid who had been stopped by another. The wind and the rain went on. And the rain, the stones and the birds fell on us, beating us with their wings, scratching us with their talons, pecking at us with their beaks, and it was hard to tell which hurt the most, the birds or the stones, the birds being more frightening to us because they themselves were more frightened than the stones. The wind could tear us away from the stones, but it couldn't tear the birds away from us. And the hail came down on us like gravel, and the cries of the birds drowned our cries. At one point six or seven of us got onto our feet, stepping lightly on the stones, and as streams of air and spiny tips of wings brushed against us we moved fast, now in this direction and now in that, one moment ducking our heads and the other leaping, now seeking any kind of contact, and now avoiding contact with anything that we couldn't see. It was like dancing. And since we were determined not to let go of one another, we let ourselves dance. We danced, now following the leader, the wind, now turning around, and I felt a surge of laughter in my chest as though we'd left fear behind and the pain was already gone. It was joy. We had overcome the danger, had learned to dance, to fly and to swim all at once, and the birds were ahead of us and behind (we could feel the tips of their wings but no longer their talons), and I thought there was no end to that devilish energy, so we might as well dance, fly and swim until morning. But then the island was too small for something like that to go on. This thought occurred to me as I stepped on a stone, and a moment later I heard the stone tumble down the cliff. "Back," I shouted, fighting the push of the wind and the pull of the stone. And the kids on my right turned left, and the kids on my left turned left also, and even the wind turned around as if to change direction. Terrified anew, the birds stood in our way, opposing us, their wings a wall, and their beaks battlements. We attacked, fighting with fists and feet to break through their ranks, and before we knew it they'd broken through ours. Separated from the others, I pressed away from the cliff as I heard the sea gulls fly off the sharp edge and over the sea. I fought alone until I no longer remembered the purpose of fighting. I kicked and clawed and punched each stone, each gust of wind, while the rain left tiny pockmarks on my face and chest. The wind gnawed my forehead with teeth of salt, and the seawater streamed off the corners of my mouth and eyes. And I fought the wind and every element and creature of the storm with equal abandon, because when I measured myself against the wind I was wind and I was I, and when I fought the rain I was rain and I was I, and when the birds went through me I was a bird myself—as I was a stone and a grain of salt.

And when in the dawn of next day the quiet of the sea and the sky awoke me, my first thought was, how could there still be a sea and a sky.

·18·

Way up in the eastern sky, a sea gull. Up as high as that so he can be the first to see the sun rising. The sea below was so calm it made me remember the closed sea of Nafpaktos. Saturday morning. Up as early as that because of the haymarket and the bazaar. The rest of the week only the fishermen caught the sea asleep. At the town square, farmers and merchants, horse traders and shepherds, tanners and carpenters, Gypsies and Gypsies: they'd sell you a Persian rug made in Italy; they'd fix your rush-seated chairs; change the cotton batting of your mattress; tell your fortune: all important events in your life to come about in three terms of time. Always. In three days, three months or three years. Don't forget the weeks: better in three weeks than in thirty years. If you can't wait, put silver in the hand, and it'll come faster. Three drachmas. You're a lucky one. Born to get rich and happy. Good luck to you. I mean it. Craftsmen snored in the sun, leaving the peddling of the craft to their wives. Here were clay pitchers, fine tin cups, bread stamps carved patiently in hardwood, distaffs for spinning wool . . . There were shoemakers, blacksmiths, tailors, a monk who fixed dislocated bones, a nun who sold amulets, a magician who pretended to be a tailor (measuring and marking with a stick of chalk fantastic figures in the air, then pinning pockets, collars and sleeves onto them, contouring the sides, stitching the flaps, cutting the buttonholes against the sky), and a real

224

tailor who couldn't talk because his mouth was full of pins just smiled, wondering. What happened then? Did the magician cut a real jacket from the sky, or did the real tailor expose him to the public? More likely that the magician produced the jacket that the real tailor had just finished. But I couldn't remember for sure. What I did remember were the Gypsies, the sun and the calm sea at dawn—a sea that was as calm as the sea I saw after the sea gull let me have a glimpse of the sun long before the sunrise.

The whole island was littered with bodies: bodies sleeping, twitching or crawling about on all fours. A few stood on their feet, wandering in a daze as though they were trying to remember who they were and what they were supposed to be doing. The landscape was not familiar. I myself crawled about, joining other crawlers, who were trying to wake up those who were still asleep.

My injuries were not bad: a twisted ankle, scraped knees and elbows, a big scratch and bruise across my chest. Others were hurt so much they had to be carried to the main barracks. There I saw Minos, Avramakis, Fotis, Polyvios and the Naxians, who were in good shape, helping others and counting heads. According to Prassinos' tally eight kids were missing. According to Polyvios' count the missing were not eight but nine. Petty Officer Palioras' own tally was the same as Prassinos'. The missing kids were eight, but we knew only two of them: Pavlos and Alekos. A search party had already gone out, combing Antikalamos, and Ensign Tsakalos started his motorboat and made circles around the island, looking for the missing in the water. Once again Palioras put the padlock on the gate of the main barracks, making sure he wouldn't have to count heads again, and went to write his report.

By noon two bodies had been found: one down the quarry, showing head and chest injuries, and another in the water. Their names were not announced. For a few moments all crying and moaning stopped inside the main barracks, then it

began again even more loudly. Overhead, the corrugated tin
creaked and crackled as the sun grew warmer. The assembly
room had no windows.

Minos now wondered aloud if Pavlos hadn't actually been
taken away by the wind and dropped off in Italy, or near
enough for him to reach the coast by swimming.

"More likely he's still flying," said Avramakis.

I tried to imagine Pavlos dead from head injuries or drowning. I couldn't. I could imagine him flying, swimming, convers-
ing in the streets of Naples or Messina like a native, eating
spaghetti and eggplant with melted cheese, but I couldn't imagine him dead, so when Minos asked me next if I thought Pavlos
might still be flying, I said, "Why not?"

"Because there isn't any wind," said Minos.

"Aren't you getting a little too technical?" said Avramakis.

"Look, we're all so thin, so light," I tried.

Minos wasn't convinced, but he hadn't given up hope yet.
All he needed was a good argument, the right answer. "You
still need some wind," he muttered.

"That's no problem," said Avramakis. "Just because it's so
quiet around here it doesn't mean that there isn't any wind
down south, north or west."

"That true?" asked Minos, smiling. The right answer was at
hand. But then his face became serious again. "What if . . ."

"What now?"

"What if he got dropped into the sea, though? What about
the sharks? Remember those three guys who escaped from
Makronesos and tried to get to Lavrion swimming?" Two of
them had been torn to pieces by sharks; only one had made it
to the mainland."

"There are no sharks in those waters," Avramakis reassured
him. "Only dolphins. Remember the singer who was thrown
overboard by the pirates, and a dolphin picked him up off Ancona and carried him on its back all the way to Korinthos?"

"No," said Minos, always eager for a good story.

But whether or not Avramakis intended to tell the story of Arion and the dolphin, there was no time. The tin creaked, and the key turned in the padlock, and in burst Ensign Tsakalos of the Children's Navy, followed by Petty Officer Palioras and two seamen recruits.

"On your feet!" yelled Palioras, knowing that some of us were unable to stand up.

Tsakalos slapped his crop into his left hand and cleared his throat. "What happened last night is nothing short of a riot," he started off. "For those of you who are unaware of the magnitude of such an offense in the armed forces, let me assure you that riot and mutiny are crimes punishable by death."

"Wouldn't you know it?" whispered Avramakis.

"What?"

"He's going to send the weather to the firing squad."

But that wasn't what Tsakalos had in mind. "The Coast Guard has recovered two more bodies from the sea, and the search for the remaining four will continue until dark. I will see to it that you are charged with these deaths as well as with the injuries that you have inflicted on one another, and with the destruction of Navy property such as the six tents, your blankets and, of course, the two flagpoles. I intend to submit my report and recommendation for disciplinary action immediately, but until such time as the Ministry can decide, work at the quarry will go on as usual. Until the new tents arrive, you will be allowed to use the assembly room as your dormitory. But your daily rations will be reduced to half, so that in the future you will lack the excessive energy that went to work last night, destroying everything." That's all he had to say, and once he'd said it he turned around, heading for the gate, but he was stopped.

"Liar!" It was Fotis.

The seamen recruits moved against him, but Tsakalos stopped them with a gentle movement of his crop.

"I didn't hear," said Tsakalos, looking around to locate the shouter.

"Liar!" Fotis' voice and entire body trembled with anger.

"Come here!" ordered Tsakalos.

"You go to hell! And there will be no work at the quarry— we're on strike!"

"Say that again."

"No food, no work." Having regained some of his compo- sure, Fotis stood tall, determined to lead us regardless of whether we wanted to be led by him or not, his missing arm making him look even more dramatic.

"You are not free to strike," said Tsakalos. "You are pris- oners."

"Prisoners, yes. Slaves, no!"

Tsakalos took a deep breath and turned to Palioras. "Put him in isolation," he said, his voice calm, but his eyes were already bloodshot.

· 19 ·

Many small kids were crying throughout that afternoon, but you couldn't tell if it was from pain, for those who were dead or missing or for what Ensign Tsakalos might have done to Fotis, or what Fotis might have done to us.

Trakas, Polyvios, Ke-kes and a few others had joined the Parians and the Naxians, who were thinking the situation over. A few kids mentioned the work "strike," but the Parians didn't respond. They were thinking. And so were the Naxians, perhaps, who had been silent most of the time, anyway.

Mastro-Kyrillos' mouth, silent as it was, kept as busy as if it worked on a piece of candy: now sucking on it, now turning it around between his tongue and his teeth, now rolling it from one cheek to the other; once I even heard its sound on his teeth. Where in the world had he found the candy? That kid Mastro-Kyrillos now looked old enough to have been a deserter in at least two wars. No doubt he was deported not because he joined the Andartes but because his stonecutting skills were needed here. Yet the hardships of the previous night had drained him, made him look old. His lips were a pitcher's spout, and his nose the rest of the pitcher. Above his nose, his wrinkles formed a felled Corinthian column. His gray eyes had receded in their sockets as if they'd shrunken, but they still gleamed past the white thickets of his eyebrows. He'd learned most of what he knew from the stones, and his body was prob-

ably like the trunk of an ancient olive tree, a trunk with many
rings and much history: here the 1896 disaster, and here the
First Great War, and after that the Asia Minor catastrophe.
Here the Italian attack, and here the German and Bulgarian
atrocities, and here the Resistance, and more Resistance, and
more and more Resistance: terror, the civil strife, the islands of
detention and the death camps. Year by year our glorious history, the whole history, and throughout the years the starving
and the dispossessed, the disabled and the thoroughly dead—
unnamed and unclaimed forever. And here, among the finest
rings, the lean years in which the children were taken away to
be saved, some by this side and some by that, and were not
saved (including those who still lived in Tashkent, in the
Queen's "Children's Cities" and in the detention camps), for
some of them were to die, and the others never to grow up: to
go gray, and to wrinkle, and to shrink, but to be somewhere
between five and fifteen forever—never to outgrow the heroic
age.

Did Mastro-Kyrillos know that he knew all that history? If so,
maybe he had an answer to the question "What is to be done?"

He put the thumb and forefinger of his right hand between
his lips and took out of his mouth a smooth white pebble that
looked like wedding candy. "The stone says, 'Patience,' " he
said.

"Is that all?"

"The stone *is* patience."

Trakas took the pebble from Mastro-Kyrillos' hand and put it
into his ear.

"Don't lose it," warned the stonecutter.

Trakas spoke as he did his own listening. "We can't go to
work on half-rations," he said. "If we go on strike, it means no
food at all. What else is there? Try and take over? They'll open
fire, and it's not only the rifles; they have two big rattlers and
enough hand grenades to put us out of our misery once and
for all."

"So what's it going to be?" said Polyvios.

Trakas stood up, securing the pebble in his ear and listening, but then he changed his mind and sat down again. "No, I don't think so," he said.

"What?" said Minos.

"The stone says, 'Patience,' " repeated Mastro-Kyrillos.

Once again Trakas stood up. "No, I don't think it's going to work, but maybe we should give it a try."

"What?" insisted Minos.

"All right, we'll give it a try," said Trakas, and, taking the pebble out of his ear, he put it into his mouth and sat down again.

And Polyvios grabbed Mastro-Kyrillos from the shoulders and shouted to him, "That stone of yours is crazy! Do you hear? That stone is cuckoo! Take it from him and put it back in your mouth, and swallow it, or throw it in the water and let the fish worry about it. . . ."

·20·

The following morning we went to work limping, hopping, crawling and dragging one another to the quarry as though it were an outdoor theater and we were the actors, although many of us were still in pain from injuries and had to limp, hop, crawl and drag one another, anyway. Minos wasn't much help as a water boy, since he had to hold one cheek after the other, faking toothaches, and the same could be said for Varant. Ke-kes handed stones backward through his legs, and Avramakis held on to his foot though no one had dropped a stone on it, and everybody else went along in his own way, turning and bending, and sitting down and standing up, and fooling around—everybody except Polyvios, who was there and wasn't, who was too indignant about what went on to have any part of it, until Trakas sat down and stood up behind him and hit him with a steel rod across the legs, which like a miracle brought Polyvios back into the fold. Minutes later we saw Palioras coming down the hill, accompanied by Prassinos and another guard. No doubt they'd noticed that something was wrong somewhere and were coming to find out more. When they stopped before our group, Trakas stood up and sat down. The rest of us carried on, limping, hopping and crawling, exchanging stones or insults in Serbo-Croatian. Even Polyvios. Palioras' face turned yellow, his lips white with patches of blue. He walked on. Everywhere the same. After having toured the

work site, he returned to the barracks, leaving the two guards
to keep an eye on us.

It was a mild, sunny day, and as the afternoon wore on, so
did our Babel. The day was completely wasted, and if we'd
made a point of linking work with food, Tsakalos could always
make his point by linking food to work.

We'd said, "No food, no work," without actually going on
strike.

Tsakalos could say, "No work, no food," and let us limp, hop
and crawl around the island until we'd lost enough weight to
be swept off the face of the earth by a gust of wind—to say
nothing of the disciplinary action that Tsakalos had already
promised for the destruction of Navy property and for the
deaths.

Back in the main barracks at the end of the day, Polyvios was
massaging his legs and wondering if there wasn't some truth in
Tsakalos' charges.

"Sure. Some truth," said Trakas.

"I thought it was the storm," said Polyvios, "but after what
happened today I can't be sure about anything."

"Why don't you side with Tsakalos and Palioras? They'll treat
you special," sneered Ke-kes.

"Don't listen to that," advised Avramakis. "Tsakalos' charges
are all false. You see, he can't report the truth to his superiors
because they'll hold him responsible for not taking measures to
protect the camp from the storm. But if he reports that we went
on a rampage, they'll probably praise him for restoring order
without suffering any real casualties."

"I am not sure," said Polyvios. "What about the dead and the
missing on our side?"

"Suicides," said Mastro-Lambros. "He can always report that
they took their own lives, like the kids in the Leros camp."

"Did kids kill themselves there?"

"Last year. Someone sneaked a message out."

"I don't know," said Polyvios.

"I'm not sure, either," said Varant. "Maybe Tsakalos made that accusation just to scare us off—to make sure we didn't hold *him* responsible for what happened."

"You never can tell," said Trakas. "I mean, when you're dealing with crows like Tsakalos and Palioras, you never know what they're really up to."

"The bigger their talons, the smaller their brains," said Şükrü.

Trakas was impressed. "Is that a Turkish proverb, Mehmed?"

"It is now. And you can call me Şükrü, eh?"

"Nobody's ever happy for being who he is," brooded Trakas.

Or *where* he is. Once again we were locked up in the assembly room, hungry, tired, sleepy, confused. And this time Tsakalos didn't even bother to make a formal announcement of his intentions, leaving it up to Palioras to decide, who in turn left it up to his own subordinates, who dispatched Prassinos to tell us that we were to remain confined in the main barracks without food or water until we were ready to go work—and actually work.

Trakas stood up, sat down, and stood up again.

Ke-kes turned around, opened his legs, and looked at Prassinos backward and upside down.

Then they brought back Fotis. His face was purple, bruised and swollen all over. He said they'd worked him over with a rubber club. When he said that, we saw that he'd lost an upper front tooth. He said they'd worked him over so badly even his missing arm hurt.

"Did they find it?" asked Minos in all innocence.

I thought Fotis might smile at that, but he didn't. Instead he sucked his bleeding gum and spat.

"A martyr," mumbled Trakas. "Who can stop him from saving us now?"

"What's going on?" whispered Fotis through the gap in his teeth.

"Nothing much, we're taking it easy," said Avramakis.

"Tsalalos and his boys went on strike," said Trakas. "They won't give us any food or water, and they won't let us out of here."

Avramakis had gotten to his knees, examining Fotis' cuts and bruises "You think you got any broken bones?" he asked.

"All of them," said Fotis.

"None of them," diagnosed Avramakis. "What you need is hot compresses and a lot of rest."

"I can't sleep," said Fotis.

"If you don't sleep, the tooth fairy won't come," said Trakas.

"When I close my eyes I see those statues again. . . ."

"What's he talking about?"

"We were in isolation together. It was a large hole dug under the floor of the supply room, where they beat me. It was very dark, except when they opened the trapdoor to bring those two bodies they said they'd recovered. The bodies were completely stiff and wrapped up in burlap, but I thought one of them was Pavlos."

"Weren't you scared?" said Varant.

"I wouldn't be scared by those bodies. But when they brought them down I thought they were going to bury me alive with them, and that terrified me."

"What about the statues that you said you were in isolation with?" I asked Fotis.

"Wait. When the guards left I carefully unwrapped the burlap at the top so that the next time someone opened the trapdoor I could see who the bodies belong to."

"If there was a next time," said Varant.

"If," agreed Fotis.

And Varant said, "What nerve!"

"That's what the guards said the next time they opened the trapdoor and saw that I had uncovered the faces."

"And what did you see?"

"I saw that those bodies were not corpses. They were statues. That's right. Marble or plaster—I wasn't sure. But they were smooth and white, and their sizes were the sizes of Pavlos and maybe Alekos, but in the face they didn't look like Pavlos or Alekos, or any of the other missing kids."

We stood there, listening to Fotis, the questions now too big and too many to be asked. Had Fotis gone mad from the beating and from terror? Were Tsakalos and his subordinates insane? Or had the kids spoken in stone, saying, "We're neither missing nor lost, nor quite recovered. We're here and will be here forever"?

·21·

A barrage—no, a handful of stones. I awoke, the muscles of my stomach tensed, arms and legs shaking.

"What happened?" Everybody had jumped up from sleep, asking the same question again and again: "What happened?" So it wasn't a nightmare. Someone had actually thrown a handful of stones on the roof.

"Don t they learn anything else in the Navy?" I heard Avramakis' voice in the dark.

Some of the smaller kids had been startled in their sleep and they were crying.

"What happened?"

We heard voices outside, approaching. It was still early evening, not long after the complaining about hunger had quieted down and we went to sleep cuddled up on our straw mattresses. It was cold in the barracks, colder than it'd been in the tents so far.

"What did they do that for?"

"War of nerves." That was the voice of Theophanis, a kid from Kerkyra.

"What for?"

"For to go to work, and *work*," said Theophanis.

"While we're starved like this?"

"Eh . . . don't tell *me* about starving like this."

Nothing happened. As soon as they'd approached the gate,

the voices and the steps went away again, and we lay down, convinced that it wasn't anything serious, just a war of nerves. But minutes later, some fifteen or twenty minutes, when we'd relaxed again and were about to sleep, another barrage of stones on the roof made our bodies convulse, and Theophanis stood up, growling.

"I've got to find out what Matsoukas is thinking about all this," he said, and, getting down to his knees, he began to crawl toward the far end of the assembly room.

"Wait. What's so important about Matsoukas?" said Trakas, grabbing Theophanis by the ankle.

"Let go of my foot."

"Tell me first."

"I'm going to take a tin sheet out of the wall and I'm going to walk right out of this tin can before you know it," said Theophanis.

"The sheets are screwed in from the outside, you know," said Trakas.

"You've noticed that, haven't you?" said Theophanis. "But you didn't do anything about it while you were at the right end of the screws."

"Did you?"

"Virtue's children cook their food before they get hungry," said Theophanis.

"You're killing me."

"You took the screws out?" asked Avramakis.

"Matsoukas and I. It was so easy. We thought, Well, who knows, maybe someday we might be inside and—"

"Virtue's children," said Trakas.

"My foot!"

Right then another handful of stones hit the roof, and Trakas released Theophanis' foot and asked him to lead the way. We crawled after Theophanis, spreading the word along the way, and by the time the fourth barrage of stones sounded on the roof more than a dozen of us had sneaked out of the main

barracks, and others were coming behind us one at a time—
not as quietly but as fast. The sky was clear but without a
moon, so all one could see was the others' silhouettes against
the sky.

"Maybe we should disperse now," said Matsoukas.

We decided to split into groups of ten and climb down to the
shore, but our escape was discovered before everybody had left
the barracks, and there was shouting, and warning shots were
fired.

"What now?" said Leonis.

"We've already played c-c-c-crazy, now we c-c-c-can play
hide-and-seek," said Ke-kes.

"Keep it up and pretty soon we'll all be playing dead," said
Avramakis.

"Hide-and-seek, hide-and-seek . . ."

Three or four groups began to climb down the eastern shore,
and three more including Minos and Avramakis went down the
opposite way through the quarry. I was still with Theophanis,
Trakas, Matsoukas, Ke-kes, Leonis and a few others somewhere between the outhouses and the barbed-wire fence, di-
recting and guiding the newcomers, when we saw a dozen or
so lights moving in our direction—probably the entire guard,
armed with flashlights and storm lamps, pistols and rifles.

"Get back! Everybody get back!" I recognized Palioras' voice.

"Get back immediately and there will be no disciplinary action," shouted Tsakalos.

"We need food!" shouted back a kid somewhere east of the
barracks.

"I can't hear you," said Tsakalos.

"We need food in our stomachs, not stones on the roof!" It
was Şükrü.

The flashlight beams scanned the rocks east of the barracks,
and a pistol shot rang out.

"Missed!" shouted the same kid.

"We need food, not bullets!" shouted Theophanis.

The flashlights stretched out their long, luminous arms toward us, and a bullet went by whistling just above our heads. The lights were moving again in our direction.

"Why did you have to give away our position?" Matsoukas asked Theophanis.

"So they wouldn't get Şükrü," said Theophanis.

"I thought we were playing hide-and-seek," said Matsoukas.

·22·

"We've got to go through the fence," said Trakas.

"Are you serious? What for?"

"To hide," said Trakas.

"Don't be crazy. We can climb down to the shore like the others," said Matsoukas.

"They'll find us sooner or later," said Trakas. "They have the flashlights and the guns. We have nothing."

"C-c-c-come on," said Ke-kes, pushing me toward the fence.

"You always wanted to go through that fence; don't lie to me," said Trakas.

"That was in my sleep. I never meant to die for it."

"We've got to go through, or give ourselves up," said Theophanis. "They're coming."

"Let him go through first," suggested Leonis. "If he doesn't get killed by a mine, we'll follow him."

"Follow me, but don't run," said Trakas, pulling at the sign. "Walk fast but softly like a cat," he said.

Matsoukas and Leonis helped Trakas tear down the sign and throw it against the wire.

"Even if it's true there are mines in there, they won't blow up, I promise you," said Trakas, stepping onto the sign, pressing the barbed wire down.

"I'd rather give myself up. Don't do it!"

"Chicken shit!"

241

That was me. "Eh, Prassinos! This way," I shouted in the direction of the flashlights and the storm lamps.

"Stop!" yelled Palioras. "Don't go past that wire!"

Now the lights were upon us, but Trakas had already stepped into the minefield.

"Take a few more steps," said Leonis.

"Look," said Trakas.

We couldn't see in the dark, but I imagined him hopping lightly from mine to mine unharmed.

"Still alive!" said Trakas. "Come on."

"Let's go," said Ke-kes, stepping onto the sign.

"I've figured it out," said Trakas again.

Ha! Seven years before, the two little shepherds stared at an exposed mine and I stared at them, hoping they knew what they were doing. They didn't. They probed at the mine with a long stick (it was a simple wooden box with six cakes of dynamite in it), turning their faces the other way as though the worst they'd suffer if the mine did go off would be a slap in the face. The mine did go off as I began to shout insults at them, and one of them was blown up, thrown headfirst into a ditch full of water. His stomach had been ripped open, the water turned red. I'd rather not have seen the entrails coming up to the surface, the thin layer of flesh that stretched over rib cage and stomach all torn to shreds, the dark of the empty stomach rising like black smoke. But the other shepherd suffered no injury, and once he'd recovered from the shock of the explosion he reached out and, taking hold of one of his friend's feet, he began to pull, to get his friend out. I had no choice, I had to help. I turned back, and taking hold of the other limp, heavy foot I began to pull also. But the young shepherd didn't approve of what I was doing. "What are you doing there? They're mine—they're both mine," he barked. He wasn't pulling at the feet but at the shoes.

"Go on, you can explain later," I said to Trakas.

Another bullet whistled by. "I am warning you, that's a mine-field," yelled Palioras, running ahead of the others toward us.

"Let's go," urged Ke-kes. "That swine would rather k-k-k-kill us with his own bare hands."

Trakas had vanished, and Theophanis was gone, too, and Ke-kes was third in line.

"C-c-c-come on," urged Ke-kes, pulling Matsoukas by his shirt.

And Matsoukas followed him quietly.

Then I felt Leonis' hand on my shoulder, and I shuddered. No mine had gone off yet, but the idea of walking through a minefield still frightened me, and I began to suspect that Trakas and the others might want to commit suicide and were leading me to certain death. "No, I won't!" I shouted, pushing Leonis' hand away.

"Come on," urged Leonis.

"Hold it right there!" shouted Palioras, panting.

Then there were several shots, and the rest of the kids pushed me over the sign and the fence, and kept pushing me until we were all halfway between the fence and the shore and there was no going back.

"Gently now," advised Trakas, who waited for us, probably yellow with fright.

"Tell me, what makes you think that the mines won't go off?" asked Leonis.

"I'll tell you: I just think we're too light to set off a mine, that's all," said Trakas.

"You mean the mines are good only for grown-up soldiers?"

"Oh, they're good for kids, too, but you must have some weight to set it off, and we have none."

"I never thought all that starving c-c-c-could be useful some-day," said Ke-kes.

·23·

I awoke, sensing on my face the increasing light that each incoming wave brought to the shore. The night before, we'd walked the rest of the way down without incident. Soon the flashlight beams had not been able to reach us, and in a little while even the shouting stopped, the guard having probably given up and returned to the barracks to plan the next day's operations, how to round us up and herd us back to the assembly room, or force us back to work at gunpoint. At any rate, the next move was theirs.

I washed my mouth and face with seawater, and although I felt weak and dizzy from hunger I decided to walk around exploring this forbidden corner of Antikalamos before everyone else was up. The barbed wire came all the way down to the sea on both sides, and along the wire there were two rows of tall boulders that had either been part of the formation of the rock or been raised as protective walls hundreds or thousands of years ago. Some of the boulders bore chiseled recesses that seemed to be as old. "Throughout its glorious history our country has used several uninhabited islands such as this one to rid itself of subversive and seditious elements," Tsakalos had mentioned in his welcoming speech. Could it be that the ancient deportees had also been forced to mine and cut stone? Why not? Somewhere on Kalamos, probably in the foundations of the Church of St. Thalassios, the foundations of the Temple

of Poseidon had been built with stones from Antikalamos. Far
to the left, the sloping rock had been cut vertically and hol-
lowed, if one was to believe that the small wooden door that
hung from two rusty hinges and an old-fashioned latch on the
face of the rock weren't fake. I pressed down the cock of the
latch with my thumb and pulled, and the door opened, creaking, letting out into the sharp morning air the dark of untold
nights. I stood at the entrance, sniffing the musty history of the
cell that deepened moment by moment as my eyes grew accustomed to the dark. And then a shiver ran through my entire
body and I had to close my eyes and rub them, and when I
opened them I shuddered again. Strewn all over the floor or
leaning against the walls of the cell were about two dozen boys
and girls between six and fourteen years of age, and the more
my eyes became accustomed to the dark the more it looked like
the Tatoi cave: in one row the dead and in another the dying:
lean limbs freezing in sleep never to thaw again, a fine web of
frost spreading slowly to cover every part of the body, even the
hair, so neatly and evenly that each dead body turned into a
smooth white statue in a few days' time. Here too the bodies
had turned into statues, though not from cold. They'd turned
into stone, into cool white marble as if they'd seen the head of
Medusa or some other Greek beast, never again to leave their
cell, never to return to the quarry to cut more stone for the
Temple of Poseidon. And the authorities let them stay in their
cell, their perfect tomb, for the rest of time, leaving it up to the
Department of Ancient Antiquities to send a carpenter once
every hundred years or so to replace the door. Stepping back, I
latched the door, and I returned to join the others, who were
slowly waking up and ordering breakfast:

"Milk, honey and white bread!"

"A deep bowl of rice pudding with cinnamon!"

"A deep dish of tripe with eggs and lemon!"

We chewed on a few small crabs which we caught under the
stones, and waited for Tsakalos' move. The sun was up now,

drying the damp air, and in the light breeze we heard voices, other kids waking up among the stones all around the island. Then, while Trakas and Theophanis were away having a look at the statues in the cell that had been cut out of the rock, we heard the sound of an outboard motor approaching around the rock from the west, and we saw a large rubber boat steering toward us. In it, four sailors of the Greek Royal Navy, armed with pistols and rifles. We rolled behind a boulder, arming ourselves with stones.

"You there, come on board!" shouted one of the sailors, jumping out of the boat. "All of you!"

Ke-kes aimed a stone at him, but Leonis stopped him.

"C-c-c-come and get us!" Ke-kes shouted at him instead.

"You are too silly for words," said the sailor.

"Eh?" Ke-kes was surprised.

"Nobody's going to hurt you," said the sailor.

"Where have I heard this before?" said Leonis.

Now it was the sailor's turn to be surprised. He turned to look at the other three sailors who waited in the boat, as though he was asking for help.

"Tell them about the 'leniency measures,' " said one of the three.

Leniency? None of us knew what that word meant.

The first sailor didn't know, either. "Our captain will tell you all about that, and more," he said, and before we knew it he was standing among us, pointing to the boat. "Let's go now," he said.

We dropped the stones and stood up, just in time to see Trakas and Theophanis walking down from the little cell.

"Who are they?" asked the sailor.

"More of the same," said Ke-kes.

"What's going on over there?" shouted Trakas.

"We've just c-c-c-captured four spies of the Children's Navy," shouted back Ke-kes. "They're getting a little too old for it," he said.

"You must be the silliest one," said the sailor.

"Hurry up," said Ke-kes. "The new government is handing out lots and lots of leniencies."

"So you gave yourselves up without a fight," said Trakas, shaking his head as he stepped into the rubber boat.

And Theophanis said, "What's leniencies, anyway? Something one can eat?"

"I'm not sure," said Ke-kes.

Theophanis glanced at the rest of us. "Does anyone know?" he asked.

"I think it has something to do with the afterlife," said Trakas.

·24·

Spring had finally come to Antikalamos, riding the soft south-west breeze over the sea, over the red rock, and we couldn't even find a single wildflower to decorate her hair or put behind her ear. We spent a whole Sunday morning searching all over the island, but we couldn't even find a green leaf to give her as a down payment, as proof that the single flower was late bloom-ing that year. So we went down to the quarry with the Parians and cut a crocus in stone, but the stone crocus had no scent and, besides, it was too heavy for her delicate ear. And she asked if there were any little birds on the island. We spent a whole Sunday afternoon looking all over the island, and since she didn't really care for sea gulls we turned over every stone, hoping at least to find a nest with a single egg in it, proof that the single bird was late hatching that year. No luck. So we went down to the quarry again with the Parians and cut a young swallow in stone, but she didn't care for that either. And Spring punished us by making us smell wildflowers all over the place without seeing them, and by causing our hearts to flutter to exhaustion like birds that were too heavy to fly. And Spring wouldn't stay another day on Antikalamos. And when she flew off, riding the southwest breeze that Sunday evening, we went to hide in our tents in anticipation of another winter.

For the new tents had arrived a few days before, and now we had a place to hide in. As a surprise, what arrived on Monday

morning was the summer. It rose with the sun, filling the lucent air over the rock and the sea, and the rock warmed up and
began to creak, and the sea sighed and quieted down, and it
was that sudden quiet that awoke us—a good thing, too, for
summer had just crawled into our tents for inspection, for body
search, for surprise. And summer counted and counted again
the bodies, but some were still missing.

We'd never seen the bodies of those who perished in the
storm, and no one knew if they were to be given a funeral, to
be buried in stone on Antikalamos, or in soil on Kalamos, or at
sea, or not to be buried at all. Maybe Tsakalos, Palioras and
Prassinos and the other apprentices and recruits planned to
bring them all back and force them to work in the quarry, to
pretend day after day they were alive and in as fine health as
the rest of us.

The unannounced visit of the torpedo boat *Tombazis*, its
captain, and crew had restored order on the island within a few
hours, and that same day, we got a taste of the leniency that
the new government was about to adopt, when our ration of
black-eyed beans and galleta was doubled. So leniency was
something that one could eat, after all, just as Theophanis had
hoped. And more was coming our way, once the new government was through studying Captain Zenakos' report about the
conditions of life on Antikalamos. In return we had to go back
to cutting stone for the rebuilding of the Church of St. Thalassios, which we did gladly.

Then Ensign Tsakalos of the Children's Navy took a vacation, leaving Petty Officer Palioras in charge. And Palioras
moved to Tsakalos' quarters as though his superior officer was
never to return from leave. One day, without any provocation
whatever, Palioras showed us his gold tooth. It was meant to be
a proof that he could even smile if he had to, but several kids
thought that the petty officer might just be buckling under the
burden of his new responsibilities. As for the seamen of the
guard, they became so friendly overnight that we worried about

what they'd all be up to next. The answer occurred to us soon enough: Tsakalos' leave, Palioras' threat to smile and the seamen's friendliness proved that the Children's Navy was troubled about the change in government and the change of weather in Athens, and our guards were preparing themselves for the worst.

Ensign Tsakalos was never to return to Antikalamos, and Petty Officer Palioras never to replace his superior officer as commander, for the new government decided to turn the camp over to the Army. When Second Lieutenant Müller arrived to take command, everyone was concerned about his name, a name Avramakis swore was German.

"No more stones," said Avramakis. "From now on it's going to be soap."

"Bite your tongue," said Varant.

"The first time our hopes go up, our pants go down," said Şükrü.

And Fotis said, "We can't afford to be caught with our pants down. We've got to get organized."

Accompanying the second lieutenant were Corporal Laïos and Privates Spathis and Kalfopoulos. The changing of the guard took place without ceremony. And only when Palioras and the seamen apprentices and recruits were gone did the new commander speak directly to us, but even that occasion was very informal. After having introduced himself and his subordinates, Second Lieutenant Müller said that the government of General Plastiras was determined to pacify and reunite our nation, but that it wasn't in a position to grant a general amnesty yet. Still, our case was a special one, and a special way to deal with it could be found. Sooner than later. At any rate, his presence and the presence of his carefully chosen subordinates on Antikalamos meant two things: an improvement of our living conditions, and an effort on the part of society to prepare us to become free again. He then allowed questions, and

Trakas asked how many more soldiers were coming to join the guard.

"None," was the second lieutenant's answer. And he explained that he and his subordinates were not there to be our guards.

Corporal Laïos and Privates Spathis and Kalfopoulos had studied to become teachers, and the lieutenant had hand-picked them to teach us Greek and arithmetic, but all three of them spent their first two weeks on Antikalamos helping the Naxians and the Parians build a little stone house for the lieutenant, who wanted to bring his wife and newborn child to live with him. The rest of us cut stone for the restoration of the Church of St. Thalassios. The stone thought it was a matter of a few months before we'd leave our place of exile forever. But then the stone had already seen enough of us not to worry about missing us.

·25·

It took no effort on our part and no time whatever for us to adjust to the second lieutenant's idea of running the camp. Besides the usual black-eyed beans and galleta, we now had powdered milk for breakfast, and fresh dandelion greens from Kalamos with our dinner, and every Sunday there was a big supper of stewed lamb and potatoes with lettuce salad. At the same time, our workday was shortened by two hours, during which Corporal Laïos and Privates Spathis and Kalfopoulos, and sometimes the second lieutenant himself, taught us reading and writing, history, geography and religion.

One evening, after class, Avramakis walked to the main barracks with one of the soldiers, and he learned that Second Lieutenant Müller had been born and raised in Greece, but that his parents were German—as German and as royalist as the Queen herself. In fact, the Müllers were relatives of the Queen. Did that have anything to do with the second lieutenant's appointment as the new commander of Antikalamos?

"Yes and no," said Avramakis, quoting the soldier, but he himself thought definitely yes: The new government wanted to give a general amnesty, but the Court and the American Mission in Athens opposed it, so the Prime Minister gave orders at least to improve the living conditions of all political prisoners and detainees until he could afford to give a general amnesty, but once again the Queen and the American Mission opposed his move as premature. Finally, the government decided to do something at least about the younger prisoners and detainees. The idea was that if the Free World did something about us, maybe the Russians would do something about all those Greek kids who got stuck behind the Iron Curtain.

"Maybe," thought Avramakis, and he said, "Ha!" because the Queen and the American Mission in Athens thought that the new government in general, and General Plastiras, the Prime Minister, in particular, were too pink to be trusted, and they said this and that, such as, We're not ready to buy your merchandise, General, go peddle it someplace else. "But who's there besides the Queen and the Mission?" said Avramakis, probably quoting the soldier, and he said, "Nobody." And the Russians couldn't hear a thing from behind the Iron Curtain. Then the government suggested a young officer of German extraction as the new commander of Antikalamos, and apparently the Queen could not say no, and the American Mission said nothing. This had to be more complicated than it sounded, but anyone can tell that somebody in the new government knew what he was doing, and Second Lieutenant Müller was allowed not only to sail to our island and take over, but to have a free hand at it as well—that is, if he was willing to carry out the new government's measures of leniency. Oh, we had no trouble at all adjusting to Second Lieutenant Müller's style of running a detention camp.

It was that same day, while we ate lunch, that Lieutenant Müller had to go to Kalamos, and asked Fotis to run off and tell his wife that he'd be back before dark. And as one tells a cat to go away and the cat passes that command on to her tail, so did Fotis ask me to go instead.

"Please," said Fotis. "I think I am going to be sick," he said. Fotis was a leader, not an errand boy.

"Sure." I was everything that Fotis was not. I didn't mind taking the message to the lieutenant's wife. I gobbled up my beans and I was off, first running, then slowing down to enjoy being alone for a few minutes.

The atmosphere was so clear that when I stopped and peered southward across the sea, once again I saw the main town of Kalamos, Hora, but this time there was something different about it. And it couldn't just be the brighter light falling on the houses, shops and churches vertically, from the middle of the sky. Putting my hand over my eyes, I peered at it so intensely and for so long that everything around Hora, the sea, the hill and the sky, receded into blackness, while Hora itself seemed to be a brand-new town: its crown, the Church of St. Thalassios, its hotels, shops and houses had been repaired and whitewashed, obliterating overnight the pockmarks of war and the smudge of poverty, to say nothing of the earthquake rubble that preceded the war. "Whitewashed!" I kept saying, imagining Saint Thalassios restored to his seat, his see, blessing the hardworking islanders for their determination to mark the nine hundred and fiftieth anniversary of his martyrdom with a great Mass and procession reinaugurating the annual festival that had not been held in the war years.

Hora had suddenly been reborn from the sea, or from the lime pit, and I thought that that might be true for the rest of the country.

Turning left, I ran the last two hundred or so meters down to the second lieutenant's house, and knocked.

"Come in, the door is not locked," answered Mrs. Müller.

I opened the door and went straight to the kitchen, although the voice had come from another room.

"No, no, I am here." She was in the bedroom, nursing her infant child.

I walked back, stopping by the open door of the bedroom, staring at my shoes.

"What is your name?" she asked. There was a glow about her

and about the baby that made me feel as though I were in church.

"Well?" she said.

I kept staring at my shoes.

"You don't have a name?" she said again. She leaned against a pillow, most of which was covered by her long light hair, probably the source of that glow, nursing the baby.

"The lieutenant had to go to Kalamos, but he said to tell you he'll return before dinner," I muttered, thinking, It's probably her breast that makes the face of the baby glow.

Then the infant stopped suckling and turned toward me, its mouth moist with milk, and it hiccupped.

"To Kalamos," she repeated absentmindedly. What else could she say?

The child took the nipple in its mouth again, pressing its soft lips to the pale moon around the nipple and trying to focus on a lock of hair that hung down its mother's shoulder.

"I am going now."

"Aren't you going to tell me your name?"

I had lost my name, and the name I had was not mine. I took a deep breath, stealing some of that scent of milk that filled the air, but she stopped me.

"Wait, you can't leave like that. It's all right, you don't have to tell me your name. But do go to the kitchen and help yourself to a handful of cherries."

I looked at her, trying to understand. Then, unable to hold my breath any longer, I exhaled noisily and turned toward the exit.

"Wait! Oh, never mind, just stay where you are and I will get you some myself," she said, getting up, and she went into the kitchen still holding the child to her breast. "Cherries," she said. "They are ripe and sweet."

Cherries, I had read in a story once, were a kind of olive that ripened in May up north, and were dark red and sweeter than wild plums, but I'd never believed they existed in real life.

άπελευθέρωση. Εἶναι ὅμως καὶ ρεαλιστική;  βανε τήν ἑλληνική, γιουγκοσλαβική καὶ

Ὁ Πέτρος Ροῦσος, στὸ βιβλίο του «Ἡ Μεγάλη «Πενταετία», ἀπευθυνόμενος πρός ἀριστερούς ἀναγνῶστες καὶ προσπαθῶντας νὰ δικαιολογήσει τό «ὄχι» τοῦ ΚΚΕ, ἰσχυρίζεται πώς ἡ ἡγεσία του δὲν ἀρνήθηκε τή συγκρότηση τοῦ Βαλκανικοῦ Στρατηγείου οὔτε τό τορπίλλιασε. «Ζήτησε ἁπλώς – γράφει – ἀναβολή τοῦ ζητήματος μέχρι νὰ δημιουργηθοῦν οἱ ὅροι». Γιατί αὐτές οἱ μασημένες δικαιολογίες; Ὁ ἴδιος ἀναφέρει ὡς ἑξῆς τούς λόγους ποὺ ὤθησαν τό πολιτικό γραφεῖο τοῦ ΚΚΕ στήν ἀπόφασή του:

«Πρώτο, νὰ στερεώσουμε τὴν ἐθνικοαπελευθερωτική συμμαχία, νὰ μήν προκαλέσουμε δυσανασχέτηση τῶν συμμάχων μας στό ΕΑΜ καὶ σὲ ἄλλους ἐνδεχόμενους συμμάχους μας. Δεύτερο, νὰ μήν ἐπισπεύσουμε ἔνταση τῶν ἀντιδράσεων καὶ ἐπεμβάσεων τῶν Ἄγγλων στήν Ἑλλάδα προτοῦ προλάβει νὰ στερεωθεῖ τό ἐπαναστατικό κίνημα στήν Ἑλλάδα ἤ τουλάχιστον στή Γιουγκοσλαβία. Τρίτο, νὰ μή δημιουργήσουμε πρόωρα ἐμπόδια στήν παγκόσμια ἀντιχιτλερική συμμαχία, τὰ ὁποῖα ἄγνωστο ἄν θὰ μπορέσουμε τελικά νὰ ὑπερπηδήσουμε ὅσο βαστάει ὁ πόλεμος κατά τῶν καταχτητῶν».

Μακεδόνες καὶ Μεγαλόσερβοι

Ὁ Κώστας Καραγιώργης ὅμως, ποὺ ἀναμείχθηκε ἄμεσα στό θέμα, ὅπως εἴδαμε, σὲ ἰδιαίτερη συνομιλία ποὺ εἶχε μὲ τόν γράφοντα τά...

«... Ἡ σκέψη τῶν Γιουγκοσλάβων καὶ τῶν Ἀλβανῶν συντρόφων νὰ ἐπηρεάζουν πρός ὁρισμένη πολιτική τίς ἀντίστοιχες ἔνοπλες δυνάμεις τῶν ἐθνικῶν μειονοτήτων στήν

–"Ἄκου...
γοι ποὺ...
λιτικό μ...
ὅτι τό Ε...
λουθοῦσ...
ματα. Δ...
λίγο πρίν...
Διεθνῆς...
τῆς δέν...
ὅπως κα...
ἔδειχνε...
πολύ με...
χρεωμέν...
σίες γι...
ἑνότητα...
θεῖ τό π...
Τέμπο κ...
ὅμως δι...
χαιριά σ...
Γιατί κα...

ὀρθωνόμαστε μαζί με τοὺς Ἀλβανοὺς καὶ Γιουγκοσλάβους κατά τῶν Ἄγγλων. Ὅλα αὐτά ὅμως ἦσαν δευτερεύοντα μπροστά σὲ ἕναν ὀγκόλιθο ποὺ θά σοῦ ἀποκαλύψω».

Καὶ καθώς ὁ γράφων τέντωνε τόν λαιμό του καὶ τά αὐτιά του γιά νὰ ἀκούσει, ὁ Κώστας Καραγιώργης συμπλήρωσε:

– Ἐκεῖνο ποὺ μᾶς τρόμαξε εἶναι ἄλλο: Εἴχαμε πληροφορίες ἀλλά καὶ ἀντιληφθή-

...χώρα...
...χει σ' ὅλον τόν ἑλληνικό ἀγώνα καὶ στόν ἀγώνα τῶν βαλκανικῶν λαῶν ἡ ἄμεση υἱοθέτηση ἀπό μᾶς τοῦ συνθήματος «ἑνιαία Μακεδονία στά πλαίσια τῆς νέας Γιουγκοσλαβίας». Ὑπάρχουν ἀκόμη καὶ σήμερα ὁρισμένοι ποὺ λένε πώς καὶ ἄν ἀκόμα δέν ἐλευθερωνόταν ἡ Ἑλλάδα ἀπό τόν ἰμπεριαλισμό, θὰ εἶναι ἐλευθερωθεῖ τουλάχι-

Ὁ Τίτο κατά

Καὶ τώρα ἕνα...
γνώση τοῦ Τίτο...
Τέμπο: Ἀσφαλ...
ὅσο τελικά ὅρίσ...
πρόσωπος τῆς...
σχεδιασμό στρα...

Ὥστε ὁ Τίτο υ...
Μεγαλοσέρβων...
γκοσλαβίας;

Ἡ ἀπάντηση...
δοξο, εἶναι καὶ...
στοὺς πολλούς...
μὲ ἐντολή του...
τερα τά γιουγκ...
ψαν τό ἀντίθετο...
καὶ ἀδιάψευστα...

Ὁ Τίτο πράγμ...
σύσταση Βαλκ. Σ...
κούς λόγους. Κ...
ταν στόν στρατι...
ἦταν κακή. Ἀλλά...
μεγαλοσέρβικοι...
κοί κύκλοι – ὑπο...
νιστικοῦ θρασμο...
νησου – γιά νὰ ἄ...
τόν τόν μηχανισ...

Ἄργησε νὰ τ...
τῆς ἀραιῆς ἐπικ...
τό καλοκαίρι τοῦ...
μάχη ζωῆς ἤ θα...
τῶν. Ὅταν πληρ...
γίνει, ἡ ἀντίδρα...
σε νὰ δια...
αγγειλατ...
Τέμπο κα...
ηγεῖο γιατ...
ωστό».

γράμμα το...
αμμίζει:
...σημεριν...
...ὁποιουδ...
αν λάθος,...
ἡ χαριστικ...
λή του πε...
δημιουργ...
νησία».
...ἡγνώματα...
...γό του δ...
...εἶχε λάβ...
τοῦ Σιάντ...
στε τό θέμ...
ριστικά.
...ωστε, τώ...
αν ὅπως...
νταν μπρ...
ἀνατροπή: Ἡ Ἰτ...
Καὶ στόν βαλκα...
σποτος ἕνας ὀλό...
γέρας τῶν δυν...
χώματα τῆς Γιου...

Τό ΚΚΕ λέει:

ATHENS—After four days of debate, the Greek Parliament has granted a confidence vote to the Plastiras government by a majority of 41 votes.

Political observers stress that the mere size of the majority is not the only point for rejoicing. The Plastiras victory opens the way for a constructive reform effort. Moreover, the high level of the parliamentary debate disproved the belief that the Greeks are tired. From it a new internal policy started to emerge in its first general outlines—economic liberalism with state intervention whenever necessary to break monopolistic power and excesses, political liberalism bent on gradual abolition of court-martial and the reduction in the numbers of political prisoners and detainees. . . .

—Reuters dispatch, May 1950

·26·

On the first Monday of June Corporal Laïos distributed a printed sheet of paper to everyone, asking those who could read and understand the writing on it to report to Lieutenant Müller in the main barracks immediately. The document contained two paragraphs, the first of which sounded like a confession and the second like a pledge of loyalty to the King and to the National government of Greece, and bore the seal of the Ministry of the Interior, Department of Public Security. About forty-five of us, including Trakas, Avramakis, Polyvios, Ke-kes, Leonis, Matsoukas and Varant, gathered in the main barracks, wondering what all this meant.

The second lieutenant walked in with a broad smile on his face and quickly glanced at everyone as if he were counting heads. At the end of his smile waited a grimace of surprise. "Where is Fotis?" he asked.

"He's still at the quarry, sir," said Polyvios.

Could it be that Fotis had trouble reading the two paragraphs on the document?

"No, sir, but he said he had trouble understanding it."

That was Fotis, all right, but the lieutenant thought maybe he could explain any rough spots, and since he didn't want to do that twice he was willing to wait until Fotis had joined us. Polyvios went to get him, and when the two returned, the lieutenant asked Fotis if it was true that he had trouble understanding the document.

"It says here," said Fotis, pointing to the first paragraph, "that I have been a Communist and have committed criminal acts against my country."

The document also said that we were no longer Communists, and that, having regretted our crimes, we were ready to prove our loyalty to the Crown and to Mother Greece.

"Get to the point, Fotis," said the lieutenant.

"That's just it, there is no point, sir. Most of us here have never been Communists, and none of us has committed crimes. The government is lying, and it does so on our behalf, and you expect us to understand and to lie also. Are these the ideals of the new government?"

Somehow, the lieutenant found all this amusing, but he managed to suppress a smile that came at the end of his surprise at Fotis' statement.

"Furthermore, you expect us to sign this, perjuring and incriminating ourselves for the rest of our lives. This is also a part I do not understand. Do you understand it, sir?"

"Fotis, were you ever a Communist?" asked the lieutenant.

"If you have the right to ask that question, I must have the right to refuse to answer it," said Fotis.

"That sounds nice and I am impressed, but you are at a disadvantage."

"I will not answer."

"Fine, but you shouldn't blame the government for answering it on your behalf. Or are you still a Communist?"

Once again, Fotis was challenged to come up with an answer. He glanced at us, and I knew he'd fallen for it. With red cheeks and shining eyes he turned toward the lieutenant, lifting his chin in defiance. "I have been, I am now, and I always will be a Communist," said Fotis loudly enough to be heard at Kalamos.

"I see," said the lieutenant colorlessly, trying to play down the impression that Fotis' answer had made. "Now, how many others are still Communists?"

"They should answer for themselves," said Fotis. "But they won't."

"Well, how many?" repeated the lieutenant, this time to us.

No one spoke.

"How many of you have been Communists in the past but are not now?"

No one answered.

"Hm," said the lieutenant, somewhat puzzled.

"They've never been, and they are not now," said Fotis. And he added, "They don't even know what Communism is all about. So they'd better not sign, or they'll be perjuring themselves, and worse: they'll be giving the government the rope with which to hang them anytime it pleases."

"Is that so," said the lieutenant.

"This," shouted Fotis, showing us his copy of the document, "is the same piece of trash that one government after another has been giving all the political prisoners around the country to sign, and they refuse to. Communists and non-Communists alike, they read it, and then they take it to the shithouse and they wipe their asses with it. That's the kind of signature it deserves."

"That's enough!" The lieutenant was turning whiter and whiter.

I wondered whether or not Fotis knew what he was doing, and I wondered if he hadn't chosen the wrong moment to defy the whole world. I for one had sensed something false in the lieutenant's composure, and I shuddered, fearing the worst, that Fotis and perhaps the rest of us had fallen into a trap from which we'd never recover, a trap that the second lieutenant had set cleverly enough on behalf of the new government.

"Now, what makes you so sure that I am asking you to sign?" said the lieutenant.

Surprise. If we were to guess among one hundred questions

which one the lieutenant would ask next, nobody would have guessed right. Why shouldn't everyone assume that we were expected to sign?

But Fotis was still searching for the right answer. "Well . . ." he offered.

"I didn't ask you to sign it, did I?" interrupted the lieutenant.

"No, but the government did. Right here, at the bottom of the sheet, it says: 'Signature.' Who could that be for? My guardian or my next of kin?"

"The government does not require your signature, and no one will be asked to sign for you," said the lieutenant convincingly, but not without some irritation. If he didn't mean what he said, he had to be a great actor.

This time around Fotis found it more difficult to overcome his surprise, and in any case he couldn't come up with anything to say right away.

Then why bother to hand out the shithouse paper? I thought to myself, wishing that somehow Fotis would read my mind and say it out loud—the typical wish of a coward.

"Still, your release from Antikalamos will not be unconditional," the lieutenant went on.

Release? What release? I looked at Fotis again, only to realize that everybody else was doing the same. As for Fotis himself, he was still quiet, the redness of his cheeks giving way to paleness.

"Let me explain," said the lieutenant. He contemplated for a moment, and then he said, "Let me admit, too, that I am interested enough in you to appreciate knowing what's on your minds, even if that is contrary to what I've allowed myself to wish. So let me say this before I go on, and I am saying it mostly for you, Fotis: Whatever I know about you will not necessarily be documented and used against you."

"Now, that's different," whispered Matsoukas.

"Now, then." The lieutenant cleared his throat, as though

he'd heard Matsoukas. "I have drafted a plan according to which those of you who already know reading and writing would qualify for immediate release to any respectable business in Kalamos that is willing to offer you a job. Room and board will be the only compensation for your work, but in a few years' time you will have learned enough profitable skills to move on, free to travel to any part of the country or abroad, to be on your own. But until then you will depend on your sponsors, who will be filing progress reports with the police regularly. If the reports are negative, you will be sent back here, and if this camp has ceased to exist, as I hope it will, or if in the meantime you have reached the age of fifteen, you will be taken to an adult camp or prison."

"What are the chances of the government's approving that plan?" asked Fourkas.

"The government has already approved it, and several shop-keepers, businessmen and craftsmen have expressed interest in the sponsorship program. I know, there are people who might think all this is happening too fast, but if they ask me I'll say it's long overdue."

We were struck dumb. Sure, this was long overdue, but all the same things were going a little too fast, even to our way of thinking. The lieutenant went on talking about his plan and its advantages for us and for society, but I was no longer listening. A hot wave rose in my blood like fever, and I felt my hands shaking. I needed to think; I needed to go out and be by myself, to go out and breathe. Then the whispering among us became a constant buzz, the main barracks vibrating like a beehive.

"Any questions?" shouted the lieutenant.

Fotis raised his hand, and the noise quieted down. "If we are not required to sign this document, why was it given to us?"

"A good question, but I do not have the answer," grinned the lieutenant. "I suppose that someone at the Ministry of the Interior thought that this is an appropriate text for your literacy test. Or maybe this is the only printed matter that was available at the Ministry—stacks and stacks of it, I mean it. But you do not have to sign it. In fact, you don't even have to return it."

And then Polyvios raised his hand. "What about all those who haven't learned reading and writing yet?" he asked, as the noise began to increase again.

"They better hurry, before there is another change of government. Unless they prefer the detention camps," was the answer.

There were no more questions from us. Just noise.

"Is there anyone among you who would rather spend more time in detention camps?" shouted the lieutenant.

One single hand was raised, and once more the noise lessened.

"I," said Fotis. "Three hundred times," he said.

·27·

Saturday morning, Avramakis, Varant, Ke-kes and I and seven
more kids were boarding the lieutenant's motorboat for Kalamos. Everybody but Fotis had come to the mole to see us off,
and Miros was crying and doing all he could to make us feel
awful for going away without him. Ever since he woke up he'd
been reciting the alphabet and counting to a hundred, and
although he wasn't far from passing the literacy test of the
Ministry of the Interior, his being so little couldn't be to his
advantage in finding a sponsor in Kalamos. As for the remaining thirty-five who had passed the test, they would be sent to
the mother island at the rate of a dozen or more a week, depending on the arrival of summer vacationers and later on of
pilgrims for the Festival of Saint Thalassios.

They were all behind us now, waving at us from the rock,
looking smaller and smaller each time I turned to wave goodbye. Was all this real? One part of me believed everything, and
another believed nothing. And a third part, the littlest part of
all, was just asking questions.

"The sea," said Avramakis, shaking his head.

"What about it?"

"It's just too calm. And the air . . ."

"What about the air?"

"Too mild, too lovely. And the sky . . ."

"What about the sky?"

263

"I don't remember it being more beautiful."

"You're right, it's the clearest blue—a brillant morning."

"Too brilliant, I'm afraid. Everything's almost perfect."

"I don't mind it a bit."

"I don't, either. I'm just suspicious of it. I'd rather sail a stormy sea and find good weather on Kalamos," said Avramakis.

"Don't worry, the weather is general," said the lieutenant, who was showing Varant how to handle the rudder, and who'd heard only Avramakis' last sentence.

"Right," agreed Ke-kes. "This weather c-c-c-came all the way from Athens."

We all took turns at the rudder, and then, halfway between the two islands, the lieutenant turned off the motor and we scanned the area, hoping to locate the whirlpool that was supposed to be surfacing there from time to time, revealing the position of the old volcano.

"In Kalamos they say that the whirlpool is the eye of the volcano," said the lieutenant. "So if the eye is shut it probably means that the volcano is asleep, fast asleep," said the lieutenant, starting the motor again.

We moored the boat at what the lieutenant said was known as the Poor Fisherman's Mole, avoiding Skala, the deep-water harbor, and the attention of too many islanders and summer vacationers. That made us feel as if we were invading the island in broad daylight. During our climb up the hill to Hora we turned to look right and left and behind, to make sure we were not being spied on or followed by gendarmes or informers.

Already I could identify some of the scents that I'd detected on Antikalamos whenever the wind blew from this direction. Here, alongside the goat path, were thyme and oregano, the minty pennyroyal and the bitter chicory and other herbs sighing and filling the clean morning air with their sharp smells as we stepped on them in mock splayfoot stride, feet in dusty shoes spilling over the trail's borders of dust-over-green. And underneath the green, small workers sweating for their daily bread, and bread for the winter: bees, beetles and ants, and other summery bugs I hadn't seen in years.

Farther up the hill we were greeted by long-forgotten sounds: goat bells; the braying of a donkey hidden behind a drywall— all but his ears; the deaf cicadas, who deafened themselves with their own noise; a motorbike climbing up the other side of the hill; and even voices, words nipped at random by the breeze and scattered randomly like seeds: "July . . . ," "Cousin . . . ," "Well . . . ," ". . . carpenter," and ". . . the nets."

Soon enough we were walking in the narrow winding streets of Hora, greeting the old woman who whitewashed the front steps of her house and the curb and the greengrocer who followed his donkey, his roving stand loaded with baskets full of early tomatoes, cucumbers, squash, eggplant and peppers, stringbeans and herbs. Farther up, a young woman still in her nightgown watered the geraniums on her balcony, the dripping water causing the passersby to cross the street: we and the trash collector on this side, the trash collector's donkey on that—its own baskets, face and rump harassed by flies.

"Good morning, and where to?" we were greeted by a woman who dressed her little boy at the open window.

"Good morning, good morning," is all we said.

Kids playing with clay marbles, other kids shaking mulberries down from a heavy branch that bent over a courtyard wall, spilling streetward, the kids' hands and faces purple as though bruised from the mulberries.

Basil and marjoram, rosemary and dianthus and small white roses thriving in whitewashed cans on balconies, gates, steps— every house with its own collection, and the flower gardens too lush for the stone-disciplined eye. More likely to linger at the austere beauty of the one and only abandoned house on that street, a two-story house that had settled on one side over the years and now sat askew but freshly painted (by the next-door neighbor, perhaps), the fig tree having in the meantime broken

through a window on the north side and entered to take posses-
sion.

"Look!" said Ke-kes.

We looked. Someone had whitewashed a bougainvillea.

"C-c-c-couldn't get under its skirt to paint the wall," he
chuckled.

A priest had returned from Skala and stood by the well scal-
ing and cleaning the fish he'd just bought for his lunch. *"Kali-
mera, paidia,"* he greeted us.

"Kali orexi, Pater." Bless the fish that it may increase—so
fresh from the sea that once it's fried on one side it leaps into
the air and lands in the pan on the other, all by itself.

·28·

Lieutenant Müller took us to the police station, where we lined up while the chief of police and a gendarme did the paperwork for our transfer. We remained lined up for about an hour and a half, and then the chief of police ordered us to take off our clothes so that our sponsors could make sure that we were all right. The lieutenant thought this was unnecessary, but he didn't make a case of it. After all, it was summer. We were fine. Lean but hardy, and in good spirits. We were billy goats and rams, ponies and prized donkeys and mules, ready to change hands as at a country fair or a saint's festival.

"So what?" whispered Avramakis.

"Did I complain?" I said, glancing at his penis.

"Half the shame theirs, and the other half ours," said Avramakis.

"Speak for yourself," whispered Varant, covering his crotch.

First went Varant, to a barrel-maker from Skala, and then I was assigned to Kyr Thymios, a mild-mannered, stocky man of about sixty who owned the Leto, one of the two hotels on the island. He told the lieutenant that he'd just finished renovating the old hotel building and added another floor to it, thanks to a low-interest loan from the Commerce Bank, and was hoping to attract more guests this year, now that the war was over and people could travel again.

"Let me see your teeth," said Kyr Thymios.

I showed him my teeth.

"Purple," he said. "What have you been eating? Mulberries?"

I looked at the lieutenant, wondering if I could tell.

"Black-eyed beans," said the lieutenant. "They have a lot of iron, you know."

"So it's rust," decided Kyr Thymios.

I was allowed to put on my clothes while Kyr Thymios kept asking me questions: "Can you make additions? . . . Subtractions? . . . What do you want to become when you are a grown man? A Bolshevik? . . . Who are the Three Hierarchs of the Orthodox Church? . . . The last Emperor of Byzantium? . . . The current King and Queen of Greece? . . . Who was Apollon?"

"The son of Leto," I answered.

"By Zeus!" exclaimed Kyr Thymios. "But Apollon is also the name of the other hotel in Hora—the one that's competing with ours."

Ours? Ours was a three-story L-shaped building with a small entrance on the outside of the base of that L, and a terrace overlooking the sea on the inside. There was nothing special about it, except, first, that the new floor that had been added recently made the other two look their age, for the effort at uniformity was a token effort limited to the paint, and, second, that the Leto soared way above all the houses and shops of the neighborhood, claiming to be in the same league with buildings that housed such institutions as the city government, the Commerce Bank and the relics of Saint Thalassios, although each one of them was built at a different level of the hill town.

We went through a small unattended reception room straight to the kitchen, where Kyr Thymios' wife and a young girl prepared the meals and washed water carafes and glasses.

"Here he is!" announced my sponsor, presenting me to his wife. "Well, what do you say, Kyra Tassia?" Her full name must have been Anastasia, her name day celebrated on Easter Day.

She looked younger than Kyr Thymios, but not as lively; her pale skin and straight white hair that was combed back to a neat round bun made me think that she'd probably gone through a serious illness, or an unhappy marriage. And the color of her eyes was so light a blue it seemed unnatural: a bleached color, all the good blue washed out by the sea as if she made a habit of gazing at it for hours on end. Or else it had been washed away by tears. When she spoke, her voice sounded calm but not colorless: "Come closer, let me see your eyes."

"Never mind his eyes," joked Kyr Thymios—or maybe he wasn't joking. "Just check his fingernails and his ears," he said.

Kyra Tassia glanced at her husband as though reprimanding him, and, turning to me, she smiled, saying, "What is your name?"

"He can read and write," said Kyr Thymios. "He can add up sums, too. He even knows who Leto was!" he said.

"You don't say. What else do you know?" said Kyra Tassia.

I didn't like that question, but then she didn't mean it, either. Just the same, I didn't want to miss that opportunity to impress her, so I raced through my mind, trying to remember a few worthwhile items, but all I could think of that moment was how to graft an apple shoot to a quince tree, how not to cry in front of others but to wait for when I could be all alone, and how to endure pain without complaining. No, I wasn't going to mention any of these, and naming the twelve sons of Jacob would be as juvenile as naming the twelve gods of Olympos.

"Do you know any secret meanings?" she asked.

Now, that's entirely different. Once again I raced through my mind, digging up one after another the most exciting secret meanings that I'd discovered, and smiling.

"I think you know quite a few," said Kyra Tassia, pleased with herself.

"Well, tell us some," Kyr Thymios urged me.

"He won't," said Kyra Tassia.

"What? The first time he disobeys, back to Antikalamos he sails!"

"Some poet!" smirked Kyra Tassia at her husband's attempt to rhyme his warning. And she said, "A secret told is a secret lost."

"Nonsense," muttered Kyr Thymios, quite impressed by his wife's wisdom. Taking a cigarette out of his No. 3 carton of one hundred that was perched on a little shelf next to the stove, he broke it in two, and after putting the first half back into the carton he fitted the other half into a hand-carved cigarette holder. "You like my cigarette holder?" he said, noticing that I was looking at it. "It was made by a prisoner in the St. Stratis camp. And here's *my* secret meaning of the day: if he'd won the war it would be he running this hotel now, and me making the cigarette holders."

Maybe. But why did the blood rise to my eyes? Why did I feel like crying?

"You won't be a prisoner here," said Kyr Thymios, looking for his lighter, "but you won't be as free as the other boys of your age, either."

The girl who was washing a large copper pot now dried her hands on her apron and lit Kyr Thymios' cigarette with a match.

"This is Triantafyllia," said Kyr Thymios. "She's like a daughter to us." He then went on to describe my duties: Up at six, and first chore to sweep the terrace and wash the tabletops for breakfast. When the ice block is delivered, quickly into the icebox before it turns into a puddle out on the sidewalk. Next comes the milk and it sits on top of the ice. Don't forget this, or it'll turn into yogurt. Off to the baker then, for fresh bread. My own breakfast, bread and milk (or yogurt) left over from the day before. "You'll need a hearty breakfast before following Kyra Tassia to the market for food shopping," said Kyr Thymios. Serving the guests' meals and making sure to write everything down on each guest's account would be as important as any duty I performed. "But you won't be allowed to go to a guest's room, except with my permission, and stealing from the guests is punishable by death," warned my sponsor.

·29·

In the first few days of my internship at the Hotel Leto I was so terrified about doing something that would cause my being shipped back to Antikalamos that I ended up making several mistakes and breaking two water glasses and a dessert saucer. Kyr Thymios wrung my ear, lectured me, and in the evening he dutifully wrote everything down in a special notebook which he said was my record. It was to be a record of wrongdoing, and there would be no other record. Whatever I did right, it didn't seem to matter or to count. Because of the fear of being sent back, I had already lost all sense of excitement for my new life, and by Sunday I was so scared about Kyr Thymios' displeasure at my performance that I decided not to take any time off, and instead to take care of the terrace flower beds, cultivating and watering the geraniums, and looking around for other things that could be improved.

Triantafyllia, the girl who always seemed to be washing and drying pots and dishes in the kitchen, came out to the terrace all dressed up and said that it was wrong for me to be doing this kind of work on a Sunday. Didn't I already have a record-keeper of wrongdoings capable of missing nothing?

"If you think Kyr Thymios is unfair, you haven't seen anything yet," said Triantafyllia.

I didn't think he was unfair. I just wished I could learn everything faster, or that he could be a little more patient.

Triantafyllia had originally been adopted from the orphanage by a wealthy couple on the island, but a few months later she ran away and told the police that her stepparents beat her every day and that she wanted to return to the orphanage. The chief of police went around asking people if they could use some help at home, or at work if they owned a business, and Kyr Thymios and his wife talked about it and offered to take Triantafyllia in. This was her third year at the hotel. She worked hard. But she couldn't complain. "If you think Kyr Thymios is unfair, you haven't seen anything." I thought the reason I was granted a second life was exactly the opposite: that I had seen everything.

That Sunday Kyra Tassia baked a corn-almond cake, and when it set and it could be cut into neat triangle and trapeze-like portions, she called on Kyr Thymios to go into the kitchen and have a taste of it. She and Triantafyllia had already taken a bite or two, but they said nothing, waiting for Kyr Thymios' verdict.

Kyr Thymios took a bite, and then another before he'd even swallowed the first, rolling up his eyes.

"Well?" asked Kyra Tassia and Triantafyllia in one voice.

"No good," said Kyr Thymios categorically, guiding the rest of his portion into his mouth.

"I thought so myself," admitted Kyra Tassia.

I was still staring at my helping, a slave of the rich almond aroma and flavor, the snowy cloud of milk and powdered sugar.

"Aren't you even going to try it?" Triantafyllia asked me, mistaking my reverence for hesitation.

Quickly, I took a bite before anyone could put words into my mouth.

"He doesn't like it, either," said Triantafyllia.

And Kyra Tassia had to confess that the cake was too dry.

"Bitter too," added Kyr Thymios. "It's those wild almonds again."

I didn't understand. The cake was neither dry nor bitter. I took another bite, and it tasted even better. The soft, moist mouthful dissolved and slipped down my throat even before I swallowed.

"Too much cinnamon, too little sugar," fussed Kyr Thymios, finishing off his second piece.

The cinnamon was just right, and so was the sugar, especially on the top, each ingredient right and in the right proportion.

"The whole thing's for the birds," said Kyr Thymios, returning one-half of his third piece.

"I take no offense," said Kyra Tassia. "If something's for the birds, to the birds it goes."

"Take it to the coop, feed it to the chickens," Kyr Thymios told Triantafyllia.

Putting the rest of my helping into my mouth, I spread arms and legs in the opening of the door, intercepting Triantafyllia, who had already taken the cake and was on her way to feed it to the chickens. The world had gone mad and I was at a loss, ready to disobey my sponsor and risk being sent back to the camp just because I couldn't sit back and watch the chickens eat up the rest of the cake. "Please, don't," I was trying to say, but my mouth was too full for words.

"What did you say?" asked Kyr Thymios.

"Phmlfs vom-mum."

"Eh?"

I swallowed hard, and the words poured out of my mouth breathlessly: "Please don't feed it to the chickens I really don't see anything wrong with the cake it's the most wonderful thing that I've ever tasted I mean it honestly I like it very much let the chickens eat scraps . . ."

The three of them looked at one another and then at me again in amazement, and they burst out laughing, and in a few moments' time I knew without being told that I had made a perfect fool of myself. Of course, they weren't about to give the cake to the chickens, of course I could have another piece, any good entertainer deserves more than one piece of cake at the end of his act.

·30·

Later that Sunday afternoon Kyr Thymios and Kyra Tassia went to visit relatives in Skala, and I was left in charge of the reception desk. Triantafyllia had gone to her room, but she showed up again in a little while, carrying a small embroidered purse. I wondered if she too was going out.

"I am not allowed to go out alone yet," she explained. But then she realized that I was staring at her freshly pressed dress and her purse. "It's Sunday," she added. She took a newspaper from the magazine rack and began to turn the pages. "Kyra Tassia is thinking of buying some new clothes for you too, you know," she said, smiling from the top of the paper.

I wasn't sure I was going to believe anyone for a while after what had happened with the cake, but then I heard someone coming down the stairs and that was a good enough excuse for me to be distracted.

"Ah, Mrs. Becca," said Triantafyllia in pleased surprise.

Mrs. Becca was coming down the staircase carefully, left hand on the rail, right hand fanning herself with an oversized envelope. "*Ti zesti*," she said with a foreign accent, glancing now at Triantafyllia and now at me.

"Very hot," Triantafyllia agreed in English.

Mrs. Becca was from America, and this was her third trip to Greece, the second since the death of her husband. She was sixty-two according to her passport, and she looked thin and tall among Greeks. She had a long, bony face and an inexhaustible repertoire of expressions and grimaces that sometimes seemed theatrical because of her plucked eyebrows and bright makeup. Her hair was short but dark, without any sign of graying—the result of vitamins, according to Triantafyllia, of new improved dyes according to Kyra Tassia. She owned many dresses, which made one think of her as a rich woman, but she wasn't spending much on the island, and she never tipped. She was friendly, always with a nice word to say, and when she could say it in Greek everybody around was impressed, amused and flattered all at once. Mrs. Becca had learned some of her Greek from Triantafyllia, who in turn learned some English from her.

Since Triantafyllia wasn't going out, I decided to get my bucket of lime and a brush and give the front steps and the curb a fresh coat of paint. Those steps had been whitewashed so many times that they had lost their original lines, the sharp edges of the stone all rounded over, and the stone itself buried under two fingers of onionlike layers of lime—each layer representing not one but fifteen to twenty coats. Once in a while a bubble of air or a slow-dissolving speck in the lime would burst through and the small crater would allow a glimpse at the history of the place: prosperous layers, lean layers, layers separated by layers of dirt, each new layer whitewashing another layer, another paragraph, another chapter of history.

It was then, while whitewashing my first week's footsteps and history at the Hotel Leto, that I heard someone approaching from the street, and, turning, I saw Avramakis smiling, with open arms.

"You working on Sundays?" he said. "What is this?"

I stepped back so I could have a good look at him from head to toe. Avramakis wore a new shirt, a new pair of shorts, a new pair of sandals, and his hair was still wet from swimming. "Let's go in," I said, picking up my bucket and brush.

Triantafyllia and Mrs. Becca were still in the reception room, talking, so I led Avramakis straight to the terrace, where in the shade of the eucalyptus tree we could catch up with each other's news.

"Who is your friend?" asked Triantafyllia as we went through the second door. "Mrs. Becca wants to meet him."

"We'll be back," I promised.

We sat at a table in the shade, and I asked Avramakis if he cared for a cold lemonade.

"Maybe later," he said. Avramakis worked in a taverna down at Skala, and Kyr Nikos, his sponsor, let him take time off for siesta and, on Sundays, for a swim at the beach.

"How's the sea?" I asked.

"The sea's fine, thanks, but you've got to watch out for your clothes," said Avramakis. "If the gendarmes see you swimming in the nude they take your clothes to the police station, and you'll have to get there stark naked in order to claim them. It's an old custom, they say, and when you cross the square everybody comes out of the shops to poke fun at you."

"Did you have to go through that?"

"No, but Varant did. Poor Varant! You know how he hates to be caught with his pants down."

There was already a different air about Avramakis. In one week's time he'd loosened up, showing in every word and gesture how much he'd learned, how much he'd changed because of what he'd learned. He had even begun to pick up the local accent. I wasn't sure that I liked what was happening, what was bound to happen, and I wondered whether or not I was changing, too, without knowing it.

"You look well fed, but unhappy," observed Avramakis. "A swim in the sea can make a lot of difference, you know, and besides, if you don't come to the beach on Sundays, we'll never see each other."

I told him my troubles, told him about the record that Kyr Thymios kept of everything I did wrong, and how this could be my ticket back to Antikalamos.

'Nonsense," said Avramakis. "In a few more days they'll depend on us. In a few more weeks we'll be running this island." Avramakis said that that morning Lieutenant Müller had brought another dozen kids to Kalamos, including Trakas and Polyvios, and as the word spread on the island about the poor orphan kids the police station was flooded with requests. "Everybody wants to help the poor orphan kids," said Avramakis. "And why not? All one has to do is put the poor orphan kids to work—twelve hours a day," he said.

Back in the reception room, I introduced Avramakis to Triantafyllia and to Mrs. Becca, who wanted to know if he'd also graduated from the Antikalamos school.

"Yes," translated Triantafyllia, disregarding our chuckles about the words "graduated" and "school."

"What sort of school is it, anyway?" asked Mrs. Becca, intrigued by the grin on Avramakis' face.

"An experimental school. Can you translate that?"

"I can, but I don't understand what it means," complained Triantafyllia.

And Mrs. Becca said, "What sort of school, honey?"

"I've got to go now," said Avramakis.

"Wait, what's your hurry?"

"I have to work tonight. I have to light the charcoal and turn the lamb on the spit and then serve wine. It's going to be a big night down in Skala."

"Wait," said Triantafyllia. "Mrs. Becca wants to know what kind of name is Avramakis."

"It's from Avraam, a name like any other."

"And what about your second name?"

"We don't have second names," I explained.

"Like the ancient Greeks," said Mrs. Becca. "But Avraam is a Hebrew name, like mine."

"Becca?"

"Rebecca. What was your father's name?" she asked through Triantafyllia.

"I don't remember," said Avramakis. And, turning to Mrs. Becca, he said, "Father *kaput.*"

"*Kaput,* yes, *Alles kaput.* I know all about it," said Mrs. Becca, reaching out to touch Avramakis' head.

"I've got to go now. The lamb . . ." said Avramakis, moving toward the door.

"*Alles kaput,*" Mrs. Becca murmured again as though speaking to herself. There were tears washing her eye shadow and painting two purple trails down her cheeks.

·31·

My efforts to improve my work and think up jobs to do beyond my regular duties made a lot of difference during my second week at the Hotel Leto. Kyr Thymios seemed to have a hard time keeping up with me, but he didn't mind limiting his supervision to what he thought were the most difficult tasks of the day. Then came the first signs of approval by him, which startled me, but I didn't mind them as much as the lectures, the threats and the frequent entries into what soon proved itself to be a useless record of uselessness. "Eh, bandit!" Kyr Thymios would shout at me when I least expected it, and I'd freeze wherever I was, whatever I happened to be doing, thinking, What now?, but he'd only smile or wink at me, or just shake his head and fit half a cigarette to his hand-carved cigarette holder, the one made by the prisoner in the camp of St. Stratis, without bothering to explain his shouting to me, or his calling me "bandit."

By not having to worry too much about Kyr Thymios' rating of my performance, I now felt freer to look around and enjoy the small pleasures of waking up early in the morning and gazing from the hotel roof at the tiny Goat Island and the port town of Skala and the narrow streets of the neighborhood, wondering about all the people that I would meet, all the new things that I would see or hear about that day. There were pleasures to be enjoyed in the ways that people greeted one

another, the ways in which they bargained and did their shopping or trading of goods at the market where Kyra Tassia and I
bought fresh fish and vegetables each morning. How amazed I
was at the variety of goods displayed on shop shelves and
stands, inside baskets, barrels, boxes and cans, now wondering
and now asking how could anyone afford to buy so many
things, how could anyone eat so many different things without
getting a stomachache or constipation. Kyra Tassia would often
tease me and say that I was probably missing the black-eyed-
bean soup and galleta, that I probably preferred black-eyed-
bean soup to her cooking. Imagine it! But the truth was that
most of the time I sat down to eat I'd remember the hunger,
and the black-eyed-bean soup, and the kids who were still on
Antikalamos, and I'd play with my fork for a while, or put food
into my mouth but be unable to swallow it, and everybody
probably thought that the black-eyed-bean soup had destroyed
my taste buds, if not my brain. That's why Kyra Tassia teased
me. Then, when she realized how much harder I now worked,
she seriously advised me to start taking a little rest between
three and four in the afternoon, so I wouldn't feel tired in the
evening when some of the guests stayed on late having more
wine or brandy on the terrace. I tried that once, but I fell asleep
and had awful dreams, dreams that I was still in the cave, and
I got to be moody for hours after that. I must have had those
dreams because it was too hot to take my cot out into the open
air as I did in the night, and instead I lay down on it in the
washroom, which was narrow and dark. So instead of taking a
nap, I decided to spend that hour in the reception room, looking out at the empty street or leafing through the weekly magazines. One of those magazines, the *Bouquet*, carried several
novels in two-page installments. I began to read them and to
detest them. I went on reading them. They were about poor
and rich people who detested each other but kept falling in love
with each other just the same. Their private lives, their petty,
awkward, devious, dishonest and sorry ways were an embar-

rassment to anyone who could read, but I couldn't make up my mind about how much of the responsibility for that embarrassment was mine. And then I felt exactly the same way when I read the page about movie stars. Here there were even photographs to consider, making the embarrassment more personal. The stars were beautiful, rich, famous, and so their ways were more unusual than the ways of the novels' characters, and therefore difficult to understand. They seemed to get married and divorced as often as in their movie roles, which only meant that they were more confused about their lives than anyone who read that page. Since I hadn't seen a movie yet at that time, I wondered if going to the cinema would help me make some sense out of that confusion, or at least stop feeling bad about learning the secrets of those people's love affairs, marriages, broken promises and contracts, and in- and out-of-court settlements. Somewhere between the story characters and the movie stars were these nice-looking girls who liked to be photographed in their underwear, and who, according to the captions, were on their way to Hollywood to become famous stars. In the meantime, you could clip the photos and pin them to the wall so you could look at them all the time. Fine, but the captions were so foolish they didn't bear looking at twice. I began to clip and paste the photographs on individual sheets of notebook paper, and to write new captions and stories for them. I liked that. But when Kyr Thymios found out, he said I was destroying the magazines and wasting good writing paper, and he wouldn't have any more of that.

Mrs. Becca planned to stay at the hotel through the summer, perhaps until the Festival of Saint Thalassios, which was celebrated on the twenty-eighth day of August, but all the other guests had checked in for only a week or two each. Most of the rooms were still unoccupied, and Kyr Thymios spent about an hour every day answering inquiries by mail, making connections with travel agencies in Athens and Patras, and writing notes on the calendar, trying to keep as many rooms as possible filled at all times, regardless of how many guests checked-in and out of the hotel. No one else, not even Kyra Tassia, was allowed to make reservations, or to write a single word on the calendar. According to Kyr Thymios' predictions, the Leto would be full to capacity in July and the first three weeks of August, and full beyond capacity the week of the saint's festival.

The most recent arrival at the hotel was Mr. Hans, an elderly man from the Transvaal, South Africa. Mr. Hans seemed to know Greek well, but he rarely spoke any, and even then only in broken and unfinished sentences, as if his extensive repertoire of nonverbal sounds, gestures and grimaces was more in concert with his general feebleness and absentmindedness. Mr. Hans would say, "Yes, indeed," and then proceed to clear his throat, or blow his nose, or unplug his ear with his pinky, or press the corner of his handkerchief to the corners of his watery eyes, and if all these did not fill the silence he might add another word or repeat the word "Yes." Kyr Thymios said that according to his passport Mr. Hans had been born in Greece, but that his second name was as foreign as his given name. That was Bremer, a German name, all right, according to Mrs. Becca. And Mr. Larry, an Englishman who also stayed at the Leto, thought it could very well be a Dutch name. From time to time a significant word like "diamonds," or "friend," or "General," would sneak out of his mouth between a yawn and a sneeze, and we'd prick up our ears in hopes of learning something about Mr. Hans, but the inevitable "ah-choo!" and subsequent sounds and gestures would wipe out hint and hope alike. Mr. Larry wondered if Mr. Hans weren't a victim of amnesia or of some other form of forgetfulness, the result of senility, or arteriosclerosis, a kind of disease that causes old people to slow down so they can die gracefully.

· 32 ·

Kyr Thymios had known Mr. Larry since the war, when the English did the spying here and the Greeks the fighting. Mr. Larry got to know the islands so well he now wrote books and articles about them, and some tourists came from England and America straight to the Leto thanks to his published recommendation. In return, Mr. Larry's favorite drink, Masticha (the mastic retsin-flavored ouzo), was permanently on the house. Mr. Larry drank a lot of Masticha. He'd return to the hotel after having spent the early part of the evening drinking with the fisherman at Skala, and, finding an empty table on the terrace, he'd order a *karafaki*, a small carafe, and sip quietly, raising his glass each time a fishing boat or a liner sailed aglow between the Goat Island and the southern promontory.

One evening we ran out of Masticha, and Mr. Larry didn't even want to hear about the plain old ouzo that came from Lesbos and was praised by everyone on the island.

"Pf," he said. But when he heard Kyr Thymios sending me off to Diakos' taverna to fill the demijohn with his heart's delight, Mr. Larry was embarrassed. "Never mind," he said. "It's too late, the taverna is probably closed. It's all right, I'll take a pill."

"A sleeping pill? A-*pa-pa-pa-pa!*" Kyr Thymios would rather send me to the taverna.

I wondered what a sleeping pill was and what happened when

285

it woke up. In a way Masticha was a sleeping drink as long as it was kept in the bottle, but I had trouble imagining a little pill substituting for a *karafaki*. A-*pa-pa!* I was off to Diakos' taverna. Kyra Tassia had shown me the little yellow basement door of the place one morning during our shopping expedition, so I didn't have trouble finding it. I climbed up the stair to the street carrying the full bottle as the last customers gathered by the door, stalling and chatting, wishing each other well till tomorrow, and I heard one of them say: "Keep an eye . . . youngsters. . . . Everyone . . . dangerous."

He must have referred to me—to every one of us coming from Antikalamos, the red-stone island. I decided to take a back road to the hotel, to get there faster and to avoid drawing the attention of any more law-abiding, peace-loving islanders.

And then I got lost. It happened when I heard steps behind me and thought that someone was following me. The wind seemed to have increased, or just the running made the sea breeze feel stronger on my face. There were no street lights and no moon; the little houses were quiet behind their shuttered windows. Some people always slept in their courtyards or terraces in the summer. I kept running forward, although I was sure I'd already taken one wrong turn. I didn't want to turn back, from fear I might run into whoever was coming after me. I could still hear his steps clearly on the cobblestones. I held the bottle by the wicker handle and the bottom and tried to run faster. I could see the whitewashed walls of the houses on both sides of the street, the lime glowing as though it had its own source of light, but each stretch of covered walkway was pitch-black, and I worried I might run into a dead end. I thought I had a good sense of direction, but what's the use of it without side streets to turn to? A *frrrt!* across the street, a cat climbing the honeysuckle on the wall, then staring at me with glowing eyes, terrified. The cat had crossed the street because the street had come to an abrupt end, just what I was afraid of. I hid in the darkest corner I could find, panting. Whoever was running behind me must have stopped also. The top of a hibiscus tree heaved gently, shedding the neatly rolled blossoms of the day. Past the treetop, along the edge of the terrace, a row of whitewashed tin pots of basil and marjoram.

Moving to the opposite side of the street, I saw an abandoned house, the wrought-iron gate to its front yard open. Cautiously, I walked in. Dried-out plants and thorns rustling between my feet, scratching me. It was even darker there, since the house hadn't been painted recently. A wooden stair took me to the second floor and to a balcony from which I thought I might see the lights of the hotel. It must have been quite some time since I'd left the taverna, and I wondered what Kyr Thymios would be thinking. I could imagine him looking at the clock every two or three minutes, then apologizing to Mr. Larry, saying how crazy kids are nowadays, promising to wring my ear full circle.

Another house nearby blocked my view, but there was enough light for me to see the little footbridge connecting the two houses at the second-floor level. A few days before, I had seen two similar houses linked by a footbridge, and I smiled. I'd seen them from the roof of the hotel, and I wondered about the relationship between the two families, and what became of them. Were they friends, getting together during the long winter evenings to pass the time, or were they close relatives, brothers and sisters who visited back and forth too often not to want to save some footwork? It occurred to me then that all this must have come to an end sometime during the war, during one of the wars: was it hunger? illness? prison? the firing squad? It often took more than one cause for families such as these to perish.

Out of the gate and into the street, I ran into a man, who grabbed me by the shoulders and lowered his face closely to mine.

"No!" I screamed, shaking.

"Shh. I mean no harm," he said, his breath smelling of wine.

"What do you want?" I shouted, hoping someone would hear.

"You are from the camp—from Antikalamos," he said. He was one of the men I'd seen in the taverna.

Terrified, I waited.

"Tell me. Is there someone by the name Pavlos in that camp?"

Still trembling, I tried to understand.

"Here," he said, putting some money into my hand. And he said, "Pavlos Vafiades. He's your age. Blond hair . . . speaks Italian . . ."

"But who are you?" I asked.

"His uncle. I have been trying to find him and take him home for almost two years now."

"I am sorry," I said. "He was here, but he escaped. They say he's in Ancona, Italy. I know nothing else." And, returning his money, I began to run.

I ran, feeling the briny wind on my cheeks and through my hair, my saliva streaming from the corner of my mouth, the smells of basil and marjoram stronger than before, as if somewhere in the sea there were vast gardens of basil and marjoram. I took two more turns, both to the right, and I ran the last hundred meters competing with the wind that blew in the same direction. I rushed into the kitchen breathless, not knowing how to start apologizing, how to explain my being so late, what to say. I just handed Kyr Thymios the bottle and collapsed into a chair, saying nothing.

"Back already?" he said. He wasn't being funny.

According to the clock, I had gone to the taverna, bought the Masticha ouzo, gotten lost and found my way back to the hotel in exactly fourteen minutes. It couldn't be possible.

"Slow down," said Kyr Thymios, filling a *karafaki* from the demijohn. "You could have stumbled and fallen and lost all this ouzo. Slow down, I'm not going to send you back to the camp."

Mr. Larry was delighted to see me. He moved an English magazine and a notebook to the far end of his table to make room for the *karafaki* and a saucer of olives on toothpicks, smiling, then rubbing his hands with anticipation. "Excellent!" he said. And he said, "Now, if I were you, I wouldn't give up sticking pictures into notebooks and writing captions for them."

How did he know?

"Kyr Thymios showed me," said Mr. Larry. "Not bad," he said again. "Not bad at all. If I were you I wouldn't give it up just like that."

"Well, maybe if I were you I wouldn't give it up, either."

"Ha! That's the spirit." Mr. Larry raised his glass, toasting me.

And I nodded, feeling like a ghost ship sailing with some of its lights out between the Goat Island and the promontory.

·33·

As the days grew longer and the midday sun seemed to stand
still for hours on end and the period of noontime rest throughout Kalamos was extended to 5 P.M., the morning and evening
hours became increasingly busy. Now the S.S. *Glaros* docked
twice a week at Skala, unloading dozens of vacationers in colorful dresses and funny hats and with all sorts of luggage: suit-
cases, baskets and bags. And as Kyr Thymios predicted, by the
beginning of July every room of the Leto was occupied, and we
had to send anyone who had not made a reservation off to the
Hotel Apollon, where Trakas now worked. And there were so
many rooms to be cleaned, and beds to be made twice a day,
that Kyr Thymios had to hire a woman so that Kyra Tassia and
Triantafyllia could meet the increased demand in the kitchen.
Several of the old guests were still there, and although we paid
special attention to them, we saw less of them and rarely had
the time or the peace of mind to carry on a long conversation
with them. The coming and going of so many people, single,
elderly, and couples with children, their routines and unpre-
dictable needs and requests, even between two and five in the
afternoon, forced a new rhythm to our lives, and a tenser atmosphere throughout the hotel. Kyr Thymios became frantic
trying to satisfy his guests and to keep track of their accounts.
Kyra Tassia, on the contrary, was able to retain her calmness
despite the additional work and responsibility. Triantafyllia and

I tried to emulate Kyra Tassia, but ended up running about as confused as Kyr Thymios.

Skala was always more crowded, especially in the evening, when the cool sea breeze attracted hundreds of islanders and guests to the pleasures of the promenade along the crescent of moored fishing boats, the outdoor tavernas and Kyr Nikos' restaurant, where Avramakis offered octopus and crab on the grill with each *karafaki* of ouzo or bottle of retsina wine, while Ioanna the Rebetissa sang to the accompaniment of guitar and bouzouki. When, late at night, I went to the roof of the Leto and pulled my cot out of the washroom and lay down exhausted, I listened to Ioanna's songs in the distance, and I slowly fell asleep thinking about her and about the people in her songs. Those people were homeless, living in ruins, or they were desperate lovers, or criminals who spent the rest of their lives in prison. It was never too clear, though, what crimes they had committed, and sometimes I thought they sounded too good to be common criminals; more likely they were political prisoners, and if there was a crime connected with them it was probably the crime that was committed against them. Avramakis, who could see and listen to Ioanna closely every night, was crazy about her, especially since that Friday night when she pinched his cheek and told him to quit shaving his mustache, because she liked only men wearing thick black mustaches. What a tease!

The most impressive mustache in those days belonged to a new guest at the Hotel Leto. Mr. Elias, a tall middle-aged man from Piraeus, had checked in with a much younger woman whom he introduced as his sister, Loula. Mr. Elias had a black handlebar mustache which he kept perfectly groomed at all times, even at noon when he'd just returned from the beach, but he never went to Skala to hear Ioanna sing, so she never got to see the greatest mustache on the island. Mr. Elias and Miss Loula slept in adjoining single bedrooms on the second floor, and every morning they walked down to the beach, hold-

ing hands. Miss Loula was a blonde and wore bright-orange
lipstick and rouge and an unusually strong perfume that
smelled like camphor. Mr. Elias had something fake about
him, but I couldn't tell whether it was his mustache or everything except his mustache that gave me this impression. At any
rate, I doubted that he was Miss Loula's real brother. But then,
as Mr. Larry remarked one morning over his first glass of Masticha after breakfast, Miss Loula's heavy makeup and unpleasant perfume made her an unlikely sister for anyone.

Later that very same day, though, Mr. Elias and Miss Loula
took me by surprise when after dinner they went to introduce
themselves to Mr. Hans, the old man from South Africa, and
then to join him at his table for dessert and coffee. It was a
pleasant surprise, especially since by that time everybody else
at the hotel seemed to have given up on poor Mr. Hans on
account of what they said must be a case of advanced senility.
Still, the old gentleman showed no excitement, nor even interest, at Mr. Elias and Miss Loula's kindness to him, and from
what I overheard as I took their order for brandy, Mr. Hans
was as vague, as forgetful and finally as eccentric as ever. I was
sorry for him. No doubt it was a matter of time before Mr. Elias
and Miss Loula would lose all interest in his company and
would find someone who was more talkative to associate with
in the five or so remaining days of their vacation.

Throughout that summer I saw many interesting and even
fascinating people come and go, but the Hotel Leto also had
more than just a share of the world's least interesting, most
boring and outright awful characters, who demanded all of our
attention, did most of the complaining, and seemed to have no
sense of their place in the world, and no sense of humor whatever.

As the number of vacationers arriving from Athens and Patras increased, so did the number of friends arriving from Antikalamos. They were in every part of the island, working and
learning skills in bakeries, restaurants, grocery stores, fields,

fishing boats and offices—painting houses, washing windows, selling vegetables, delivering cases of gazoza and mineral water, repairing shoes, weaving chair seats, soldering or galvanizing copper, sweating over the bellows with blacksmiths, sweeping wood shavings and sawdust in carpenters' shops, bleaching sponges. And on Sundays some of them could be seen in church, and most of them at the beach. One had to be decently dressed to enter the church, but one had to leave his clothes behind to take a dip; at the beach, we could also see how well each of the others was being fed.

Minos had been at Hora for almost two weeks, but I'd seen him only once, briefly, while Kyra Tassia and I did the day's shopping. Minos worried about being late, so he couldn't talk much, except to say that each time he returned from an errand Kyria Marianthe, to whose household he was assigned, would glance at the clock and make a note in a special book with his name on it. Minos had been released to Kyria Marianthe on condition that she would send him to school in September. Later on I learned that Kyria Marianthe was confined to a wheelchair and never left the house, not even on the day of Saint Thalassios' Festival. Kyra Tassia said that the old woman was well off and could afford a cleaning woman and a gardener. Minos was her new gardener. The next time I saw Minos, he confessed that one of his most important duties was to go to church every Sunday morning—but to go on Kyria Marianthe's behalf: to pray on her behalf, and to confess and take Communion on her behalf. Still, she didn't believe in miracles.

άπελευθέρωση. Είναι όμως καὶ ρεαλιστική;

Ὁ Πέτρος Ροῦσος, στὸ βιβλίο του «Ἡ Μεγάλη «Πενταετία», ἀπευθυνόμενος πρὸς ἀριστερούς ἀναγνώστες καὶ προσπαθώντας νά δικαιολογήσει τὸ «ὄχι» τοῦ ΚΚΕ, ἰσχυρίζεται πὼς ἡ ἡγεσία του δὲν ἀνήθηκε τή συγκρότηση τοῦ Βαλκανικοῦ Στρατηγείου οὔτε τό τορπίλλισε. «Ζήτησε ἀπλῶς – γράφει – ἀναβολή τοῦ ζητήματος μέχρι νά δημιουργηθοῦν οἱ ὅροι». Γιατί αὐτὲς οἱ μασημένες δικαιολογίες; Ὁ ἴδιος ἀναφέρει ὡς ἑξῆς τοὺς λόγους ποὺ ὤθησαν τό πολιτικό γραφεῖο τοῦ ΚΚΕ στήν ἀπόφασή του:

«Πρῶτο, νά στερεώσουμε τὴν ἐθνικοαπελευθερωτική συμμαχία, νά μήν προκαλέσουμε δυσανασχέτηση τῶν συμμάχων μας στό ΕΑΜ καὶ σὲ ἄλλους ἐνδεχόμενους συμμάχους μας. Δεύτερο, νά μήν ἐπισπεύσουμε ἔνταση τῶν ἀντιδράσεων καὶ ἐπεμβάσεων τῶν Ἄγγλων στήν Ἑλλάδα προτοῦ προλάβει νά στερεωθεῖ τό ἐπαναστατικό κίνημα στὴν Ἑλλάδα ἤ τουλάχιστον στή Γιουγκοσλαβία. Τρίτο, νά μή δημιουργήσουμε πρόωρα ἐμπόδια στὴν παγκόσμια ἀντιχιτλερική συμμαχία, τά ὁποῖα ἄγνωστο ἄν θά μπορέσουμε τελικά νά ὑπερπηδήσουμε ὅσο βαστάει ὁ πόλεμος κατά τῶν καταχτητῶν».

Μακεδόνες καὶ Μεγαλόσερβοι

Ὁ Κώστας Καραγιώργης ὅμως, ποὺ ἀναμείχθηκε ἄμεσα στό θέμα, ὅπως εἴδαμε, σὲ ἰδιαίτερη συνομιλία ποὺ εἶχε· μὲ τόν ἀράφοντα τό 1946, καθαρά καὶ σταράτα ἔδωσε τὴν ἐξήγηση:

– Ἄκου...

γοι ποὺ ...
λιτικό μ...
ὅτι τό Ε...
λουθοῦσ...
ματα. Δ...
λίγο πρίν...
Διεθνής...
τῆς δέν ...
ὅπως κα...
ἐδείχνε π...ς ὁ Στάλιν ἀντιμετωπίζε ἀκόμη πολύ μεγάλες δυσκολίες. Πῶς ἦταν ὑποχρεωμένος νά κάνει κι ἄλλες βαριές θυσίες γιά νά διατηρήσει τή συμμαχική ἑνότητα χωρίς τὴν ὁποία μπορούσε νά χαθεῖ τό πᾶν. Καὶ δέν ξέρω πὼς ὁ Τίτο καὶ ὁ Τέμπο κάναν τοῦ κεφαλιοῦ τους, ἐμεῖς ὅμως διστάζαμε νά καταφέρουμε μιά μαχαιριά στά νεφρά τῆς μεγάλης συμμαχίας. Γιατί κάτι τέτοιο θά ἦταν ἄν ἀπροκάλυπτα ὀρθωνόμαστε μαζί μὲ τοὺς Ἀλβανούς καὶ Γιουγκοσλάβους κατά τῶν Ἄγγλων. Ὅλα αὐτά ὅμως ἦσαν δευτερεύοντα μπροστά σέ ἕναν ὀγκόλιθο ποὺ θά σοῦ ἀποκαλύψω».

Καὶ καθὼς ὁ γράφων τέντωνε τόν λαιμό του καὶ τά αὐτιά του γιά νά ἀκούσει, ὁ Κώστας Καραγιώργης συμπλήρωσε:

– Ἐκεῖνο ποὺ μᾶς τρόμαξε εἶναι ἄλλο: Εἴχαμε πληροφορίες ἄλλά καὶ ἀντιληφθή

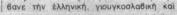

βανε τήν ἑλληνική, γιουγκοσλαβική καὶ

«... Ἡ σκέψη τῶν Γιουγκοσλάβων καὶ τῶν Ἀλβανῶν συντρόφων νά ἐπηρεάζουν πρός ὁρισμένη πολιτική τίς ἀντίστοιχες ἔνοπλες δυνάμεις τῶν ἐθνικῶν μειονοτήτων στήν Ἑλλάδα (Σλαβομακεδόνων καὶ τσάμηδων Ἀλβανῶν)...

Ὅσοι τρέφουν αὐτή τήν ἰδέα ξεχνοῦν ὅτι: Στή Γιουγκοσλαβία μὲ τὴν ἀπελευθέρωση ὑπῆρχαν 30 μεραρχίες σοβιετικοῦ στρατοῦ. Στήν Ἑλλάδα μετά τὴν ἀπελευθέρωση ἦρθαν 3 μεραρχίες ἀγγλικοῦ στρατοῦ.

Ἀλλά πολύ χαρακτηριστικά ὁ Πέτρος Ροῦσος παρατηρεῖ:

«Γιουγκοσλάβικα καὶ ἰδίως ὁρισμένα σλαβομακεδονικά στελέχη τῆς γειτονικῆς χώρας ἀψηφοῦσαν τίς συνέπειες ποὺ θά 'χει σ' ὅλον τόν ἑλληνικό ἀγώνα καὶ στόν ἀγώνα τῶν βαλκανικῶν λαῶν ἡ ἄμεση υἱοθέτηση ἀπό μᾶς τοῦ συνθήματος "ἑνιαία Μακεδονία στά πλαίσια τῆς νέας Γιουγκοσλαβίας". Ὑπάρχουν καὶ σήμερα ἀκόμη ὁρισμένοι τους ποὺ λένε πὼς καὶ ἄν ἀκόμα δέν ἐλευθερωνόταν ἡ Ἑλλάδα ἀπό τόν ἰμπεριαλισμό. θά εἶνε ἐλευθεωθεῖ τουλάνι-

Ὁ Τίτο κατά

Καὶ τώρα ἔνα ...
γνώση τοῦ Τίτο ...
Τέμπο; Ἀσφαλ...
ὅσο τελικά ὁρίσ...
πρόσωπος τῆς ...
σχεδιασμό στρα...

Ὥστε ὁ Τίτο υ...
Μεγαλοσέρβων ...
γκοσλαβίας;

Ἡ ἀπάντηση, ...
δοξο, εἶναι κα...
στούς πολλούς ...
μὲ ἐντολή του ...
τερα τά γιουγκ...
ψαν τό ἀντίθετο ...
καὶ ἀδιάψευστα ...

Ὁ Τίτο πράγμ...
σύσταση Βαλκ. Σ...
κοὺς λόγους. Κ...
ταν στόν στρατι...
ἦταν κακή. Ἀλλά ...
μεγαλοσέρβικοι ...
κοί κύκλοι – ὑπο...
νιστικοῦ βρασμ...
νήσου – γιά νά δ...
τόν τον μηχανισ...

Ἄργησε νά τό ...
τῆς ἀραιῆς ἐπικ...
τό καλοκαίρι του ...
μάχη ζωῆς ἤ θα...
των. Ὅταν πλη...
γίνει, ἡ ἀντίδρ...
Ἔσπευσε νά δια...
...αγγελίαι...
Τέμπο νά ...
γεῖο γιατ...
...υστό».

...άμμα το ...
...μίζει:

...σημερ...
...ὁποιουδ...
...τό λάθος, ...
...χαριστικ...
...λή του πρ...
...δημιουργί...
λεῖ ἀνοησία».

Τά μηνύματα ...
στρατηγό του δ...
νος τά εἶχε λάβ...
«ὄχι» τοῦ Σιάντ...
πυρώσει τό θέμ...
τήσει ὁριστικά.

Ἄλλωστε, τώ...
παρτιζάνοι ὅπως ...
βρίσκονταν μπρ...
ἀνατροπή: Ἡ Ἰτ...
Καὶ στόν βαλκα...
σποτε ἔνας ὁλό...
γέρας τῶν δυν...
χώματα τῆς Γιου...
...ι την Ἑλλάδ...

Τό ΚΚΕ λέει:

·34·

The next week Avramakis and I waited until after the liturgy to go to the beach, hoping that Minos might join us. We located the gardener's shack behind a row of apricot trees, but Minos was terrified to see us.

"That's awful," he kept on saying, glancing toward the house, afraid that Kyria Marianthe saw everything and approved of nothing.

"Get your bathing suit and let's get going," ordered Avramakis.

"What? I don't have a bathing suit."

"That's all right, we don't have bathing suits, either. We'll take the risk."

"I can't go—she'll send me back to the camp. She's writing everything down, I tell you."

"So you like it here after all," I said to Minos.

Minos shrugged.

"Well?" asked Avramakis.

"So far so good," said Minos.

"Let's go swimming now."

"I'm afraid to."

"Well, go ask her, or tell her afterward that you couldn't resist the temptation."

"Maybe some other Sunday," I suggested, dragging Avramakis by his belt.

Halfway between Hora and the beach, Minos was catching up with us, panting.

"You couldn't resist the temptation," said Avramakis.

"She gave me permission," replied Minos, panting triumphantly.

"That was too easy," brooded Avramakis. "Everything's just a little too easy around here. I don't like it."

"She also said the next time you show up in the garden, she wants to have a word with you," said Minos.

"A word of wisdom, to be sure." Avramakis led the way past the public baths to a rocky stretch of the shore which had pockets of sand and was used only by kids who didn't have bathing suits and had to swim naked. When we got there we were greeted by Trakas, Şükrü, Ke-kes, Varant, Polyvios and a dozen or so more kids from Antikalamos, who were diving from the rocks or rubbing their heels in the sandy bottom of the shallows, searching for shells. We took off our clothes and dived in, Avramakis and I from the rock, Minos from down below, and we swam for a while, cooling off, then joined the kids who played with a rubber ball, chasing and splashing one another. We felt clean and healthy; we felt strong. Many years before—"Oh, forget," I said, and everything in between, between then and now, mattered little.

The rest of the afternoon turned out to be less pleasant but not less memorable, when two gendarmes came from behind the rocks, picked up our clothes and sandals, and hurriedly made for the town without turning to look back. That was the unpleasant part. The memorable part came later, when for the last time we did something worthwhile as a group, as one body and mind. The mind belonged to the body, and the body was naked, stark naked, made up of seventeen smaller bodies and thirty-four legs. We climbed up the same rocks, heading toward Hora on the same road. We followed the two gendarmes at a distance, but when we reached the market we had to stop.

"Here they come," said Trakas, who was at the head of the column.

Several men had gotten up from their chairs under the shed of the *kafeneion* and waited for us, blocking our way.

"March on!" shouted Avramakis. "Half the shame ours and half theirs!"

When was the last time he'd said that?

"At the police lineup," said Varant, who'd already gone through this once.

A fishmonger, a barber and a waiter ran to join the others, asking what went on.

On our side Ke-kes was asking the same question.

"They're dressed and we're naked, that's what," said Varant.

We had to answer questions and more questions, take the teasing and the jokes.

"Watch out, your little Napoleons could get sunburned," chortled a little old man, probing Varant's genitalia with the tip of his walking stick.

And the barber approached Trakas, clicking his scissors in the air threateningly.

The waiter, who carried several cups of coffee and glasses of water in his tray, was asking Şükrü what pleased him.

The Turk was thirsty. "A glass of ice water," he said, licking his lips. "Please," he said.

"Coming right up!" said the waiter, and he promptly poured a glass of ice water on Şükrü's crotch.

"They're the kids from the Bandit army," said someone else. "They have no morals."

Several of them followed us all the way to the police station, and while we were waiting for the chief they stayed out in the street telling jokes and shouting.

"They'll be charged for disturbing the peace," said the gendarme, meaning us.

"Disorderly conduct too," said another.

Once again we were lined up and waiting.

At one point we heard the chief of police shouting, "Get them out of here! Out! Out! Out!" There was a brief pause and then he said, "All the others can go. And if you catch them swimming in the nude again, don't bother to bring them here. Ship them to Antikalamos!"

"Well, you heard the chief," said the gendarme, throwing the pile of clothes at our feet. And then he said, "Which one of you is assigned to the Hotel Leto?"

Everybody's eyes turned in my direction.

"You are staying," said the gendarme.

·35·

Minos and Avramakis promised to wait for me out in the street, but I doubted that I would join them again that day. I had been allowed to dress and wait in the hallway, and I was silently debating the seriousness of the situation, trying to figure out what I had done to draw the attention of the chief of the police, listing the reasons why I shouldn't be sent back to Antikalamos in the next boat, then taking a deep breath and reassuring myself that everything was going to work out all right, when a door opened up across the hall and the chief signaled to me to go into his office.

"Close the door," he said, sitting behind his desk, centering his chair between the desk and a framed photograph of the King and the Queen on the wall.

I centered my position halfway between the door and the chief's desk and stood at attention.

"At ease!" he commanded, staring into my eyes gravely, while the King looked on and the Queen smiled benevolently. "You are assigned to the Hotel Leto," said the chief, as though that were a new order. And then the tone of his voice changed completely. "How's Kyr Thymios?" he said in that relaxed, friendly tone.

"Oh, he's fine."

"He is fine, *sir*," the chief corrected me. "And how is the business?"

"There're no vacancies, sir. We're very busy."

"But you can still find time to go to the beach."

"Only with Kyr Thymios' permission, sir."

"So you can't complain."

"Not at all, sir."

"I take it you wouldn't want to be sent back to Antikalamos."

"Oh, no, sir. I like my job a lot, and my sponsors are very nice to me."

"Yes," he said. He was thinking. "Then we must make sure that you won't have to return to Antikalamos." He opened a drawer, looked into it, and pushed it shut again. He was thinking. He then reached to the front of his desk and picked up a paper knife that lay in state like a dead general at the head of an army in which a ruler was second in command, the pen holder a sergeant, and an assortment of pencils the troops, all neatly lined up as though they'd been caught on the beach without bathing suits, or had been wounded in battle and were waiting to be decorated by the King. In this fine arrangement the inkwell served as headquarters, and the blotter as barracks. Now the chief was staring at me again.

Did I owe him a response? "I agree, sir," I said, a little worried.

The chief acknowledged my attention and glanced at the pinky of his left hand, the nail of which was exceptionally long and had a fine black crescent at its base.

I was out of danger, I could sense it, but working hard at the hotel and keeping out of trouble weren't enough. The chief was about to put a new price to freedom, to my freedom anyway. "Is there something I can do for you, sir?" I asked, hoping I wasn't being too helpful.

"For me?" he said, a pretense of surprise at the corners of his stretched-out lips. "No-no-no—nothing for me, young man." His eyes were still on me, but part of his mind would not leave his right hand, the hand that held the paper knife, the sharp point of which kept inching its way toward the idle fingers of his left hand, threateningly.

"But you can do something for the law—if you are on the side of the law," said the paperknife.

"Oh, I'm on the side of the law, all right."

"Good!" said the chief. And without removing his eyes from me, he guided the tip of the paper knife under the nail of his pinky, and before I knew it the little black crescent was gone and the sky of his long fingernail was moonless and clear.

"No doubt about that, sir."

The chief laid the paper knife down at the head of the small army on his desk and, leaning back in his chair, said, "I have information that something strange is going on at the Hotel Leto, that in fact one strange thing has already led to another. There seems to be something wrong with the old man from South Africa, and something equally wrong with the couple—the two new guests who befriended him . . ."

"Mr. Elias and Miss Loula?"

"Correct."

"It's true that they showed some interest in Mr. Hans while everyone else was avoiding him," I said.

"There's nothing wrong with that. In a free country everyone is free to associate with everyone else. But the police have reason to suspect fraud, a criminal transaction or some sort of conspiracy."

"On the part of Mr. Hans?"

"On the part of anyone. It could be our old friend Mr. Larry, or Mrs. What's-her-name."

"But what can I do, sir?"

"Spy on them. On all of them. See if you can learn anything about any plans they might have. Try to pick up whatever you can from their conversations. Anything."

"There's a problem, sir. Kyr Thymios has warned me never to eavesdrop or repeat anything that I might overhear from the guests."

"I am glad to know that. Kyr Thymios is an honest man."

"Very honest, sir. If I don't follow his instructions he'll write a bad report on me, and I'll be sent back to Antikalamos before I know it." No, it wouldn't work.

"You need not worry about that. Nobody gets sent to the camps for helping the authorities."

How true.

"If you get in trouble I'll intervene," promised the chief. "But you must understand that I don't want to let Kyr Thymios or anyone else in on this right now."

"I understand, sir."

"Now, it may be that in two, three days we'll get enough information from Athens to move in on that sleazy couple or on someone else, by which I mean that you won't have to do anything whatsoever and you will still be in good standing with the authorities; but we can't always count on Athens—we have to do our part too, don't we?"

Who was I to disagree? "I'll do my best, sir."

"I thought you would. You may go now."

·36·

Friday afternoon, siesta time, I was lazily sweeping the terrace, when a crow came and perched in the eucalyptus tree and began to preen the underside of its wings, stopping now and then to stare at me or at my broom. My broom didn't like being watched while working, so up it swung in hopes of scaring away the crow. No luck. The broomstick too short. I thought the crow might just be stuffed with straw and tied to its branch with wire. If only it weren't for the sun among the leaves, through the leaves. The leaves were still, but the light wasn't. I looked around. Nothing else stirred. And the sea was no comfort. And the promontory cast no shadow into the water. Not really. The Goat Island stretched out its neck as far as it could, but there was no green leaf in the midst of light.

Friday afternoon, siesta time, except for those who resist rest and dread sleep and dreaming.

An old man who looked like a beggar sat on the front steps of the hotel, and when he saw me he stood up and pointed at me with his hardwood stick. "So you're going to be a police informer." he said.

"What?" Where did he get that?

" 'I'll do my best, sir,' " he said. " 'I thought you would,' " he added.

I wished I didn't have to lie to the chief of police, I wished I could afford to be straight with him and just tell him to go piss.

"Or maybe you won't become a police informer," said the beggar.

I would not. I had no intention of spying on anyone. Not on Mr. Elias and Miss Loula, nor on Mr. Larry or Mrs. Becca, nor even on poor old Mr. Hans.

"That Mr. Hans," said the beggar.

If the chief of police summoned me to report on my findings, I would say I'd noticed nothing unusual, heard nothing worth repeating. I would not be a police informer, and I would not be sent back to Antikalamos either.

"That Mr. Hans . . ."

I waited.

"It's nothing, forget it," said the beggar.

Unfamiliar voice, and hair gray with dirt. The wrinkled face unshaved, the wrinkles filled with dust. And when he dusted off the seat of his pants, a cloud of soot ascended in the light.

I stepped in to get my brush and the bucket with fresh whitewash, and when I got back there were six or seven children in the street, teasing the beggar. They were school-age kids who never went to school, never rested, who spent siesta time at the beach, or playing soccer in alleys.

"Go ahead, paint," said the beggar, stepping down so I could go to work.

The kids were elbowing one another, giggling.

"That Mr. Hans, yes," said the beggar once again.

"What about Mr. Hans?"

"Oh, nothing, nothing worth repeating."

"Ask him if Mr. Hans is actually sleeping with that Miss What's-her-name," said one of the kids.

"Shh, that's not very nice," said the beggar.

"Well, ask him if Mr. Hans is actually *resting* with Miss . . ."

"Lola," said another kid.

"Lulu," offered another.

"Loula."

"With all three of them?" asked the beggar. "And you call that resting?"

"Then ask him where Mr. Hans is keeping those shining pebbles of his," said the first kid.

"Stones," offered the other.

"Diamonds."

"That Mr. Hans," said the beggar coldly, his little eyes shining with spite.

"What about him?"

"He's dead," said the beggar.

There was a long silence. Then the shade of the eucalyptus tree climbed down the front steps of the hotel, and it was five o'clock, time to go in. I opened the door, but then I remembered my bucket. I looked and saw that it had tipped over, spilling the lime all over the beggar's shoes—or were those his feet?

·37·

On the third day of August those of us who'd been up before
sunrise felt the earth and the hotel building shaking, and Kyr
Thymios thought we should wake up the guests and warn them
that this might just be the prelude to a major earthquake. We
got out to the street, where many islanders had already gathered, debating the situation. This was the second tremor that
had occurred since May, and Kyr Takis the barber believed
that a third one within that summer could be catastrophic.
According to his understanding of nature, everything happened three times, and the third was the worst. But others
thought the significant number for earthquakes was seven, and
some of them were even willing to place bets against the barber's theory. Kyr Takis would welcome their challenge.

Later that morning Mrs. Becca wrote letters to America from
the terrace, telling relatives and friends where she could be
found if and when the catastrophe came, because she had no
intention of leaving Kalamos and Greece before the end of the
summer, certainly not before the Festival of Saint Thalassios.

Although the tremor was not repeated that day, everyone on
the island worried about the immediate future, and in the evening a lot of people took their blankets and pillows to the beach.
Everyone was talking about it. Everyone but Mr. Hans, whose
days had already come to an end. Mr. Hans had died in his
sleep on the last Friday of July, "between 4 and 5 P.M. from a

stroke," as the police reported. The police found no diamonds, though. What the police found was a trace of Miss Loula's perfume on the clothes of the deceased, but there was no evidence of foul play. Mr. Elias and Miss Loula were the last to have seen Mr. Hans before he passed away that afternoon, and the chief of police questioned them for twice as long as anyone else at the hotel, but he let them go in time to catch the *Glaros* to Piraeus. Mr. Hans and his mystery were buried the next day in a little cemetery north of Hora.

"Mr. Hans and his mystery, but not his diamonds," said Avramakis Sunday morning at the beach.

"Certainly not the *rumors* about diamonds," said Polyvios.

Later that Sunday the *Glaros* brought in a big load of summer vacationers, and everyone on the island had to forget the earthquake and the diamonds and had to work harder to meet the demand for food and drink and other services. The new arrivals included several Europeans, Americans and Greek-Americans. Mr. Bruce, a young man from California, occupied the room that had been vacated by Mr. Hans and his mystery, while the twin rooms that had accommodated Mr. Elias and Miss Loula were taken over by Eva and Cynthia Pappas, two young sisters from Astoria, New York. Another Greek-American, Dr. Koutsoulis, found accommodations at the Apollon, but, like most of the Europeans who had rented rooms in houses, he showed up at the Hotel Leto for his dinner. Kyra Tassia's cooking was famed all over the world. After finishing his dinner that evening, Mr. Bruce went to talk to the two sisters, whom he'd met on the ship. He pulled up a chair and sat at their table, ordering coffee for three. He looked pleased. One couldn't say that Mr. Bruce was a handsome young man. He had small, deep-set eyes, so deep-set that one couldn't see their color. Deep-set eyes and big white teeth, and a very short haircut, especially at the top, that reminded me of the haircuts the nurses give at the hospital before dressing a head wound. But the top of Mr. Bruce's head showed no sign of injury.

When I served their coffee, Miss Eva asked me my name and where I was from. I answered the first question and I was ready to leave, but she stopped me.

"Wait. Aren't you going to tell me the name of your village?" she protested. She was the younger of the two, eighteen or nineteen years old, and the more talkative one. She spoke Greek with two accents: an Epirotan and an American.

"I am from Antikalamos," I said. "Why?"

"Antikalamos," she repeated. "What is that? Anyway, Mr. Bruce here wants to know if it's true that there are sunken ships off the coast. Do you know anything?"

I told her what I knew: the earthquake, the whirlpool, the volcano. Rumors.

"What else?"

"He should talk to the fishermen," I said.

At another table Mr. Thanos, an elderly retiree from Athens, who'd been staying in Room 204, was pleased to make the acquaintance of Dr. Koutsoulis, by whom he was joined for a glass of brandy.

When some of the guests had left and the noise on the terrace quieted down, I overheard Dr. Koutsoulis asking Mr. Thanos what he thought about the Communist plot to conquer the world. Then the Pappas sisters paid for their meal, including coffee for three, and Mr. Bruce wiped his mouth, looked around, drummed his fingertips on the red tablecloth, yawned and looked around once again, his eyes stopping at Mr. Larry.

"Good evening," said Mr. Bruce, showing his big white teeth.

"Good night," replied Mr. Larry, turning his tired face in the opposite direction.

That was the direction of Mr. Thanos and Dr. Koutsoulis, toward whom Mr. Bruce then moved.

"Sure, sure," Dr. Koutsoulis welcomed him, forgetting that he himself was a guest at Mr. Thanos' table.

Mr. Bruce pulled up a chair and introduced himself, then clapped his hands, ordering brandy for three.

Soon enough Dr. Koutsoulis was busy translating from Greek into English and vice versa for the benefit of Mr. Bruce, who knew no Greek, and of Mr. Thanos, who had no idea of English.

For a while Dr. Koutsoulis, on whose translations the others depended, kept bringing up the subject of the Communist plot, or, as he said to Mr. Thanos for the third time, "the satanic machinations of international Communism and its fellow voyagers."

"I know," said Mr. Thanos, who wasn't really listening.

And Mr. Bruce laughed nervously, saying, "Well, if I were you I wouldn't worry about Greece—not for a while, anyway."

"Apparently he hasn't heard about the escape," Dr. Koutsoulis shouted in Mr. Thanos' ear.

What escape? I hadn't read the paper, I hadn't heard a word.

"Ah, yes, the escape," agreed Mr. Thanos, mildly annoyed for having been forced to listen.

Whose escape? From where?

But Mr. Thanos wasn't really listening, and he went on to say that for some strange reason for the past two and a half months he'd been losing sleep, he'd been unable to sleep at all, not a wink.

"You're probably worrying too much!" Dr. Koutsoulis shouted again in Mr. Thanos' ear.

But Mr. Thanos was not listening, and I began to think that he might even be deaf.

Mr. Bruce was talking to Dr. Koutsoulis in a low tone.

But Mr. Thanos minded that, and he shouted at Dr. Koutsoulis, as if the doctor were the deaf one, "What does our friend have to say?"

"He just told me that he's fought the reds even here, in Greece. He's in the American Mission, you know. A year ago he was dropping bombs on the Bandits!"

·38·

Soon after I had gone to sleep that night I awoke again, breathing with difficulty. The breeze had stopped, and, as always is the case before a weather change, there was a complete stillness over the sea and the island. I wiped my sweating face and chest on the bedsheet and walked across the roof to the parapet to see if it was cooler there. The tavernas at Skala had closed for the night, and only half a dozen lights were on in the harbor.

My eyes were fixed on the red flashing light at the far end of the Goat Island, when I heard someone's hearty laughter coming from within the hotel. It sounded like Mr. Bruce. I asked myself, how could he laugh like that in the middle of the night all by himself? Or was he all by himself? I recalled the last part of his conversation with Dr. Koutsoulis, the way Dr. Koutsoulis had summarized it in Greek for Mr. Thanos, and I shuddered, realizing that I had in fact recalled that part of their conversation earlier, while I slept, and I had been awakened by it: "He's in the American Mission. . . . A year ago he was dropping bombs on the Bandits!"

A layer of hot, humid air was settling over the island, pressing down on it, and the sea was breathless and still and at peace with every isolated rock and stretch of shoreline, hugging each rock and beach serenely. I remembered the bombs, the incendiaries and the scattered bodies, and it occurred to me that living might be the price, not the reward of survival. I shut my eyes to avoid the red flashing light.

I shut my eyes, but still I heard the beat of my blood in the rhythm of that red flashing light, and I asked myself, What am I doing here, catching up and adapting and functioning, in a position where I am expected to say, "Yes," or "Yes, but," or "Well, it's that kind of thing," or "Poor Mr. Hans," or "Yes, yessir, thank you," even to Mr. Bruce, who had flown the Hell-divers over Grammos a year before, "Here's your coffee, sir, here's your brandy, sir, here's Miss Eva and Miss Cynthia, sir," and "Would that be all, sir?"

Once again I heard Mr. Bruce's laughter, this time through the stairwell, not far from the roof.

I wiped the sweat from my face and, certain that Mr. Bruce was about to make an appearance on my roof, rushed to hide on the other side of the washroom

He was coming up the stairs laughing, but he wasn't alone. Another laugh or giggle, another little sound, another word— Miss Cynthia, or was it Miss Eva? The effort of climbing up the stairs was almost over.

It was that same month, just one year before, that we knew that soon most of us would die rather than surrender. And Papanikas ran out of Christ, ran out of bread and wine, and said to those who had not received Communion, "You are the flesh and the blood of the Savior, you, the flesh and the blood of Greece." And everyone knew that after that night neither Christ nor Greece would ever be the same.

What was I supposed to make of Mr. Bruce's appearance on the island? In the Hotel Leto? On the roof of the hotel where I slept? Was the next round to be fought hand to hand between him and me? What if I just jumped over the railing? What if I pushed Mr. Bruce off the roof?

From the tone of their voices I could guess they'd been to-gether all evening, and the first time I heard his laughter it must have come from his room. Now they were on the roof to cool off, not knowing that the roof was enemy territory. Holding hands, they walked cautiously to the side of the roof overlooking Skala and the sea, and I was sure that my second guest was Miss Cynthia, the more shy of the two sisters.

"Aaaah!" I heard Mr. Bruce inhaling deeply, as if there were actually enough air to breathe.

A hollow sound of thunder, and then another nearer, clearer, distracted me from my guests, briefly. The weather was changing fast. Soon a cool breeze and the first drops of rain, sparse, sizable, on my face and feet, and all over the roof, and then the rain.

Would Miss Cynthia suggest going down? Would Mr. Bruce refuse? Would Miss Cynthia return to her room, to his room, without him? Would he stay on the roof alone, cooling off, balancing the books of the day? Would he lean against the rail, convinced he was alone, unaware that the enemy waited in the dark for the right moment?

If Miss Cynthia gave up on the rain and on him, and if he gave up on her but not on the rain, I, who had moved in the foul weather, should have no difficulty pushing Mr. Bruce over the railing. But could I?

·39·

When I saw Avramakis at the beach the following Sunday, he said that Mrs. Becca had been at Kyr Nikos' restaurant a few times, and that at first he had wondered about the quality of the food at the Hotel Leto, but then he noticed that Mrs. Becca was having long conversations with Kyr Nikos and his wife, and he began to suspect that what went on might be more serious than Kyra Tassia's menu. He was right. Mrs. Becca had been inquiring about him. She had told him so only the day before when she asked him if he would like to go to America someday.

"I didn't know what to say," said Avramakis. "So I said, 'Sure I'd like to go to America someday. Someday I'd like to go to Israel too. There are a lot of places I'd like to see.' "

But Mrs. Becca wasn't just talking about traveling for fun. She was talking about living in America and going to school there. Mrs. Becca had property but not children, and what she had in mind was adoption. "We Hebrews are always trying to help one another," she said to Avramakis.

Avramakis appreciated that, but he wondered how come the Hebrews did not help one another move to Israel now that they had a country of their own.

"Never mind about Israel, honey," was her answer. "The promised land is America."

"Honey," said Avramakis, meant *meli*. That's what Hebrews called one another once they got to know and like one another.

"So you are going to America," I said in order to say something, hoping for a negative answer.

"I'm not sure," said Avramakis. "To begin with, I'm not sure that the police will let me."

When Mrs. Becca announced a few days later her intention to adopt Avramakis and take him to America, she said nothing about his reservations or any difficulty with the police. All she mentioned was the paperwork for the adoption and a trip to Athens, as soon as the Festival of Saint Thalassios was over, to obtain a visa from the American Embassy. "No sweat," said Mrs. Becca.

"Sweet," said Kyr Thymios. "Baklava."

"No, no, no."

The conversation stopped abruptly when Mr. Bruce and the Pappas sisters returned from the beach, asking if there was anything left for lunch. It was 3:25 P.M. and no, there was nothing left; that is, nothing besides omelettes and salads and frying fish, of which we never ran out. Omelettes it would be; omelettes and a big country salad, and beer. Off to the terrace then, under the eucalyptus.

"*Schmuck*," hissed Mrs. Becca once Mr. Bruce and the sisters were out of hearing range.

Triantafyllia didn't know what that word meant in English.

And Mrs. Becca would not help. She just filled a pitcher with ice-cold water and returned to her room, muttering something or other disapprovingly. At about five she would come downstairs again, fanning herself and complaining about the heat ("*Ti zesti paidi mou!*"), and about the commotion in the room adjacent to hers, where Mr. Bruce and the Pappas sisters were going at it again ("as if there was no tomorrow").

For a few more days and nights Mr. Bruce's laughter resounded inside the hotel and out, up on the roof and down the terrace, and farther down at Skala, he now playing with the sisters separately and now together, now diving in search of treasure from a rented boat that for all practical purposes was

too small for two and far too small for three passengers, and
now sunbathing at the beach, his head resting comfortably on
Miss Cynthia's stomach and his feet on Miss Eva's ass. But
after those few days Mr. Bruce's laughter no longer echoed
over land and sea—not that he grew tired of searching, nor
that he fell from the sisters' favor, no, but because the saint's
anniversary and festival were not far off, and the pilgrims had
begun to pour into the island by the hundreds, and collectively
they sounded at least as loud as Mr. Bruce, so no one was
surprised when his laughter did not crown the general pande-
monium but instead succumbed to it.

The one and only taxi on the island seemed to be everywhere
at the same time, carrying pilgrims and packages from Skala to
Hora—to the Hotels Leto and Apollon, or to the rooms and
dugout cells that the church assigned to the poorest among
those who could not afford proper accommodations. The pilgrims spoke Greek in a great variety of accents, which proved
that they were coming from every class and part of the country.
Likewise, those who were afflicted made all sorts of pathetic
sounds and noises or let their faces and limbs suggest silently
that they were coming from every region and corner of suffering. Some were excitable, prone to sudden fits of rage, others
were convulsed and rolled left and right on their backs like
vessels on a stormy sea, and some just laughed unconvincingly,
as if that were a distant memory of laughter, not the laughter
itself, unlike their crying, which always seemed spontaneous
and often spread to others who were vulnerable to similar fears,
obsessions or pains. Some made faces, others limped. Some
made vulgar gestures which mortified their custodians, others
twitched and cursed. And the crowds filled the streets with
smells of medicine and body odor, and the daily trash increased
far beyond the poor donkey's two-basket capacity per block, so
the smell of refuse became noticeable, too—at least until late
afternoon, when the south wind would pick up and sweep all
smells and most of the noise out to sea. And the islanders

showed signs of exhaustion even before the preparations for the great event were over. Kalamos looked, sounded and smelled like a madhouse, and by the eve of Saint Thalassios' Festival it wasn't an easy task for anyone to tell who were the possessed and who the plain exhausted.

The pilgrims seemed to be devouring an inordinate amount of food each day. Big meals and desserts, and sandwiches between meals, sweets-of-the-spoon and coffee, ouzo, beer and wine, more food, pastries, pies, fruit juices, club soda and cordials. Sandwiches between meals and, between sandwiches, snacks. "Eat," they advised each other. "Finish your meal." And to the have's reasoning, "It's great island cooking," the have-not would add, "It costs money!" Some of the afflicted consumed more food than any healthy person could manage, while others, sickened at even the idea of food, ate nothing at all, tiring and tormenting their relatives or nurses, who somehow related affliction to hunger, and good health to food. As a rule, the physically disabled ate too much and the mentally disturbed too little. But there were more categories in between, including the seemingly well and the obviously dying, who either ate beyond their capacity while pretending to be on a diet or had their leftovers wrapped in waxed paper for later. The veal was vital and the lamb lovely; fresh fish had iodine and calcium; dandelion greens had iron; feta cheese and fruit helped digestion.

It was during that week that Mr. Larry quit eating altogether and then packed his small suitcase and took the boat to Piraeus.

·40·

On Wednesday morning, the day before the Festival of Saint
Thalassios, Mrs. Becca went to the chief of police and to a
lawyer about the paperwork for Avramakis' adoption, and when
she came back she brought a newspaper from which we learned
that there had been an escape from a maximum-security prison
in Piraeus. According to the paper, the government had first
denied that some thirty political prisoners who'd been sentenced to death, and whose final appeal had been turned down,
had broken out of prison, but now the Deputy Minister for
Public Security had admitted it, adding that public knowledge
could help in recapturing the dangerous criminals. That must
have been the escape that Dr. Koutsoulis had been talking
about with Mr. Thanos. The article said that the escape had
been made through a sixty-five-meter-long tunnel that the former Bandits had dug out during the night for the past ten
months. I could imagine at least a couple of Naxians among
them. The tunnel had gone through the foundation wall of the
prison building, under a paved road and a storage shed, and
had ended in the basement of a small bleach factory. Amazing!
And Mrs. Becca, who was still struggling with the headline,
wanted to know why I kept smiling over her shoulder.

After lunch Mrs. Becca filled her pitcher with ice-cold water
and went to her room, but she didn't come downstairs later on
complaining about noises. As it turned out, Mr. Bruce had not

yet returned from his diving expedition. Generally he came back early, eager to show the Pappas sisters whatever fragments of ancient pottery he'd just recovered. So it was Miss Cynthia and Miss Eva who came downstairs for coffee earlier than any other guest that afternoon. I took pains to assure them that the source of my cheerfulness had nothing to do with developments at the hotel.

Then the guests began to arrive early for dinner (even the Greeks who usually ate an hour or two after the Americans) as if they feared there wouldn't be enough food in the kitchen. There were several new faces: an elderly couple from Samos, three well-to-do friends (Messrs. Mitsos, Georgios and Kotsos) from Rhodos, Miss Marianna from Athens, and Mrs. Domna and her sixteen-year-old son, Nakos, also from Athens. Mrs. Domna had already been complaining to Kyr Thymios about the service in general, and about his insistence on sending "that boy" upstairs instead of Triantafyllia, in particular. Nakos preferred Triantafyllia a thousand times.

Kyr Thymios kept wiping his hands in his apron, waiting for his turn. It seemed to be taking forever. "I understand, madame . . ."

"Do you really?"

Roasted breast of chicken and cucumber-yogurt salad for Mrs. Becca. And two more beers for Miss Cynthia and Miss Eva. Lamp chops and artichokes *à la polita* for Mr. Thanos. And a beefsteak with fried potatoes for Dr. Koutsoulis. Fried smelts, kalamarakia, and octopus stewed in wine for the three friends from Rhodos. And a broiled red snapper for Mr. Cloutier, plus tomato and cucumber salad, plus retsina. Kokkineli for Mr. Thanos, and two more beers for Miss Cynthia and Miss Eva.

"How do you do, Miss Marianna. Here's our dinner menu. Take your time."

"I will, I will," she said, showing me her fine profile as she blew her cigarette smoke away. Warm, friendly voice, seasoned by strong tobacco. "Tell me," she added, looking me straight in the eyes this time, "do you always perk up like that when you read the paper?"

She must have seen me stretching out my neck over Mrs. Becca's shoulder and grinning about the jailbreak. "I don't read the paper very often," I said, blushing.

She looked into my eyes, saying nothing, her lips just a twitch away from smiling. She looked into my eyes as if she had known me before, and I thought I was about to recognize a relative, a dear cousin, whom I hadn't seen since childhood.

But then she could be a police informer, spying and filing reports, getting kids shipped back to Antikalamos. For a few moments I just stood there, unable to take my eyes away from hers. And then I noticed again that she wore black, and I began to think about that also.

"So what was it that you read in the paper that cheered you up?" And this time she half smiled.

"I no longer remember," I lied, my voice choking.

"It got washed from your memory?"

"Sort of."

"Soapsuds." She smiled.

"No. Bleach," I said.

"The little bleach factory in Piraeus," she said. "It had to be."

"Well, Miss Marianna," I said.

"Well, Panagis."

I looked into her eyes. I wanted to tell her how strange that name sounded to me now, but I didn't.

·41·

The news of Mr. Bruce's disappearance spread rapidly throughout Kalamos the next morning. The police had been alerted, and, in spite of the busy schedule of arrivals and departures in the harbor, the Coast Guard sent out its one and only patrol boat, searching for him. Around noon the captain of the S.S. *Kanaris*, the second passenger ship that had been added to the line that week, reported that he'd sighted a small empty boat some three miles off the coast toward Antikalamos, but when the patrol searched the area the little boat was not there. What *was* there was a whirlpool, the whirlpool that from time to time became visible and was supposed to be the eye or the mouth of an underwater volcano. According to some, it was only a sinkhole at the bottom of the sea, and last week's earthquake had unplugged it, causing huge amounts of seawater and fish to go down the drain. Maybe that's where Mr. Bruce had gone also. It was that very noon, too, that Kyr Takis the barber closed shop. Convinced that the end of Kalamos was at hand, he placed a half-dozen more bets and boarded the S.S. *Kanaris* to Piraeus. And why not? If he truly believed that the end of the island was so near, why shouldn't he run?

In the meantime, Lieutenant Müller's motorboat and a hired caïque went back and forth between Antikalamos and Kalamos, bringing in the rest of the kids for the festival. I saw two groups of ten in the street, wearing blue armbands for quick identification. They looked neat, and delighted to leave the camp even for a few hours. Only Fotis had refused to come. The camp was scheduled to close down by Easter, but Fotis would stay on, a prisoner of himself, a hermit. We were growing apart now in different ways. I realized that when I ran out to the street to greet the newcomers from Antikalamos. It just wasn't like old days. Maybe it was the time and the distance, whatever little time and distance had separated us that summer. We looked different, sounded different to each other, and I took all this to mean that something was wrong with me. I was neither too friendly nor too embarrassed to be friendly, but they were shy enough to sound polite, and I didn't keep them long. Then, when I thought about it more, I knew that there was distance even between me and the kids who'd been in Kalamos for some time, even between me and Avramakis and Minos, who'd been my closest friends for so long. How strange, I thought. Could it be that someday we might not even care for one another?

Around noontime I saw one more group passing through the street, wearing blue armbands, but Kyra Tassia called me in to start taking orders for lunch, so I just greeted them and followed them with my eyes until they turned the corner. How did Lieutenant Müller trust them? What made him so sure that some of them wouldn't sneak out of Kalamos in one of the fishing caïques that brought goods and pilgrims from other islands? Had they become so predictable? Or did he actually hope to get rid of them that way?

Lunch was the last meal to be offered at the hotel on Saint Thalassios' Day. The guests and the other regular patrons had been warned about it, and they'd made dinner reservations elsewhere. The Pappas sisters ordered lunch but did not touch it. They talked little between themselves, and every time I went to their table they stopped so that I wouldn't hear their worried comments about Mr. Bruce's disappearance. But the next time I came out of the kitchen with a loaded tray I couldn't believe what I saw: both of them were sitting at the table of the three

Stratis Haviaras

gentlemen from Rhodos, debating whether they should have
some beer or dessert and coffee.

"It's odd," I heard Mrs. Becca saying to Kyra Tassia. "Five,
like three, is an odd number."

·42·

As the day wore on and the shade slanted its way down the sidewalk into the deserted street, and the zephyr picked up enough strength to revive Hora from its midday stupor, an old woman saw Saint Thalassios walking along the whitewashed fringe of the shade, and she fainted. The saint, dressed in blue and white, walked on, blessing the geraniums of his martyr-dom, the carnations of all innocent blood, the sunflowers of the turning-to-look and returning-the-blessing: Holy be his name and his name day, Saint Thalassios who triumphed over evil, this nine hundred and fiftieth anniversary of the removal of his relics; holy his miraculous mercy for the mindless cap-tives of Satan; holy his grace that soothes our passions, that absolves our transgressions . . . Overlooking the street, orna-mental and broadleaf basil, honeysuckle, bougainvillea and the purple-cross clematis murmured a prelude to exorcism: Off with you, evil spirit, the molester of twigs and new leaves! Off with you, the thrice accursed blossom-end rot, the unnameable rapist of youth, the defiler of innocence! And right above herbs and trees blew the blue-and-white wind of the national fervor; for the nation itself, only recently rescued from the crooked talons of Communism, had allied itself to the saint and his followers the sunflowers, and the others that remained behind: the geraniums, the carnations, all the everyday plants in white-washed now-empty cans of feta from Tyrnavos, tarama from

Turkey, and sardines and anchovies from Portugal. And the
lesser plants chanted: Blessed be the saint and the nation, the
immaculate skies that shelter and the seas that surround this
island; blessed be Paul, King of the Hellenes, and also Frederika, the Queen, his royal wife, Crown Prince Constantine, and
Sophia and Irene the princesses; blessed be the Army, the Navy
and the Air Force, the Coast Guard, the police and the Gendarmerie, and all the paramilitary and secret societies, on this
nine hundred and fiftieth anniversary of his martyrdom; blessed
every shade of blue, every shard of white; the wind-tattered
banner; every shore, every rock, every snow-capped or foam-
crested ridge regardless of altitude—our martyred saint and
nation emerge triumphant.

Two boys stepped down the sidewalk, helped the old woman
back into the shade. There, now. And when she came to, they
had to agree that they too had witnessed the saint, but she
wouldn't believe them, ah.

Soon there were more people: pilgrims and islanders suffering in their clothes—some old, some new, but all special for
this day. Most of them poor, men without land or license to
fish; widows; wives of political deportees and war victims; children, children, and children. And children whose clothes were
not different from the clothes they wore every day, except
that they'd been carefully washed and specially ironed, and
mended, and patched with patching that resembled the original
fabric—not as the fabric originally looked, but as it looked at
the time that it needed patching. The children held cotton
candy or pinwheels in their hands, colorful pinwheels made
from expensive glossy paper and bought for a drachma or made
from pieces of newspaper by their fathers or older brothers.
And the sea breeze was strong enough to spin any kind.

Wave after wave of children and workingmen and -women
poured out of the ships and made the climb to Hora, carrying
baskets and packages, long white or golden wax candles and
other votive offerings. Most of them were poor. One could tell

from their clothes, the way they felt in their best clothes, the way they walked, sat and stood up in their clothes, and how once in a while their clothes seemed to disobey their bodies or certain limbs of their bodies, making them look awkward, sad, even comical—the way their sleeves hung, a bit shorter, a bit longer, the way their shirts were hitched up, the way their collars swung up ready to take off like paper kites, the way their trousers bent at the knees on their own, as if they'd traveled in the suitcase in a kneeling position, worshiping the Lord and the saint even as their owner dozed off on the deck of the *Glaros*.

But the air was festive with goodwill and anticipation, and in any direction that one turned to look something interesting happened: This way, a detachment of the Children's Navy marching toward the church. That way, the musicians of the city's band rehearsing their program with their shining instruments, and already there was an audience of children around them. In the little square the photographer leveling his box camera on its tripod, then setting up the screen that depicted the Church of St. Thalassios recently restored with red stone from Antikalamos and freshly painted, just as the church itself looked in the distance. This way the municipal councilmen ironing out their last differences, that way the mayor and the chief of police checking out the cordoned-off section of the boulevard in front of the church where the great procession was supposed to begin at the end of the special service specially presided over by the bishop. That way, and that, Boy Scouts and Wolf Cubs spreading out along both sides of the cordoned-off section of the boulevard to help control the largest concentration of pilgrims. And here and there, throughout Hora, the kids from Antikalamos: those already apprenticing on the island, in relative freedom, and those just visiting for the day, always in groups of ten and wearing blue armbands.

Vendors on every square, every road and sidewalk, peddling prayer books and balloons, cotton candy, small icons of

Saint Thalassios engraved in tin, dolls in island costumes, sunglasses, grapes, straw hats, sesame buns and almond paste,
halvah, samali, baklava, kataif, and French pastries with lots
of whipped cream on top, and ice cream, and sherbet . . . And
the smells that filled the air were so many and different they
made me imagine faraway places, and the whole town smelled,
sounded and looked so lovely and sad that it made me imagine
faraway lands and islands that one day exist and are there and
the next day don't and are not, the next day they vanish: eastward, past the cedars of Lebanon, or south into the deserts of
Africa, or even down into the cold gaps of volcanos.

So Kyr Takis the barber had a better chance of winning the
bet, after all, than anyone thought till that day.

·43·

I was back at the hotel, on the terrace, but still browsing in the open-air market of colors, sounds and smells, when I heard footsteps. Miss Marianna, I predicted hurriedly, and, turning, I saw that it was she. It could have been a wish.

"What is it going to be?" she said, sitting down, tapping a cigarette on the nail of her left thumb.

I raised my shoulders, smiling. The question was too general.

"Let me put it this way," she said. "Where were you before Antikalamos, and what did you do to be sent there?"

Surprise. A dry, curled-up leaf fell from the eucalyptus tree onto the table. Why should I tell? I was taking my time.

"You don't have to tell me if you don't want to," she said.

What do you say to that? I was staring at the leaf.

"It's not just curiosity," said Miss Marianna, picking up the little dry leaf by the stem and giving it a spin between her thumb and forefinger.

"What about yourself?" I asked. "Where were *you* before?"

"Before what?" she said, squinting her eyes, trying not to smile.

"Before Antikalamos."

Miss Marianna burst out laughing. "You!" she said, pointing at me. "You and I are going to have a man-to-man talk, once this carnival's over."

Stratis Haviaras

Why not now? If Kyr Takis the barber was right, we might not have another chance.

"The camp I was in is called Trikeri," she said.

"And before then?"

"The Averof Prison, in Athens."

"What for?"

She'd fought the Germans in Boeotia, the English in the suburbs of Athens, and our own scum between Eleusis and Mégara. "Very little else," she said, and that included some studies in France, journalism, a long affair with a man who'd been court-martialed and sentenced to die, but the sentence hadn't been carried out, not yet.

"Which prison?"

She wouldn't tell me, not yet. "Your turn now."

I started from Kalamos, going backward: Antikalamos, Kavalla, Grammos, the journey to the borders. "Very little else," I said.

"What about Grammos?" Miss Marianna wanted to hear more about the battles. "You really were there," she said, and a sheaf of fine wrinkles began to form on her forehead. "How much did you see? What did you see?"

"I saw everything. I was there at the end . . . I saw the end," I said.

She reached across the table and took hold of my hand. "Don't say that," she said, biting her lower lip. "It wasn't the end."

"If that wasn't the end, then there isn't any such thing as the end," I said.

"There is no such thing as the end," she repeated, and her eyes welled up with tears. Then she pulled back her hand and lighted her cigarette. "That's what's killing me," she added, forcing a smile.

"You in the Party?" I asked.

She rubbed her eyes without answering, as though I ought to know better.

"Your turn," I said again.

No, she wasn't in the Party. Not anymore. She'd been accused of having grown doubtful, restless. And after her man was captured she could not work, not effectively. She was accused of indulging in bourgeois attitudes. Her comrades forced her to open up her heart. "Self-criticism," they called it. Worse than confession. Far worse than interrogation. But she turned it against them. And the next morning the Nationalist security police knew where she could be found. "One hand rinses the other, says a proverb," said Miss Marianna.

And both hands rinse the face, said the rest of the proverb. How did that fit into Miss Marianna's story? Whose face was it?

"Death's?" she said, exhaling her smoke. Miss Marianna had fought her own private Grammos, made her last stand, and was wounded mortally, but she didn't admit it. She went on smoking cigarettes and rubbing her eyes.

"Maybe Saint Thalassios," I said.

"I thought you were my friend," she complained.

"Why Kalamos, then?"

"I had to leave Athens in a hurry."

"What for?"

"I can't tell you now."

I was in no position to continue. Even as we sat at the table she was taller than I. Even as her eyes watered at the remembrance of personal loss, once she had fought bravely. Never mind her passion for tobacco and her easy tears. The way she still held that dry leaf between index finger and thumb . . . The way she looked at me and at everything else . . . The way her body in that simple black dress turned toward me . . . What was it I meant to say to her?

"Be my friend," she whispered as if we weren't alone on the terrace.

"Maybe Minos and Avramakis won't show up, after all." I was choking again.

"Are you changing the subject?" she said.

"I am not. I just wished I didn't have to go with Minos and Avramakis," I confessed.

"Women always come between friends. Maybe you and I can see each other when the carnival's over." She smiled.

"We can try, but it might be too dark to see each other."

"We can meet down below the concrete terrace by the shore. There is a night-light over the stairway. What do you say?"

"Thank you."

"By the way, don't call me 'Miss.' I am not *that* old."

"I'll wear a red carnation on my lapel." I smiled back.

άπελευθέρωση. Είναι όμως καί ρεαλιστική; βανέ τήν ἐλληνική, γιουγκοσλαβική καί

Ὁ Πέτρος Ρούσος, στὸ βιβλίο του «Ἡ Μεγάλη Πενταετία», ἀπευθυνόμενος πρὸς ἀριστερούς ἀναγνώστες καὶ προσπαθώντας νά δικαιολογήσει τὸ «ὄχι» τοῦ ΚΚΕ, ἰσχυρίζεται πώς ἡ ἡγεσία του δέν ἀρνήθηκε τή συγκρότηση τοῦ Βαλκανικοῦ Στρατηγείου οὔτε τὸ τορπίλλιασε. «Ζήτησε ἁπλῶς – γράφει – ἀναβολή τοῦ ζητήματος μέχρι νά δημιουργηθοῦν οἱ ὅροι». Γιατί αὐτές οἱ μασημένες δικαιολογίες; Ὁ ἴδιος ἀναφέρει ὡς ἑξῆς τούς λόγους πού ὤθησαν τὸ πολιτικὸ γραφεῖο τοῦ ΚΚΕ στήν ἀπόφασή του:

«Πρῶτο, νά στερεώσουμε τήν ἐθνικοαπελευθερωτική συμμαχία, νά μήν προκαλέσουμε δυσανεσχέτηση τῶν συμμάχων μας στὸ ΕΑΜ καὶ σὲ ἄλλους ἐνδεχόμενους συμμάχους μας. Δεύτερο, νά μήν ἐπισπεύσουμε ἔνταση τῶν ἀντιδράσεων καὶ ἐπεμβάσεων τῶν Ἄγγλων στήν Ἑλλάδα προτοῦ προλάβει νά στερεωθεῖ τὸ ἐπαναστατικό κίνημα στήν Ἑλλάδα ἢ τουλάχιστον στή Γιουγκοσλαβία. Τρίτο, νά μή δημιουργήσουμε πρόωρα ἐμπόδια στήν παγκόσμια ἀντιχιτλερική συμμαχία, τά ὁποῖα ἄγνωστο ἂν θὰ μπορέσουμε τελικά νά ὑπερπηδήσουμε ὅσο βαστάει ὁ πόλεμος κατά τῶν κατακτητῶν».

Μακεδόνες καὶ Μεγαλόσερβοι

Ὁ Κώστας Καραγιώργης ὅμως, πού ἀναμείχθηκε ἄμεσα στὸ θέμα ὅπως εἴδαμε, σὲ ἰδιαίτερη συνομιλία πού εἴχε μὲ τὸν γράφοντα τὸ 1946, καθαρά καὶ σταράτα ἔδωσε τήν ἐξήγηση:

«Ἀκο...
γοι πού...
λιτικ...
ὅτι ἡ Ε...
λουθοῦσ...
ματα. Δ...
λίγο πρ...
Διεθνής...
τῆς δέν...
ὅπως κα...
ἔδειχνε...
πολύ μετα...
χρεωμένος νά κάνει κι ἄλλες βαριές θυσίες γιά νά διατηρήσει τή συμμαχική ἑνότητα χωρίς τήν ὁποία μπορούσε νά χαθεῖ τὸ πάν. Καὶ δέν ξέρω πῶς ὁ Τίτο καὶ ὁ Τέμπο ἔκαναν τοῦ κεφαλιοῦ τους, ἐμεῖς ὅμως διστάζαμε νά καταφέρουμε μιὰ μαχαιριά στά νεφρά τῆς μεγάλης συμμαχίας. Γιατί κάτι τέτοιο θὰ ἦταν ἂν ἀποκαλυπτά ὀρθωνόμαστε μαζί μὲ τούς Ἀλβανούς καὶ Γιουγκοσλάβους κατά τῶν Ἄγγλων. Ὅλα αὐτά ὅμως ἦσαν δευτερεύοντα μπροστά σὲ ἕναν ὀγκόλιθο πού θὰ σοῦ ἀποκαλύψω».

Καὶ καθώς ὁ γράφων τέντωνε τὸν λαιμό του καὶ τὰ αὐτιά του γιά νά ἀκούσει, ὁ Κώστας Καραγιώργης συμπλήρωσε:

– Ἐκεῖνο πού μᾶς τρόμαξε εἶναι ἄλλο: Εἴχαμε πληροφορίες ἀλλά καὶ ἀντιληφθή-

«... Ἡ σκέψη τῶν Γιουγκοσλάβων καὶ τῶν Ἀλβανῶν συντρόφων νά ἐπηρεάζουν πρὸς ὁρισμένη πολιτική τὶς ἀντίστοιχες ἔνοπλες δυνάμεις τῶν ἐθνικῶν μειονοτήτων στήν Ἑλλάδα (Σλαβομακεδόνων καὶ τσάμηδων...

Στή Γιουγκοσλαβία μὲ τήν ἀπελευθέρωση ὑπῆρχαν 30 μεραρχίες σοβιετικοῦ στρατοῦ. Στήν Ἑλλάδα μετά τήν ἀπελευθέρωση ἦρθαν 3 μεραρχίες ἀγγλικοῦ στρατοῦ.

Ἀλλά πολύ χαρακτηριστικά ὁ Πέτρος Ρούσος παρατηρεῖ:

«Γιουγκοσλάβικα καὶ ἰδίως ὁρισμένα σλαβομακεδονικά στελέχη τῆς γειτονικῆς χώρας ἀψηφοῦσαν τὶς συνέπειες πού θὰ ᾽χει σ᾽ ὅλον τὸν ἑλληνικό ἀγώνα καὶ στὸν ἀγώνα τῶν βαλκανικῶν ἀπαιτήσεις καὶ ἄμεση υἱοθέτηση ἀπό μᾶς τοῦ συνθήματος: ᾽ἑνιαία Μακεδόνια στά πλαίσια τῆς νέας Γιουγκοσλαβίας᾽. Ὑπάρχουν καὶ σήμερα ἀκόμη ὁρισμένοι πού λένε πώς καὶ ἂν ἀκόμη δέν ἐλευθερωνόταν ἡ Ἑλλάδα ἀπό τὸν ἰμπεριαλισμό, θὰ εἶναι ἐλευθερωθεῖ τουλάνι-

---

ATHENS—Collapse of Greece's moderate coalition government appeared imminent as Liberal Party leader Sophocles Venizelos announced the resignation of five Liberal Party ministers. Mr. Venizelos has demanded the resignation of Premier Plastiras, who has been under fire for demanding amnesty for Communists convicted for treason. . . .

—Associated Press dispatch, August 1950

Ὁ Τίτο κατά

Καὶ τώρα ἕνα... γνώση τοῦ Τίτο... Τέμπο; Ἀσφαλ... ὅσο τελικά ὁρίσ... πρόσωπο τῆς... σχεδιασμό στρα...

Ὥστε ὁ Τίτο υ... Μεγαλοσέρβων... γκοσλαβίας;

Ἡ ἀπάντηση, δόξο, εἶναι κατ... στούς πολλούς... μὲ ἐντολή του... τερα τά γιουγκ... ψαν τὸ ἀντίθετο... καὶ ἀδιάψευστα...

Ὁ Τίτο πράγμ... σύσταση Βαλκ. Σ... κούς λόγους. Κ... ταν στὸν στρατι... ἦταν κακή. Ἀλλά... μεγαλοσέρβικοι... καὶ κύκλοι – ὑπο... νιστικό βρασμο... νήσου – γιά νά δ... τὸν τὸν μηχανισ...

Ἄρνησε νά τὸ... τῆς ἀραιῆς ἐπικ... τὸ καλοκαίρι τοῦ... μάχη ζωῆς ἢ θα... τῶν. Ὅταν πληρ... γίνει, ἡ ἀντίδρ... Ἔσπευσε νά δια... αγγείλατ... Τέμπο ἢ ἡ... γεῖο γιατ... κοστό».

ραμμα το... μμίζει:

σημεριν... ὁποιοσδ... λάθος,... χαριστικ... λήθι τοῦ πρ... δημιουργηθ... μεραρχία».

Τά μηνύματα... στρατηγό τοῦ δ... νος τά εἶχε λάβ... «ὄχι» τοῦ Σιάντ... πυρώσει τὸ θέμ... τήσει ὁριστικά.

Ἄλλωστε, τώ... παρτιζάνοι ὅπως... βρίσκονταν μπρ... ἀνατροπή: Ἡ Ἰτ... Καὶ στὸν βαλκαν... σποτε ἕνας ὁλό... γέρας τῶν δυνι... χώματα τῆς Γιου...

Τὸ ΚΚΕ λέει:

·44·

Minos, Avramakis and I, all dressed up, each with a gift of a fifty-drachma bill in his pocket, started off our free afternoon and evening with a stroll around the boulevard, along the vendor stands, checking out the candy and the expressions of those who sampled the candy, to see what was worth spending money for and what was not. Minos bought a strip of apricot paste, Avramakis five honey-dipped chestnuts, and I a large almond cookie which was a local specialty. Minos bought a bag of roasted sunflower seeds, Avramakis a bag of roasted pumpkin seeds, and I a bag of roasted chickpeas. Minos and I split a bottle of gazoza, and Avramakis quenched his thirst with an ice-cream cone. We shared these treats with Trakas, Ke-kes and Polyvios, whom we met near the church just when they were about to do some serious shopping themselves. As it turned out, each one of them had more money than the three of us combined, so our share of their sweets amounted to a good deal. They were generous.

"First come, first go," said Trakas.

"That's wrong," said Polyvios, licking his ice-cream cone. "You say, 'First come, first served,' or 'Easy come, easy go.'"

"I was thinking about something else," said Trakas. "That's what the madame in the house of sin is supposed to be saying to the patrons who don't like waiting around for too long."

Avramakis, Ke-kes and I were staring at Trakas.

Polyvios was choking on his ice cream.

Minos wanted to know what a house of sin was.

"Go ahead, tell him," said Avramakis.

And Ke-kes hit Trakas in the stomach with his elbow, saying, "What's the matter with you, anyway?"

"Eh, I forgot about him," said Trakas, looking at Minos. "Can't you go anywhere without this old baby?"

"We didn't know we were going to a house of sin," said Avramakis.

"I only said a joke I heard the other day," protested Trakas.

"You are the joke and the house of sin," said Polyvios.

"Come on, tell me," said Minos.

"Tell him."

"Let's keep walking," said Trakas. "If we stay here we'll get trampled to the ground."

To avoid the crowds, we decided to take a walk around the church. Inside the church, the special service commemorating the removal of Saint Thalassios' relics was in progress.

"Tell me."

"All right, all right, let me think. Where was I?"

"In the house of sin," said Polyvios.

"Little did I know," said Trakas. "Well, I've never been in a house of sin, so everything I know is secondhand, okay?"

"Tell him what you know," said Avramakis.

"And be c-c-c-careful how you tell it, if you don't want a black eye," said Ke-kes.

"Easy come, easy go," said Polyvios.

And I said, "First come, first served."

"All right. If you know what's going on in a house, and you think that that's sinful, chances are that it is. If, on the other hand, you happen to feel that what's going on is all right, or even wonderful, chances are that it's not all that sinful."

"He's lying," said Minos.

"I swear. The man I overheard talking about it thought it was lovely, miraculous even," said Trakas.

"Watch your language," warned Ke-kes.

"Secondhand, remember? Anyway, he said there's this old woman and her beautiful niece who are staying in one of these cells, because they're really poor," said Trakas.

"These cells?" said Avramakis, pointing to the dugouts forming a horseshoe around the back side of the church.

"Yes. Anyway, the man I overheard talking about it thought that this was a typical example because some of the patrons were describing it as a house of sin and others as a house of pleasure."

"What's a house of sin?" asked Minos.

"Help," said Trakas. "Anyway, he himself visited the house, and he said that when he saw the old woman he was sure this was a house of sin, but when he saw her young niece he was convinced that it was a house of miracles. The young niece actually worked miracles, he said."

"Which cell?" asked Avramakis.

"I forgot the number."

"What's a house of sin?" again Minos asked.

"According to the man I overheard, it all depends on who you are and how you look at it," said Trakas. "Now, if you can't tell for yourself, try guessing."

"A whorehouse?" said Minos.

·45·

The occupants of the cells were now leaving to join thousands of other pilgrims who had already filled the boulevard from the Church of St. Thalassios to the market, and the main street from the market to the shore, sparing for the time being a narrow strip in the middle of the way, which had been cordoned off for the procession. I saw spastics and paralytics, deaf mutes, men and women suffering from nervous and mental disorders, rheumatism, TB, epilepsy, and I imagined others with all sorts of rare or secret ailments, and still others whose ailments the doctors had failed to diagnose and people called "invalid" or "demonic." And each time one of them wept or groaned with pain, another would say, "Poor soul," as if the body part had already succumbed. The demonics spread out their arms and whirled, now whispering and now howling threats, now laughing madly and now seriously, and now refusing to follow their relative through the crowd. And the crowd kept thickening and expanding, and each time the church bell sounded I saw thousands of people crossing themselves and blessing the name of the saint, or asking for a miracle, good health, peace of mind, deliverance from passions and poverty. But when would that bishop finish the service so the procession might start? Soon, very soon. Maybe. One couldn't really tell, because nothing could start or finish without the bishop's decision, and the bishop had refused to offer the mayor and his council a timetable.

The crowd was pushing to keep from being pushed, being forced in the wrong direction, being stepped on. And how to protect the frail child and the crippled youth, the elderly trembling with age and fear of death? The crowd seemed to increase not from the side streets but from within its own midst, as though people actually multiplied or climbed up from a hole in the ground. And among several currents distinguished by color, direction or rhythm of movement, the black scarves of widowed women formed the most striking one within that river that walked and stumbled its way through Hora on thousands and thousands of feet. It heaved this way and that like some mythical serpent that had been blinded and charred by fire: now struggling to advance toward the church and now toward the opposite direction, the shore, now toward the left bank and the three-story houses, now toward the right bank and the office buildings of the shipping and travel agencies, and now sensing fire or some other danger or threat, and recoiling. And above the crowd, way above, the echoing hubbub, the warm human haze, every breath, every smell, every sigh—or was it just dust? And now and then a harsh, prolonged scream would tear at the crowd's nerves and startle the birds into flight. And many among the sick would panic and go into fits of rage, baring their teeth and beating their chests, adding their own screams. But before this, all other sounds subsided and the river stood still, as if that great scream had not been issued from its midst, but been thrown at it from the sky.

A stocky man in his late forties came out of Cell 172, combing his hair with the fingers of both his hands. He didn't see us, or the three pilgrims who stood in line ahead of us, or maybe he pretended not to notice us. As he went by, we tried to read the expression of his face, to read anything at all, but his face yielded nothing.

And then an old woman showed up at the door, carrying a chipped enameled pail of soapy water. She threw the water out so close to our feet that we had to jump.

"Tomorrow," she said to the three men who were ahead of us. "That's it for today."

The three men drifted off without saying a word. Somewhere in all this was an unwritten dialogue. We didn't know how it went, so we couldn't participate. The three men drifted off without protesting. We stayed on.

"That's it, I said," the old woman barked at us now. She was very short and heavy, shifting her weight from one hip to the other, a sign that she couldn't rely on either foot or wooden clog for more than a few seconds. "How old are you, anyway?" she said in general as though she wanted to know our collective age.

"Eighteen," said Trakas.

I thought she'd laugh.

The shaded areas of her face, what were they—powder? ashes? stubble? Did she shave her mustache and beard regularly? The very image of Megaera, one of the Furies, as I'd seen her years before in our schoolyard, cooking bean soup that had no beans in it, and serving it with an aluminum scoop full of holes. When the Germans retreated, they took her along.

"Sixteen, going on seventeen," said Minos.

I thought she would laugh, she would scream.

"You don't say," she said, vaguely impressed. And she said, "Tomorrow's also God's day. Come back tomorrow."

"But tomorrow's a working day, Aunt."

"A-a-a-a-a. I'm not your aunt. I can't afford to be your aunt."

"Won't you even let us see her, have a glimpse of her?" pleaded Trakas. "We've heard that she's so beautiful, and that she makes things happen. Miracles and things like that."

The old woman seemed flattered, amused. The wrinkles around her mouth stretched sideways and down, lengthening her lower lip, and her eyebrows shot up, about to fly out of her face. She was smiling.

"C-c-c-come on," pleaded Ke-kes.

"I said no. Not when my little partridge is so tired, so exhausted," she said. "If you really want to see miracles you ought to come back tomorrow—the earlier the better, *capito?*" She even knew foreign languages!

Avramakis decided to move in, and in an almost whispering voice he said, "I'm not going to call you 'Aunt,' because you don't like it, and I'm not going to hand you my twenty drachme, because that's next to nothing for you, but if that's what it takes, I'd rather give my allowance to you than spend it on candy and ice cream. We're not impatient or anything, you know," went on Avramakis, his voice trembling as though he were about to move himself to tears. "We'd gladly come back tomorrow morning when your niece will have gotten a good rest—God knows what a long day this has been for you two! But tomorrow's a working day for us also, you know; that's why we can't come tomorrow."

The old woman had been listening to Avramakis, unaware that her jaw had dropped and her toothless mouth was halfway open. Hadn't anyone as honest, intelligent and considerate as Avramakis ever spoken to her before?

"Well, maybe we ought to get going," said Avramakis, showing his defeated face to the rest of us.

"Wait," said the woman with some hesitation.

That was it. "May the grace of the saint be with you wherever you go, Aunt," said Trakas, leading the way into the dugout, and the old woman followed us, closing the door.

"Just a glimpse," she said. "You can have a quick look at her and make a wish, that's all. No miracles—understand?"

"No miracles."

The old woman squeezed her way to the front, and, pushing aside a crimson curtain that divided the little vaulted cell in two, she showed us the tall iron bed and the young woman whose head was shaved, propped up on several small pillows, pretty and lifeless as a manikin without its wig. The one piece of clothing that she had on was a sugar-colored robe whose flaps were held together at the waist with a belt of the same fabric, but parted lower down, showing her knees and shins and small feet—her skin pale yet radiant in the dim lamplight.

Where was I? Was I lost and found, and now lost once more? First Marianna, and now her . . . so strangely beautiful. She was lovely and at peace, every muscle relaxed, her eyes closed. But why was her head shaved? Her scalp seemed smooth, healthy, no sign of disease or injury there. Young women would clip their hair short in mourning for the death of a brother, lover or husband, but never that short. This was different, foreign. And yet the more I stared at her, the more familiar she looked.

I found myself first in line, staring at her so intensely that her eyelids trembled, as though aware of my gaze. She then opened her eyes a little and looked at me, but without focusing, the way some people look but do not see, or go on sleeping with their eyes half open.

A hand, its skin old and stained, its fingers humped by age or arthritic deformity, moved to loosen the girl's belt and part the flaps of her robe all the way up: soft silk, the reddish hair of corn in the strong sun of August, and lean long middle, her breasts small, with two pale moons shivering, pale yet radiant in the dim light. The old woman's hand guided mine to the girl's breast, saying, "Gently, ve-e-e-ery gently." And she said, "Make a wish, quickly."

I wasn't prepared for this. I didn't know what in the world to wish for, or how. The little breast felt cool in my hand, but beyond that coolness I sensed a faint heartbeat. I raced through the past twenty-two months as though they were a lifetime coming to an end. There, painted on the map of that life like the four winds, were Zaphira, Marina, Marianna, and this nameless one. The Gypsy I had failed twice so far, and if she reappeared I'd fail her again by failing to become a Gypsy. Marina was lost forever and yet was ever present and already grown up even more beautiful in Marianna. But this nameless one, this public yet secret one—where did she fit in that lifetime that had hardly begun?

My knees grew weak, my head dizzy. I closed my eyes, forcing my mind to make a wish, but something in me resisted. I stood there, holding the girl's heartbeat in my hand like someone who's taking an oath on the Gospel, until an ancient whirlwind of names and meanings came down on me, and I swooned. When I came to, I recalled having picked three words: "myself," "know" and "to." I read backwards, reversing their order, and I had a wish.

·46·

The procession was now leaving the church in full Byzantine splendor, headed by six schoolboys who held the gold and silver seraphs and other standards of the Church mounted on hand-carved oak poles. There followed the three local priests, shaking their noisy incense burners and blessing the crowds. The reliquary, the glass case that contained Saint Thalassios' mummy (the piling-on of votive offerings sparing only his shrunken face and hands), was carried by four prominent members of the community: the mayor, the director of the Ionian Bank, a shipowner and a man in his fifties who'd spent a lot of money in the last elections but failed to be elected deputy to the Parliament. Following the reliquary was the bishop, puffed up like a peacock in his glittering hieratic, hierarchic garments, wearing a large crown and making the sign of the cross now with his gold-inlaid ivory staff, and now with a diamond-studded crucifix that hung on a long gold chain from his thick neck. There were more priests and deacons and select members of the community, chanters, a detachment of the Royal Navy, the band. The veterans. The professional and commercial associations. The six members of the local chapter of the labor union. The three ladies who collected for the Queen's Fund. And finally the two teachers of the public school—who later said they'd seen the saint himself walking behind them, so the teachers were not the least important public figures in the procession!

And in the cordoned-off path of the procession lay the afflicted, piled up: some willingly, and some forced by relatives or nurses. And as the reliquary passed over them, those whom people call "demonics" screamed, or rolled over frothing at the mouth and mumbling obscenities at the relics. They beat their heads on the cobblestones as though preferring death to the healing touch of the saint's shadow: "Off with you, go fuck your mother, Thalassios, three times accursed, deadly scorpion of Kalamos! Ah, my brains! Stop burning my brains, rotten bastard of Kalamos! God damn you, God damn you on this nine hundred and fiftieth anniversary of your impalement."

But the thousands of pilgrims crowding on both sides of the boulevard crossed themselves, singing, "Great be your name, Thalassios, the miraculous martyr." All that singing, chanting, wailing and screaming ascended in the warm afternoon air together with incense and medicine, body odor and dust, and the smoke of roasting chestnuts and animals.

I felt a jolt in my stomach, and I slowed down. I slowed down and stopped, wondering what it was that had disagreed with me so violently: something I ate? a second thought? the saint? Like most people, I rarely stopped to think what bothered me, but when I did I always found out, and this time was no exception: it was this great joyous event that everybody had been talking about all summer and that had finally come. The holiday. The festival. An opportunity to get together thousands of unfortunate, broken beings of all ages, and play a joke on them. That's how it struck me, and I wasn't sure if I wanted to follow the procession all the way to the shore and watch time and again the wild scenes unfolding under the reliquary like a living carpet. This was pain as I'd never known it before, and the scale of it, the great number of tortured minds and bodies lined up on the cobblestones, and the repetition of the desperate efforts of the afflicted to resist, to escape, to run away screaming and to hide behind a rock or to jump from a rock, did not lessen my horror—on the contrary, it increased it, for this madness resembled fire: the larger it grew, the more it engulfed, and no one was safe.

I was alone and unwilling to catch up with my friends. I stayed behind, pushing hard to get out of the crowded area while being pushed by the crowd closer and closer to the cordoned-off strip of the procession. The most awesome scenes unfolded during the brief stations of the litany at the crossroads, where the chanting of hymns and the wailing grew in volume. It was here at the crossroads, said those who knew, that the few miracles and deaths took place, as the afflicted lost control of their bodies, spilling urine and blood on the cobblestones, purging soul and body.

I pushed to get out, but a huge wave of pilgrims who wanted to reach the cordoned-off strip when the procession approached pushed harder, throwing me back. I fell down on my back on top of the afflicted, just as the pallbearers of the reliquary were about to pass with their slow, rhythmical pace. I tried to get up but couldn't. Powerful hands got hold of my arms and legs, pinning me down, desperate hands got hold of my hair, dug their nails into my neck, clawing me. I panicked, struggled to free myself, and let out a scream, but that was nothing new to the heap of tortured men, women and children, who struggled and screamed with equal panic and desperation. I struggled, struck back, shook my head left and right to protect my face, and in so doing I knew I was no less afflicted than they, and no less a demonic. And as the blackened mummy of Thalassios passed overhead, I cursed him and his anniversary, just as the others cursed him, for every part of my body was violated by pain, and my brain burned. I had never known such terror; and when I shook my head left and right it was no longer to protect my face, but to ease the burning. How I burned, and bled, and screamed curses in terror as the blackened mummy of Thalassios went by! And when it went, many around me convulsed quietly, or passed out, and I felt my insides collapse. There was froth at my mouth, and my eyes burned with tears.

People began to help us up on our feet, eager to see what had happened to us, if anything. They slapped us in the face, shook us by the shoulders, forced our eyelids open, looking for miracles, any life at all. Then those who were too worn out had to be carried to the churchyard, where a physician and two nurses offered first aid to anyone who instead of being healed had gotten worse. And I, aching all over, drained, limping on my right leg, took a side street down to the deserted beach, where I took off my clothes and washed my body and covered my body with sand, and slept until the church bells sounded the end of the procession.

· 47 ·

Back on the terrace overlooking the sea the crowds were breaking up into small groups or couples who either headed home
or began to stroll back and forth on the graded walkway that
followed the shoreline closely, say twenty meters higher and
twelve to fifteen meters away from it. The well-to-do islanders,
pilgrims and tourists had a good hour to kill before they could
sit down to the dinner table, and they killed it well, breathing
in the briny air from the sea, now pausing and pondering the
body of quiet water surrounding Kalamos, now appraising the
festival and the saint's performance.

I wondered where Mrs. Domna was and how she might have
taken the refusal of the saint to restore her son to good health.
Did she suffer quietly, drowning even the mildest word of com-
plaint, or did she drag Nakos to the restaurant an hour early,
loudly informing her son and the saint that this was the last
time she would set foot on this island? But why should I be
thinking about Mrs. Domna and not about the desolate women
in black who had neither husband nor grown-up children?
These women had one small child that shone in their arms,
against the black, like beeswax, like gold; one small child who
was manic by grace of God, and who every day outgrew another hope for a miracle. I saw them hurrying back to their
dugout cells for the night, or climbing down the hill to Skala to
see if they couldn't use their return tickets to Piraeus that eve-

ning. The sooner the better; I could understand. But being poor also meant returning home and not having a glass of wine to wash down the bitterness, not even a spoonful of honey to talk the mouth out of ill talk. I'd known the poor: when they talked about the dead they called them "lucky." I'd known them well: and when their faith caved in they fought misfortune with cruelty, sometimes blaming and cursing the children, just as they cursed themselves or anyone who got in the way, advising patience, persistence, perseverance. They hurried to the dugout cells and to Skala as if the devil himself were after them. And such was the bitterness in the air in that hour that it even obscured the sunset.

I climbed down the stairs to the shore, and, taking off my sandals, I walked toward the sunset, turning now and then to look for Marianna or to greet families of pilgrims who'd spread a blanket or a tablecloth on the pebbles and were eating their dinner quietly. The soft wind blowing from the south was picking up strength, and the sea began to exhale smells of algae, seaweed and cuttlebone—smells that could stir up memories and ideas. I was not threatened by either. Memories, I thought, give the past depth; ideas give the present a future.

I had been refreshed by the water and the brief nap at the beach, and now the sea breeze was filling me again with energy and with an unusual clarity. Everything that crossed my mind seemed to fit perfectly with everything else; and in so doing it sparkled.

I saw everything clearly now. It made sense to me that I hadn't crossed the border out of the country; it made sense that I had had a chance to give up country and become a Gypsy, and that I had refused.

I saw everything clearly now. It made sense to me that we had lost the war, that we had fed the fire, that our bodies had fertilized the cracks in the bedrock. It made sense that the enemy had triumphed. Better that way. Had we won, we'd be the enemy now.

I could see clearly. It made sense to me now that we survived, that we refused to be reformed, and set out to learn
ourselves and the workings of the world, observing the greater
laws that keep the world going, wondering what makes it seem
still. It made sparkling sense that the vanquished, not the vic-
tors, should learn these secrets.

I could see clearly now. It made sense to me that Marina had
grown up, even after she died, to become Marianna. The war
was finally over, and we were still friends, and it made sense
that there be friendship even after death. And that there be
love.

I could see clearly. It made sense that Andreas and Issaris
would not part with their frostbitten legs, but would take them
along to the hot springs, according to Minos, and it made perfect sense for Minos to want to forget the worst that happened,
and yet still to remember.

I could see clearly now. It made sense that Pavlos and the
others flew off like seabirds into the gale, that they returned as
terrible statues; and it made perfect sense that the statues set
the rest of us free.

It made sense to me now that Fotis would not compromise,
but would not survive either, that he'd become a living monu-
ment for the dead heroes.

I could see clearly. It made sense that Avramakis be adopted
by Mrs. Becca and be taken to America. I hated to admit it, but
it made sense that he be the one to see the promised land, if
such a land existed.

I could see clearly now. And it made sense that Marianna's
man was among the prisoners who escaped from the maximum-security dungeon in Piraeus, and it made perfect sense
that she took the first boat to nowhere, not wanting to see him.
It made sense to me now that she needed a new friend—if not
a lover.

I could see clearly. It made sense that the fire seared the
mind without burning it through, and that I be the one to

perceive such meanings, to see which meaning fitted perfectly well with all the others, and to see to it that in so doing it sparkled. It made sparkling sense that to know myself mattered.

I went on walking long after sunset, after the western sky and the sea under it darkened. I went on, knowing that soon the formation of the rock would block the shoreline with several huge boulders that from above looked like cars of a derailed train. Here and there I would still hear small groups of pilgrims talking in a low tone of voice, or just lying back and throwing pebbles into the water. The sky was clear, crowded with stars. Farther on, though, it occurred to me that most of the pilgrims were just couples who'd chosen to be at some distance from others for the sake of privacy, and as I pressed on I had the feeling that these couples were not at all humbled by the saint's works. The few sounds that reached me were more and more lively. I could understand.

Later I came across a group of men speaking in a Lemnian accent and speculating about the identity of a bloated body that had been washed ashore. One of them had notified the authorities. Another thought that from the looks of it the victim must have drowned two days ago. It made sense. I felt a chill crawling up from my feet, and I thought maybe I ought to put on my sandals.

· 48 ·

I walked along the edge of the sea, hoping that the sounds of my sandals on the sand, though muffled, would warn any couples whom I came upon so they wouldn't be startled. But the farther I went, the less concerned these pilgrims seemed to be about who might walk by and why, and so it was I who got surprised each time I heard their whispering or thrashing about in the dark, on the noisy pebbles.

For a short while all I could hear was the sound of my own steps on the wet sand, and I was pretty sure that I'd left the last pair of lovers way behind. I was wrong. The new sounds came from some twenty-five or thirty steps away from the beach, where the ground was neither sandy nor covered with stones and pebbles, but marshy, filled up with a dark-brown silt in which grew the short, spiny bulrush that the children used as arrows in their games, and which often hurt them. The noises coming from that direction were caused by more than one couple, though, and at some point I thought I heard the Pappas sisters first giggling and then screaming, as if their skin had been pierced by those sharp spines. The men, on the other hand, kept on slipping and falling into the mud puddles. They had to be the three friends from Rhodos, but I couldn't be sure and wasn't curious enough to stop and listen more carefully, and at any rate their groaning sounded muffled, a clue perhaps that their mouths were most of the time filled with mud. Just like children, I thought. All of this changed soon, before I'd gained enough distance from them not to notice it. There was no laughing now, only moaning, weeping and a thudding of bodies or limbs, as though the men were trading blows from which the two girls couldn't be entirely safe, for their wailing was steady now but somehow in concert with the three men's struggle. I was appalled at their violence, the pain they inflicted on one another, on themselves. I shuddered, tried to understand. I couldn't. I ran along the edge of the sea until I came to the very end of the beach, where the huge limestone rocks stood high, darker than the night sky. There, not very far from pilgrims and ghosts, I sat down on a stone and cried. I thought I'd seen and heard enough that day, but between the rocks and the water I sensed the shadows: Trash and Zavos, the heroic doggies, and other animals and little birds, men and women, and a lot of children, father and mother, my little brother Teo, Aunt Evanthia and then Andreas, so fresh from life I wasn't sure if I should trust him. . . . There came Issaris, and Scorpaena, and Capetan Aetos, Papanikas and Pelekys. . . . And the children had grown so rapidly I no longer knew who was who. I decided to step into the water to have a closer look at them, but I slipped on a round stone and fell into the sea noisily. They drifted off as light as a breath of air, leaving no sense of sadness.

I was alone in the water and at peace with myself. I thought I understood enough to give the night a good, hearty laugh. I went ahead and laughed. It felt good. I thought I understood enough things to keep laughing all night. I went on laughing, I couldn't stop.

"Panagis?" She was coming from the rock, behind which the shadows had vanished.

I couldn't stop.

"Panagis? Are you all right?" said Marianna, stretching out her hands toward me.

I could even laugh at my own name.

She reached out and hugged me. She had no clothes on, and her hair was wet as if she'd been swimming.

I pulled her down, and we both fell into the water. I kissed her mouth and her small breasts, laughing.

"Panagis, stop . . ." But now Marianna too was laughing. "Come," she said. She led me by the hand to a narrow, graded path winding around the rock, and in a couple of minutes, short of breath from climbing and from the laughter, we were at the top of it, which was as broad as a small threshing floor, and as level.

I felt the wind on my cheeks, and I took a deep breath. Under my wet shirt my chest felt light, almost hollow.

"Take off your clothes," said Marianna, laughing. "It's all right."

I took them off and wrung them out and spread them at the edge so they could dry.

"Your sandals too."

I unbuckled my sandals and took them off. The wind wrapped itself around my body, drying my skin like a soft towel.

"Come, lie next to me," she said. "On your back, so you can look at the stars," she added, laughing.

Everything made perfect sense, and the stars sparkled, but I wouldn't lie down on my back—not with Marina-Marianna lying so close to me on her side. I drew closer, feeling her smooth, lean body alongside mine, kissing her.

"Panagis," she whispered. "Panagis . . . Panagis . . ."

I listened, and for the first time that name sounded real.

"Oh, Panagis . . ."

There was a taste of salt on her eyelids, on her lips, on her earlobes. I kissed her lips again and again as she spoke my name, and then I kissed the fine crystals of salt sparkling on her cheeks and shoulders.

Marianna combed my hair with the fingers of both her hands, pressing her lips onto mine in a long, breathless kiss.

Slowly, the sky had begun to turn southward. Slowly, too,

the tide had begun to circle our rock, flooding the land all around it, cutting it off. And the rock had begun to float.

That day marked the end of an era. That night the end of an age: the heroic age. I was almost fifteen, and the heroic age for me was over.

According to my Aunt Evanthia, the heroic age for women in Greece was from the moment they were born to the moment they died.